big NATE

IN YOUR FACE!

Complete Your *Big Nate* Collection

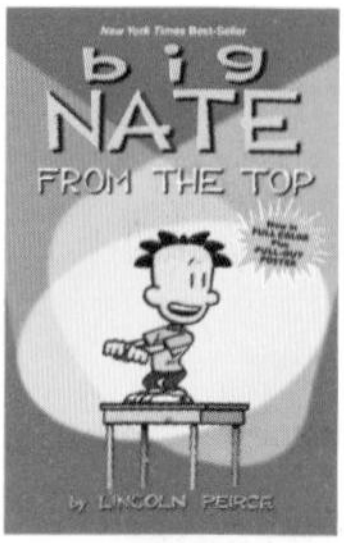
big
NATE
FROM THE TOP
by LINCOLN PEIRCE

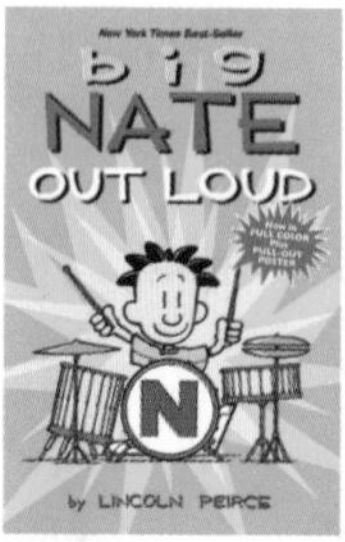
big
NATE
OUT LOUD
by LINCOLN PEIRCE

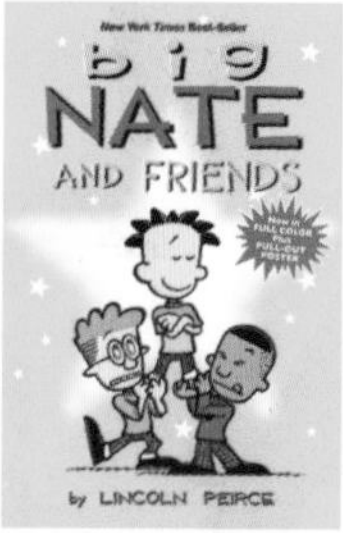
big
NATE
AND FRIENDS
by LINCOLN PEIRCE

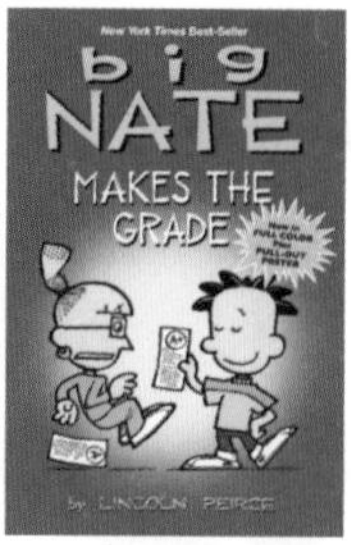
big
NATE
MAKES THE GRADE
by LINCOLN PEIRCE

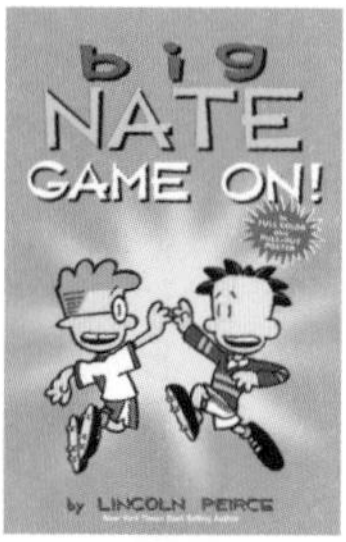
big
NATE
GAME ON!
by LINCOLN PEIRCE

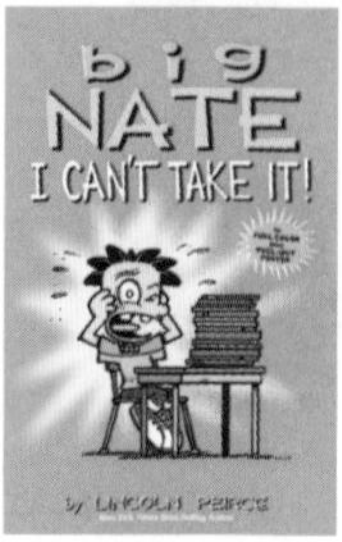
big
NATE
I CAN'T TAKE IT!
by LINCOLN PEIRCE

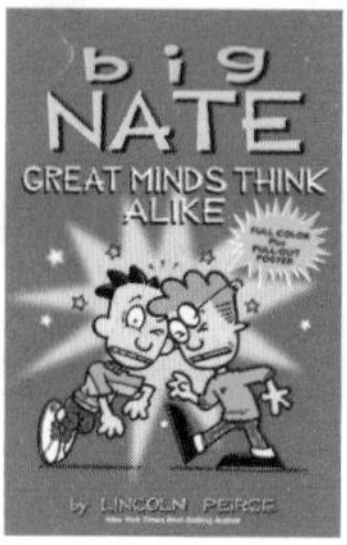
big
NATE
GREAT MINDS THINK ALIKE
by LINCOLN PEIRCE

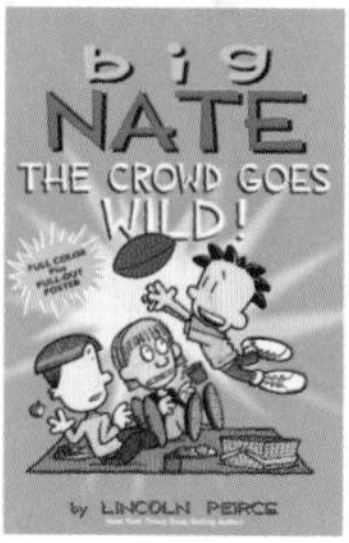
big
NATE
THE CROWD GOES WILD!
by LINCOLN PEIRCE

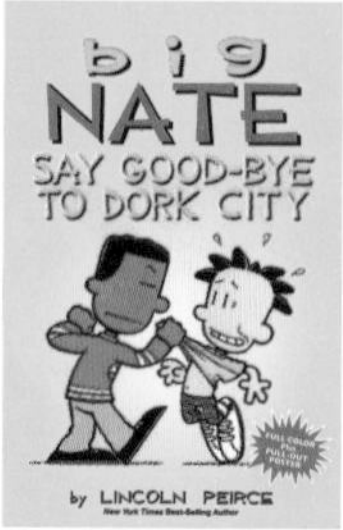
big
NATE
SAY GOOD-BYE TO DORK CITY
by LINCOLN PEIRCE

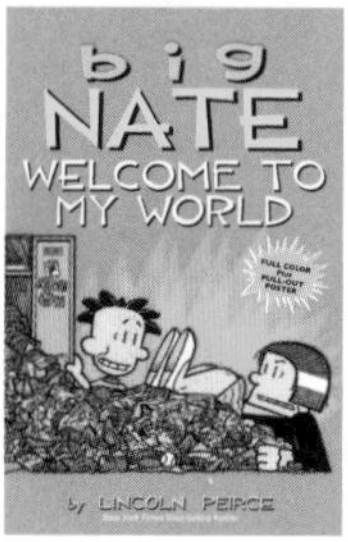
big
NATE
WELCOME TO MY WORLD
by LINCOLN PEIRCE

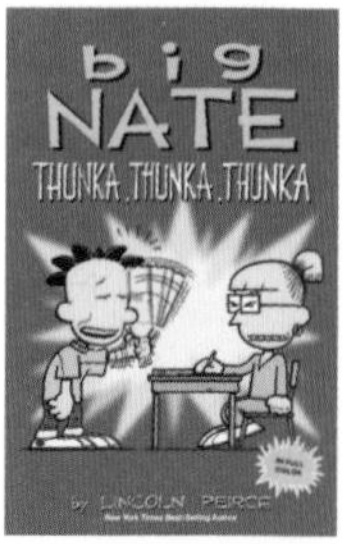
big
NATE
THUNKA, THUNKA, THUNKA
by LINCOLN PEIRCE

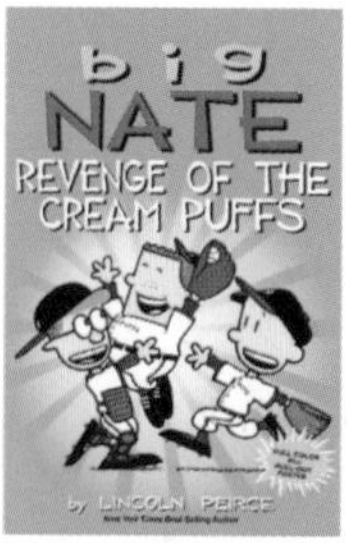
big
NATE
REVENGE OF THE CREAM PUFFS
by LINCOLN PEIRCE

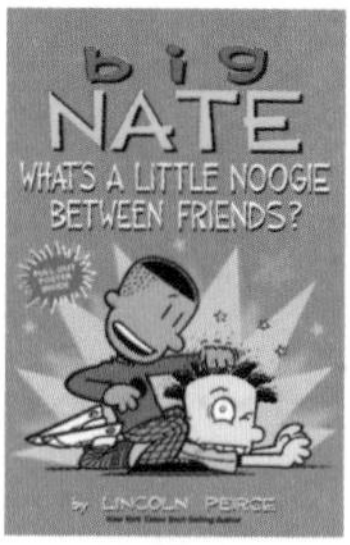
big
NATE
WHAT'S A LITTLE NOOGIE BETWEEN FRIENDS?
by LINCOLN PEIRCE

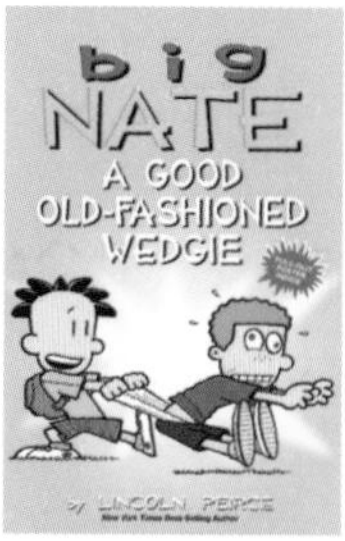
big
NATE
A GOOD OLD-FASHIONED WEDGIE
by LINCOLN PEIRCE

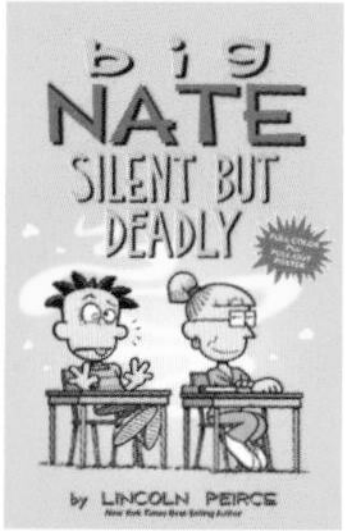
big
NATE
SILENT BUT DEADLY
by LINCOLN PEIRCE

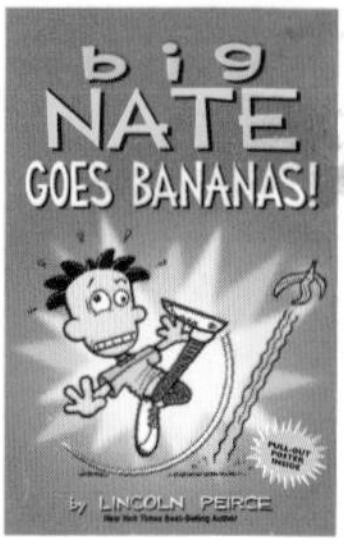
big
NATE
GOES BANANAS!
by LINCOLN PEIRCE

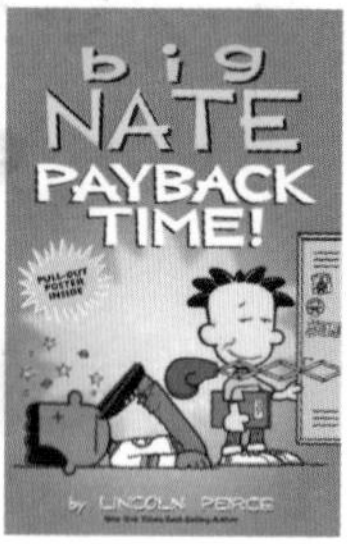
big
NATE
PAYBACK TIME!
by LINCOLN PEIRCE

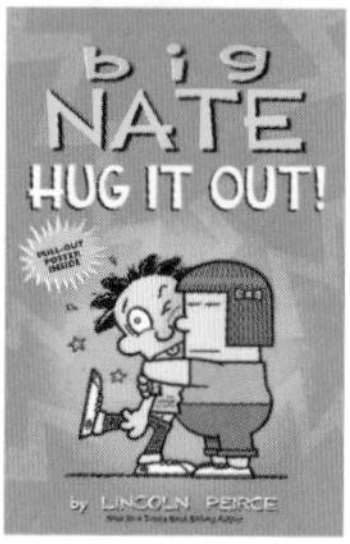
big
NATE
HUG IT OUT!
by LINCOLN PEIRCE

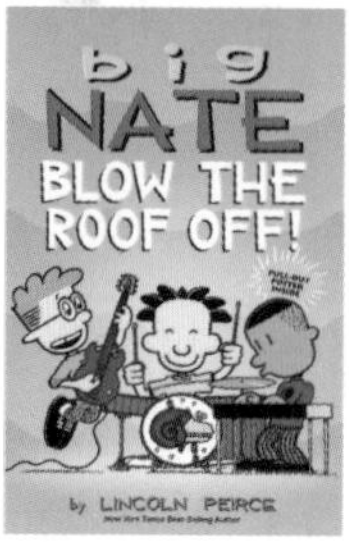
big
NATE
BLOW THE ROOF OFF!
by LINCOLN PEIRCE

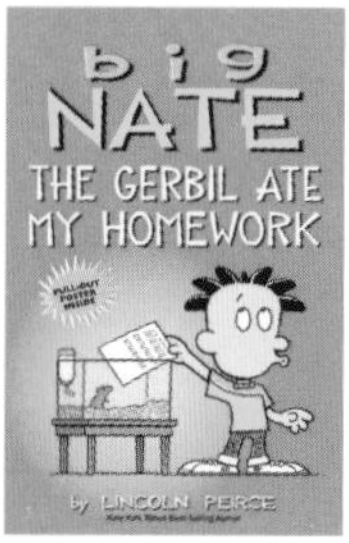
big
NATE
THE GERBIL ATE MY HOMEWORK
by LINCOLN PEIRCE

big NATE IN YOUR FACE!

by LINCOLN PEIRCE

Andrews McMeel
PUBLISHING®

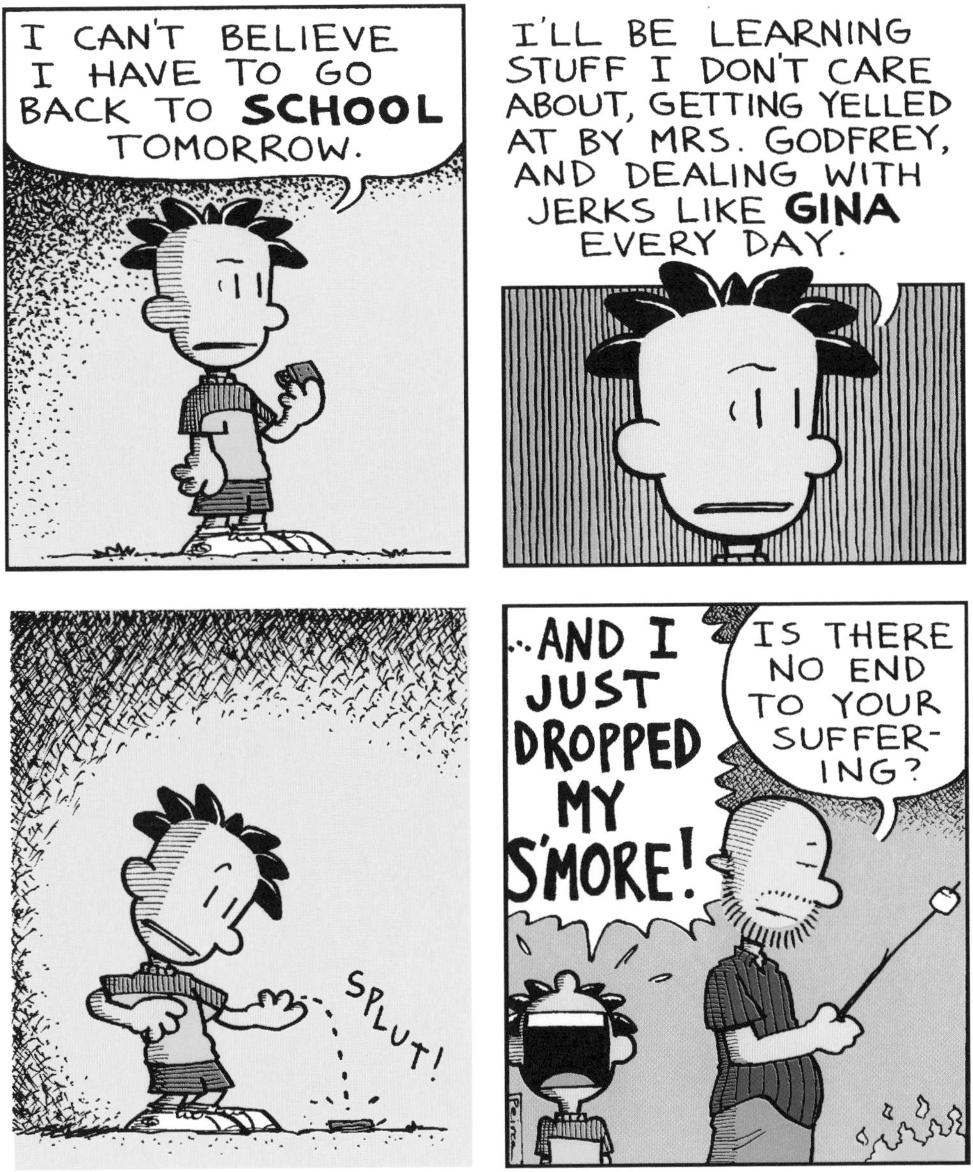
I CAN'T BELIEVE I HAVE TO GO BACK TO SCHOOL TOMORROW.
I'LL BE LEARNING STUFF I DON'T CARE ABOUT, GETTING YELLED AT BY MRS. GODFREY, AND DEALING WITH JERKS LIKE GINA EVERY DAY.
SPLUT!
...AND I JUST DROPPED MY S'MORE!
IS THERE NO END TO YOUR SUFFER-ING?

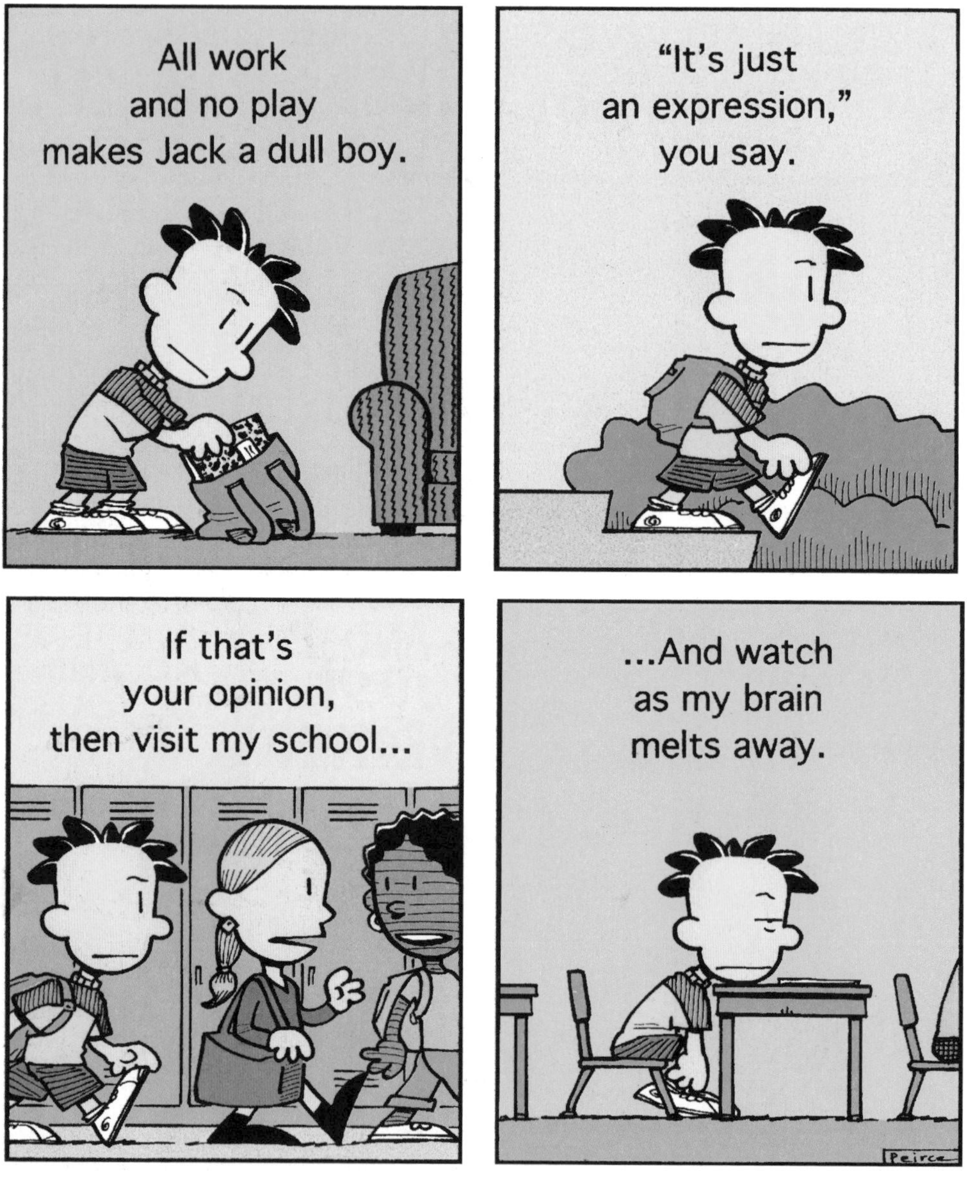
All work and no play makes Jack a dull boy.
"It's just an expression," you say.
If that's your opinion, then visit my school...
...And watch as my brain melts away.
Peirce

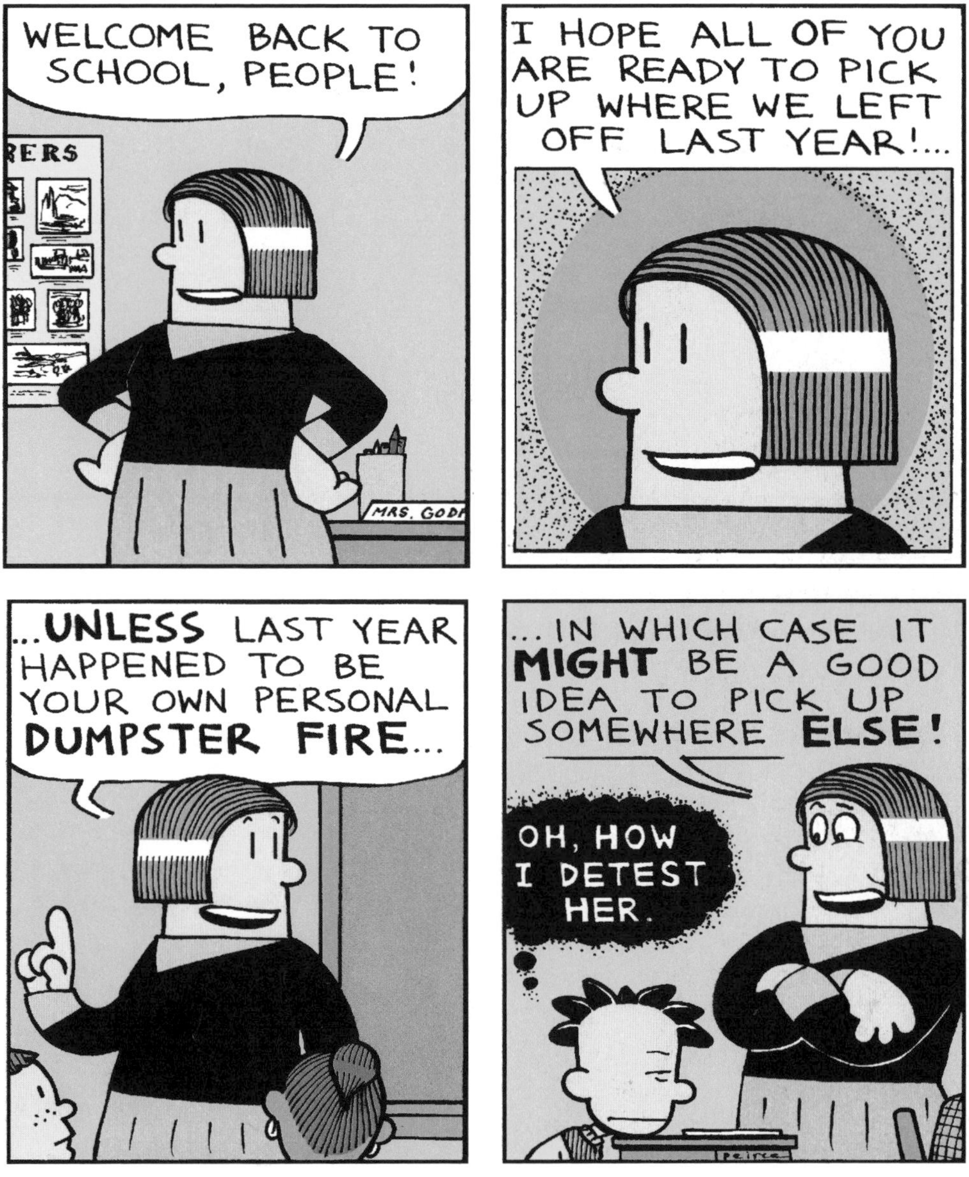
WELCOME BACK TO SCHOOL, PEOPLE!
MRS. GOD
I HOPE ALL OF YOU ARE READY TO PICK UP WHERE WE LEFT OFF LAST YEAR!...
...UNLESS LAST YEAR HAPPENED TO BE YOUR OWN PERSONAL DUMPSTER FIRE...
...IN WHICH CASE IT MIGHT BE A GOOD IDEA TO PICK UP SOMEWHERE ELSE!
OH, HOW I DETEST HER.

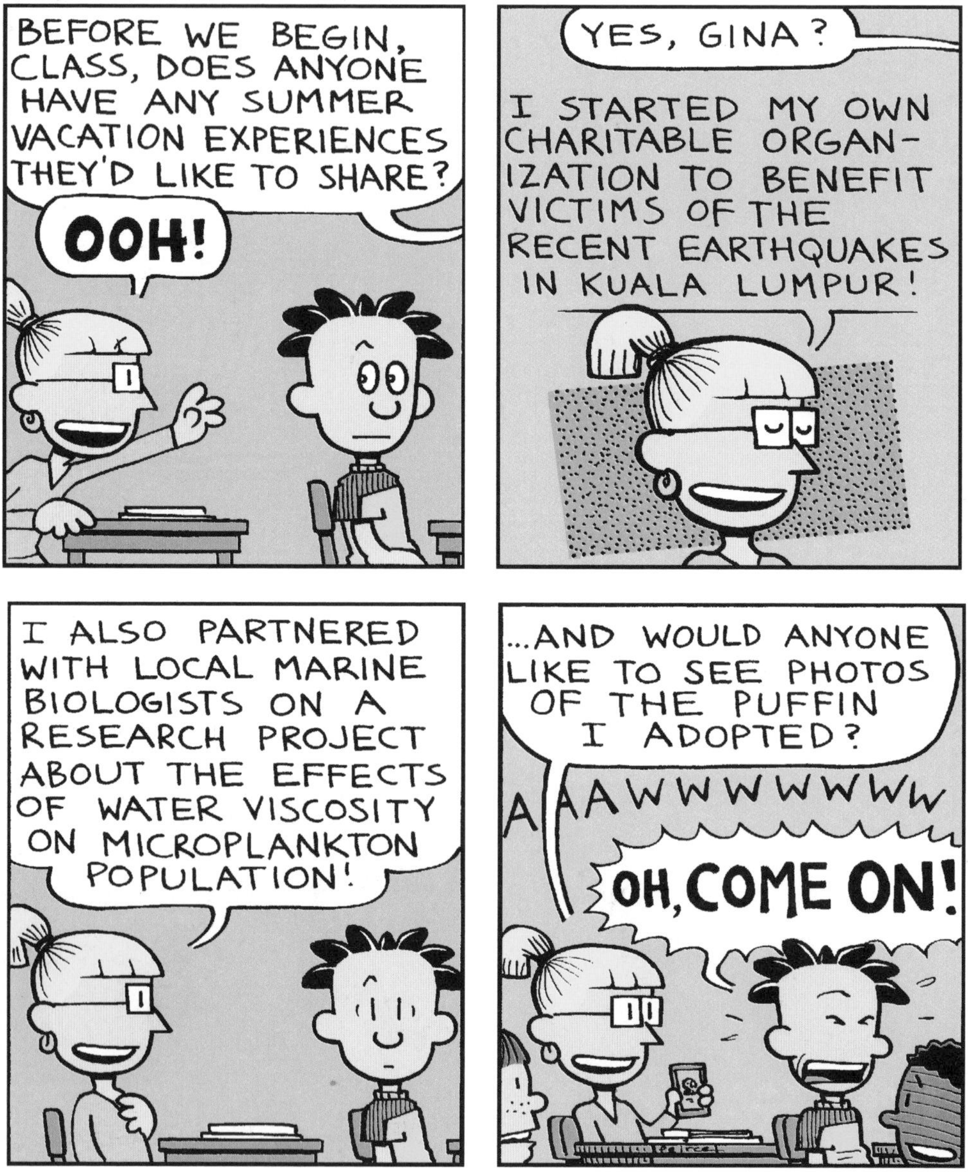
BEFORE WE BEGIN, CLASS, DOES ANYONE HAVE ANY SUMMER VACATION EXPERIENCES THEY'D LIKE TO SHARE?
OOH!
YES, GINA?
I STARTED MY OWN CHARITABLE ORGAN-IZATION TO BENEFIT VICTIMS OF THE RECENT EARTHQUAKES IN KUALA LUMPUR!
I ALSO PARTNERED WITH LOCAL MARINE BIOLOGISTS ON A RESEARCH PROJECT ABOUT THE EFFECTS OF WATER VISCOSITY ON MICROPLANKTON POPULATION!
...AND WOULD ANYONE LIKE TO SEE PHOTOS OF THE PUFFIN I ADOPTED?
AAAWWWWWWWW
OH, COME ON!

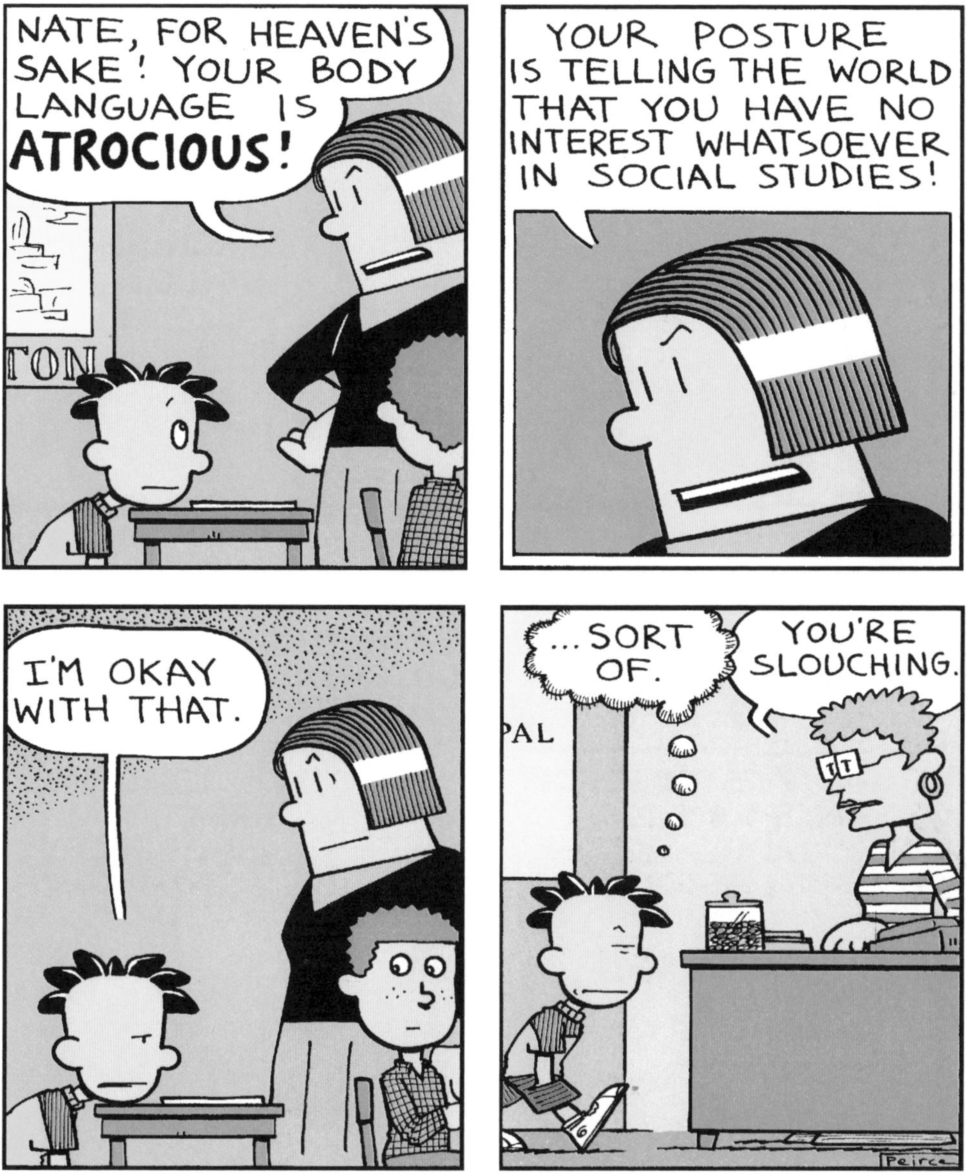
NATE, FOR HEAVEN'S SAKE! YOUR BODY LANGUAGE IS **ATROCIOUS!**
TON
YOUR POSTURE IS TELLING THE WORLD THAT YOU HAVE NO INTEREST WHATSOEVER IN SOCIAL STUDIES!
I'M OKAY WITH THAT.
...SORT OF.
YOU'RE SLOUCHING.
PAL
Peirce

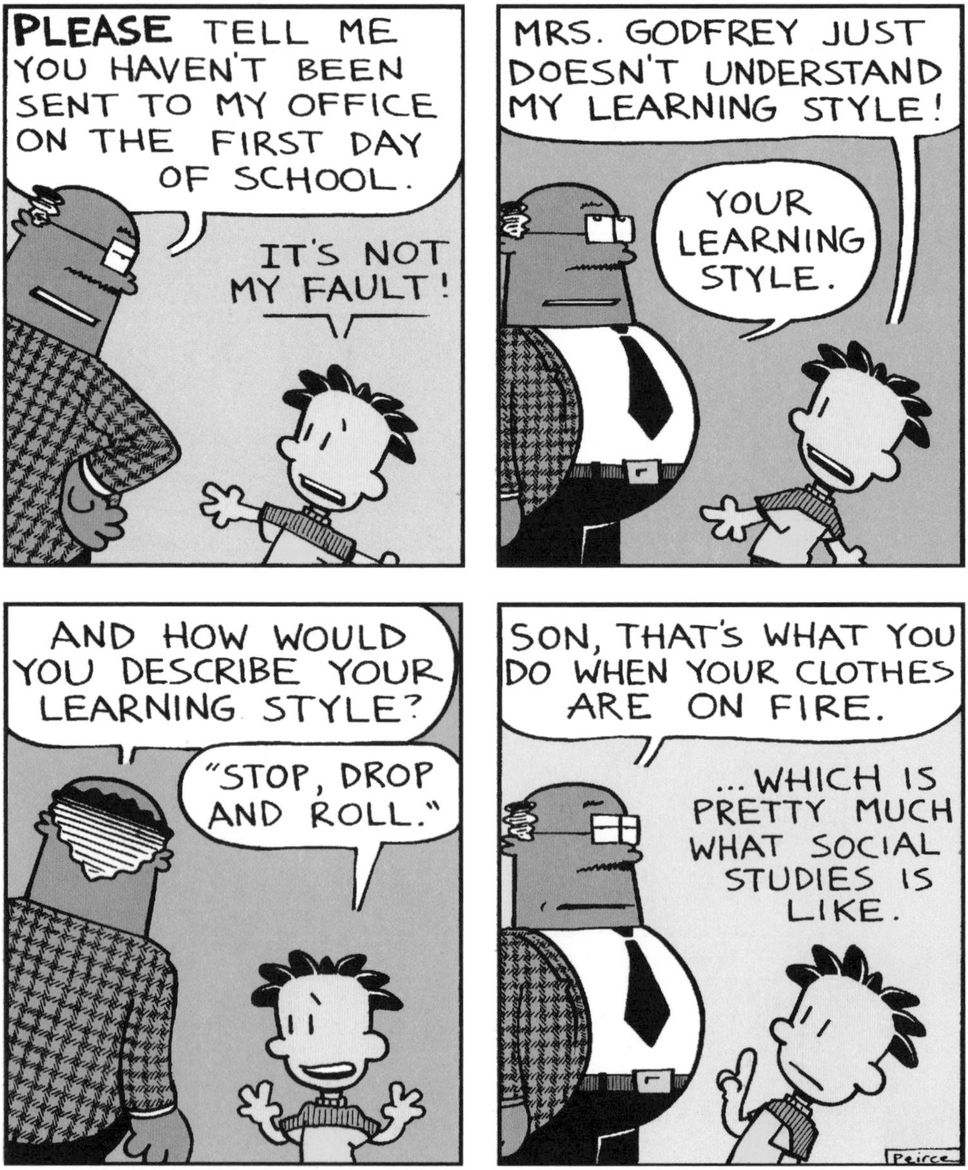
PLEASE TELL ME YOU HAVEN'T BEEN SENT TO MY OFFICE ON THE FIRST DAY OF SCHOOL.
IT'S NOT MY FAULT!
MRS. GODFREY JUST DOESN'T UNDERSTAND MY LEARNING STYLE!
YOUR LEARNING STYLE.
AND HOW WOULD YOU DESCRIBE YOUR LEARNING STYLE?
"STOP, DROP AND ROLL."
SON, THAT'S WHAT YOU DO WHEN YOUR CLOTHES ARE ON FIRE.
...WHICH IS PRETTY MUCH WHAT SOCIAL STUDIES IS LIKE.
Peirce

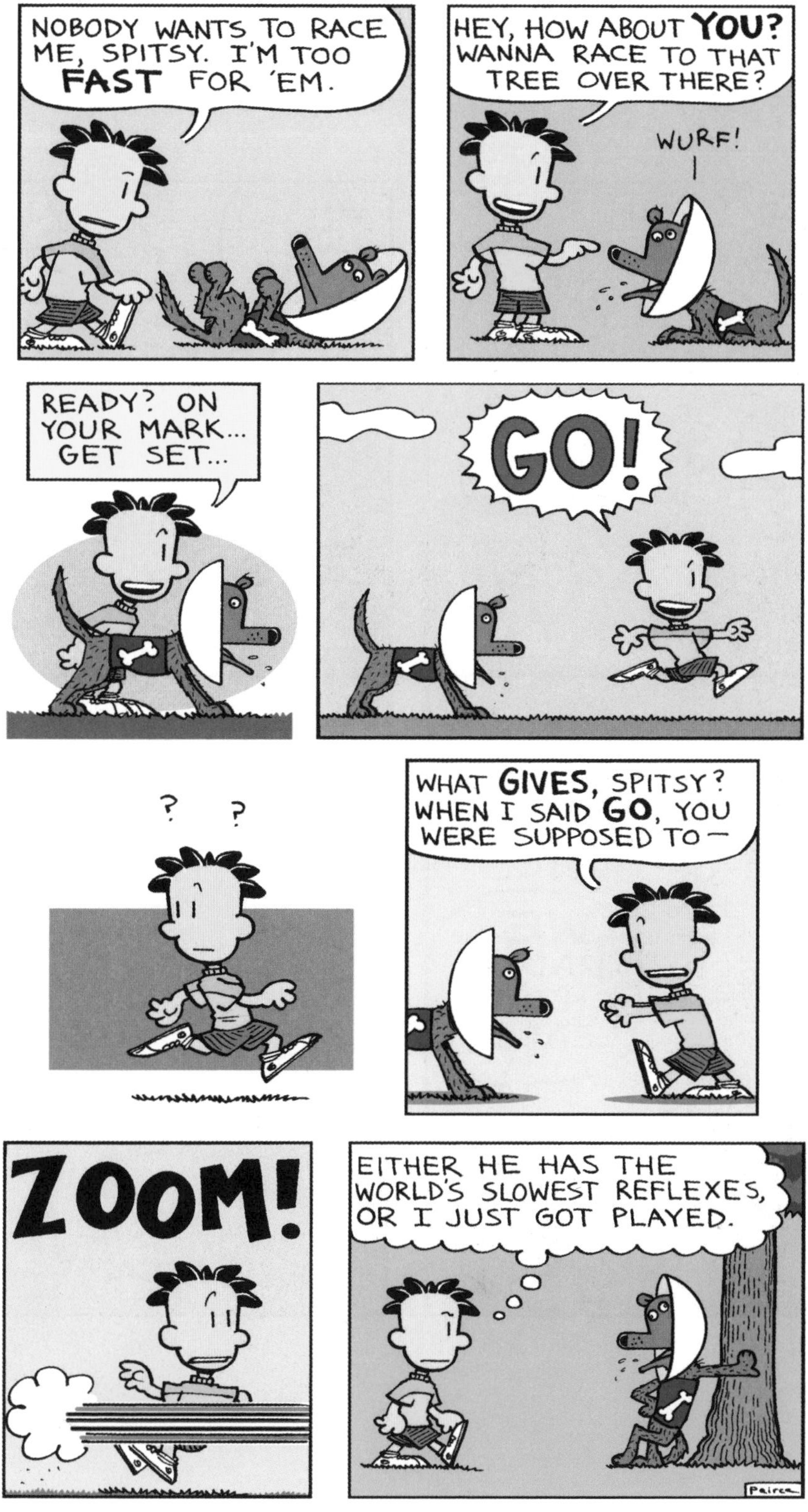
NOBODY WANTS TO RACE ME, SPITSY. I'M TOO FAST FOR 'EM.
HEY, HOW ABOUT YOU? WANNA RACE TO THAT TREE OVER THERE?
WURF!
READY? ON YOUR MARK... GET SET...
GO!
? ?
WHAT GIVES, SPITSY? WHEN I SAID GO, YOU WERE SUPPOSED TO—
ZOOM!
EITHER HE HAS THE WORLD'S SLOWEST REFLEXES, OR I JUST GOT PLAYED.
Peirce

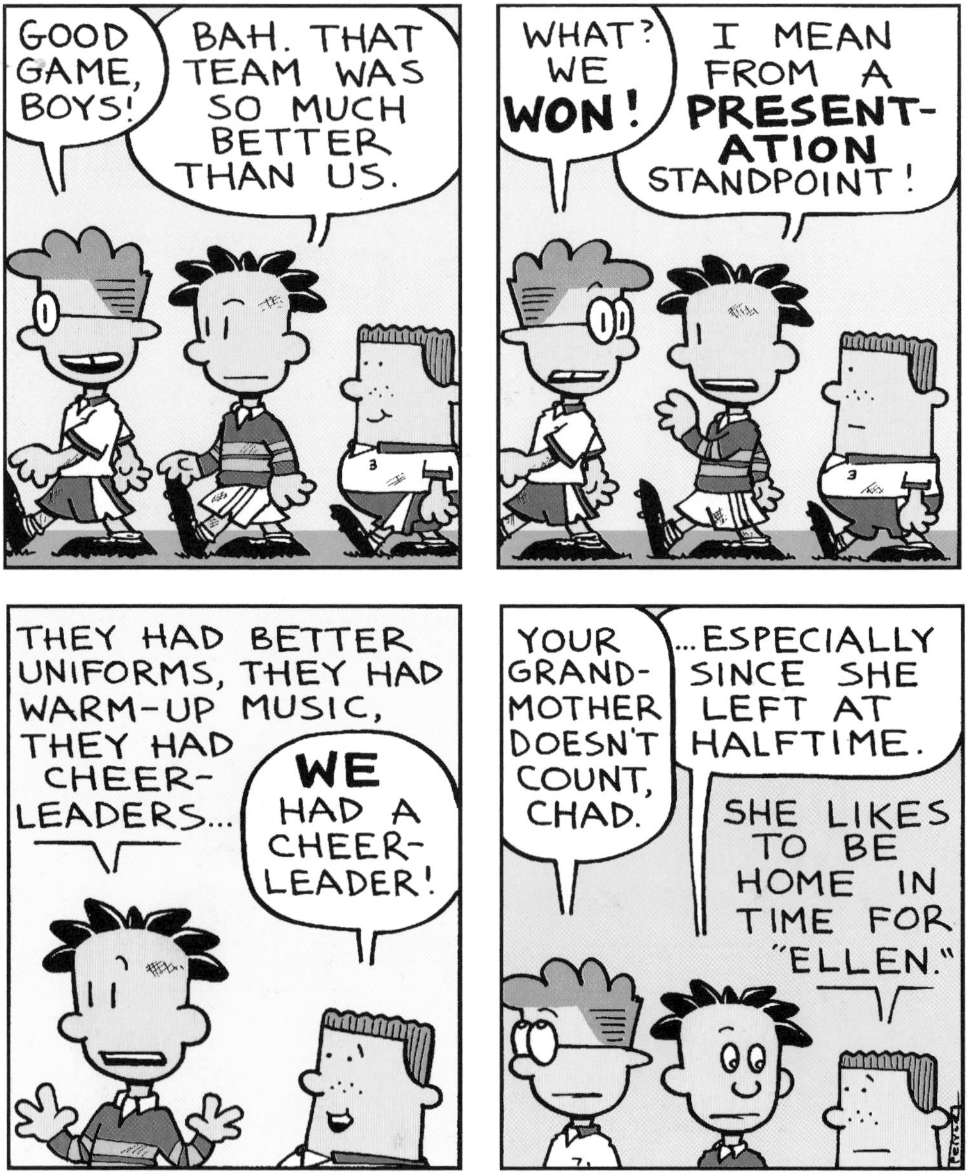
GOOD GAME, BOYS!
BAH. THAT TEAM WAS SO MUCH BETTER THAN US.
WHAT? WE WON!
I MEAN FROM A PRESENTATION STANDPOINT!
THEY HAD BETTER UNIFORMS, THEY HAD WARM-UP MUSIC, THEY HAD CHEERLEADERS...
WE HAD A CHEERLEADER!
YOUR GRANDMOTHER DOESN'T COUNT, CHAD.
...ESPECIALLY SINCE SHE LEFT AT HALFTIME.
SHE LIKES TO BE HOME IN TIME FOR "ELLEN."

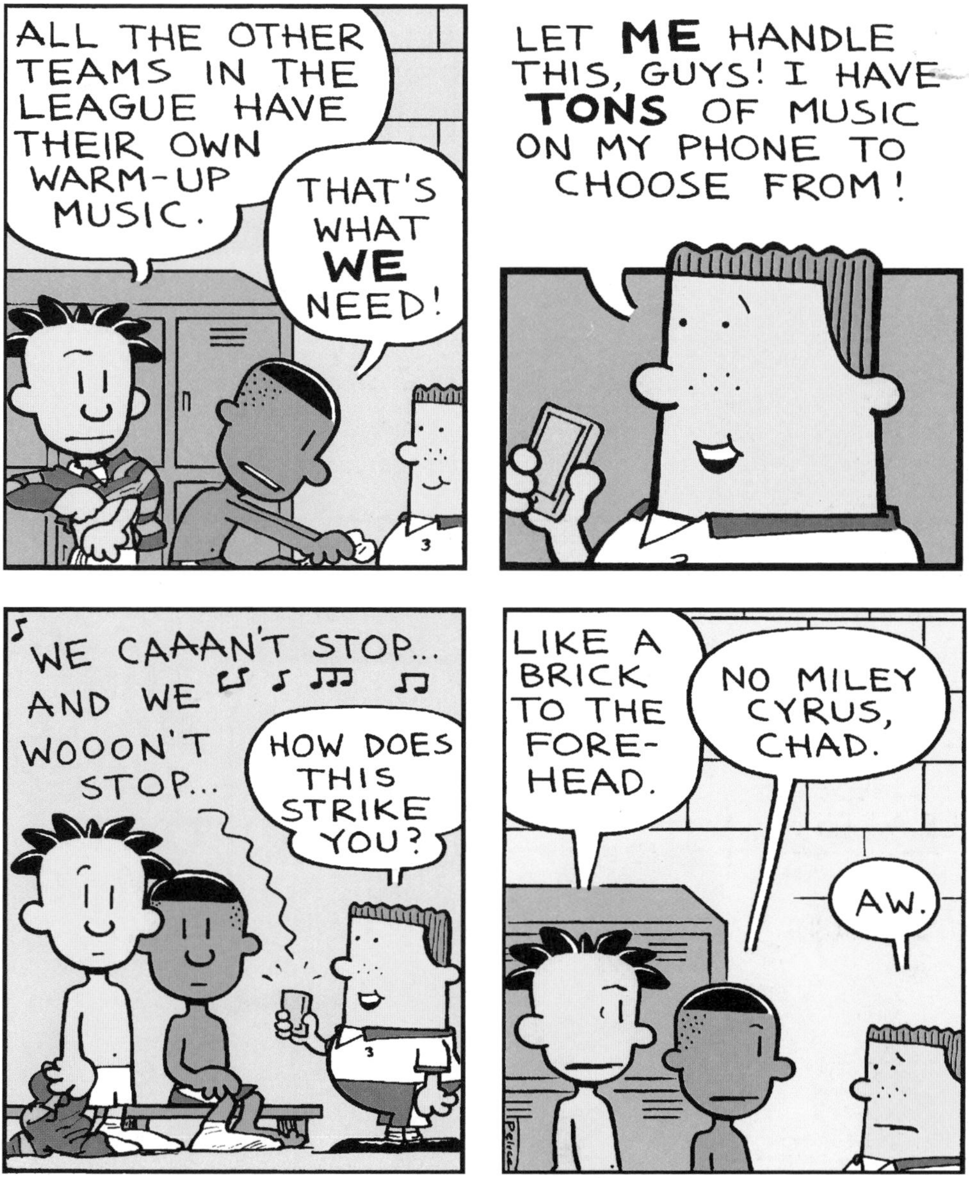
ALL THE OTHER TEAMS IN THE LEAGUE HAVE THEIR OWN WARM-UP MUSIC.
THAT'S WHAT WE NEED!
LET ME HANDLE THIS, GUYS! I HAVE TONS OF MUSIC ON MY PHONE TO CHOOSE FROM!
WE CAAAN'T STOP... AND WE WOOON'T STOP...
HOW DOES THIS STRIKE YOU?
LIKE A BRICK TO THE FORE-HEAD.
NO MILEY CYRUS, CHAD.
AW.

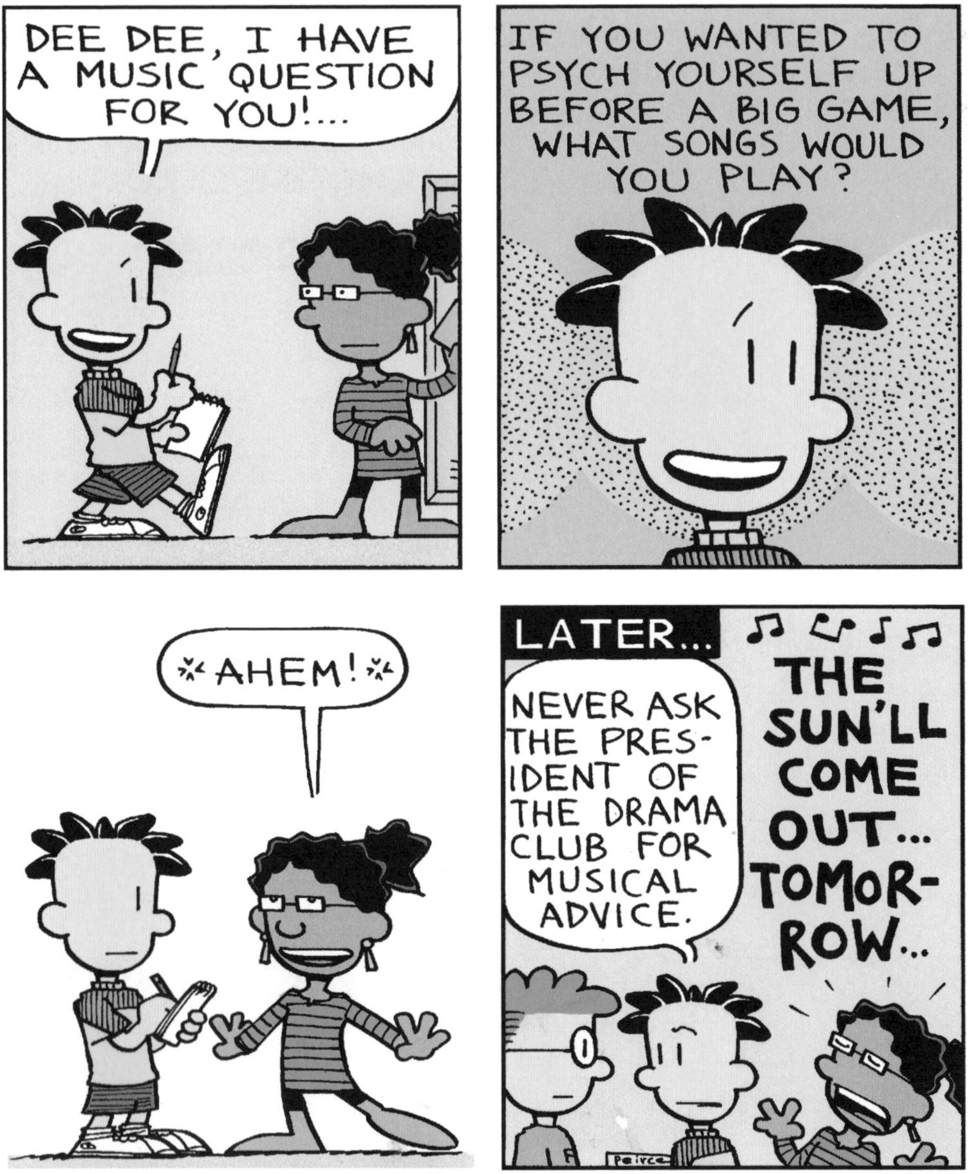
DEE DEE, I HAVE A MUSIC QUESTION FOR YOU!...
IF YOU WANTED TO PSYCH YOURSELF UP BEFORE A BIG GAME, WHAT SONGS WOULD YOU PLAY?
AHEM!
LATER...
NEVER ASK THE PRESIDENT OF THE DRAMA CLUB FOR MUSICAL ADVICE.
THE SUN'LL COME OUT... TOMORROW...
Peirce

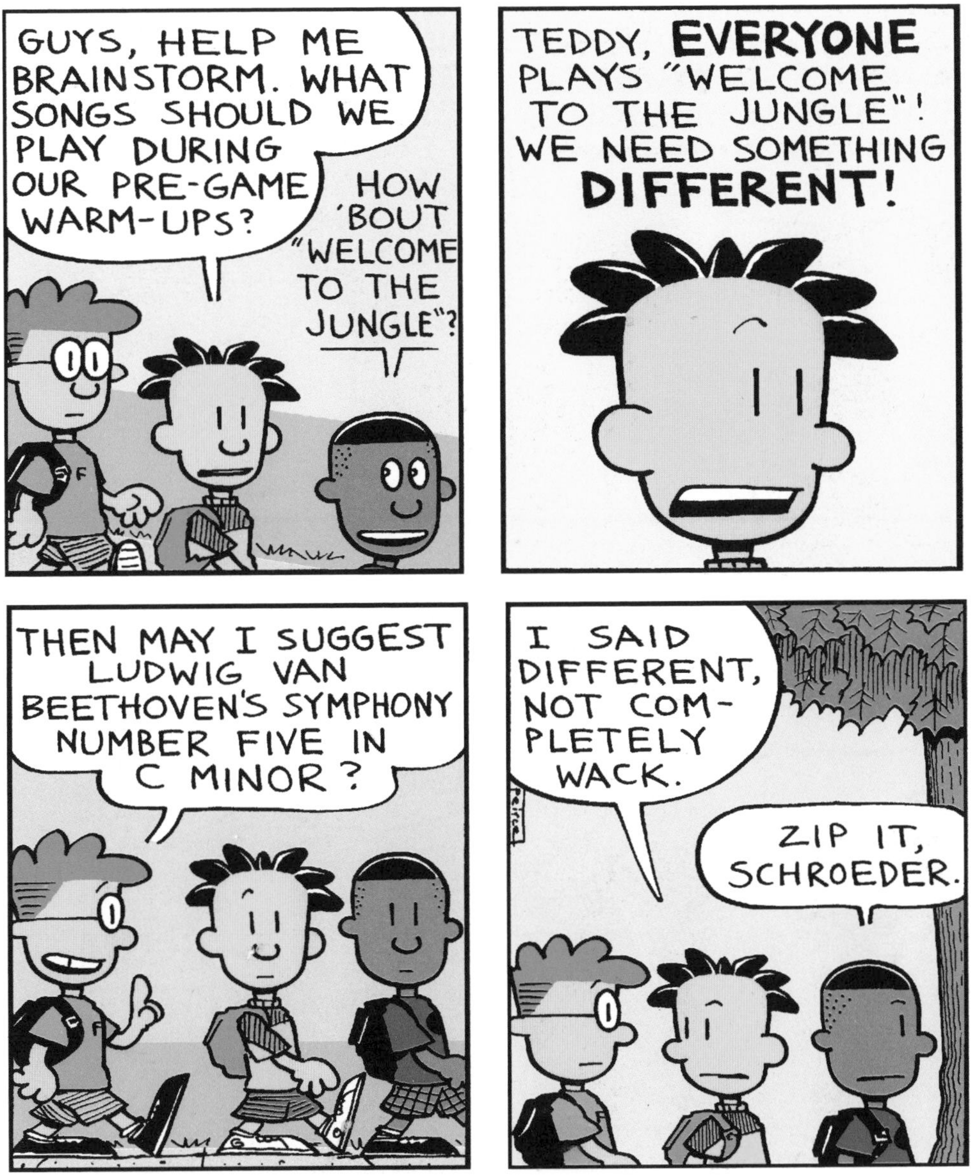
GUYS, HELP ME BRAINSTORM. WHAT SONGS SHOULD WE PLAY DURING OUR PRE-GAME WARM-UPS?
HOW 'BOUT "WELCOME TO THE JUNGLE"?
TEDDY, EVERYONE PLAYS "WELCOME TO THE JUNGLE"! WE NEED SOMETHING DIFFERENT!
THEN MAY I SUGGEST LUDWIG VAN BEETHOVEN'S SYMPHONY NUMBER FIVE IN C MINOR?
I SAID DIFFERENT, NOT COMPLETELY WACK.
ZIP IT, SCHROEDER.
peirce

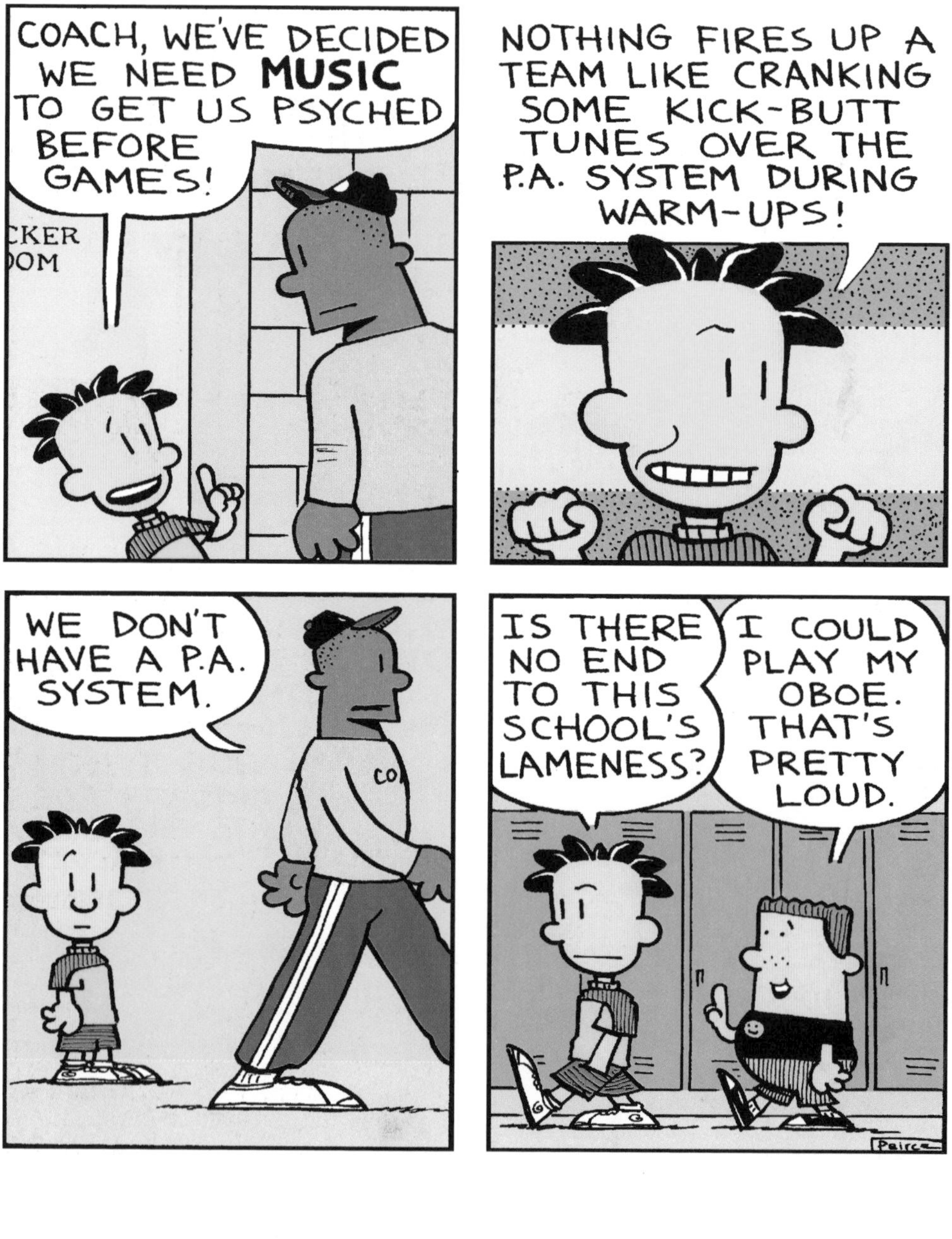
COACH, WE'VE DECIDED WE NEED **MUSIC** TO GET US PSYCHED BEFORE GAMES!
CKER
OOM
NOTHING FIRES UP A TEAM LIKE CRANKING SOME KICK-BUTT TUNES OVER THE P.A. SYSTEM DURING WARM-UPS!
WE DON'T HAVE A P.A. SYSTEM.
CO
IS THERE NO END TO THIS SCHOOL'S LAMENESS?
I COULD PLAY MY OBOE. THAT'S PRETTY LOUD.
Peirce

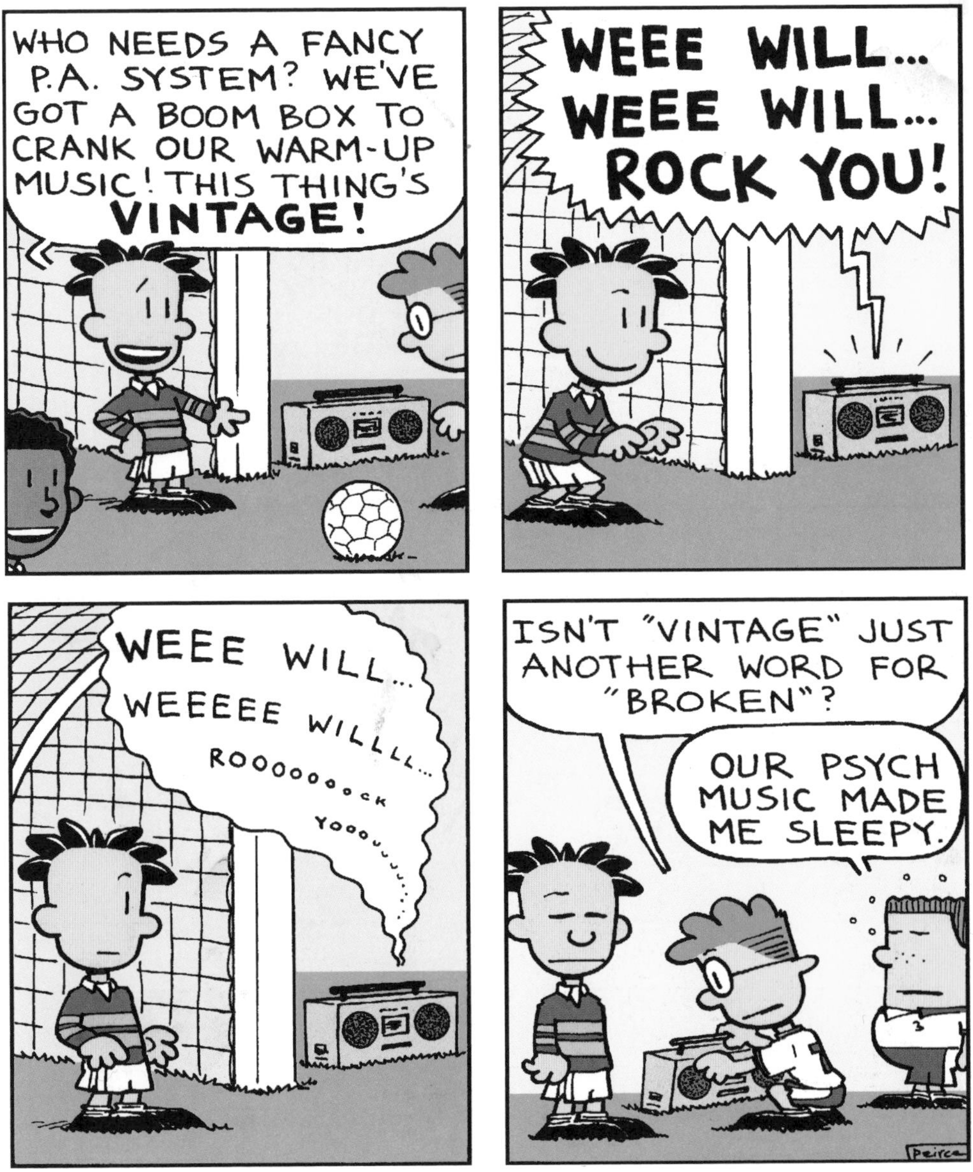
WHO NEEDS A FANCY P.A. SYSTEM? WE'VE GOT A BOOM BOX TO CRANK OUR WARM-UP MUSIC! THIS THING'S **VINTAGE**!
WEEE WILL... WEEE WILL... ROCK YOU!
WEEE WILL... WEEEEE WILLLL... ROOOOOOOOCK YOOOUUUU...
ISN'T "VINTAGE" JUST ANOTHER WORD FOR "BROKEN"?
OUR PSYCH MUSIC MADE ME SLEEPY.
Peirce

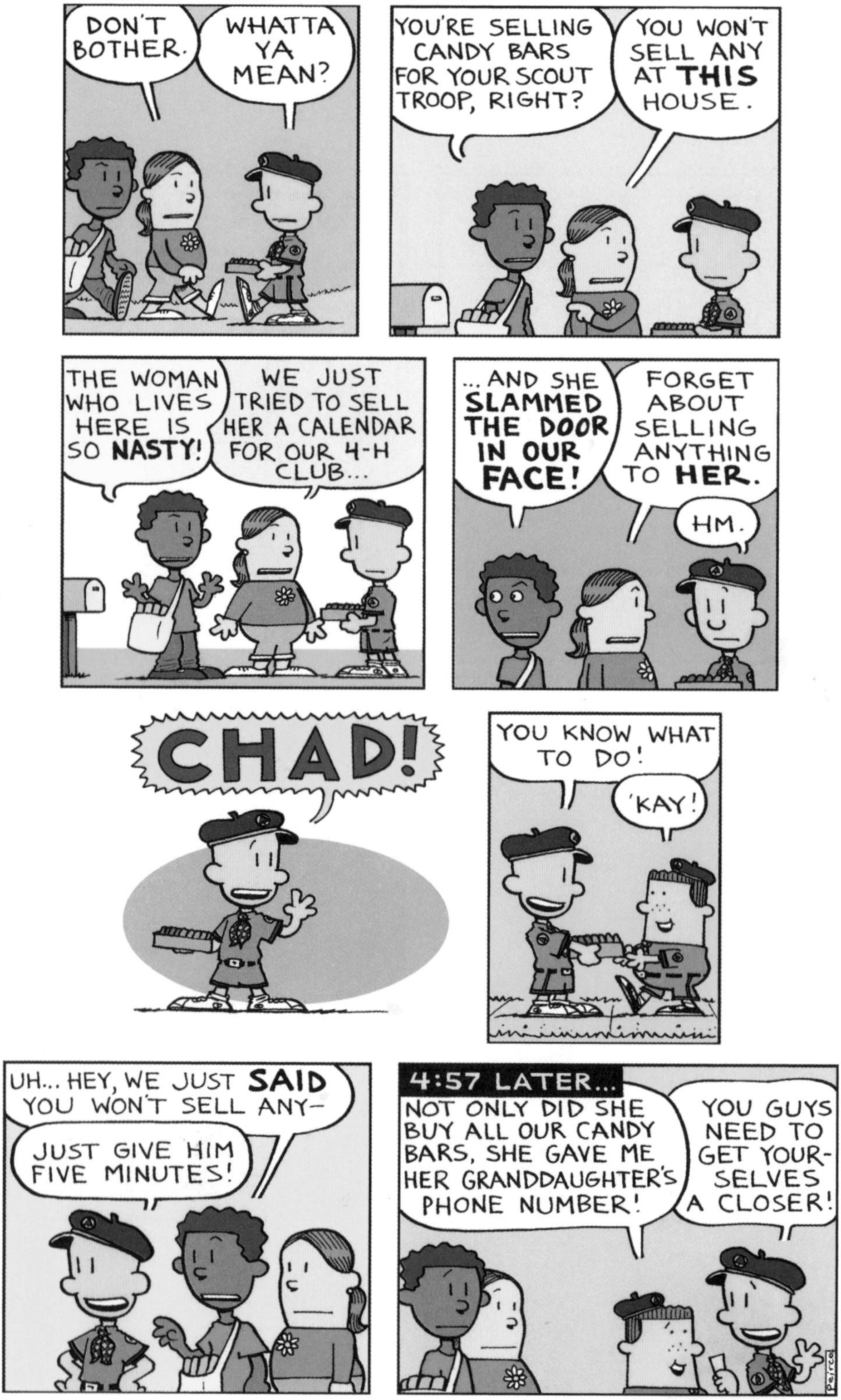
DON'T BOTHER.
WHATTA YA MEAN?
YOU'RE SELLING CANDY BARS FOR YOUR SCOUT TROOP, RIGHT?
YOU WON'T SELL ANY AT **THIS** HOUSE.
THE WOMAN WHO LIVES HERE IS SO **NASTY**!
WE JUST TRIED TO SELL HER A CALENDAR FOR OUR 4-H CLUB...
... AND SHE **SLAMMED THE DOOR IN OUR FACE!**
FORGET ABOUT SELLING ANYTHING TO **HER**.
HM.
CHAD!
YOU KNOW WHAT TO DO!
'KAY!
UH... HEY, WE JUST **SAID** YOU WON'T SELL ANY-
JUST GIVE HIM FIVE MINUTES!
4:57 LATER...
NOT ONLY DID SHE BUY ALL OUR CANDY BARS, SHE GAVE ME HER GRANDDAUGHTER'S PHONE NUMBER!
YOU GUYS NEED TO GET YOURSELVES A CLOSER!
Peirce

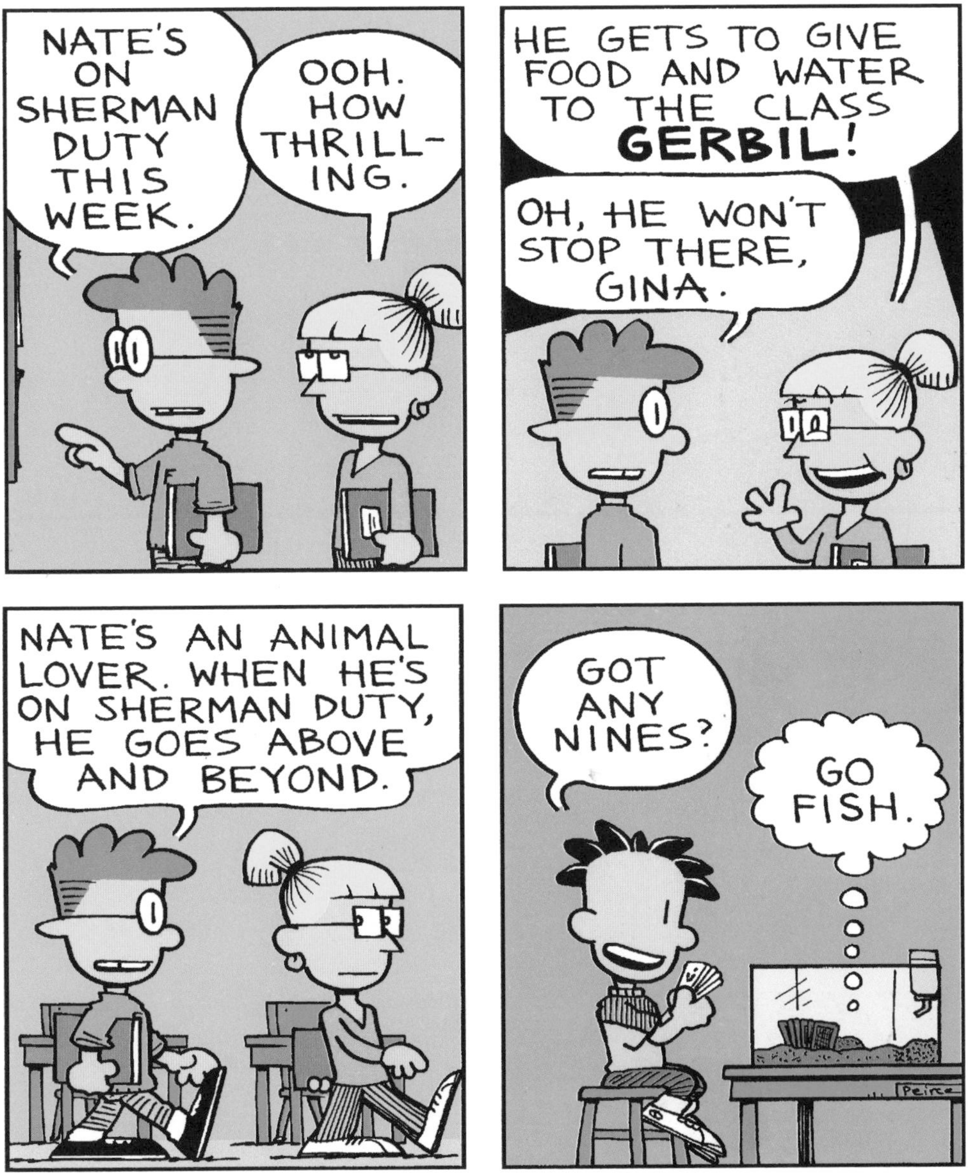
NATE'S ON SHERMAN DUTY THIS WEEK.
OOH. HOW THRILL-ING.
HE GETS TO GIVE FOOD AND WATER TO THE CLASS **GERBIL!**
OH, HE WON'T STOP THERE, GINA.
NATE'S AN ANIMAL LOVER. WHEN HE'S ON SHERMAN DUTY, HE GOES ABOVE AND BEYOND.
GOT ANY NINES?
GO FISH.
Peirce

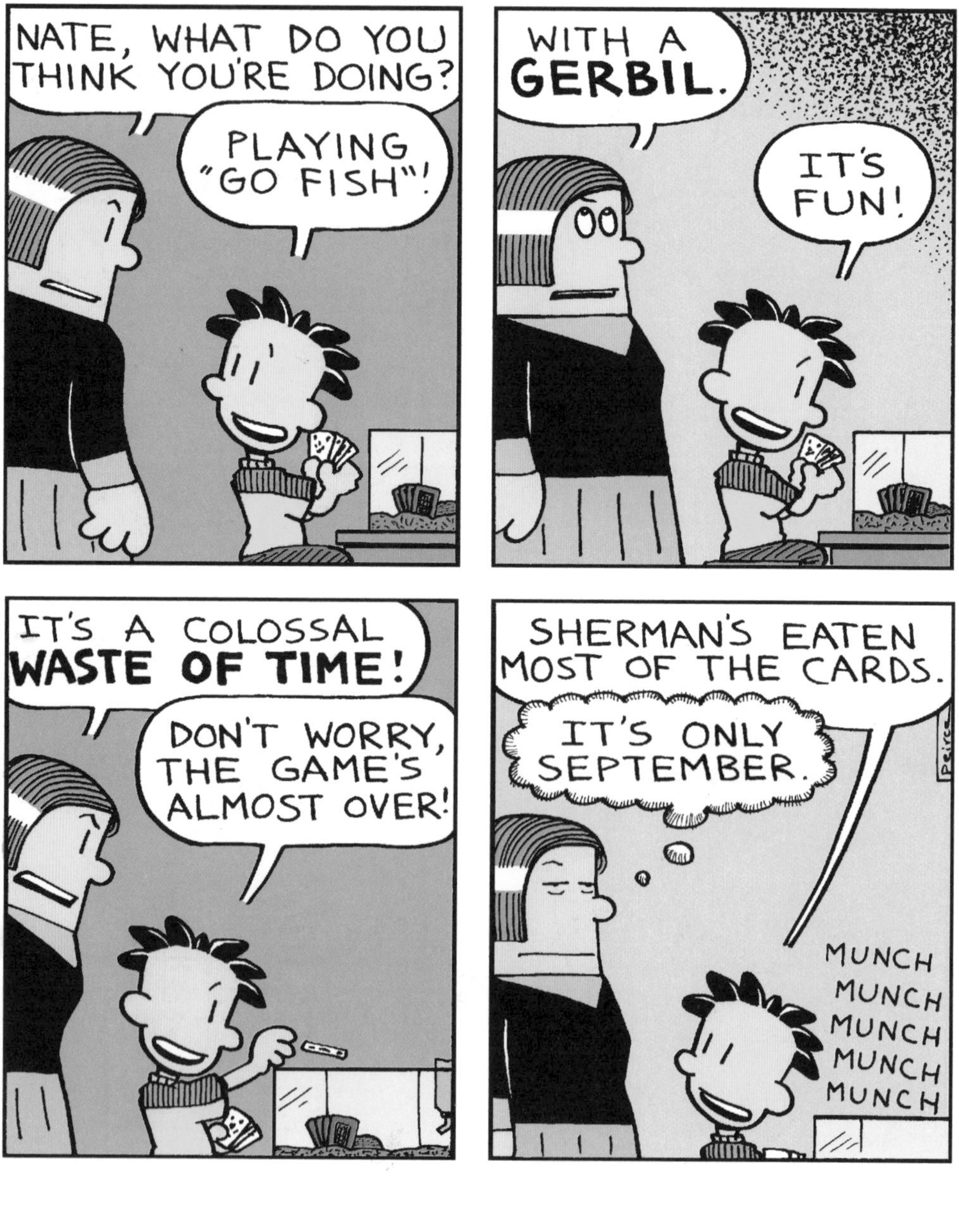
NATE, WHAT DO YOU THINK YOU'RE DOING?
PLAYING "GO FISH"!
WITH A **GERBIL**.
IT'S FUN!
IT'S A COLOSSAL **WASTE OF TIME!**
DON'T WORRY, THE GAME'S ALMOST OVER!
SHERMAN'S EATEN MOST OF THE CARDS.
IT'S ONLY SEPTEMBER.
MUNCH
MUNCH
MUNCH
MUNCH
MUNCH

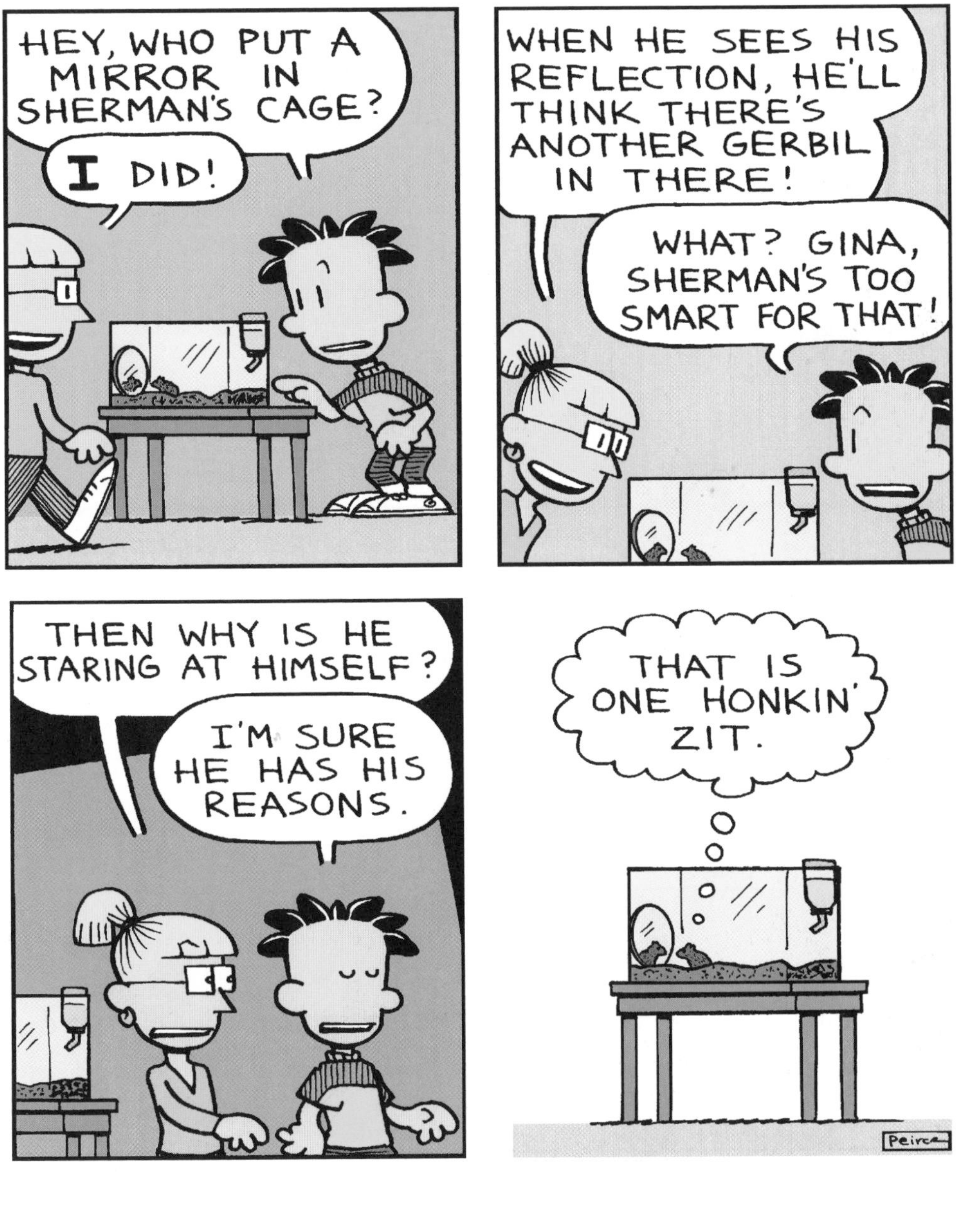
HEY, WHO PUT A MIRROR IN SHERMAN'S CAGE?
I DID!
WHEN HE SEES HIS REFLECTION, HE'LL THINK THERE'S ANOTHER GERBIL IN THERE!
WHAT? GINA, SHERMAN'S TOO SMART FOR THAT!
THEN WHY IS HE STARING AT HIMSELF?
I'M SURE HE HAS HIS REASONS.
THAT IS ONE HONKIN' ZIT.
Peirce

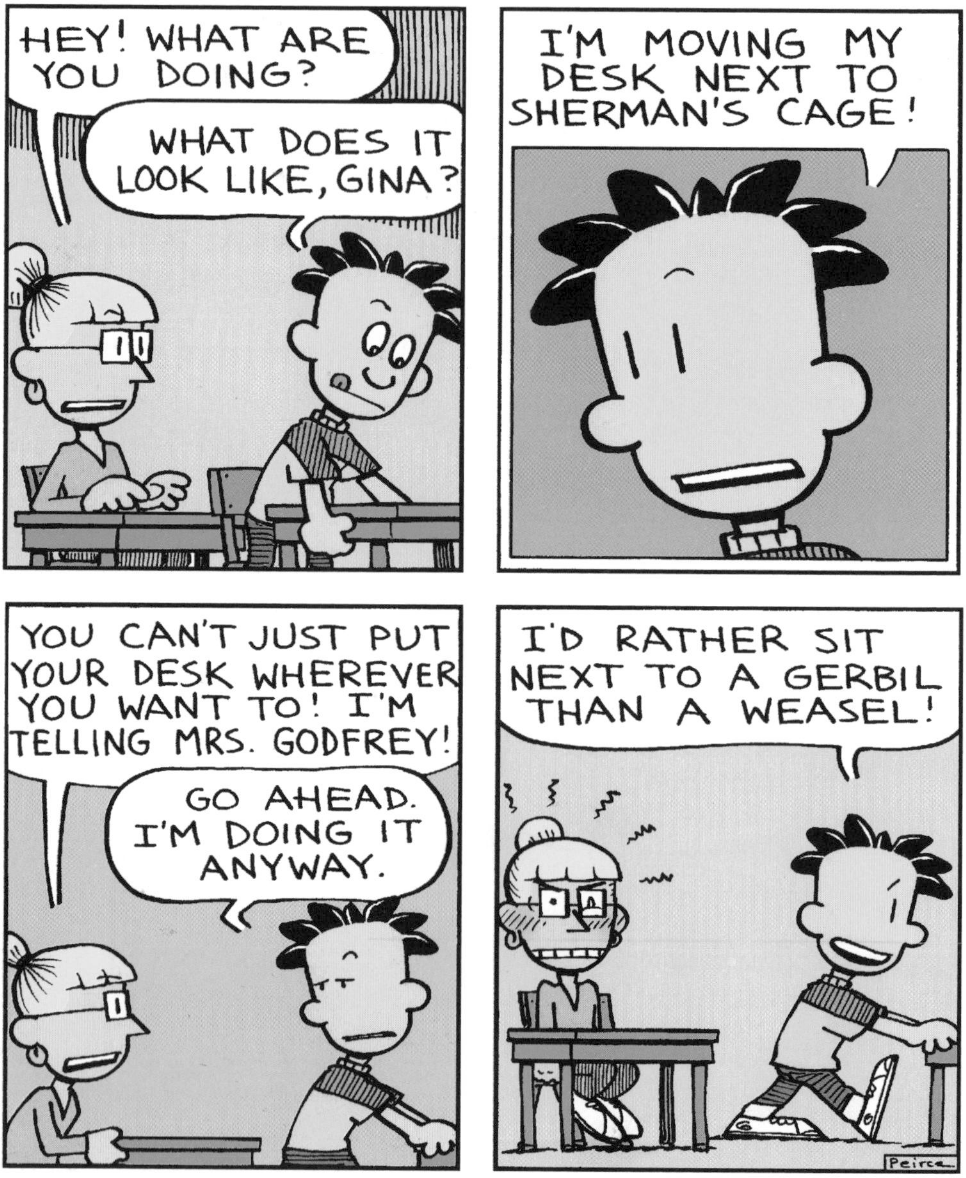
HEY! WHAT ARE YOU DOING?
WHAT DOES IT LOOK LIKE, GINA?
I'M MOVING MY DESK NEXT TO SHERMAN'S CAGE!
YOU CAN'T JUST PUT YOUR DESK WHEREVER YOU WANT TO! I'M TELLING MRS. GODFREY!
GO AHEAD. I'M DOING IT ANYWAY.
I'D RATHER SIT NEXT TO A GERBIL THAN A WEASEL!
Peirce

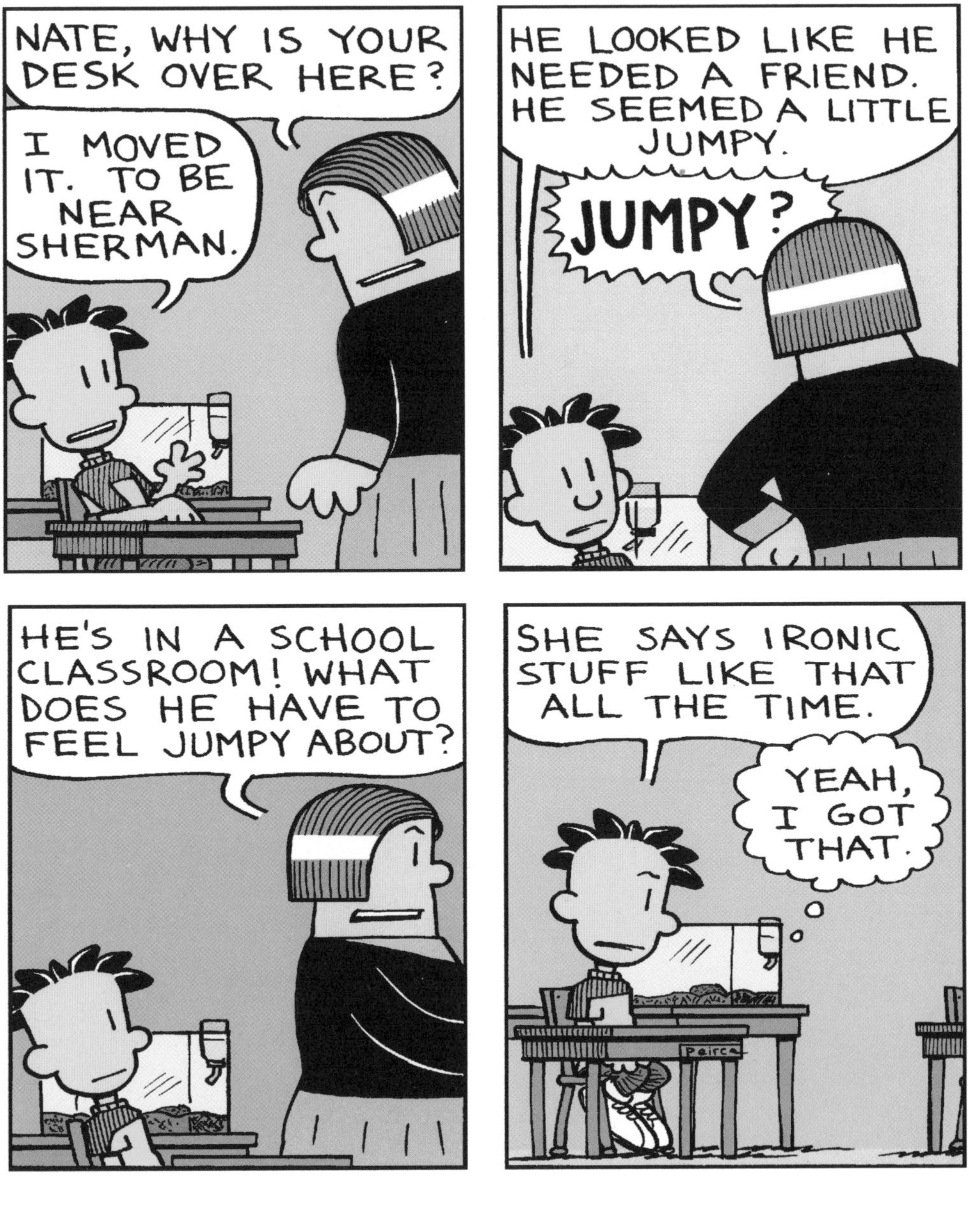
NATE, WHY IS YOUR DESK OVER HERE?
I MOVED IT. TO BE NEAR SHERMAN.
HE LOOKED LIKE HE NEEDED A FRIEND. HE SEEMED A LITTLE JUMPY.
JUMPY?
HE'S IN A SCHOOL CLASSROOM! WHAT DOES HE HAVE TO FEEL JUMPY ABOUT?
SHE SAYS IRONIC STUFF LIKE THAT ALL THE TIME.
YEAH, I GOT THAT.
PEIRCE

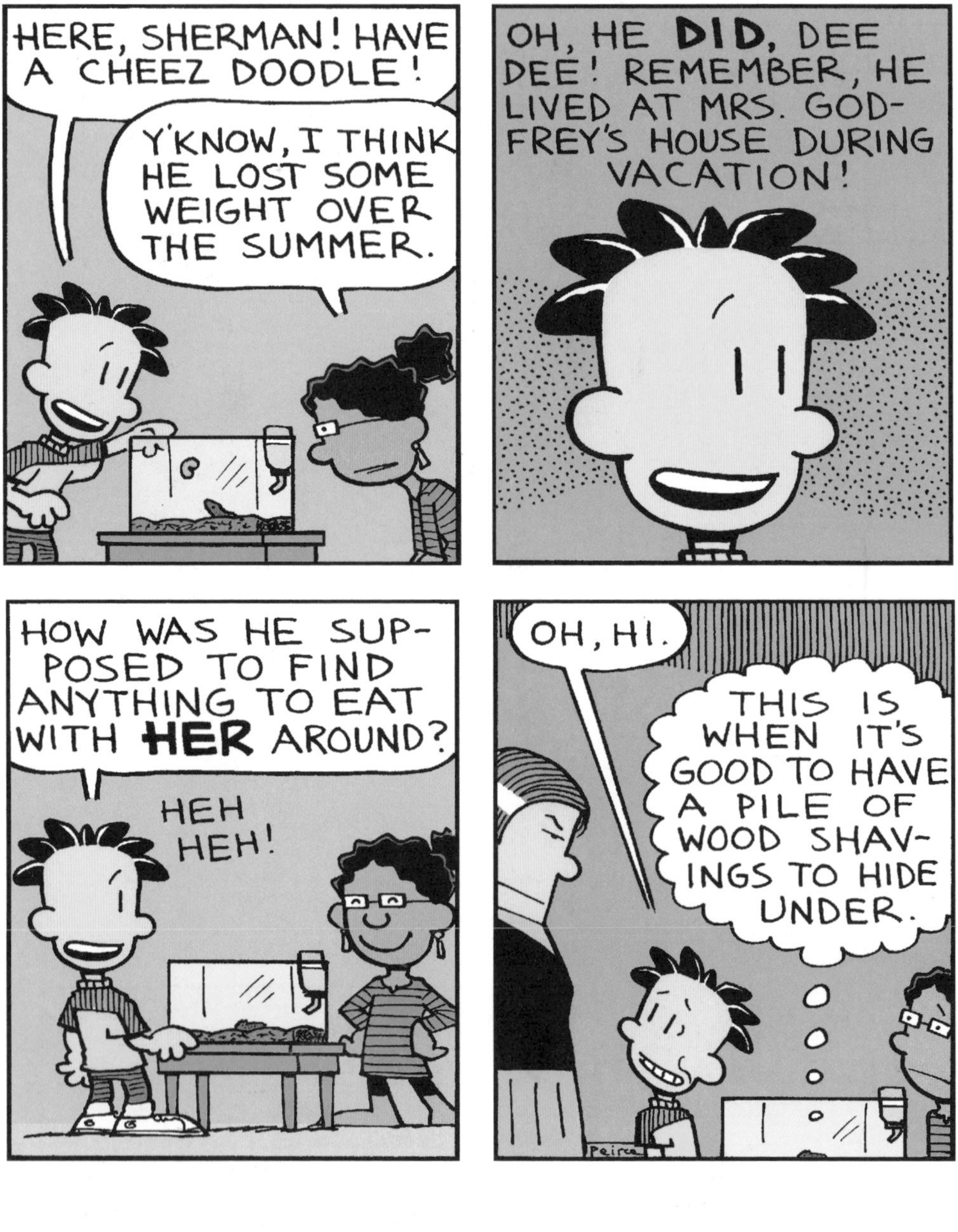
HERE, SHERMAN! HAVE A CHEEZ DOODLE!
Y'KNOW, I THINK HE LOST SOME WEIGHT OVER THE SUMMER.
OH, HE **DID**, DEE DEE! REMEMBER, HE LIVED AT MRS. GODFREY'S HOUSE DURING VACATION!
HOW WAS HE SUPPOSED TO FIND ANYTHING TO EAT WITH **HER** AROUND?
HEH HEH!
OH, HI.
THIS IS WHEN IT'S GOOD TO HAVE A PILE OF WOOD SHAVINGS TO HIDE UNDER.
Peirce

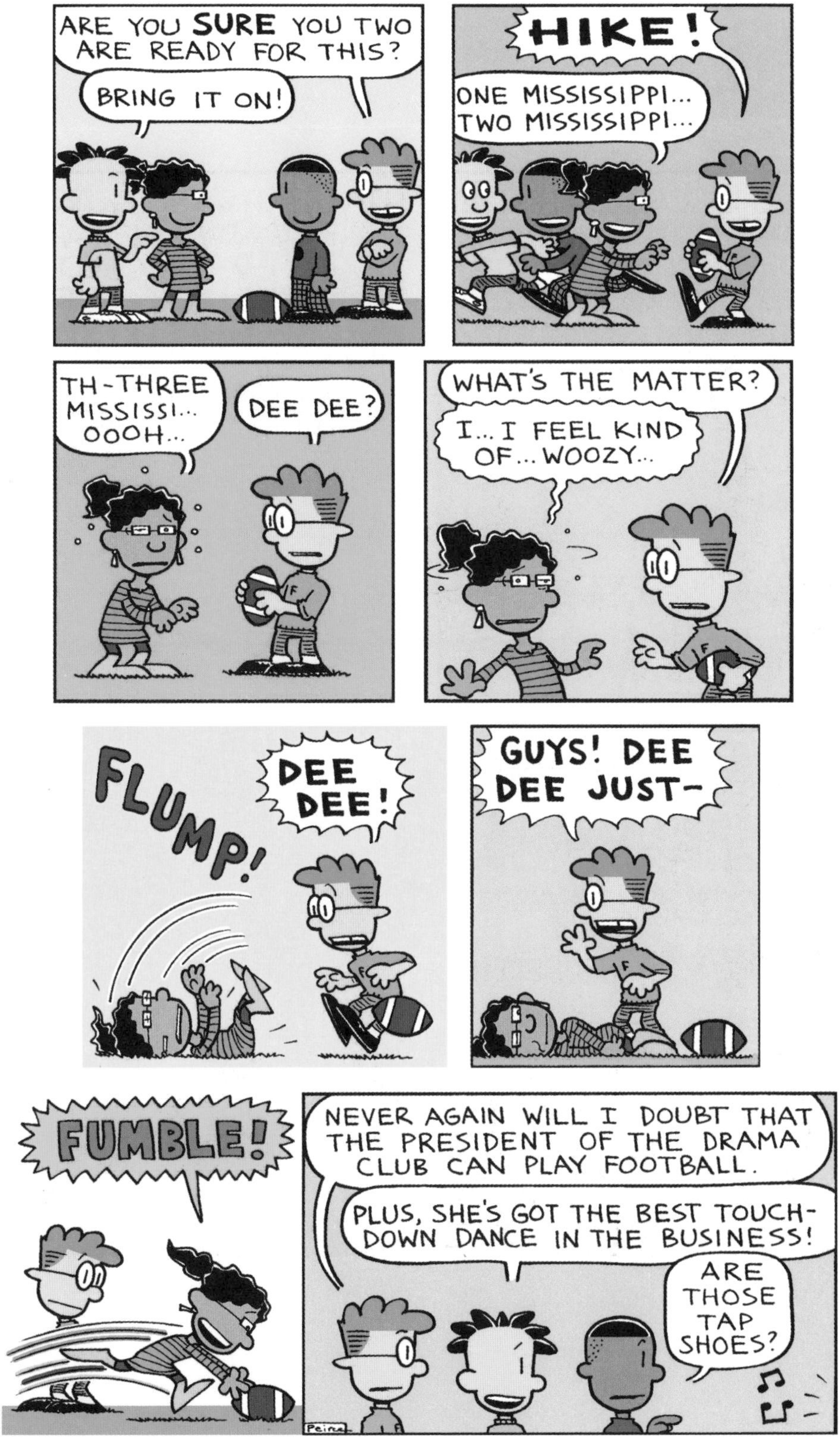
ARE YOU SURE YOU TWO ARE READY FOR THIS?
BRING IT ON!
HIKE!
ONE MISSISSIPPI... TWO MISSISSIPPI...
TH-THREE MISSISSI... OOOH...
DEE DEE?
WHAT'S THE MATTER?
I... I FEEL KIND OF... WOOZY...
FLUMP!
DEE DEE!
GUYS! DEE DEE JUST-
FUMBLE!
NEVER AGAIN WILL I DOUBT THAT THE PRESIDENT OF THE DRAMA CLUB CAN PLAY FOOTBALL.
PLUS, SHE'S GOT THE BEST TOUCH-DOWN DANCE IN THE BUSINESS!
ARE THOSE TAP SHOES?
Peirce

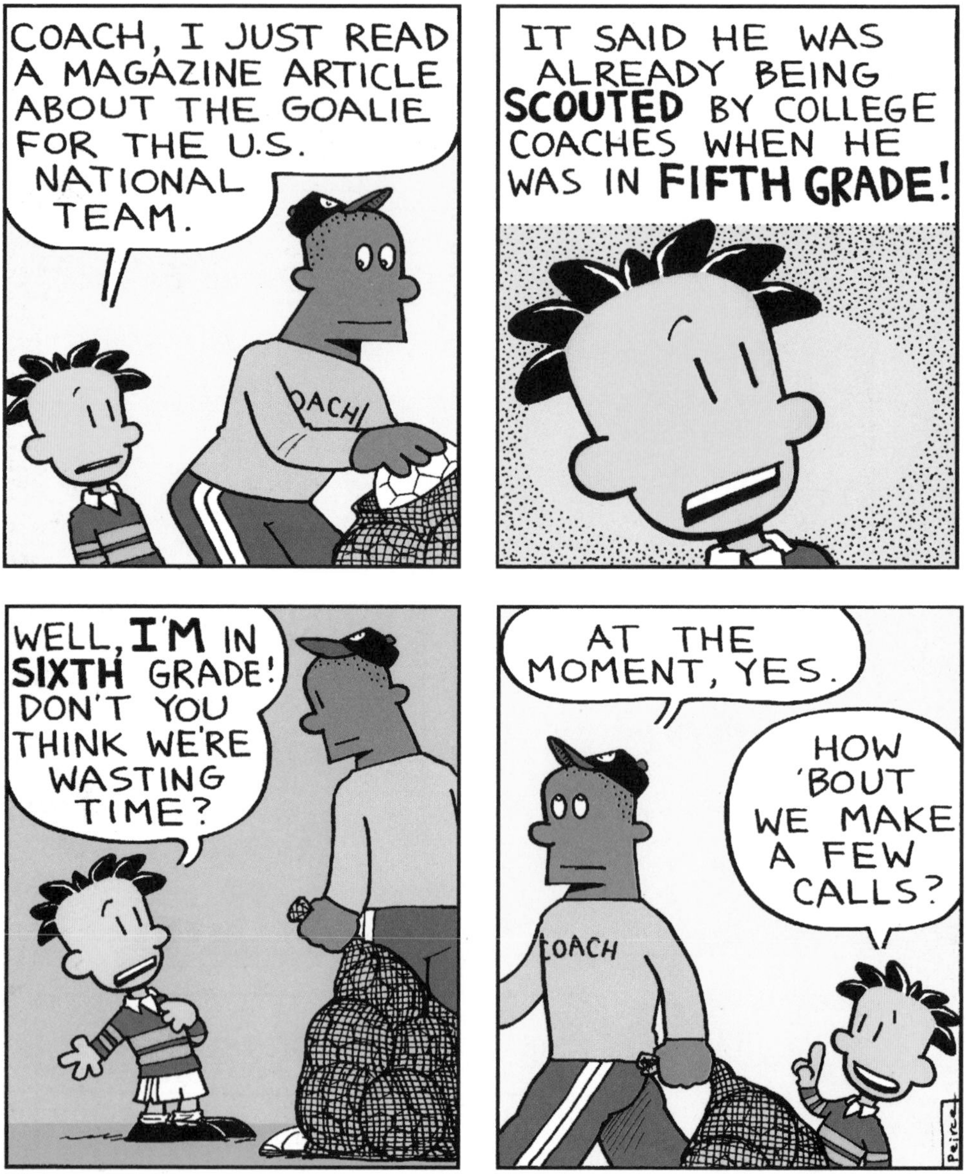
COACH, I JUST READ A MAGAZINE ARTICLE ABOUT THE GOALIE FOR THE U.S. NATIONAL TEAM.
IT SAID HE WAS ALREADY BEING SCOUTED BY COLLEGE COACHES WHEN HE WAS IN FIFTH GRADE!
WELL, I'M IN SIXTH GRADE! DON'T YOU THINK WE'RE WASTING TIME?
AT THE MOMENT, YES.
HOW 'BOUT WE MAKE A FEW CALLS?
Peirce

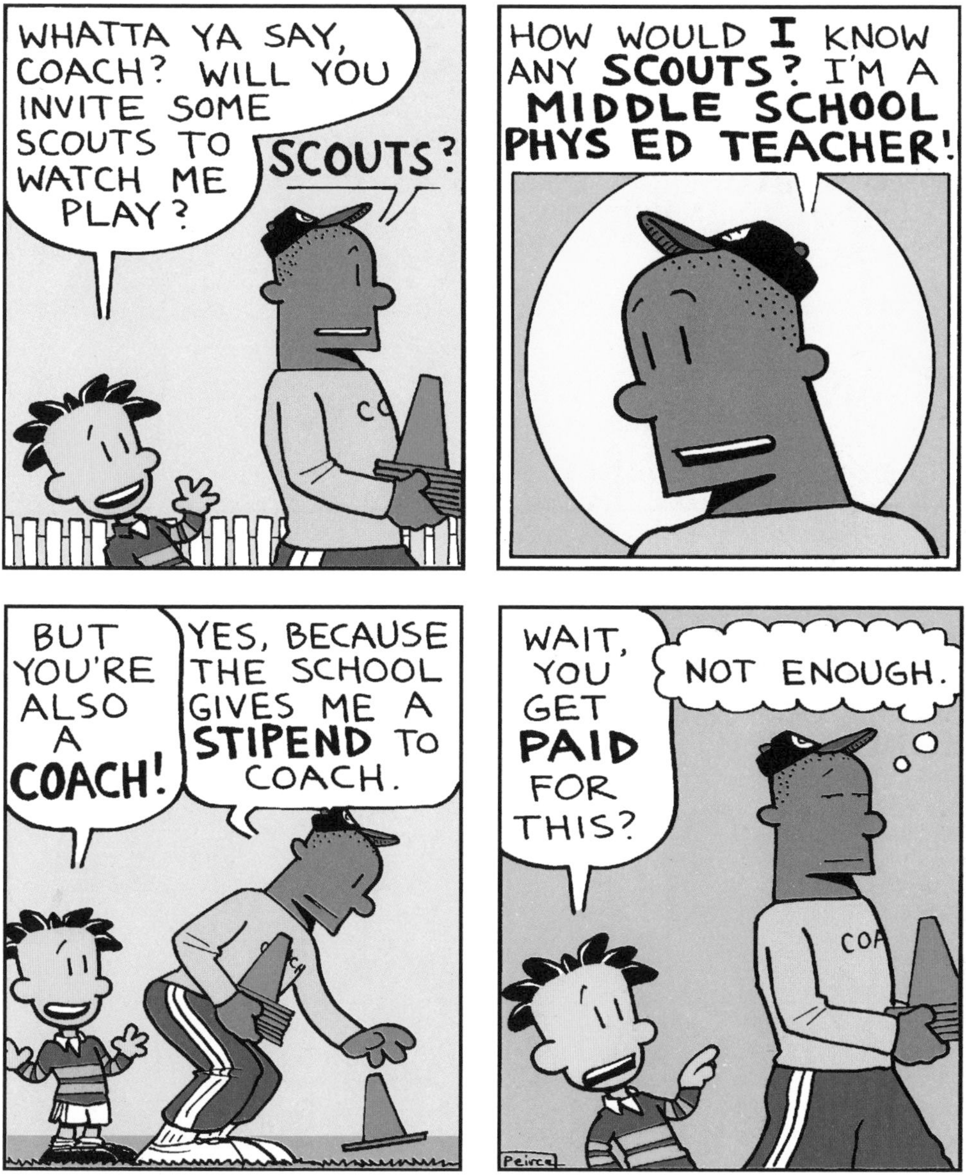
WHATTA YA SAY, COACH? WILL YOU INVITE SOME SCOUTS TO WATCH ME PLAY?
SCOUTS?
HOW WOULD I KNOW ANY SCOUTS? I'M A MIDDLE SCHOOL PHYS ED TEACHER!
BUT YOU'RE ALSO A COACH!
YES, BECAUSE THE SCHOOL GIVES ME A STIPEND TO COACH.
WAIT, YOU GET PAID FOR THIS?
NOT ENOUGH.
Peirce

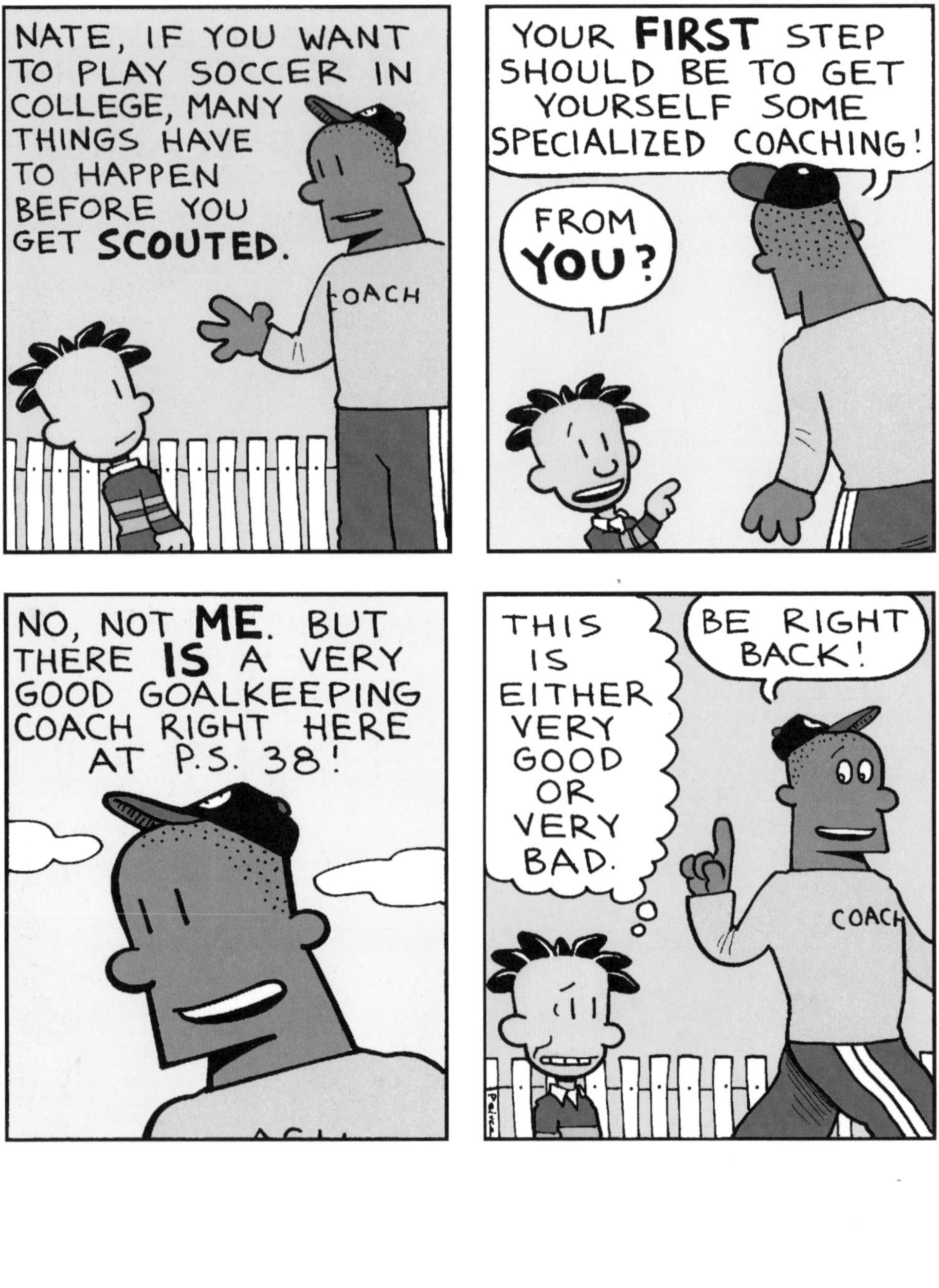
NATE, IF YOU WANT TO PLAY SOCCER IN COLLEGE, MANY THINGS HAVE TO HAPPEN BEFORE YOU GET SCOUTED.
COACH
YOUR FIRST STEP SHOULD BE TO GET YOURSELF SOME SPECIALIZED COACHING!
FROM YOU?
NO, NOT ME. BUT THERE IS A VERY GOOD GOALKEEPING COACH RIGHT HERE AT P.S. 38!
THIS IS EITHER VERY GOOD OR VERY BAD.
BE RIGHT BACK!
COACH

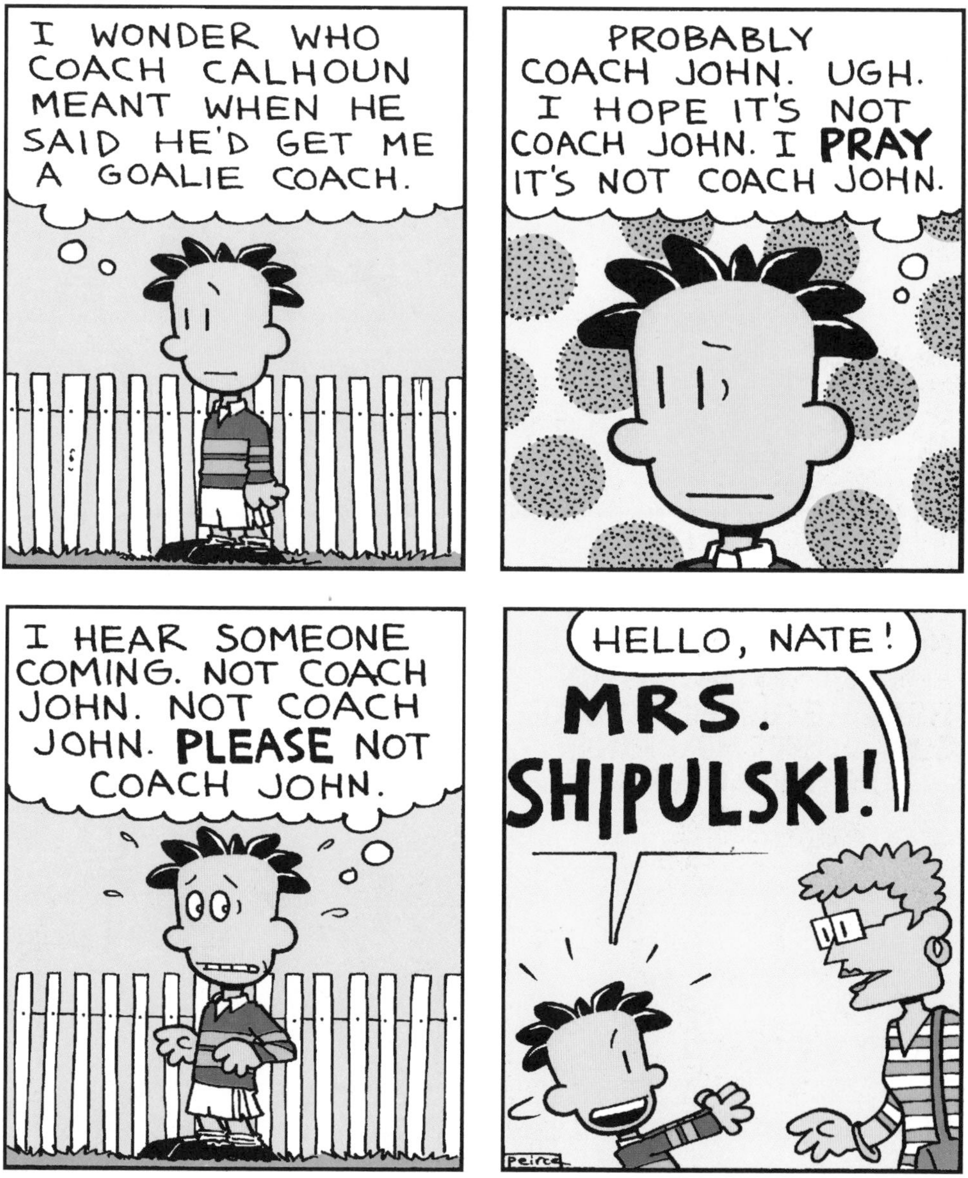
I WONDER WHO COACH CALHOUN MEANT WHEN HE SAID HE'D GET ME A GOALIE COACH.
PROBABLY COACH JOHN. UGH. I HOPE IT'S NOT COACH JOHN. I **PRAY** IT'S NOT COACH JOHN.
I HEAR SOMEONE COMING. NOT COACH JOHN. NOT COACH JOHN. **PLEASE** NOT COACH JOHN.
HELLO, NATE!
MRS. SHIPULSKI!
peirce

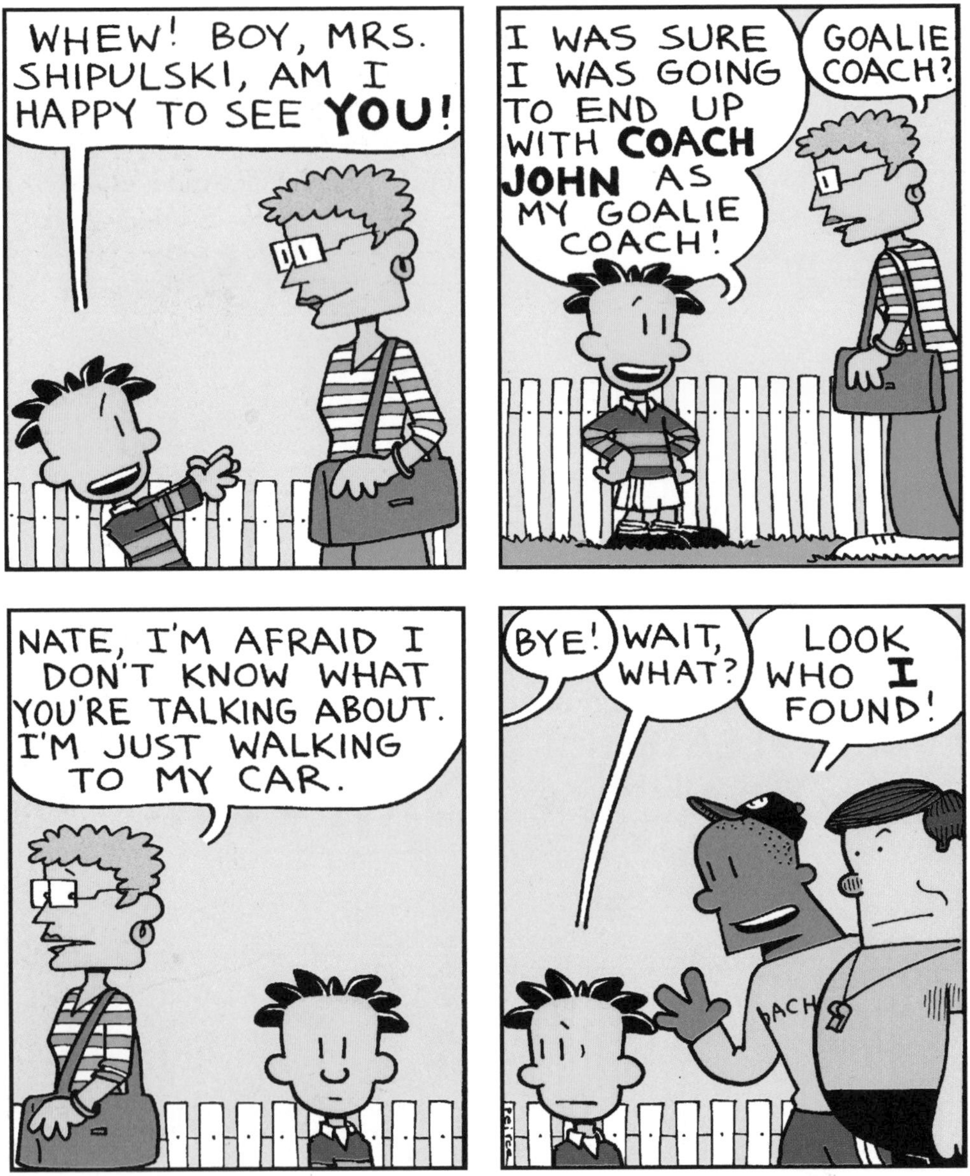
WHEW! BOY, MRS. SHIPULSKI, AM I HAPPY TO SEE **YOU**!
I WAS SURE I WAS GOING TO END UP WITH **COACH JOHN** AS MY GOALIE COACH!
GOALIE COACH?
NATE, I'M AFRAID I DON'T KNOW WHAT YOU'RE TALKING ABOUT. I'M JUST WALKING TO MY CAR.
BYE!
WAIT, WHAT?
LOOK WHO **I** FOUND!

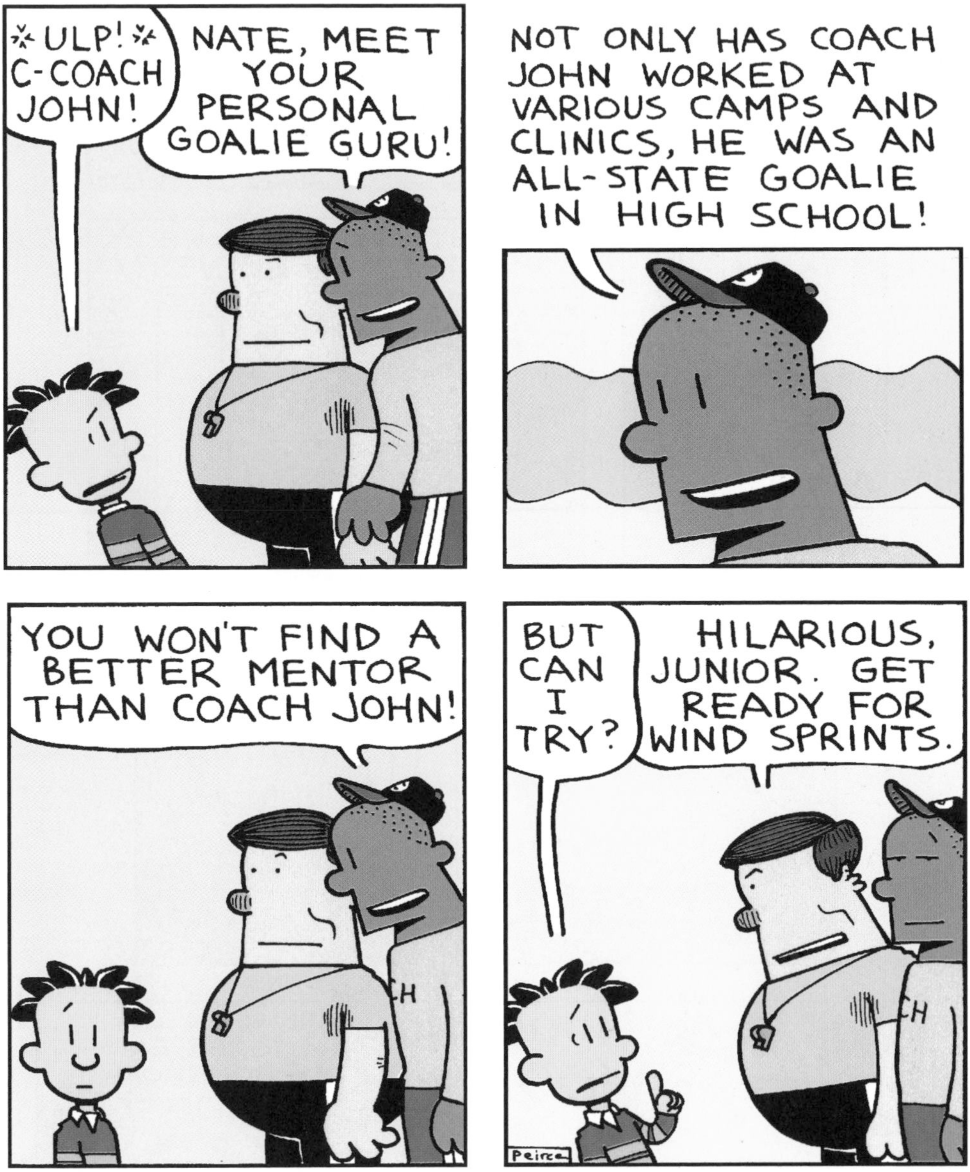

✳ULP!✳ C-COACH JOHN!
NATE, MEET YOUR PERSONAL GOALIE GURU!
NOT ONLY HAS COACH JOHN WORKED AT VARIOUS CAMPS AND CLINICS, HE WAS AN ALL-STATE GOALIE IN HIGH SCHOOL!
YOU WON'T FIND A BETTER MENTOR THAN COACH JOHN!
BUT CAN I TRY?
HILARIOUS, JUNIOR. GET READY FOR WIND SPRINTS.
Peirce

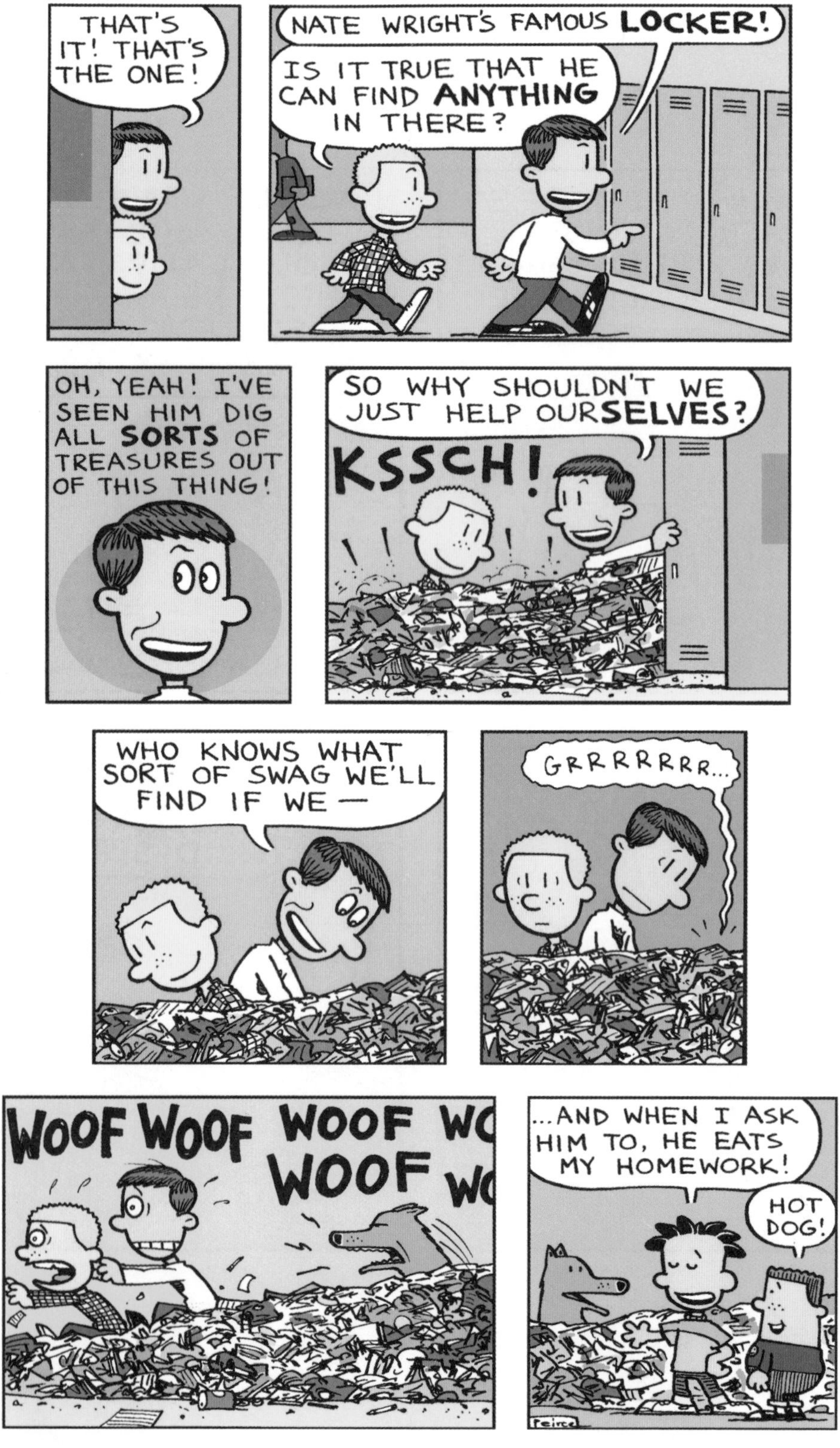
THAT'S IT! THAT'S THE ONE!
NATE WRIGHT'S FAMOUS **LOCKER**!
IS IT TRUE THAT HE CAN FIND **ANYTHING** IN THERE?
OH, YEAH! I'VE SEEN HIM DIG ALL **SORTS** OF TREASURES OUT OF THIS THING!
SO WHY SHOULDN'T WE JUST HELP OUR**SELVES**?
KSSCH!
WHO KNOWS WHAT SORT OF SWAG WE'LL FIND IF WE—
GRRRRRRR...
WOOF WOOF WOOF
WOOF
...AND WHEN I ASK HIM TO, HE EATS MY HOMEWORK!
HOT DOG!

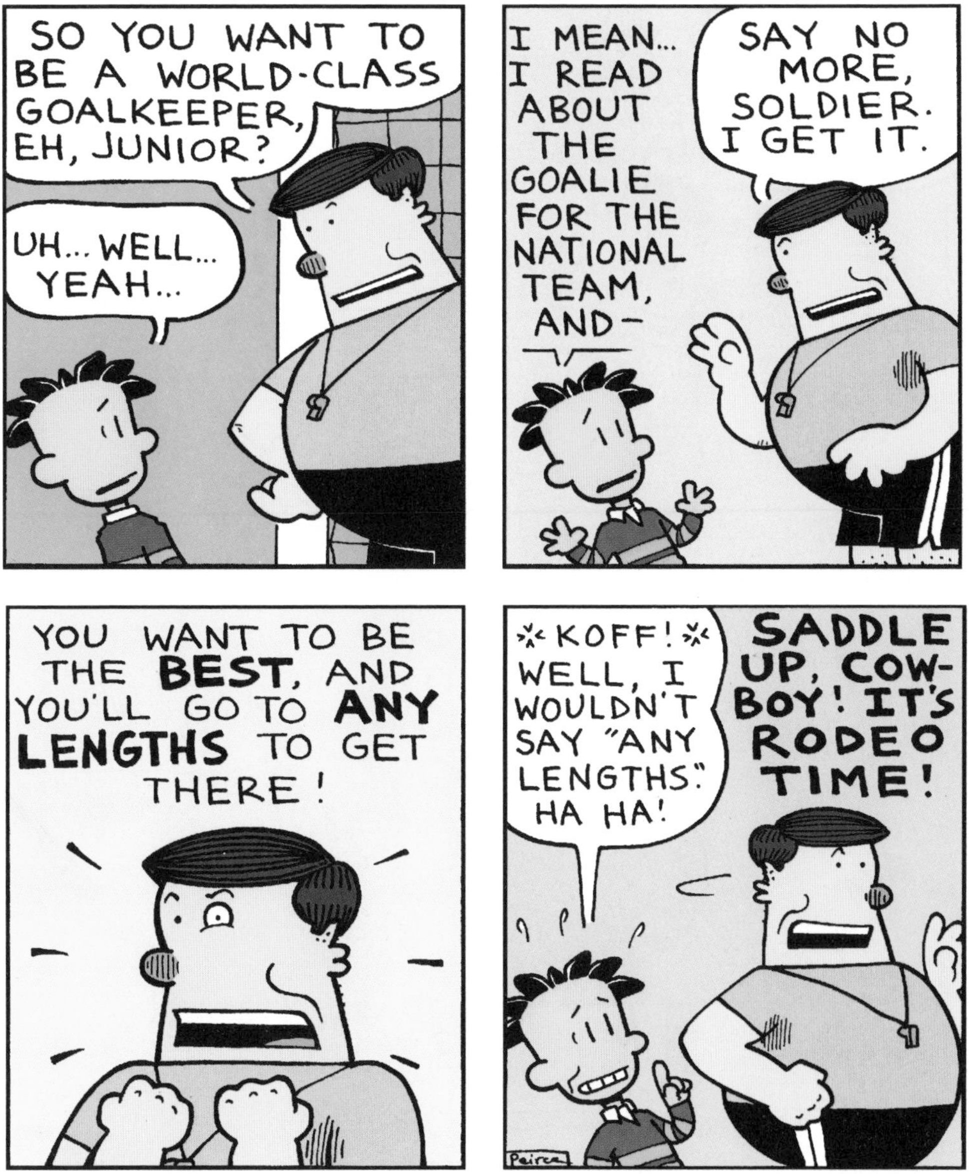
SO YOU WANT TO BE A WORLD-CLASS GOALKEEPER, EH, JUNIOR?
UH... WELL... YEAH...
I MEAN... I READ ABOUT THE GOALIE FOR THE NATIONAL TEAM, AND—
SAY NO MORE, SOLDIER. I GET IT.
YOU WANT TO BE THE **BEST**, AND YOU'LL GO TO **ANY LENGTHS** TO GET THERE!
KOFF! WELL, I WOULDN'T SAY "ANY LENGTHS." HA HA!
SADDLE UP, COW-BOY! IT'S RODEO TIME!
Peirce

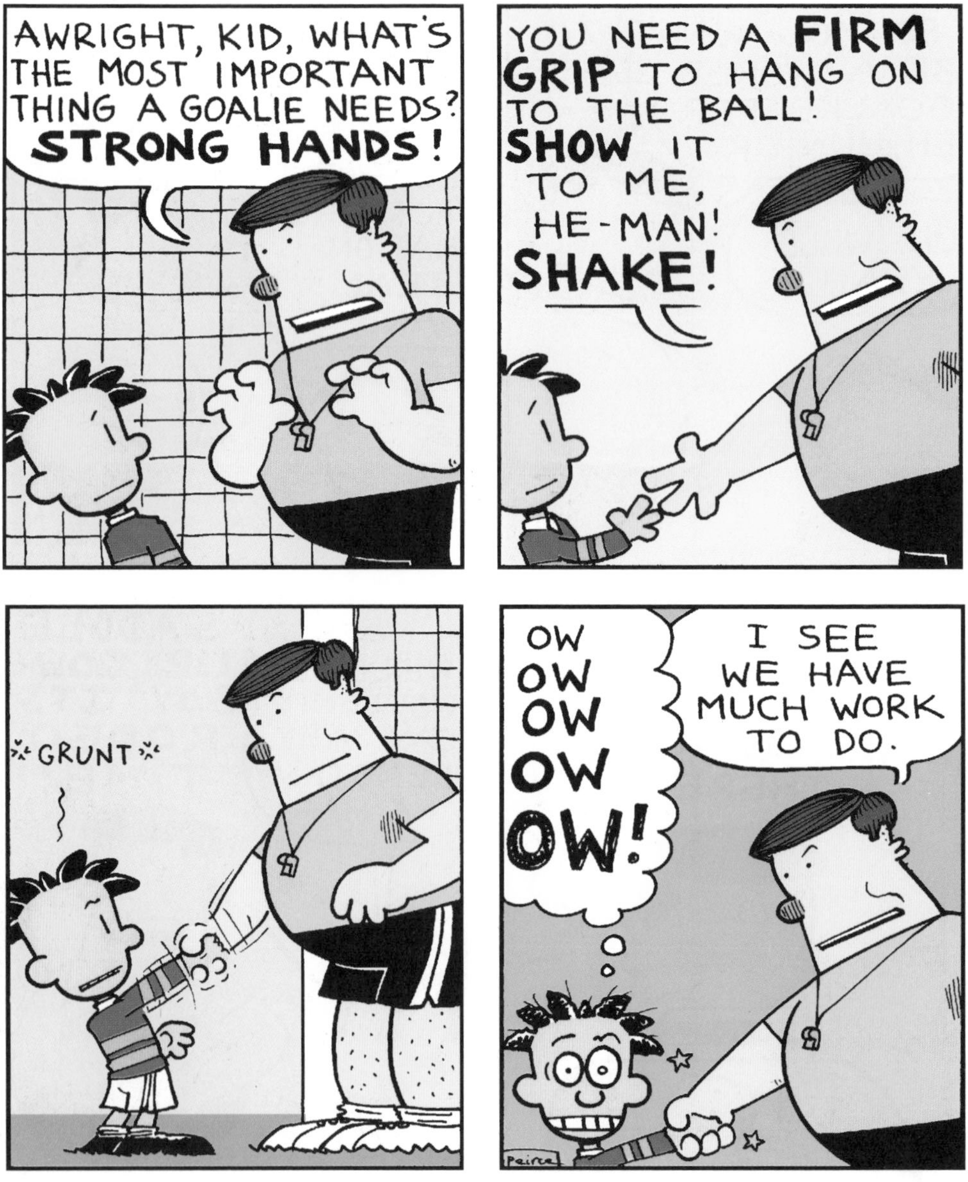
AWRIGHT, KID, WHAT'S THE MOST IMPORTANT THING A GOALIE NEEDS? STRONG HANDS!
YOU NEED A FIRM GRIP TO HANG ON TO THE BALL! SHOW IT TO ME, HE-MAN! SHAKE!
GRUNT
OW OW OW OW OW!
I SEE WE HAVE MUCH WORK TO DO.
Peirce

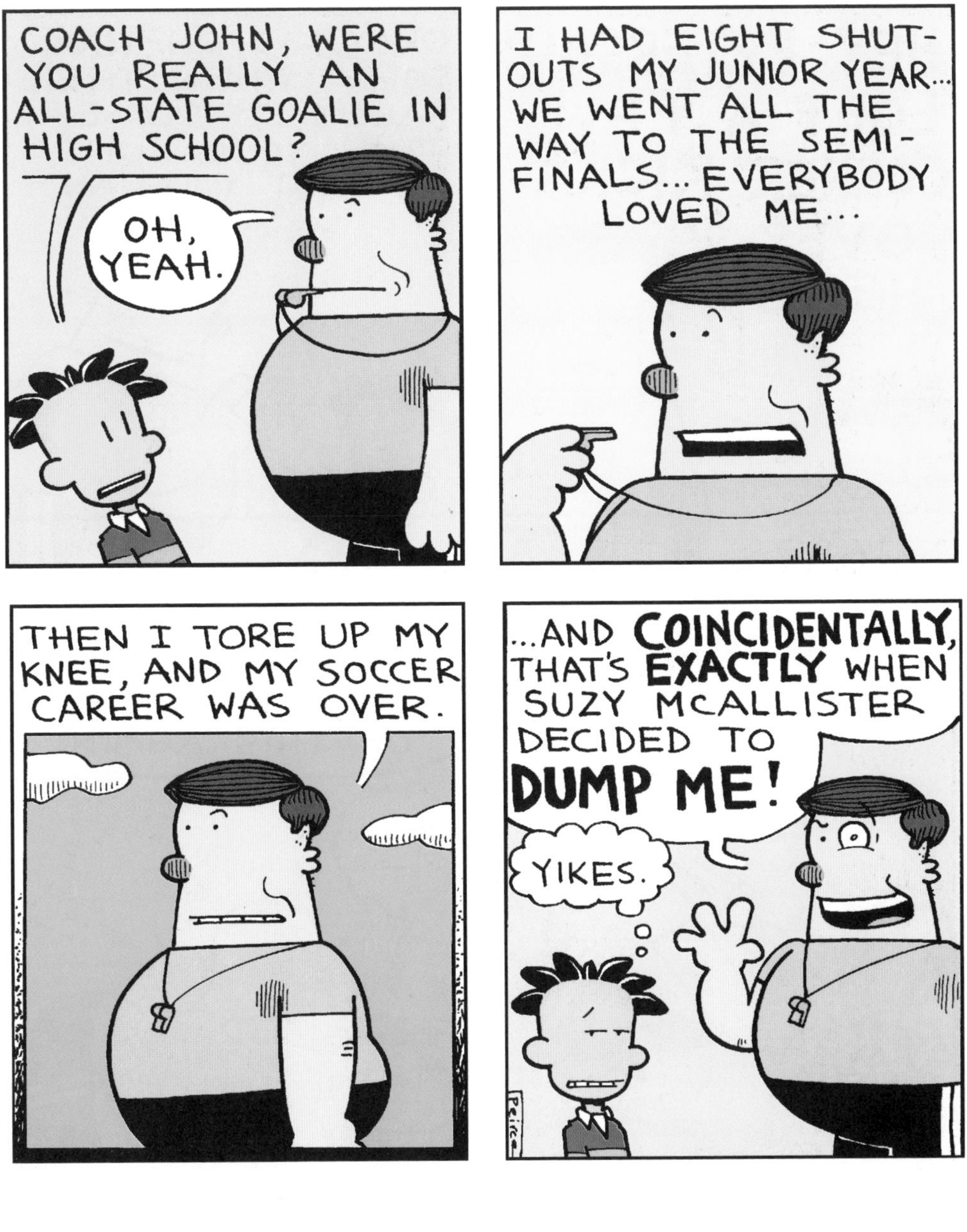
COACH JOHN, WERE YOU REALLY AN ALL-STATE GOALIE IN HIGH SCHOOL?
OH, YEAH.
I HAD EIGHT SHUT-OUTS MY JUNIOR YEAR... WE WENT ALL THE WAY TO THE SEMI-FINALS... EVERYBODY LOVED ME...
THEN I TORE UP MY KNEE, AND MY SOCCER CAREER WAS OVER.
...AND COINCIDENTALLY, THAT'S EXACTLY WHEN SUZY MCALLISTER DECIDED TO DUMP ME!
YIKES.
Peirce

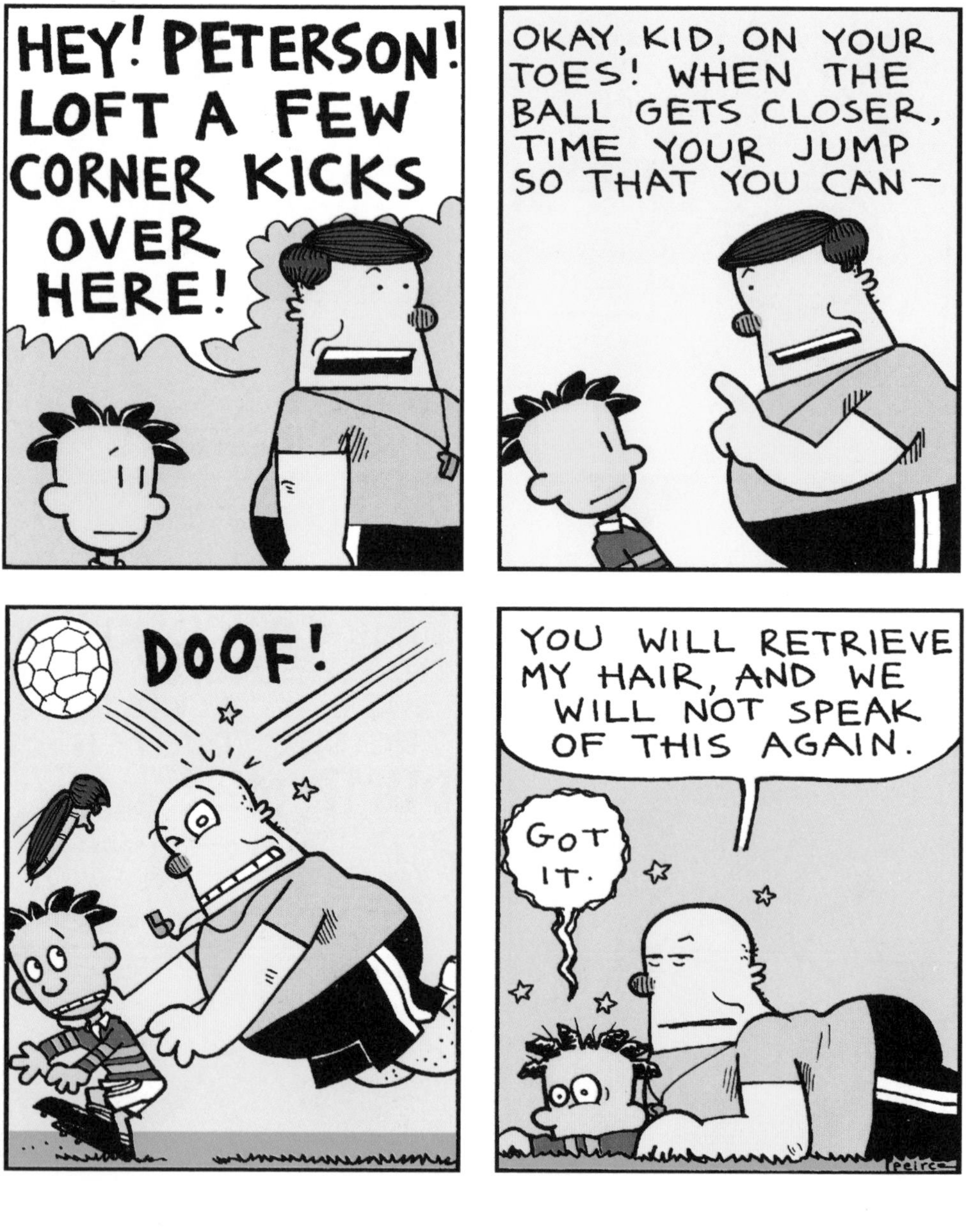
HEY! PETERSON! LOFT A FEW CORNER KICKS OVER HERE!
OKAY, KID, ON YOUR TOES! WHEN THE BALL GETS CLOSER, TIME YOUR JUMP SO THAT YOU CAN—
DOOF!
YOU WILL RETRIEVE MY HAIR, AND WE WILL NOT SPEAK OF THIS AGAIN.
GOT IT.
peirce

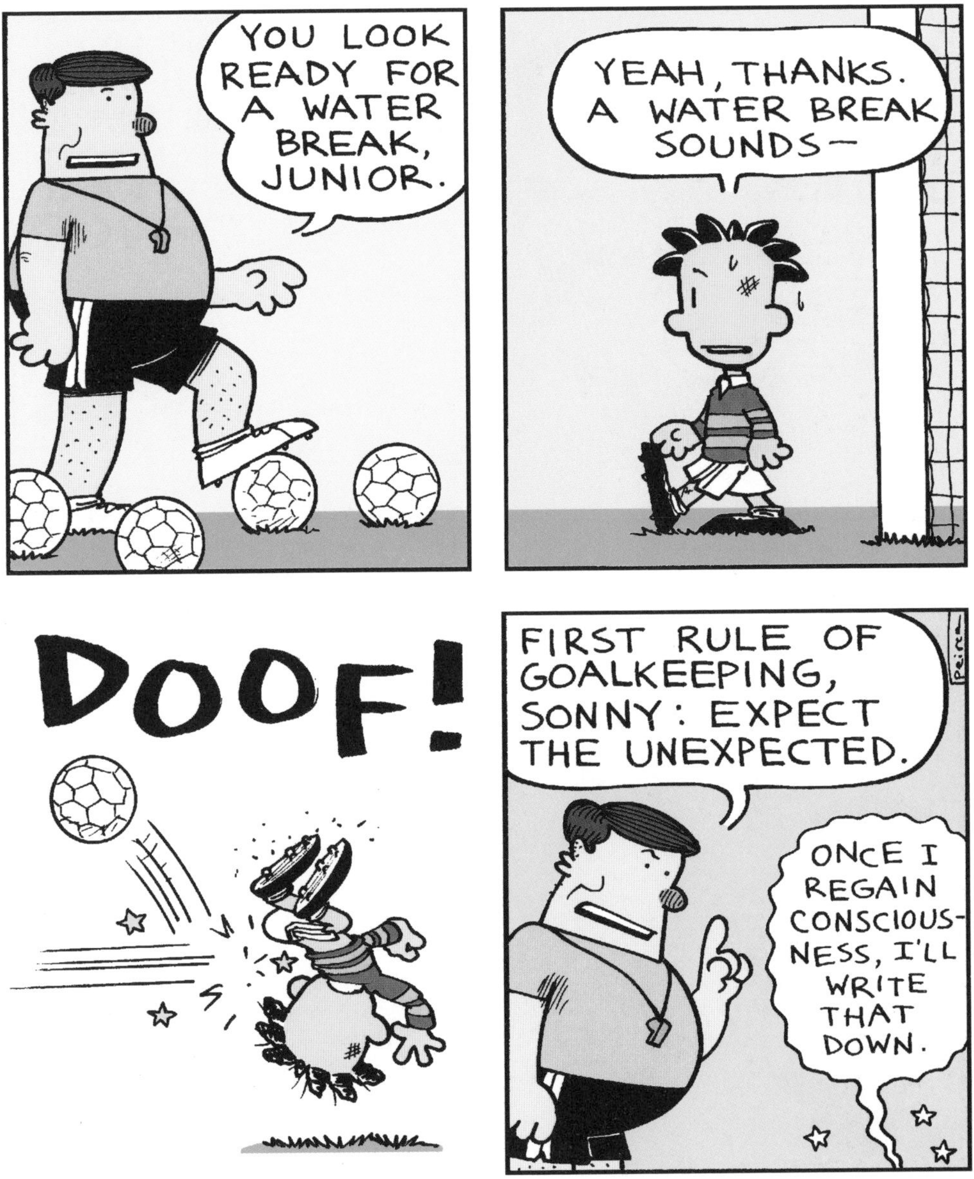
YOU LOOK READY FOR A WATER BREAK, JUNIOR.
YEAH, THANKS. A WATER BREAK SOUNDS—
DOOF!
FIRST RULE OF GOALKEEPING, SONNY: EXPECT THE UNEXPECTED.
ONCE I REGAIN CONSCIOUSNESS, I'LL WRITE THAT DOWN.
Peirce

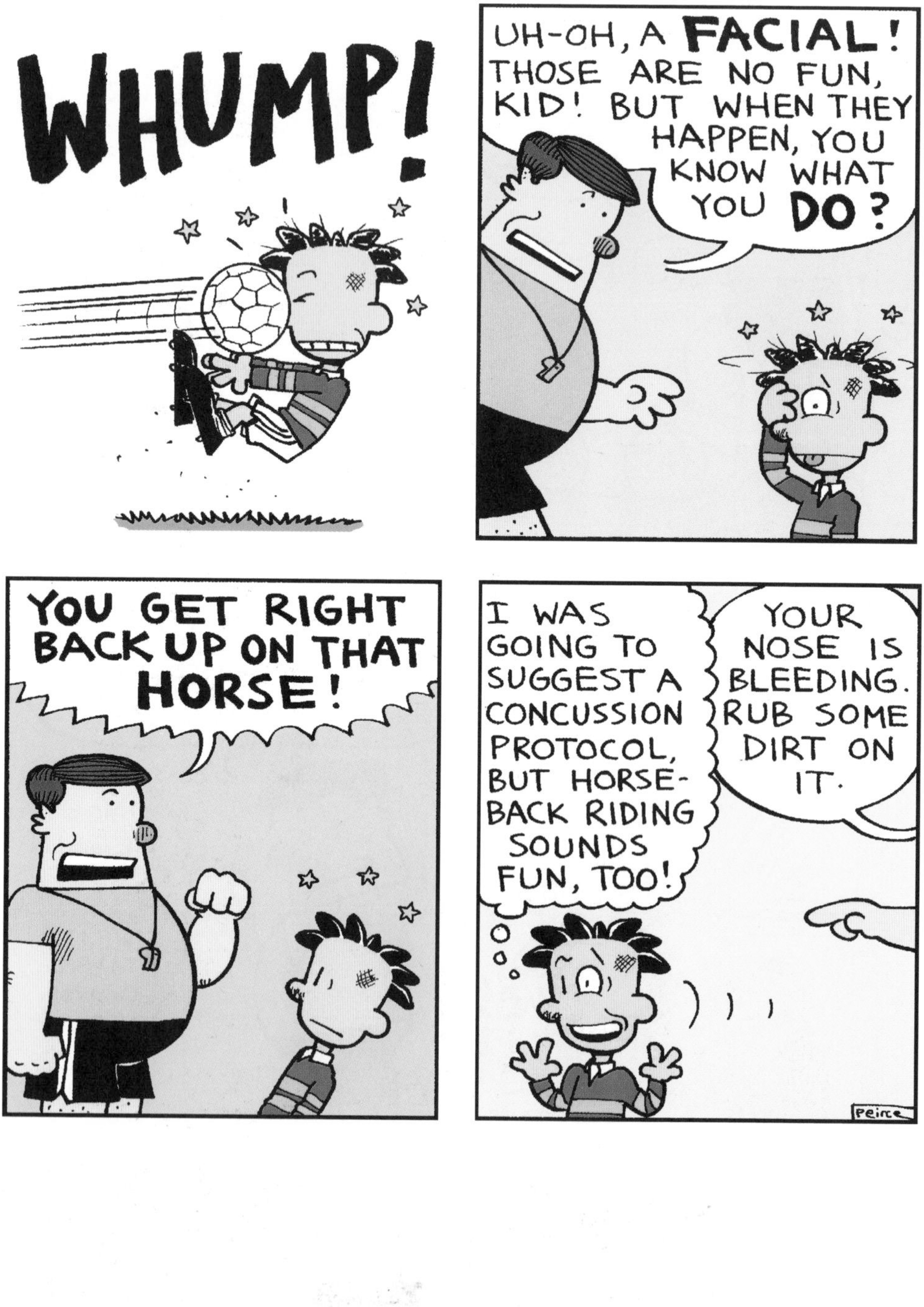
WHUMP!
UH-OH, A FACIAL! THOSE ARE NO FUN, KID! BUT WHEN THEY HAPPEN, YOU KNOW WHAT YOU DO?
YOU GET RIGHT BACK UP ON THAT HORSE!
I WAS GOING TO SUGGEST A CONCUSSION PROTOCOL, BUT HORSE-BACK RIDING SOUNDS FUN, TOO!
YOUR NOSE IS BLEEDING. RUB SOME DIRT ON IT.
Peirce

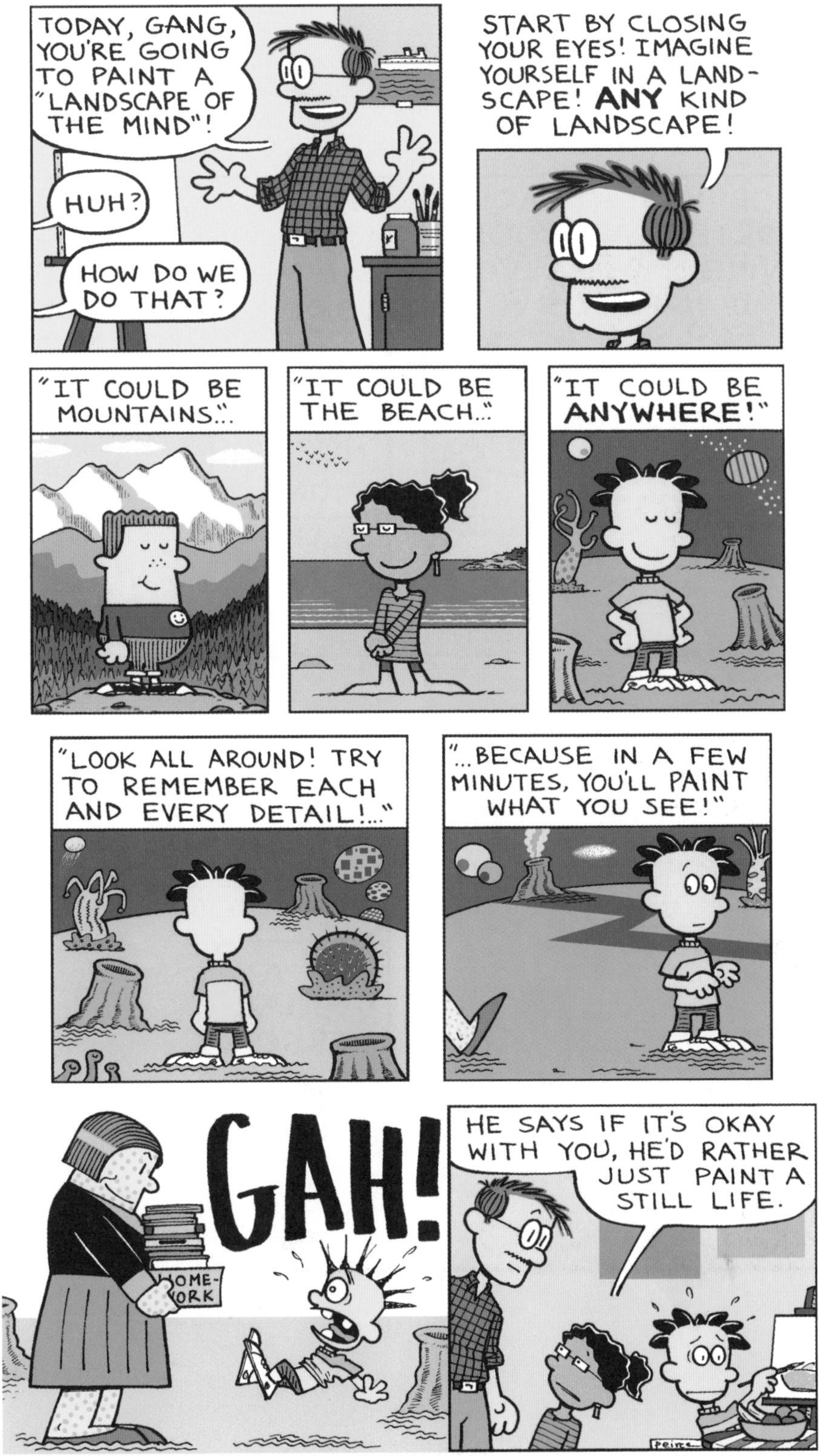
TODAY, GANG, YOU'RE GOING TO PAINT A "LANDSCAPE OF THE MIND"!
HUH?
HOW DO WE DO THAT?
START BY CLOSING YOUR EYES! IMAGINE YOURSELF IN A LANDSCAPE! ANY KIND OF LANDSCAPE!
"IT COULD BE MOUNTAINS..."
"IT COULD BE THE BEACH..."
"IT COULD BE ANYWHERE!"
"LOOK ALL AROUND! TRY TO REMEMBER EACH AND EVERY DETAIL!..."
"...BECAUSE IN A FEW MINUTES, YOU'LL PAINT WHAT YOU SEE!"
GAH!
HOME-WORK
HE SAYS IF IT'S OKAY WITH YOU, HE'D RATHER JUST PAINT A STILL LIFE.
peirce

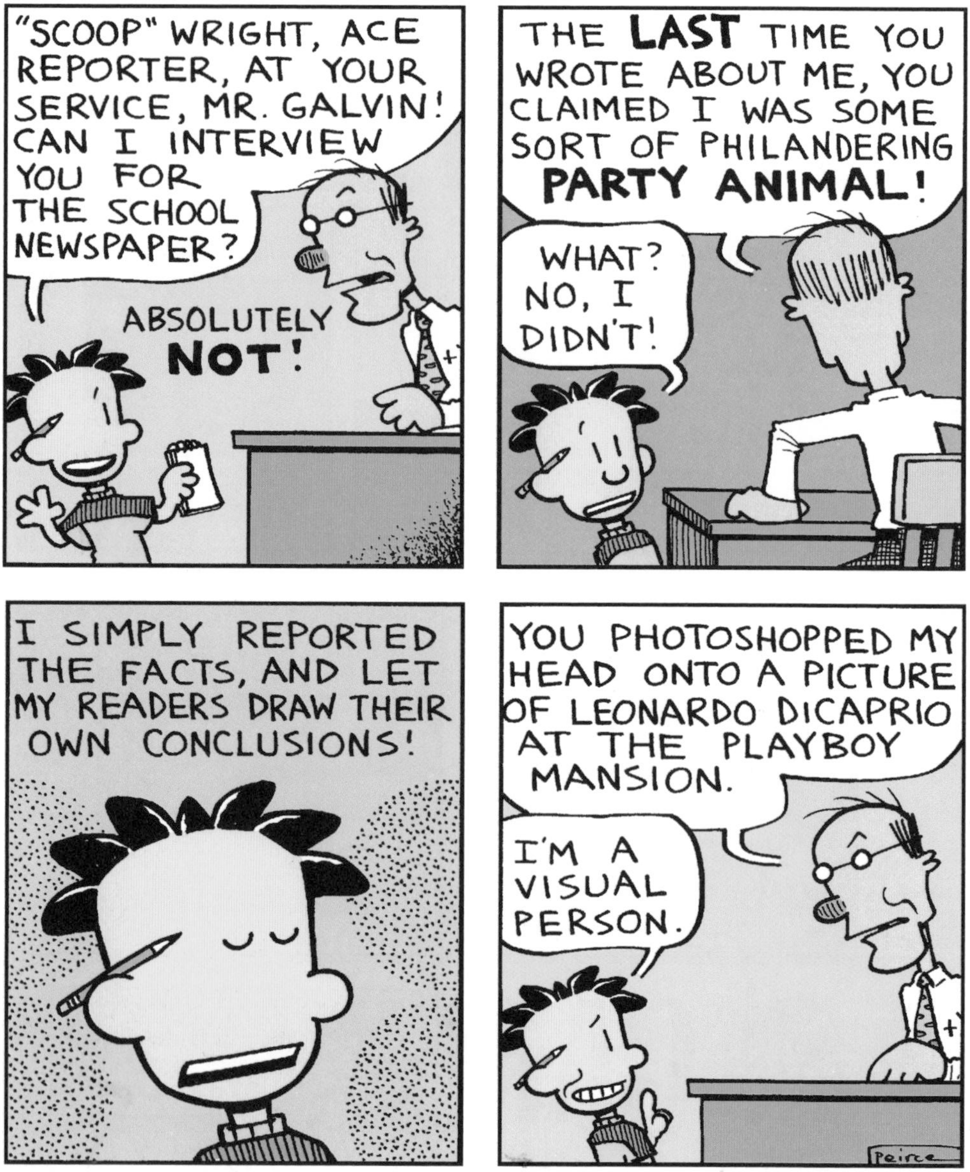
"SCOOP" WRIGHT, ACE REPORTER, AT YOUR SERVICE, MR. GALVIN! CAN I INTERVIEW YOU FOR THE SCHOOL NEWSPAPER?
ABSOLUTELY NOT!
THE LAST TIME YOU WROTE ABOUT ME, YOU CLAIMED I WAS SOME SORT OF PHILANDERING PARTY ANIMAL!
WHAT? NO, I DIDN'T!
I SIMPLY REPORTED THE FACTS, AND LET MY READERS DRAW THEIR OWN CONCLUSIONS!
YOU PHOTOSHOPPED MY HEAD ONTO A PICTURE OF LEONARDO DICAPRIO AT THE PLAYBOY MANSION.
I'M A VISUAL PERSON.
Peirce

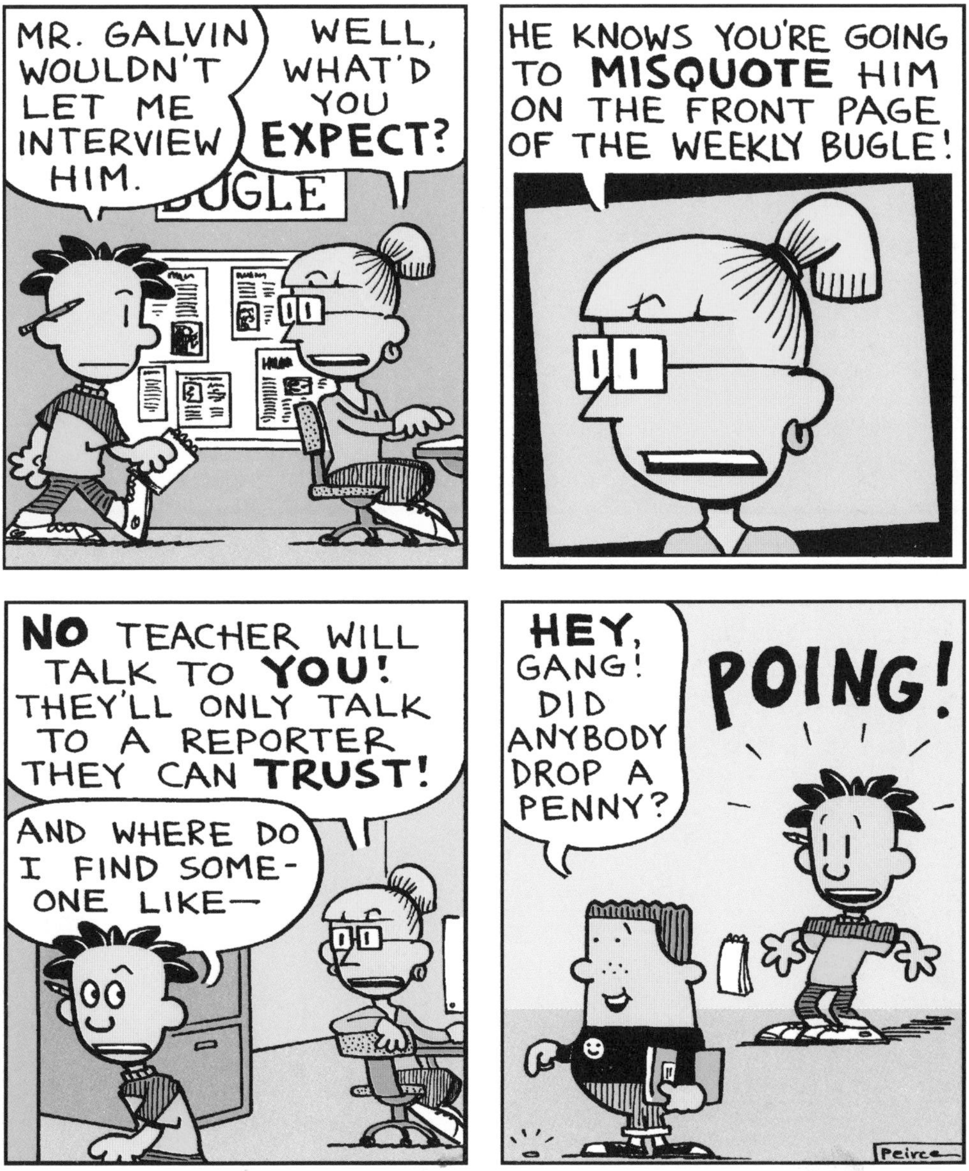
MR. GALVIN WOULDN'T LET ME INTERVIEW HIM.
WELL, WHAT'D YOU **EXPECT?**
BUGLE
HE KNOWS YOU'RE GOING TO **MISQUOTE** HIM ON THE FRONT PAGE OF THE WEEKLY BUGLE!
NO TEACHER WILL TALK TO **YOU!** THEY'LL ONLY TALK TO A REPORTER THEY CAN **TRUST!**
AND WHERE DO I FIND SOME-ONE LIKE—
HEY, GANG! DID ANYBODY DROP A PENNY?
POING!
Peirce

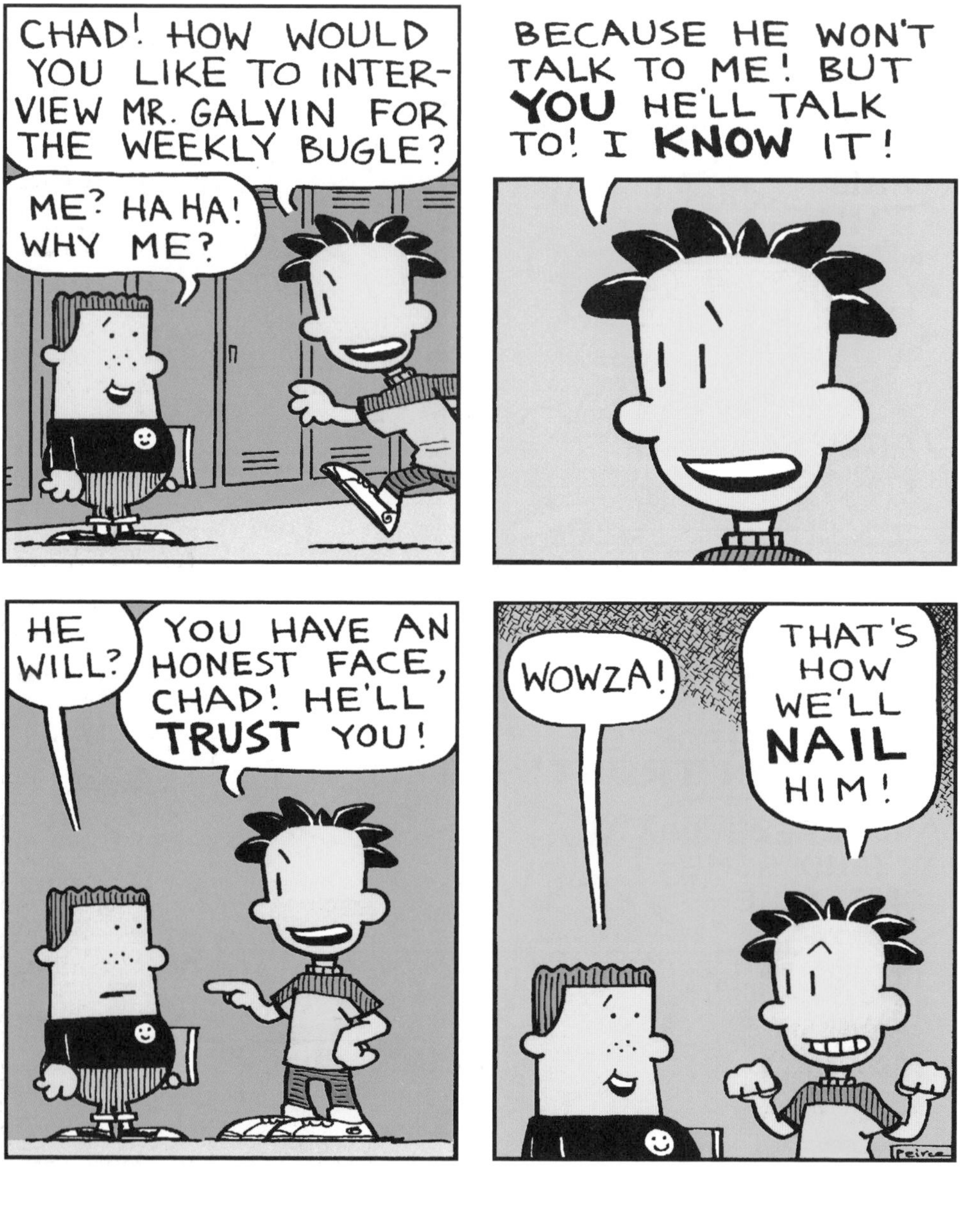
CHAD! HOW WOULD YOU LIKE TO INTERVIEW MR. GALVIN FOR THE WEEKLY BUGLE?
ME? HA HA! WHY ME?
BECAUSE HE WON'T TALK TO ME! BUT YOU HE'LL TALK TO! I KNOW IT!
HE WILL?
YOU HAVE AN HONEST FACE, CHAD! HE'LL TRUST YOU!
WOWZA!
THAT'S HOW WE'LL NAIL HIM!
Peirce

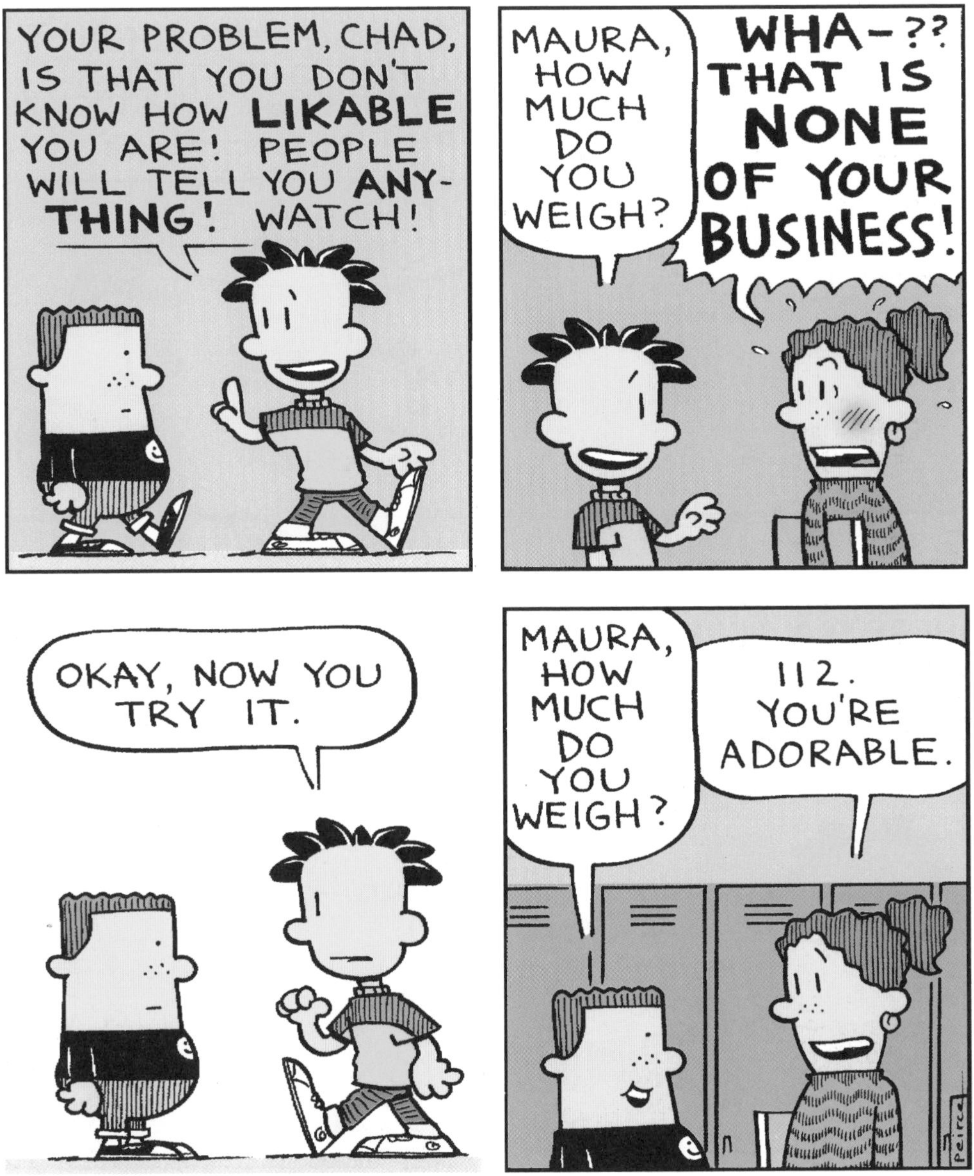
YOUR PROBLEM, CHAD, IS THAT YOU DON'T KNOW HOW **LIKABLE** YOU ARE! PEOPLE WILL TELL YOU **ANYTHING**! WATCH!
MAURA, HOW MUCH DO YOU WEIGH?
WHA-?? THAT IS NONE OF YOUR BUSINESS!
OKAY, NOW YOU TRY IT.
MAURA, HOW MUCH DO YOU WEIGH?
112. YOU'RE ADORABLE.
Peirce

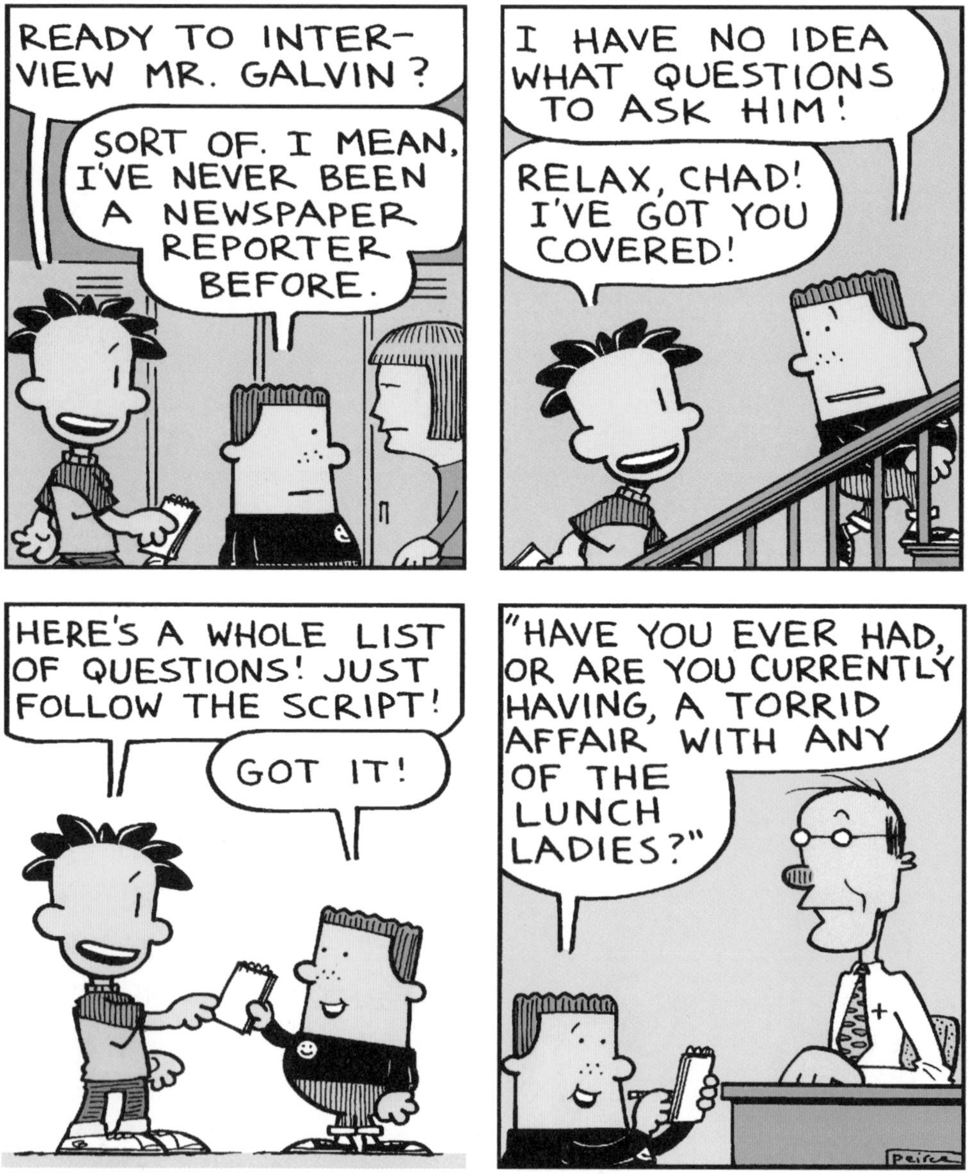
READY TO INTER-VIEW MR. GALVIN?
SORT OF. I MEAN, I'VE NEVER BEEN A NEWSPAPER REPORTER BEFORE.
I HAVE NO IDEA WHAT QUESTIONS TO ASK HIM!
RELAX, CHAD! I'VE GOT YOU COVERED!
HERE'S A WHOLE LIST OF QUESTIONS! JUST FOLLOW THE SCRIPT!
GOT IT!
"HAVE YOU EVER HAD, OR ARE YOU CURRENTLY HAVING, A TORRID AFFAIR WITH ANY OF THE LUNCH LADIES?"
peirce

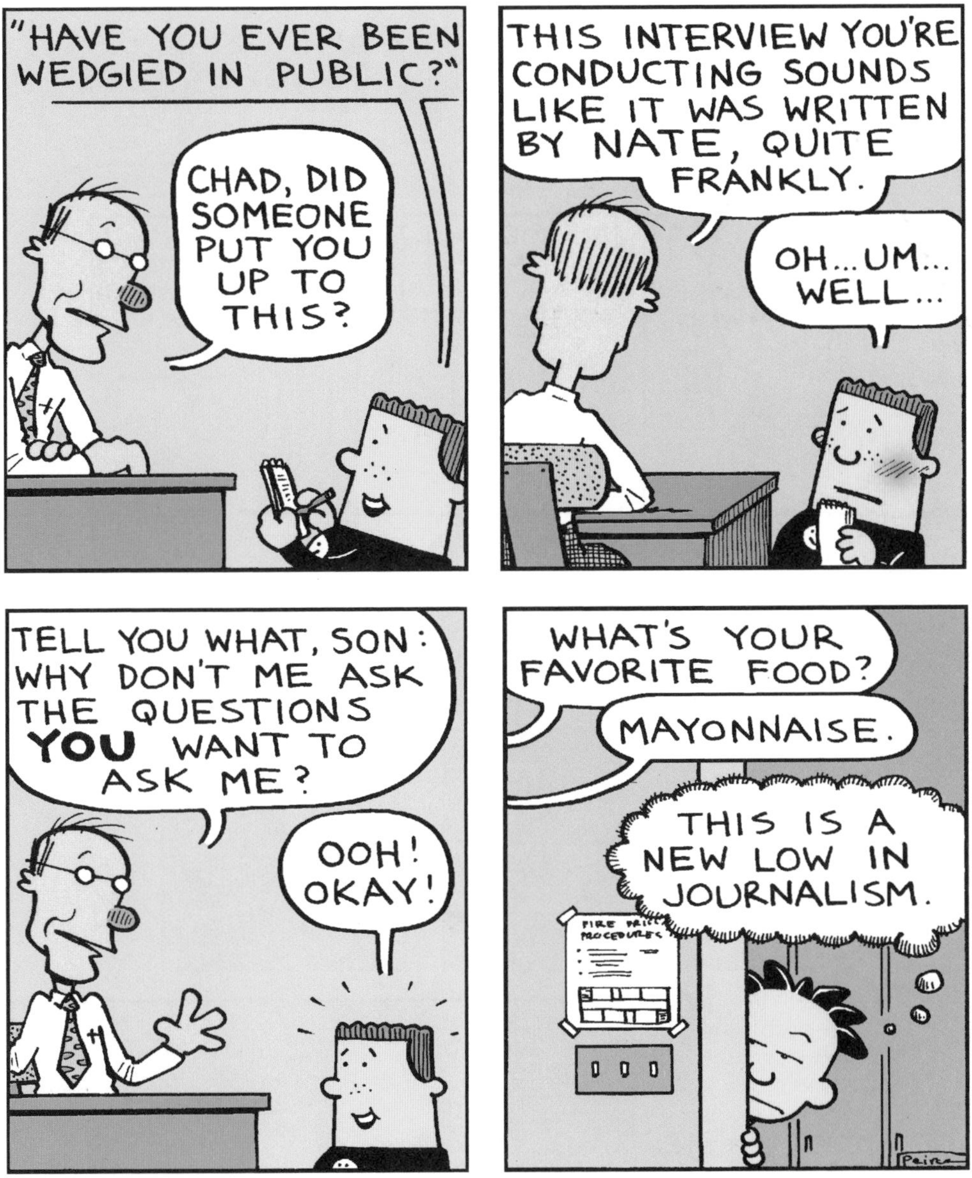
"HAVE YOU EVER BEEN WEDGIED IN PUBLIC?"
CHAD, DID SOMEONE PUT YOU UP TO THIS?
THIS INTERVIEW YOU'RE CONDUCTING SOUNDS LIKE IT WAS WRITTEN BY NATE, QUITE FRANKLY.
OH... UM... WELL...
TELL YOU WHAT, SON: WHY DON'T ME ASK THE QUESTIONS **YOU** WANT TO ASK ME?
OOH! OKAY!
WHAT'S YOUR FAVORITE FOOD?
MAYONNAISE.
THIS IS A NEW LOW IN JOURNALISM.
FIRE DRILL PROCEDURES
Peirce

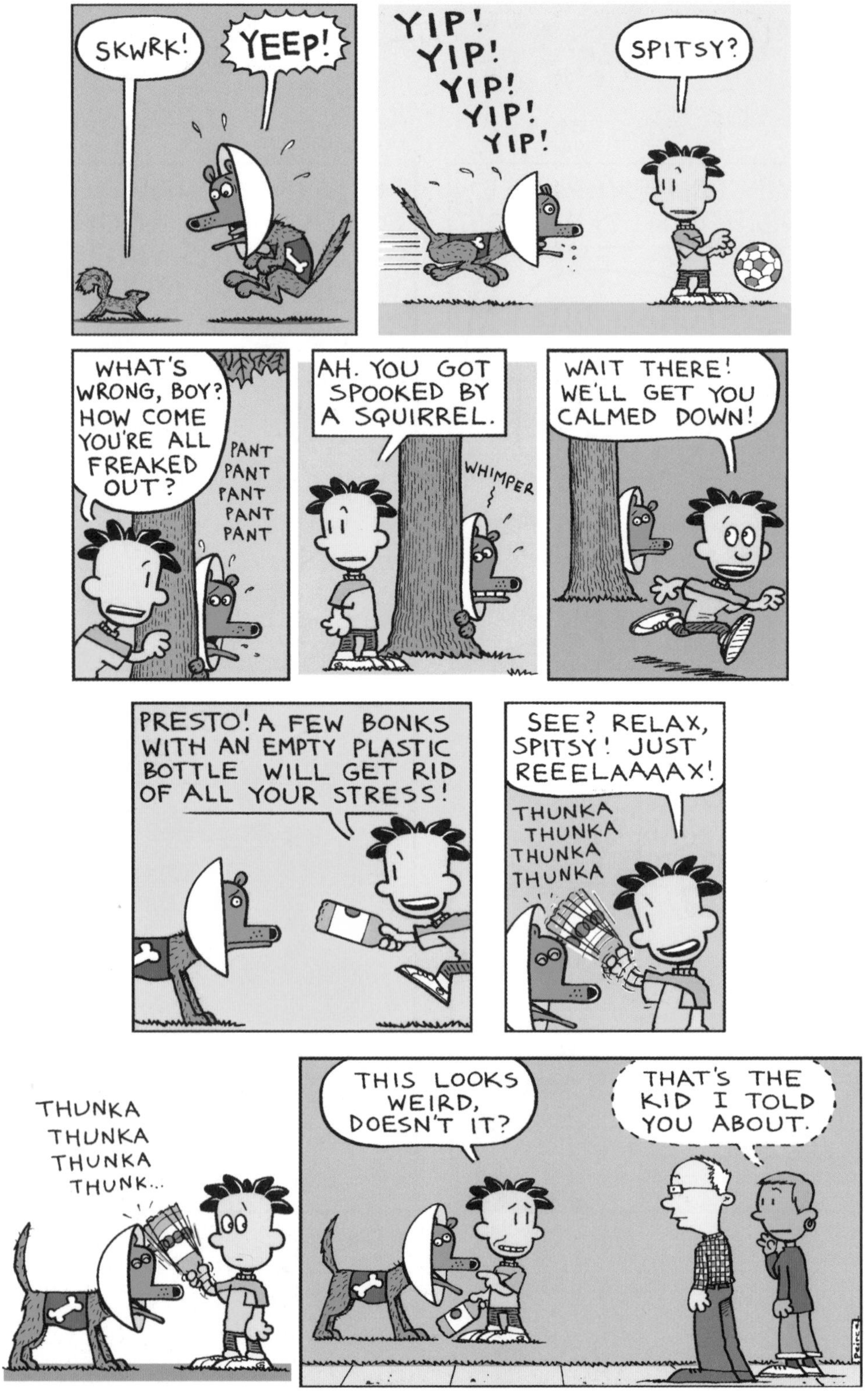
SKWRK!
YEEP!
YIP! YIP! YIP! YIP! YIP!
SPITSY?
WHAT'S WRONG, BOY? HOW COME YOU'RE ALL FREAKED OUT?
PANT PANT PANT PANT PANT
AH. YOU GOT SPOOKED BY A SQUIRREL.
WHIMPER
WAIT THERE! WE'LL GET YOU CALMED DOWN!
PRESTO! A FEW BONKS WITH AN EMPTY PLASTIC BOTTLE WILL GET RID OF ALL YOUR STRESS!
SEE? RELAX, SPITSY! JUST REEELAAAAX!
THUNKA THUNKA THUNKA THUNKA
THUNKA THUNKA THUNKA THUNK...
THIS LOOKS WEIRD, DOESN'T IT?
THAT'S THE KID I TOLD YOU ABOUT.

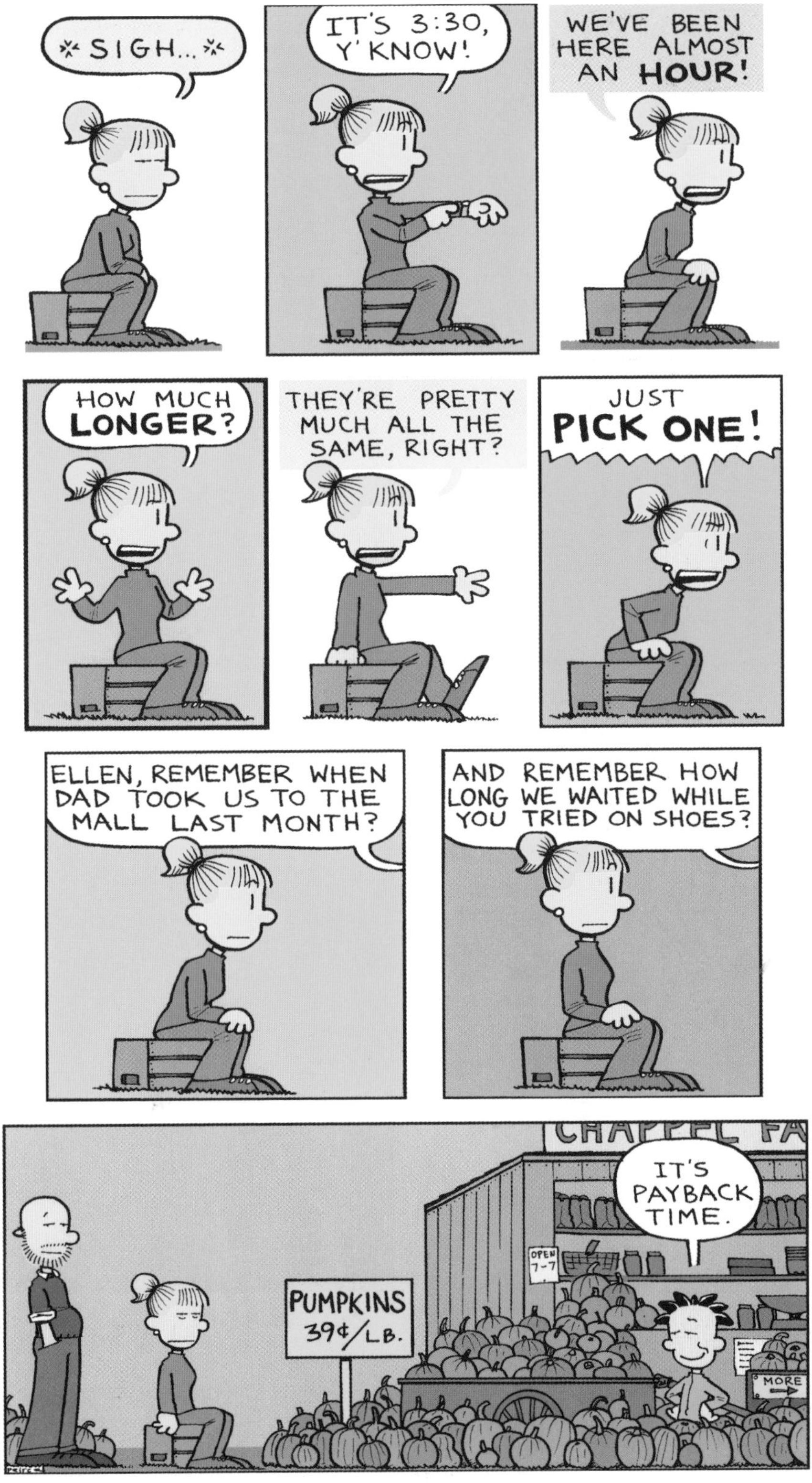
SIGH...
IT'S 3:30, Y'KNOW!
WE'VE BEEN HERE ALMOST AN **HOUR**!
HOW MUCH **LONGER**?
THEY'RE PRETTY MUCH ALL THE SAME, RIGHT?
JUST **PICK ONE**!
ELLEN, REMEMBER WHEN DAD TOOK US TO THE MALL LAST MONTH?
AND REMEMBER HOW LONG WE WAITED WHILE YOU TRIED ON SHOES?
CHAPPEL FA
OPEN 7-7
PUMPKINS 39¢/LB.
IT'S PAYBACK TIME.
MORE

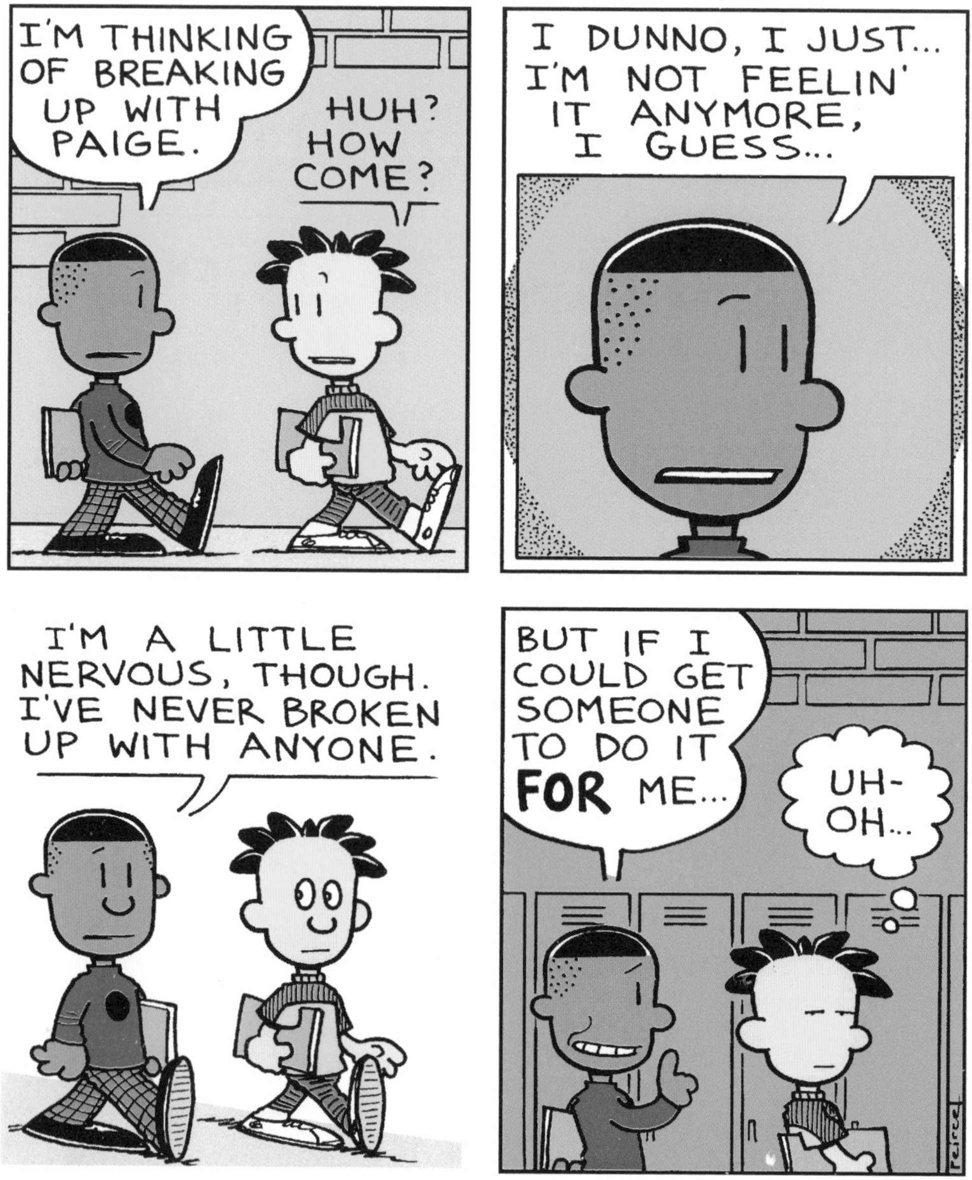
I'M THINKING OF BREAKING UP WITH PAIGE.
HUH? HOW COME?
I DUNNO, I JUST... I'M NOT FEELIN' IT ANYMORE, I GUESS...
I'M A LITTLE NERVOUS, THOUGH. I'VE NEVER BROKEN UP WITH ANYONE.
BUT IF I COULD GET SOMEONE TO DO IT **FOR** ME...
UH-OH...

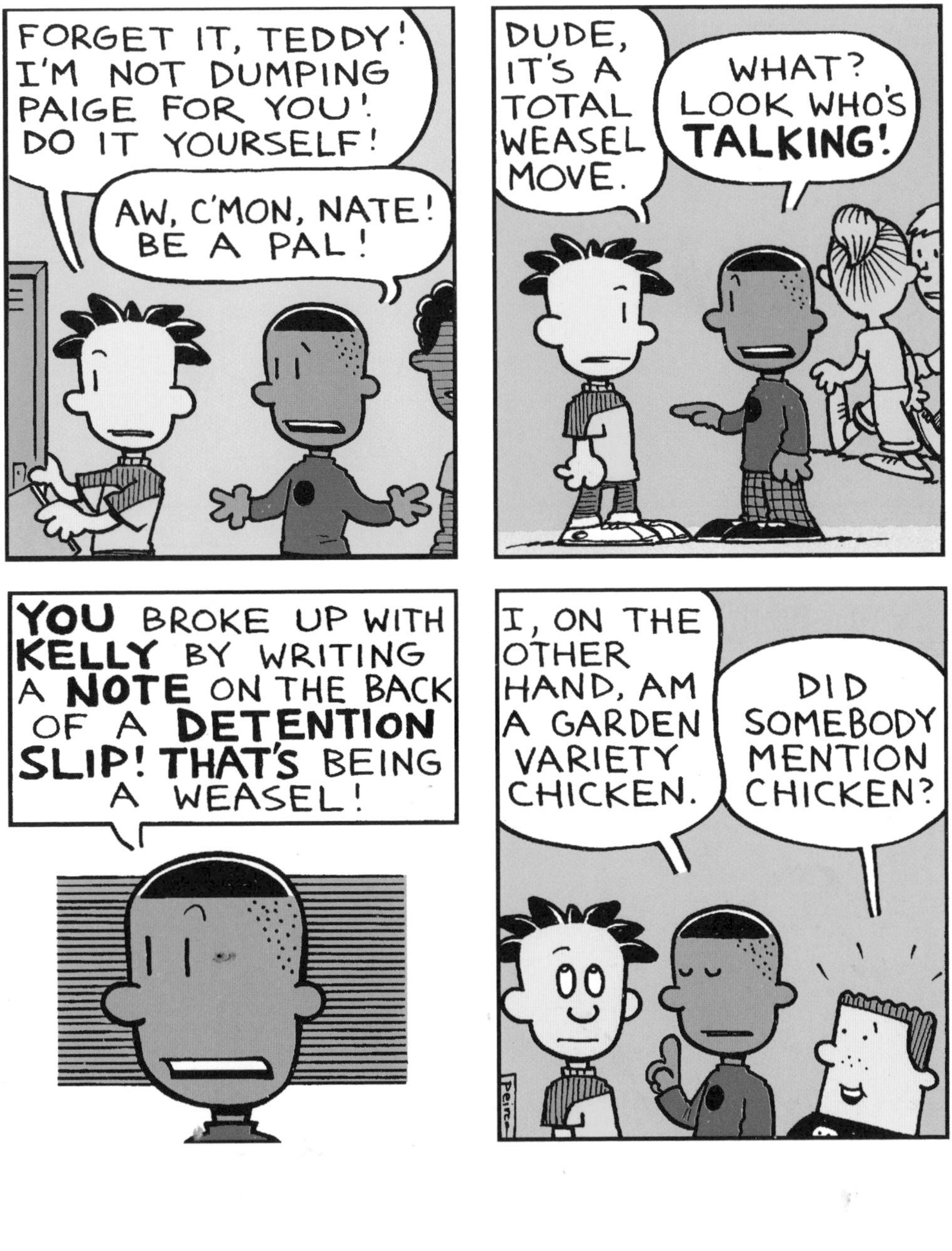
FORGET IT, TEDDY! I'M NOT DUMPING PAIGE FOR YOU! DO IT YOURSELF!
AW, C'MON, NATE! BE A PAL!
DUDE, IT'S A TOTAL WEASEL MOVE.
WHAT? LOOK WHO'S TALKING!
YOU BROKE UP WITH KELLY BY WRITING A NOTE ON THE BACK OF A DETENTION SLIP! THAT'S BEING A WEASEL!
I, ON THE OTHER HAND, AM A GARDEN VARIETY CHICKEN.
DID SOMEBODY MENTION CHICKEN?
PEIRCE

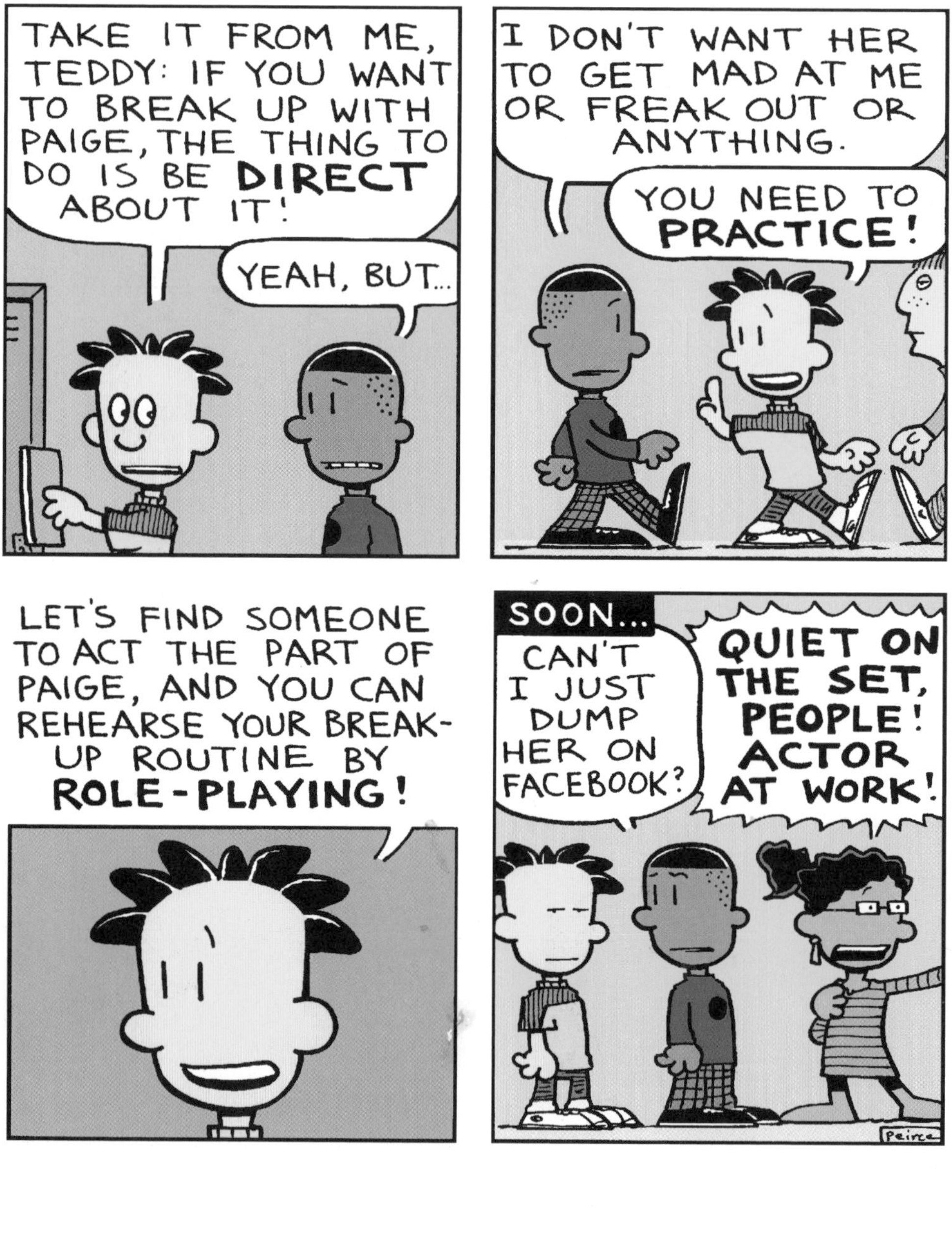
TAKE IT FROM ME, TEDDY: IF YOU WANT TO BREAK UP WITH PAIGE, THE THING TO DO IS BE **DIRECT** ABOUT IT!
YEAH, BUT...
I DON'T WANT HER TO GET MAD AT ME OR FREAK OUT OR ANYTHING.
YOU NEED TO **PRACTICE!**
LET'S FIND SOMEONE TO ACT THE PART OF PAIGE, AND YOU CAN REHEARSE YOUR BREAK-UP ROUTINE BY **ROLE-PLAYING!**
SOON...
CAN'T I JUST DUMP HER ON FACEBOOK?
QUIET ON THE SET, PEOPLE! ACTOR AT WORK!
Peirce

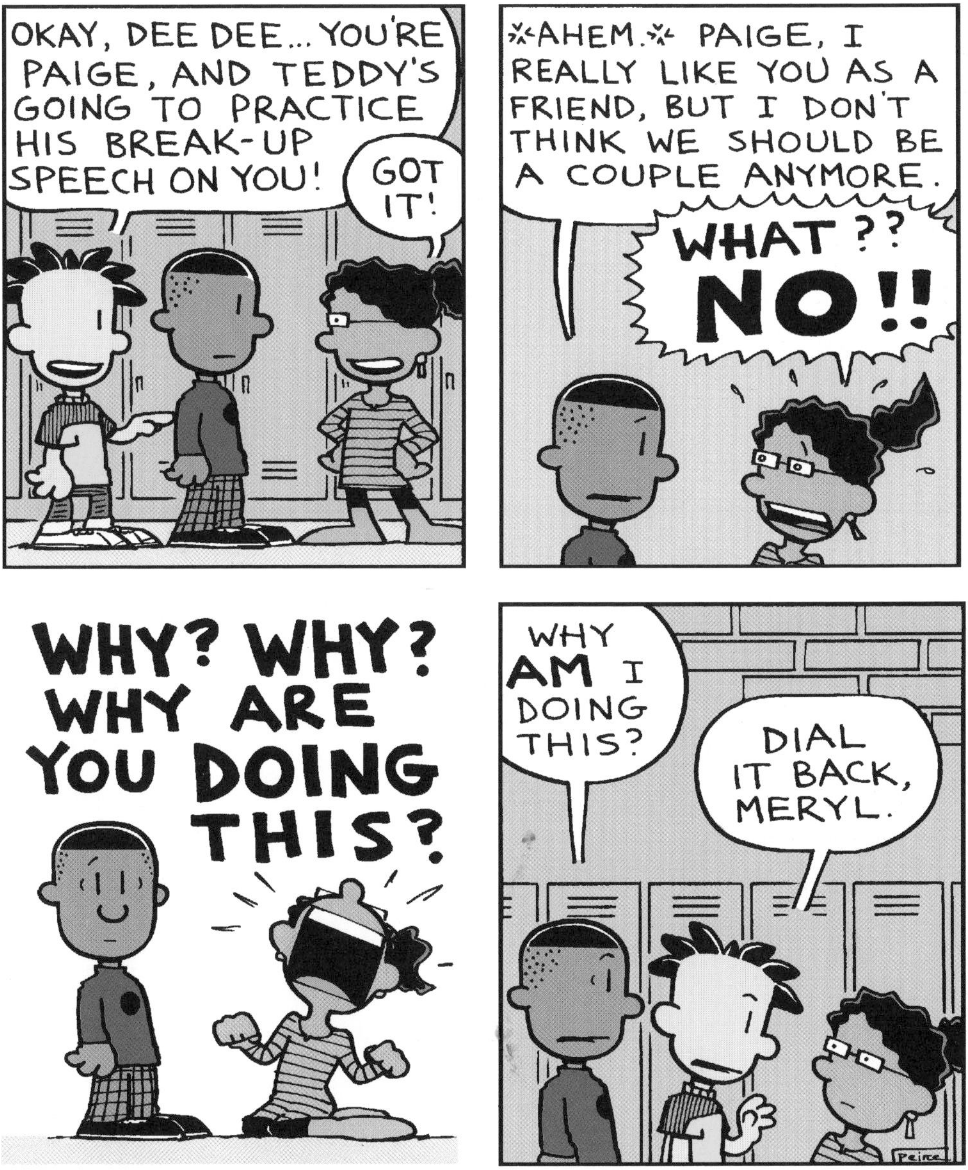
OKAY, DEE DEE... YOU'RE PAIGE, AND TEDDY'S GOING TO PRACTICE HIS BREAK-UP SPEECH ON YOU!
GOT IT!
AHEM. PAIGE, I REALLY LIKE YOU AS A FRIEND, BUT I DON'T THINK WE SHOULD BE A COUPLE ANYMORE.
WHAT?? NO!!
WHY? WHY? WHY ARE YOU DOING THIS?
WHY AM I DOING THIS?
DIAL IT BACK, MERYL.
Peirce

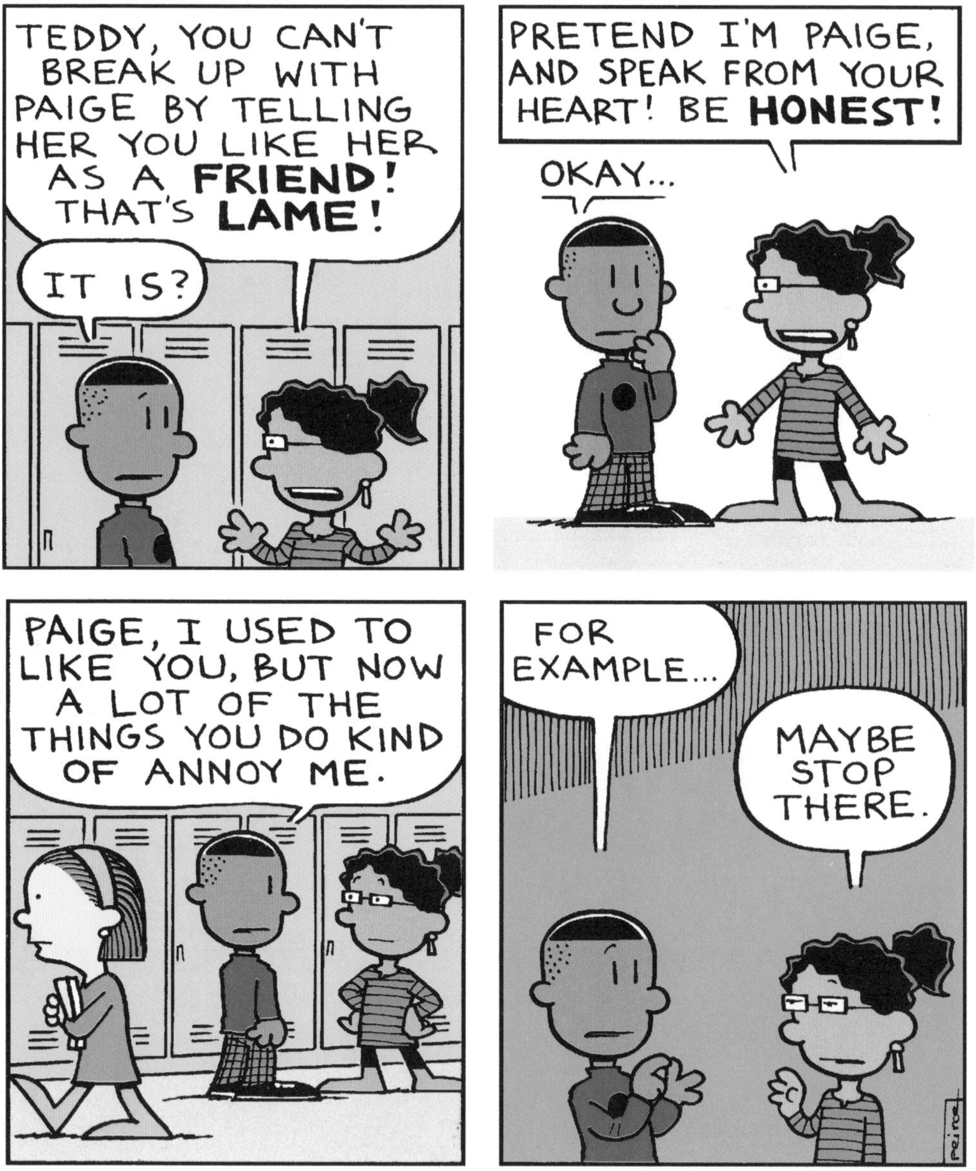
TEDDY, YOU CAN'T BREAK UP WITH PAIGE BY TELLING HER YOU LIKE HER AS A **FRIEND**! THAT'S **LAME**!
IT IS?
PRETEND I'M PAIGE, AND SPEAK FROM YOUR HEART! BE **HONEST**!
OKAY...
PAIGE, I USED TO LIKE YOU, BUT NOW A LOT OF THE THINGS YOU DO KIND OF ANNOY ME.
FOR EXAMPLE...
MAYBE STOP THERE.
peirce

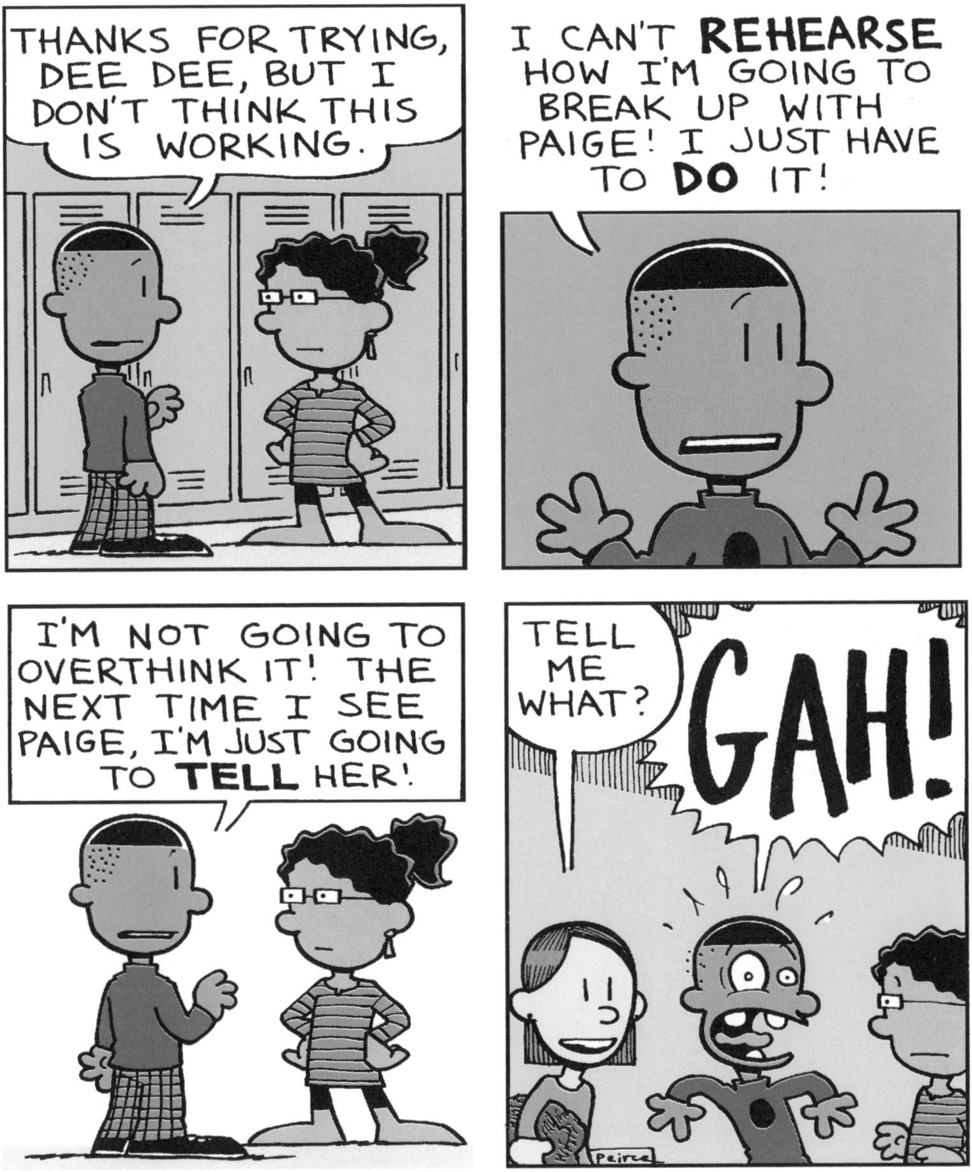
THANKS FOR TRYING, DEE DEE, BUT I DON'T THINK THIS IS WORKING.
I CAN'T **REHEARSE** HOW I'M GOING TO BREAK UP WITH PAIGE! I JUST HAVE TO **DO** IT!
I'M NOT GOING TO OVERTHINK IT! THE NEXT TIME I SEE PAIGE, I'M JUST GOING TO **TELL** HER!
TELL ME WHAT?
GAH!
Peirce

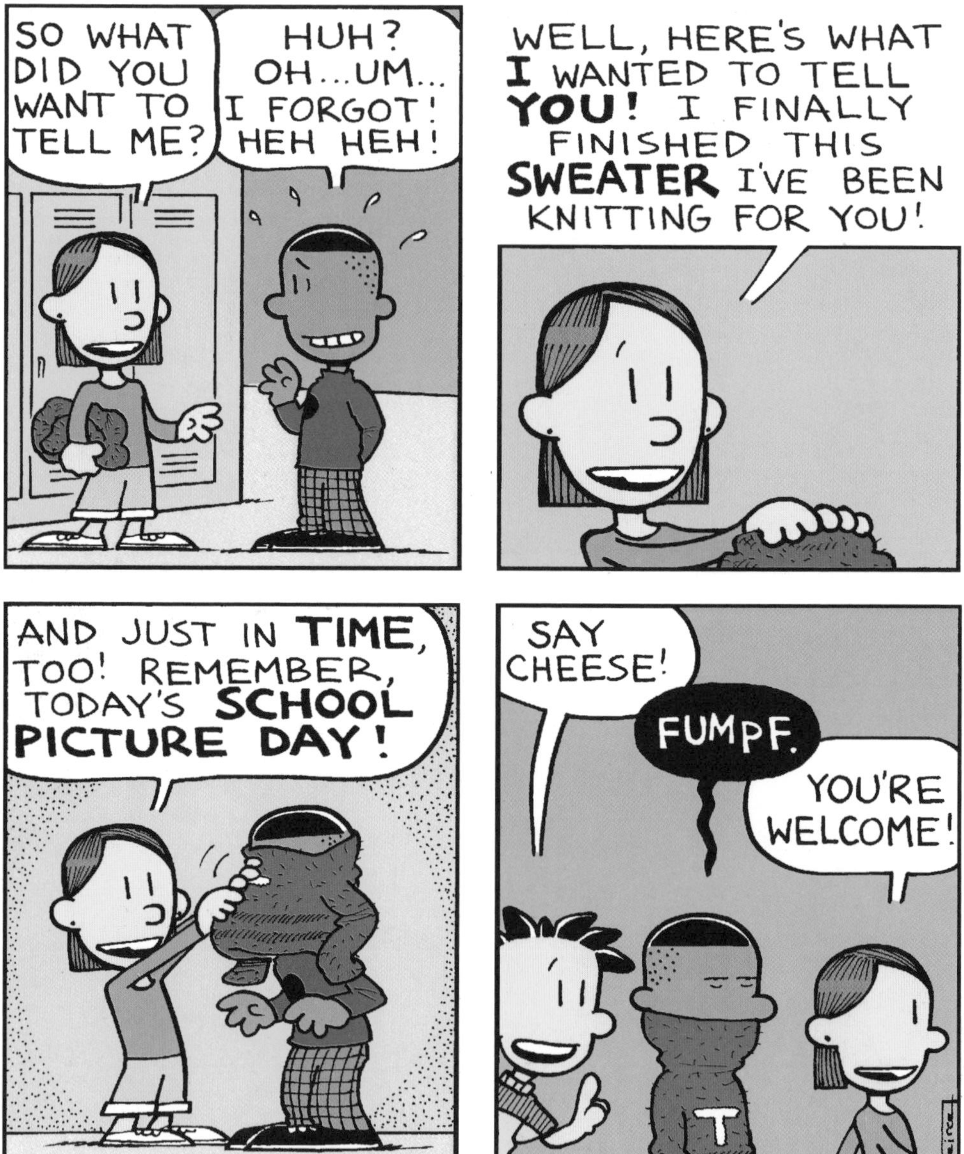

SO WHAT DID YOU WANT TO TELL ME?
HUH? OH...UM... I FORGOT! HEH HEH!
WELL, HERE'S WHAT I WANTED TO TELL YOU! I FINALLY FINISHED THIS SWEATER I'VE BEEN KNITTING FOR YOU!
AND JUST IN TIME, TOO! REMEMBER, TODAY'S SCHOOL PICTURE DAY!
SAY CHEESE!
FUMPF.
YOU'RE WELCOME!
T
Peirce

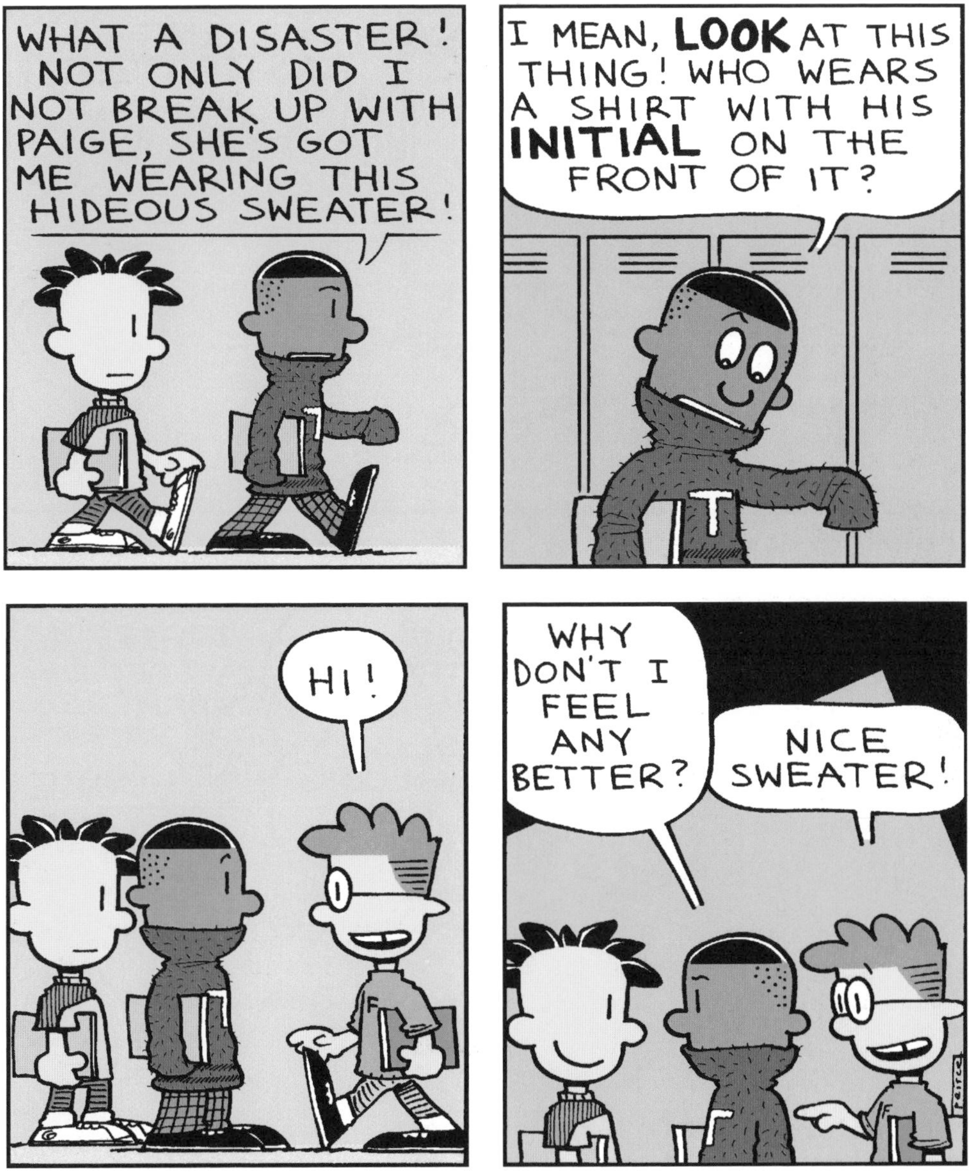
WHAT A DISASTER! NOT ONLY DID I NOT BREAK UP WITH PAIGE, SHE'S GOT ME WEARING THIS HIDEOUS SWEATER!
I MEAN, **LOOK** AT THIS THING! WHO WEARS A SHIRT WITH HIS **INITIAL** ON THE FRONT OF IT?
HI!
WHY DON'T I FEEL ANY BETTER?
NICE SWEATER!

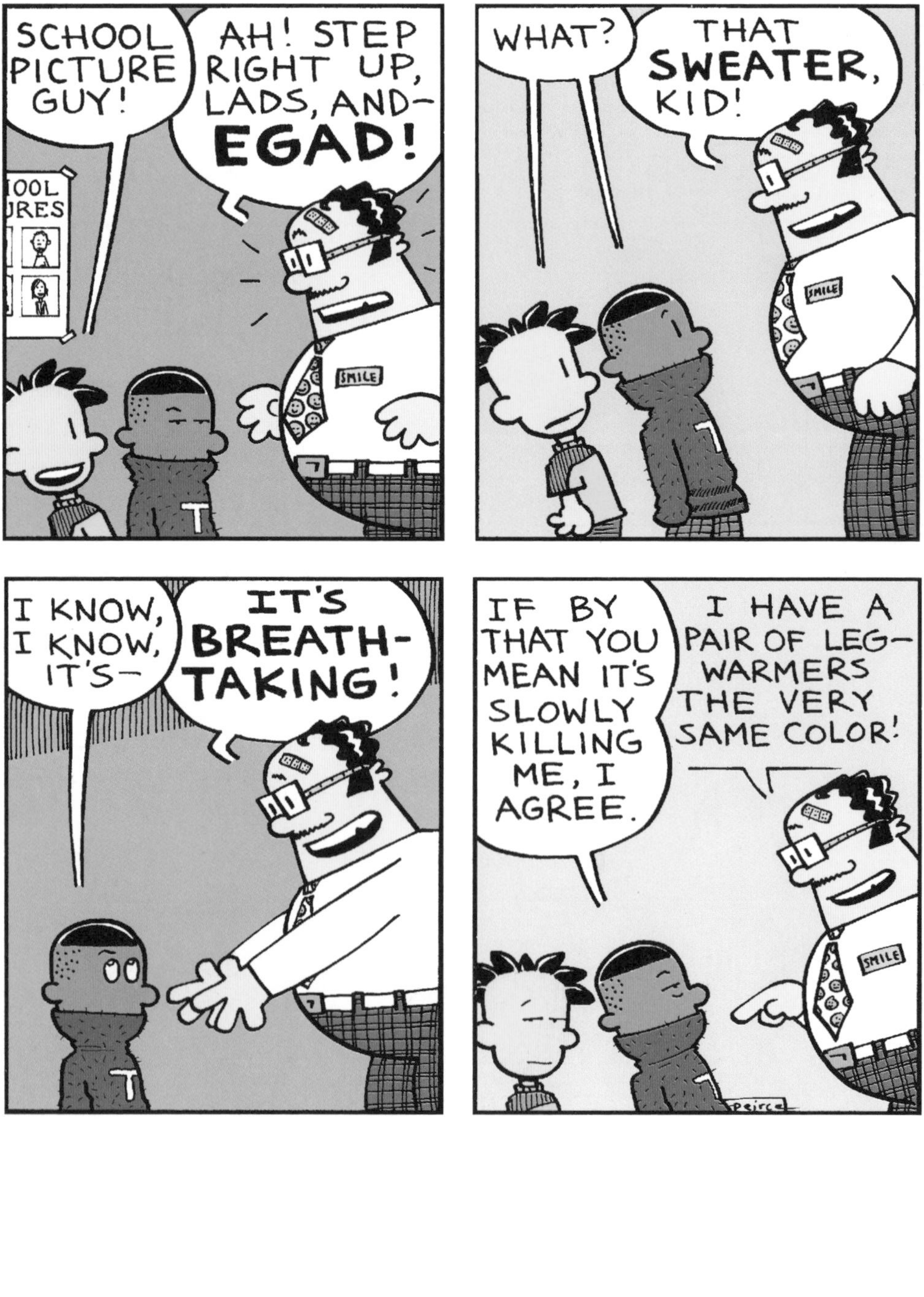
SCHOOL PICTURE GUY!
AH! STEP RIGHT UP, LADS, AND— **EGAD!**
SMILE
WHAT?
THAT **SWEATER**, KID!
SMILE
I KNOW, I KNOW, IT'S—
IT'S **BREATH-TAKING!**
IF BY THAT YOU MEAN IT'S SLOWLY KILLING ME, I AGREE.
I HAVE A PAIR OF LEG-WARMERS THE VERY SAME COLOR!
SMILE

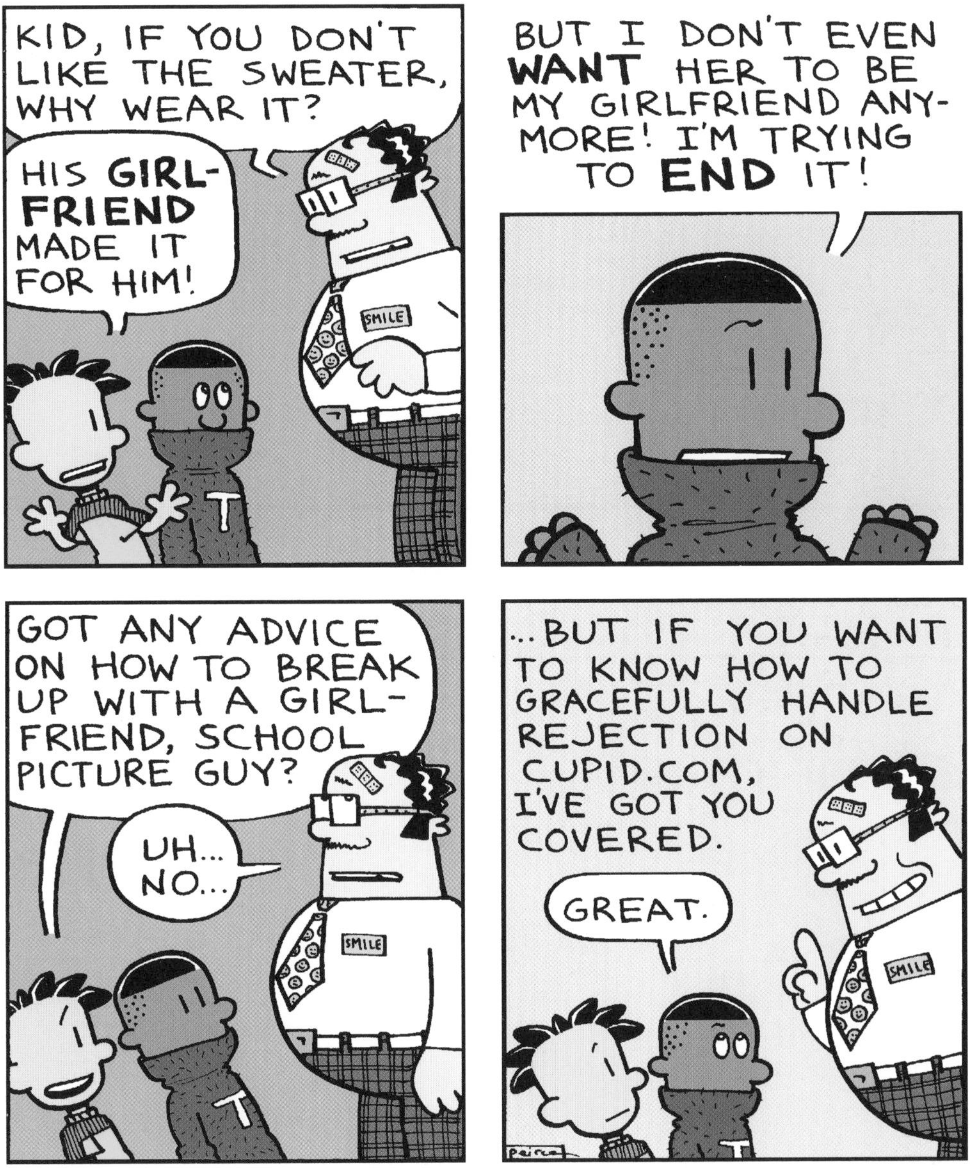
KID, IF YOU DON'T LIKE THE SWEATER, WHY WEAR IT?
HIS **GIRLFRIEND** MADE IT FOR HIM!
SMILE
BUT I DON'T EVEN **WANT** HER TO BE MY GIRLFRIEND ANYMORE! I'M TRYING TO **END** IT!
GOT ANY ADVICE ON HOW TO BREAK UP WITH A GIRLFRIEND, SCHOOL PICTURE GUY?
UH... NO...
SMILE
...BUT IF YOU WANT TO KNOW HOW TO GRACEFULLY HANDLE REJECTION ON CUPID.COM, I'VE GOT YOU COVERED.
GREAT.
SMILE
Peirce

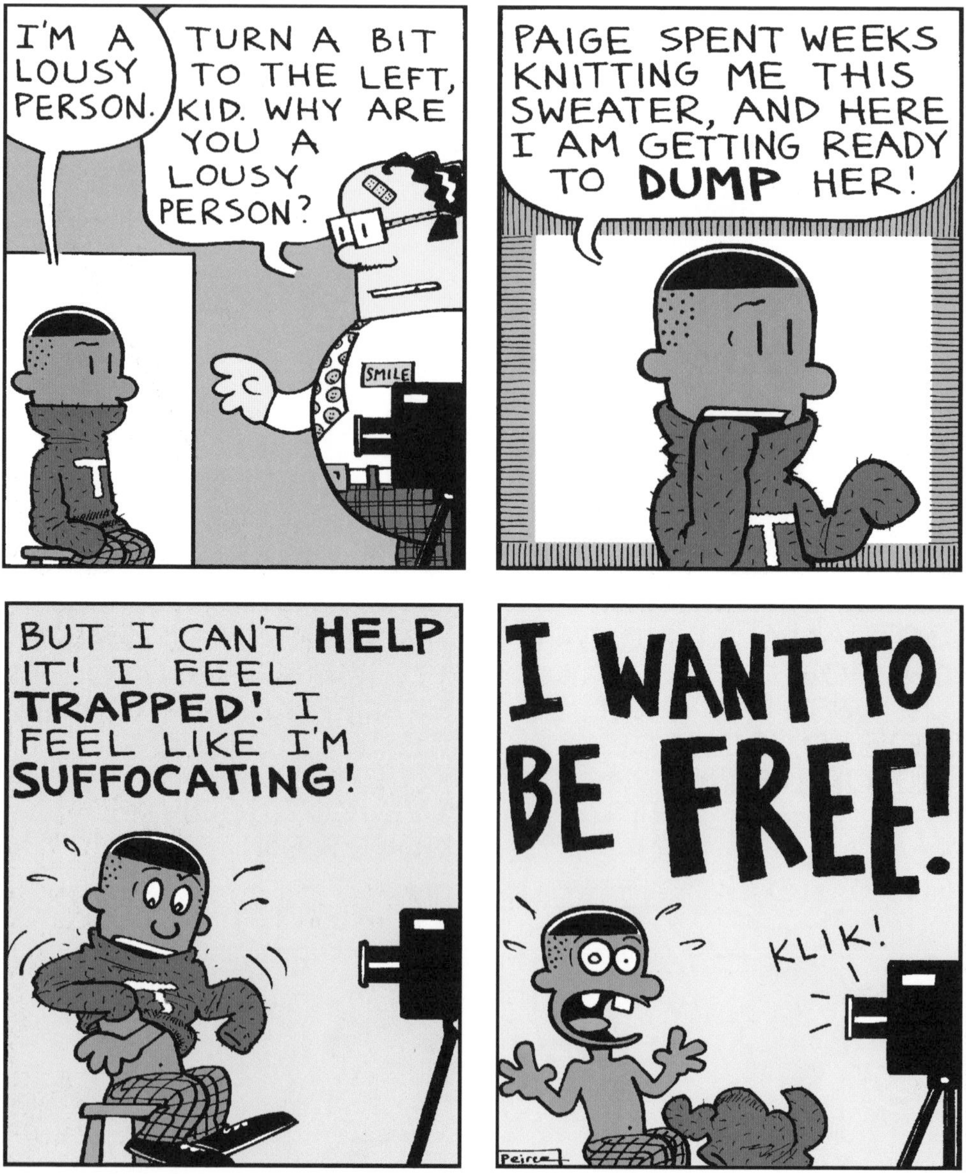
I'M A LOUSY PERSON.
TURN A BIT TO THE LEFT, KID. WHY ARE YOU A LOUSY PERSON?
SMILE
PAIGE SPENT WEEKS KNITTING ME THIS SWEATER, AND HERE I AM GETTING READY TO **DUMP** HER!
BUT I CAN'T **HELP** IT! I FEEL **TRAPPED!** I FEEL LIKE I'M **SUFFOCATING!**
I WANT TO BE FREE!
KLIK!
Peirce

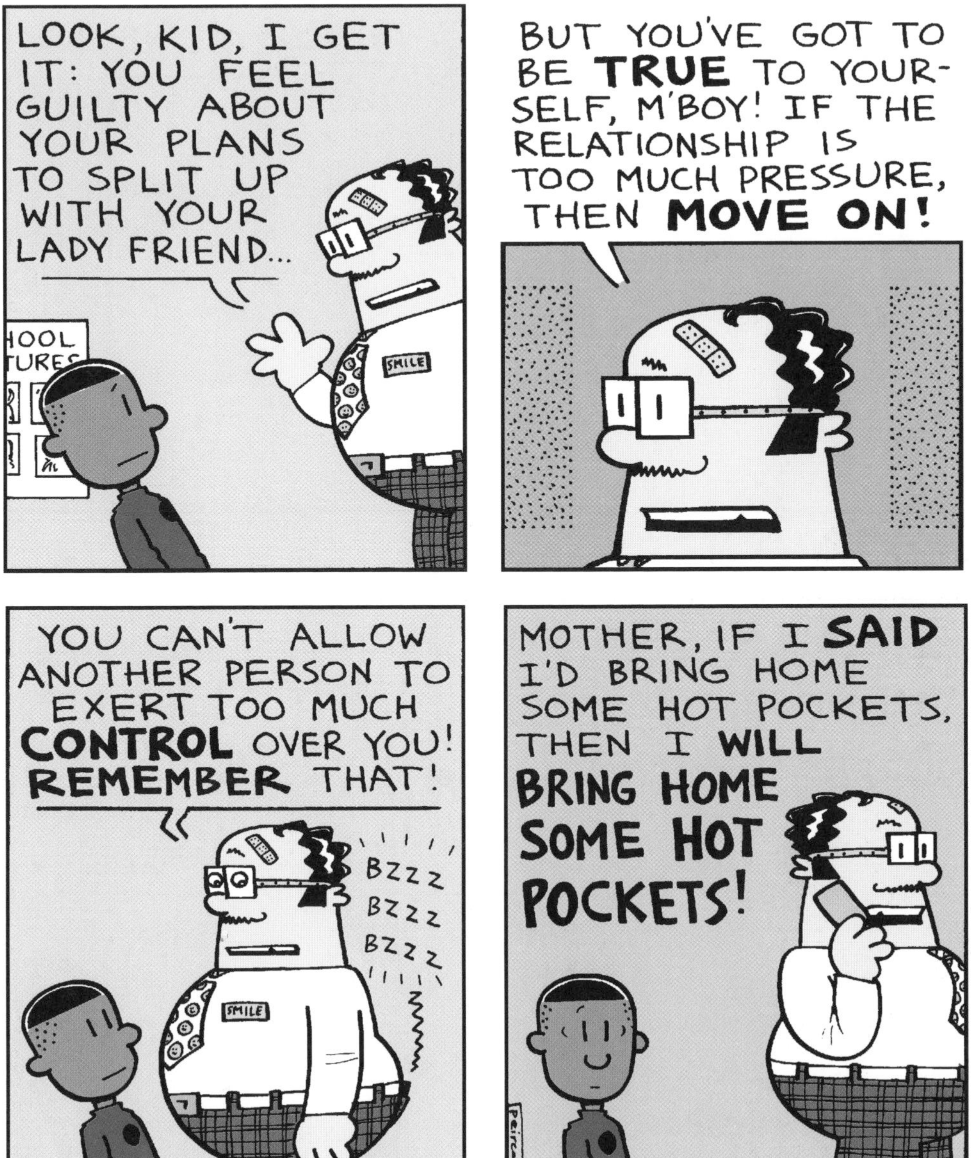
LOOK, KID, I GET IT: YOU FEEL GUILTY ABOUT YOUR PLANS TO SPLIT UP WITH YOUR LADY FRIEND...
SMILE
BUT YOU'VE GOT TO BE TRUE TO YOURSELF, M'BOY! IF THE RELATIONSHIP IS TOO MUCH PRESSURE, THEN MOVE ON!
YOU CAN'T ALLOW ANOTHER PERSON TO EXERT TOO MUCH CONTROL OVER YOU! REMEMBER THAT!
BZZZ
BZZZ
BZZZ
SMILE
MOTHER, IF I SAID I'D BRING HOME SOME HOT POCKETS, THEN I WILL BRING HOME SOME HOT POCKETS!
Peirce

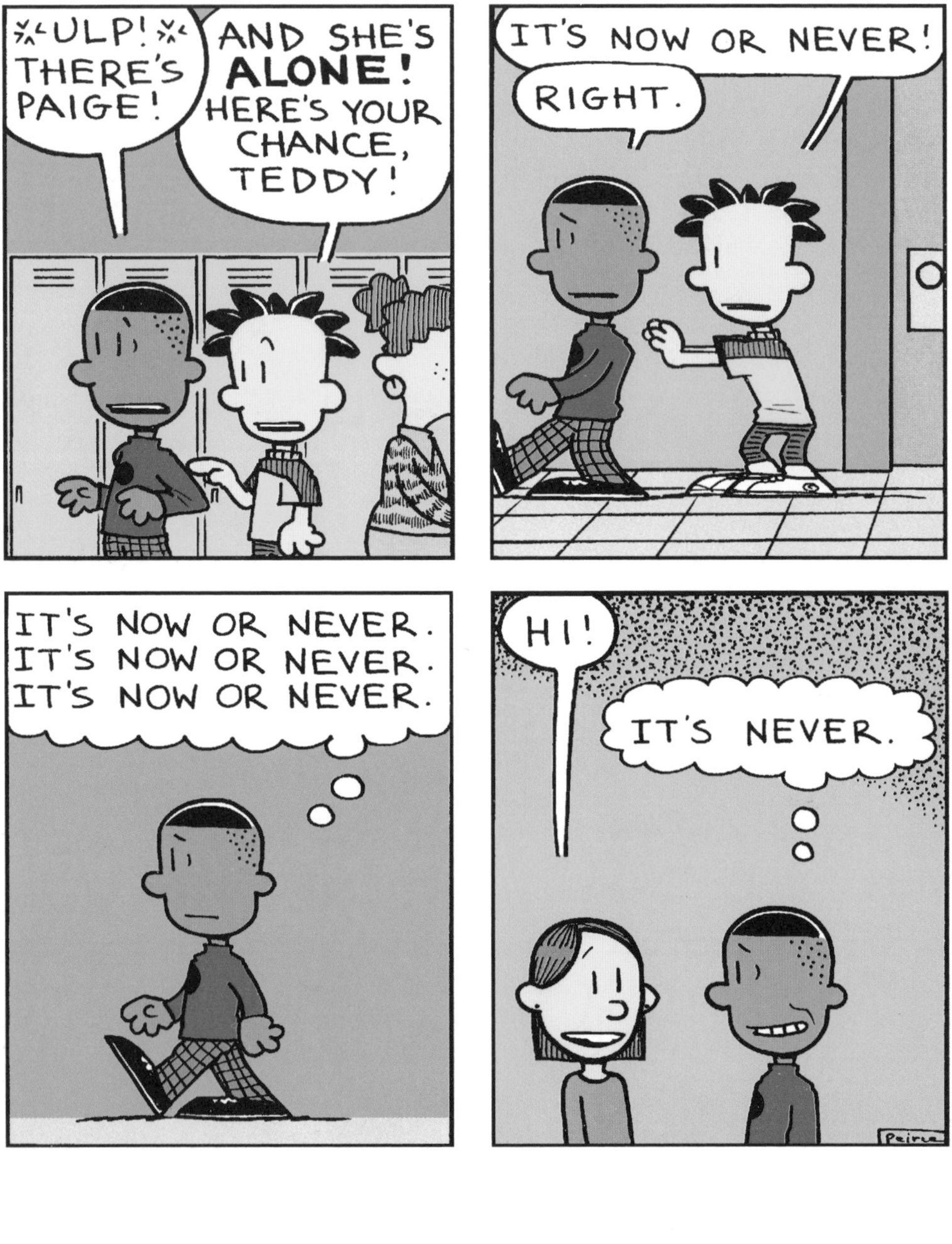
ULP! THERE'S PAIGE!
AND SHE'S **ALONE!** HERE'S YOUR CHANCE, TEDDY!
IT'S NOW OR NEVER!
RIGHT.
IT'S NOW OR NEVER. IT'S NOW OR NEVER. IT'S NOW OR NEVER.
HI!
IT'S NEVER.
Peirce

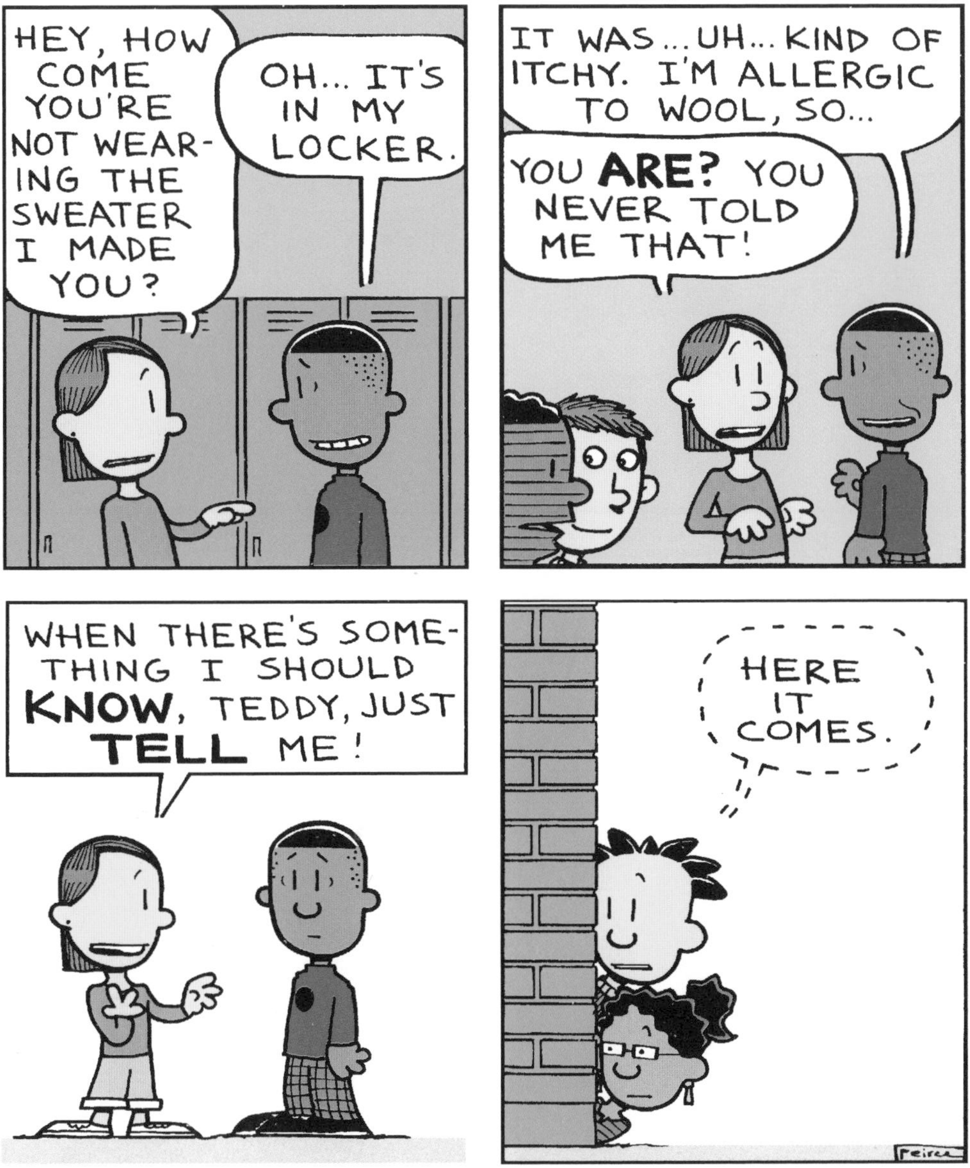
HEY, HOW COME YOU'RE NOT WEAR-ING THE SWEATER I MADE YOU?
OH... IT'S IN MY LOCKER.
IT WAS...UH...KIND OF ITCHY. I'M ALLERGIC TO WOOL, SO...
YOU **ARE?** YOU NEVER TOLD ME THAT!
WHEN THERE'S SOME-THING I SHOULD **KNOW**, TEDDY, JUST **TELL** ME!
HERE IT COMES.
peirce

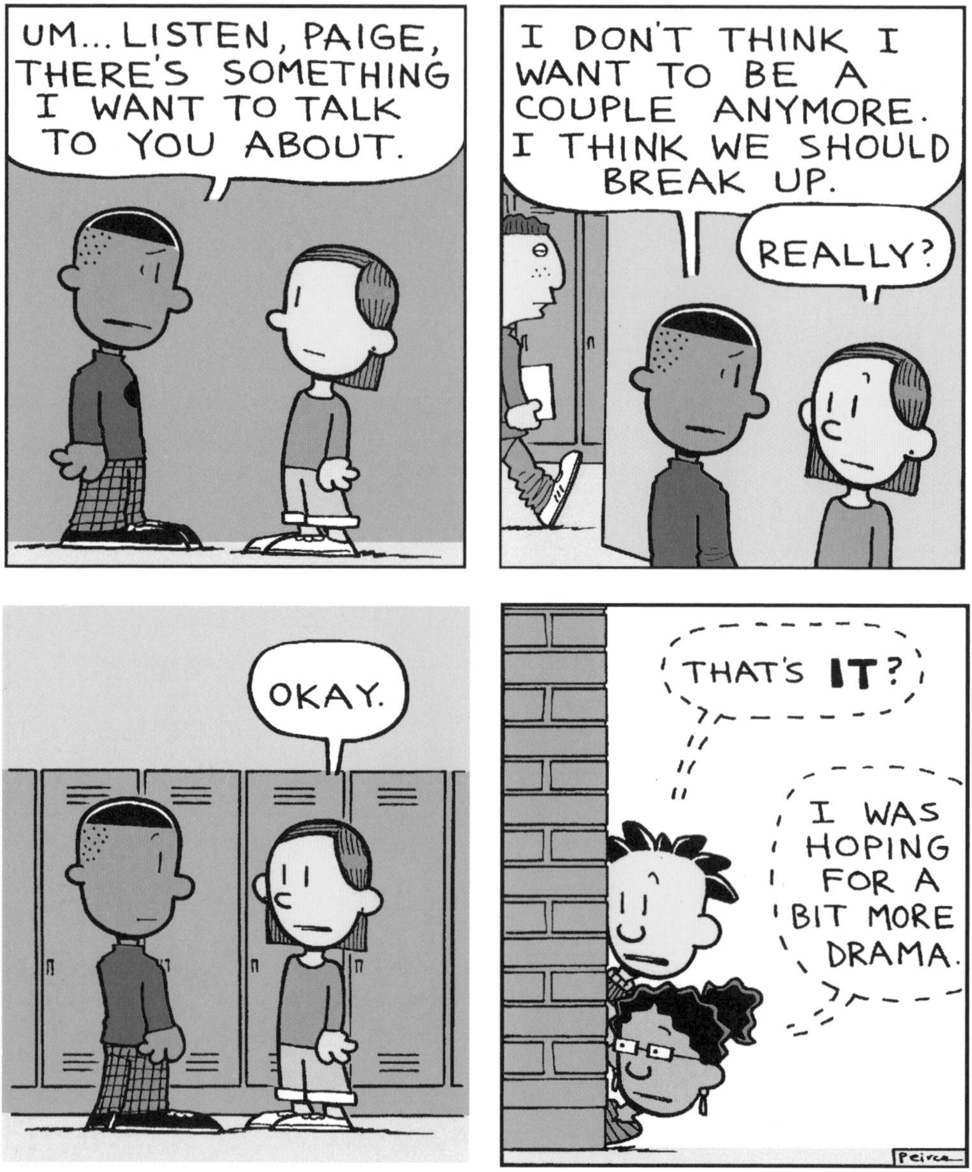
UM... LISTEN, PAIGE, THERE'S SOMETHING I WANT TO TALK TO YOU ABOUT.
I DON'T THINK I WANT TO BE A COUPLE ANYMORE. I THINK WE SHOULD BREAK UP.
REALLY?
OKAY.
THAT'S **IT**?
I WAS HOPING FOR A BIT MORE DRAMA.
Peirce

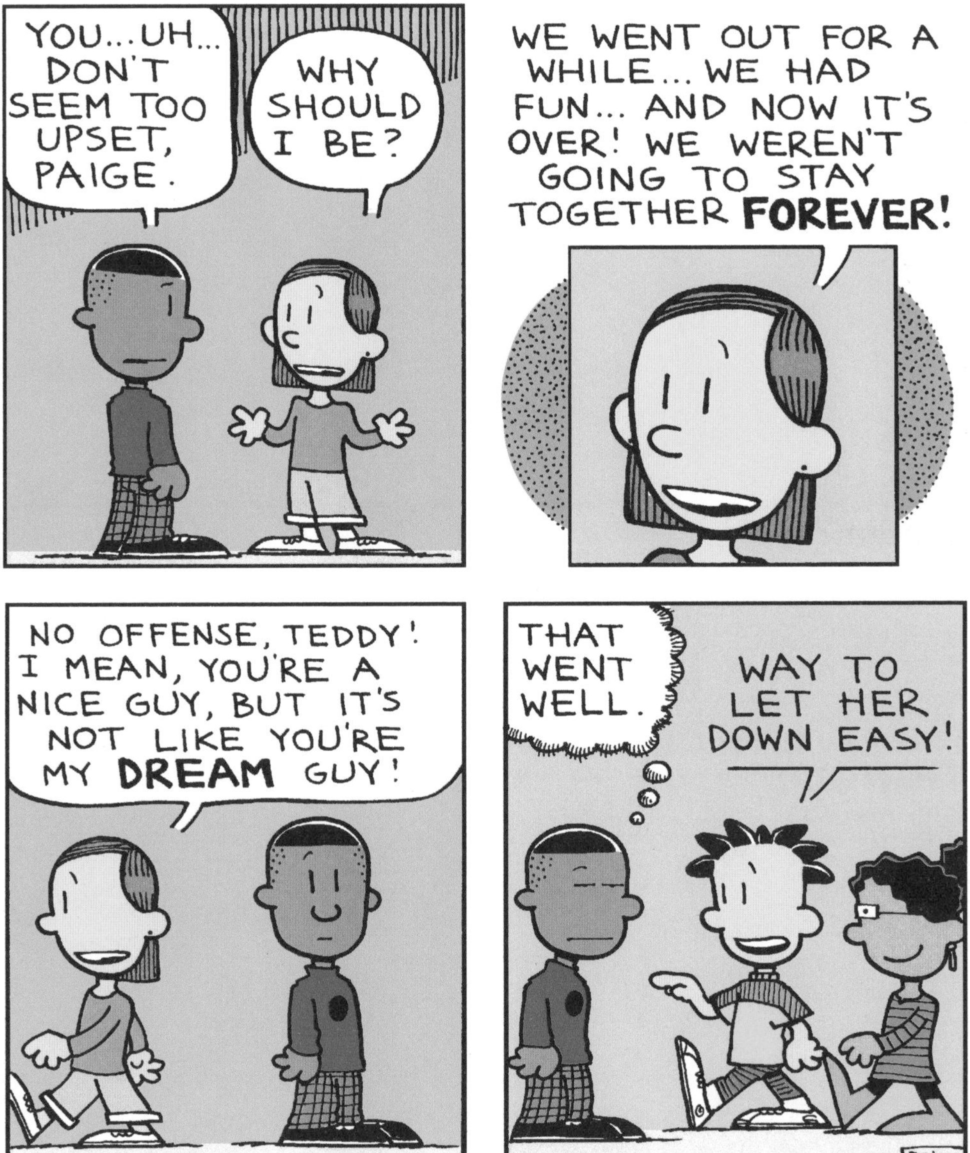
YOU...UH... DON'T SEEM TOO UPSET, PAIGE.
WHY SHOULD I BE?
WE WENT OUT FOR A WHILE... WE HAD FUN... AND NOW IT'S OVER! WE WEREN'T GOING TO STAY TOGETHER **FOREVER**!
NO OFFENSE, TEDDY! I MEAN, YOU'RE A NICE GUY, BUT IT'S NOT LIKE YOU'RE MY **DREAM** GUY!
THAT WENT WELL.
WAY TO LET HER DOWN EASY!
Peirce

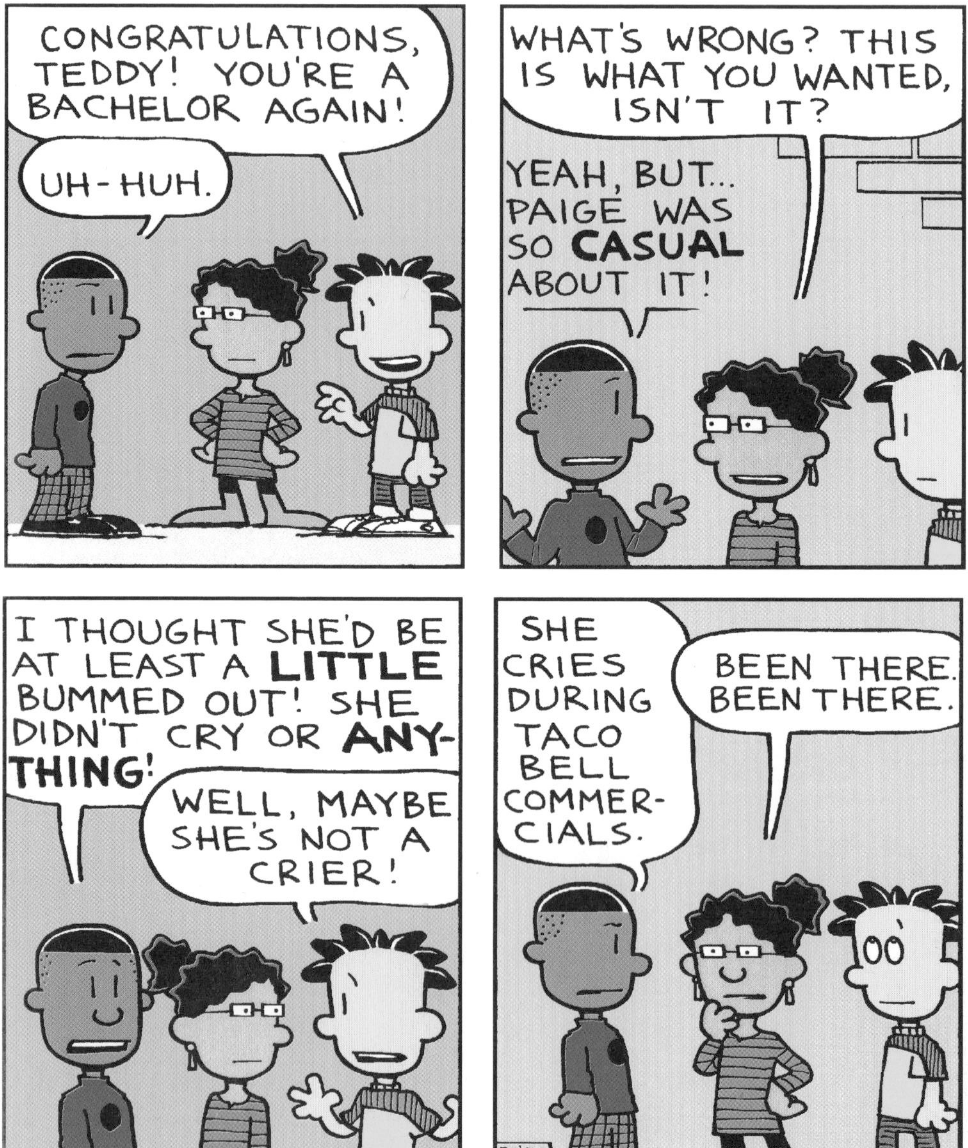
CONGRATULATIONS, TEDDY! YOU'RE A BACHELOR AGAIN!
UH-HUH.
WHAT'S WRONG? THIS IS WHAT YOU WANTED, ISN'T IT?
YEAH, BUT... PAIGE WAS SO **CASUAL** ABOUT IT!
I THOUGHT SHE'D BE AT LEAST A **LITTLE** BUMMED OUT! SHE DIDN'T CRY OR **ANY-THING**!
WELL, MAYBE SHE'S NOT A CRIER!
SHE CRIES DURING TACO BELL COMMER-CIALS.
BEEN THERE. BEEN THERE.
Peirce

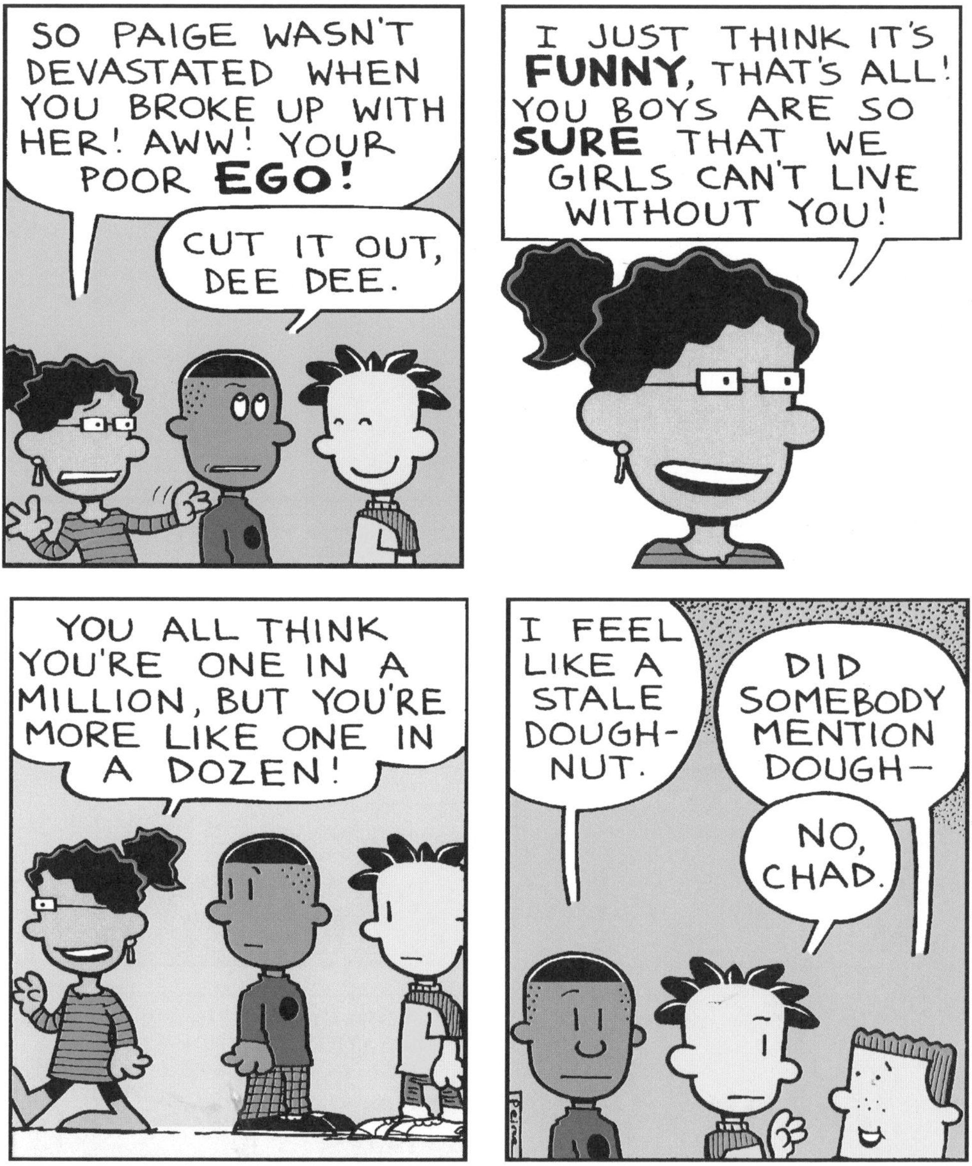
SO PAIGE WASN'T DEVASTATED WHEN YOU BROKE UP WITH HER! AWW! YOUR POOR **EGO**!
CUT IT OUT, DEE DEE.
I JUST THINK IT'S **FUNNY**, THAT'S ALL! YOU BOYS ARE SO **SURE** THAT WE GIRLS CAN'T LIVE WITHOUT YOU!
YOU ALL THINK YOU'RE ONE IN A MILLION, BUT YOU'RE MORE LIKE ONE IN A DOZEN!
I FEEL LIKE A STALE DOUGH-NUT.
DID SOMEBODY MENTION DOUGH-
NO, CHAD.

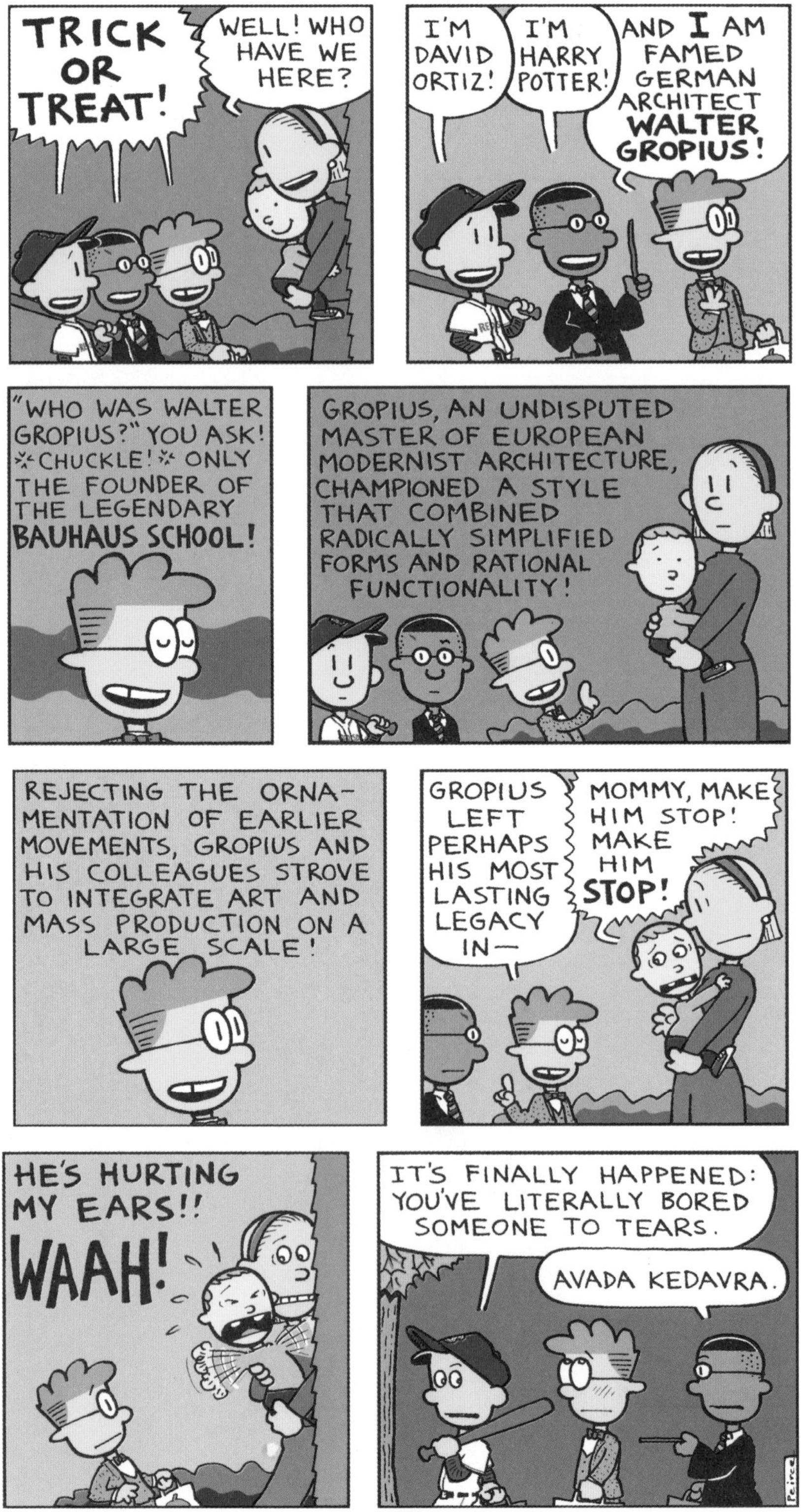
TRICK OR TREAT!
WELL! WHO HAVE WE HERE?
I'M DAVID ORTIZ!
I'M HARRY POTTER!
AND I AM FAMED GERMAN ARCHITECT WALTER GROPIUS!
"WHO WAS WALTER GROPIUS?" YOU ASK! *CHUCKLE!* ONLY THE FOUNDER OF THE LEGENDARY BAUHAUS SCHOOL!
GROPIUS, AN UNDISPUTED MASTER OF EUROPEAN MODERNIST ARCHITECTURE, CHAMPIONED A STYLE THAT COMBINED RADICALLY SIMPLIFIED FORMS AND RATIONAL FUNCTIONALITY!
REJECTING THE ORNAMENTATION OF EARLIER MOVEMENTS, GROPIUS AND HIS COLLEAGUES STROVE TO INTEGRATE ART AND MASS PRODUCTION ON A LARGE SCALE!
GROPIUS LEFT PERHAPS HIS MOST LASTING LEGACY IN—
MOMMY, MAKE HIM STOP! MAKE HIM STOP!
HE'S HURTING MY EARS!!
WAAH!
IT'S FINALLY HAPPENED: YOU'VE LITERALLY BORED SOMEONE TO TEARS.
AVADA KEDAVRA.
Peirce

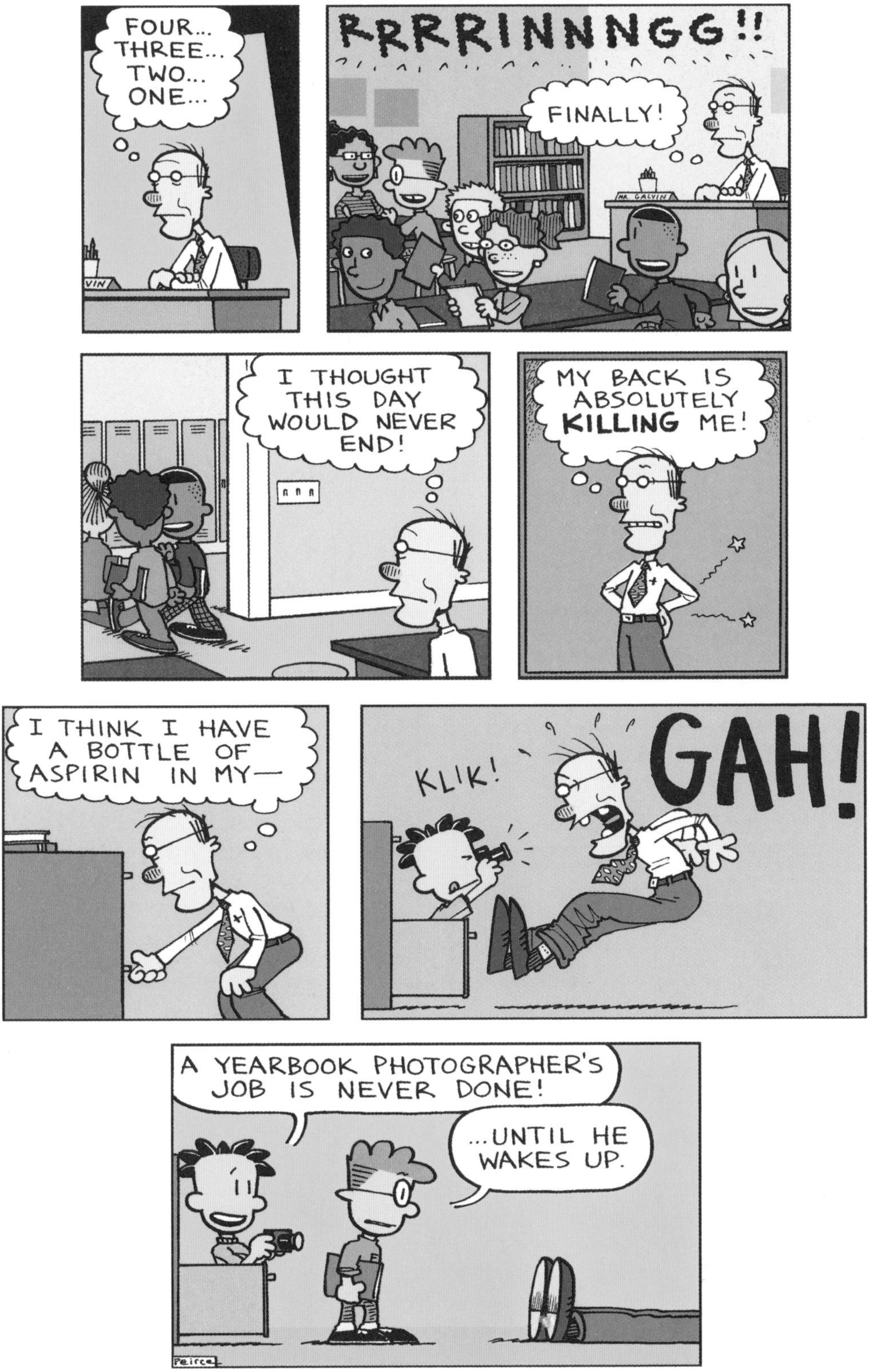
FOUR... THREE... TWO... ONE...
RRRRINNNGG!!
MR. GALVIN
FINALLY!
I THOUGHT THIS DAY WOULD NEVER END!
MY BACK IS ABSOLUTELY **KILLING** ME!
I THINK I HAVE A BOTTLE OF ASPIRIN IN MY—
KLIK!
GAH!
A YEARBOOK PHOTOGRAPHER'S JOB IS NEVER DONE!
...UNTIL HE WAKES UP.
Peirce

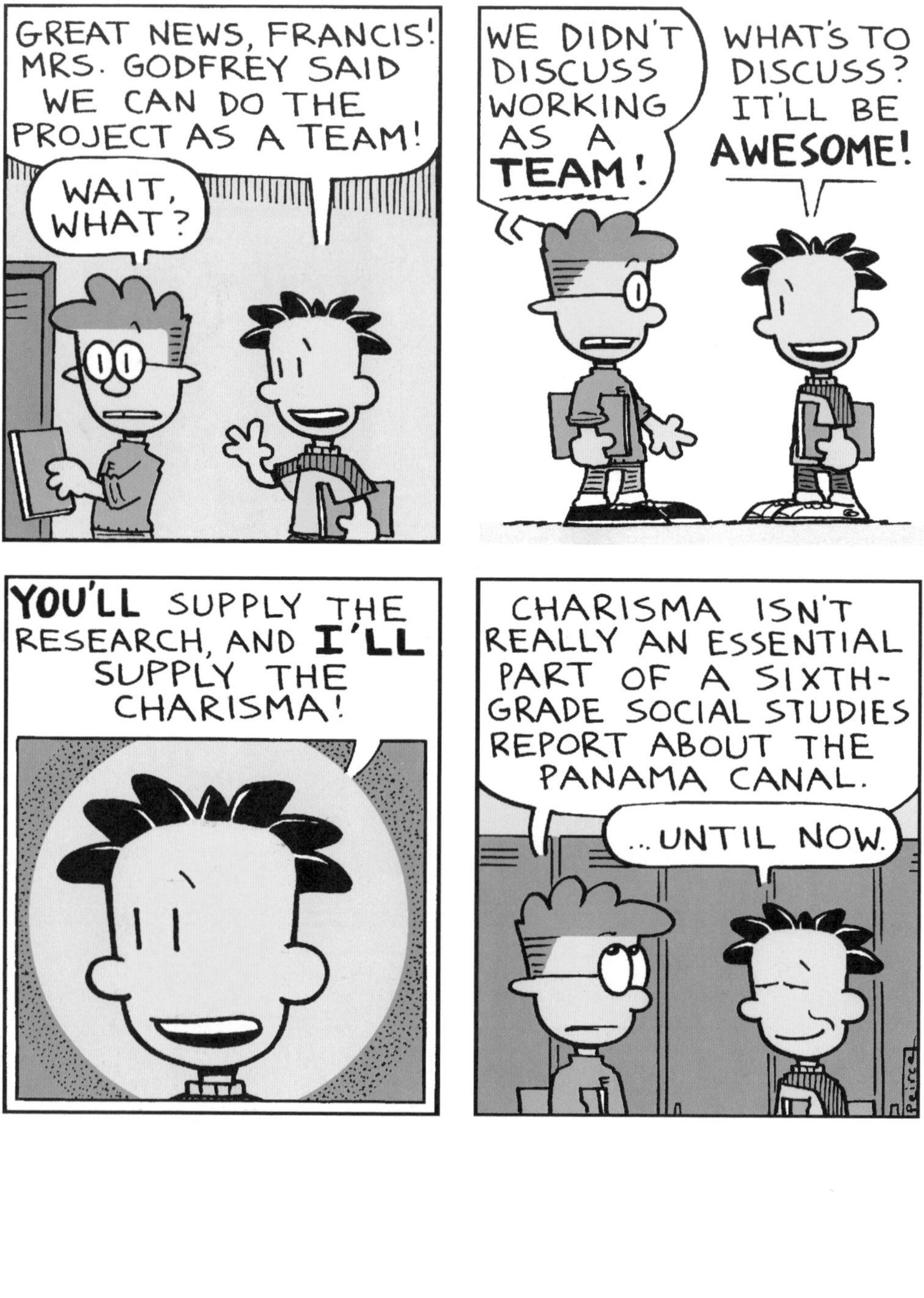
GREAT NEWS, FRANCIS! MRS. GODFREY SAID WE CAN DO THE PROJECT AS A TEAM!
WAIT, WHAT?
WE DIDN'T DISCUSS WORKING AS A TEAM!
WHAT'S TO DISCUSS? IT'LL BE AWESOME!
YOU'LL SUPPLY THE RESEARCH, AND I'LL SUPPLY THE CHARISMA!
CHARISMA ISN'T REALLY AN ESSENTIAL PART OF A SIXTH-GRADE SOCIAL STUDIES REPORT ABOUT THE PANAMA CANAL.
...UNTIL NOW.
Peirce

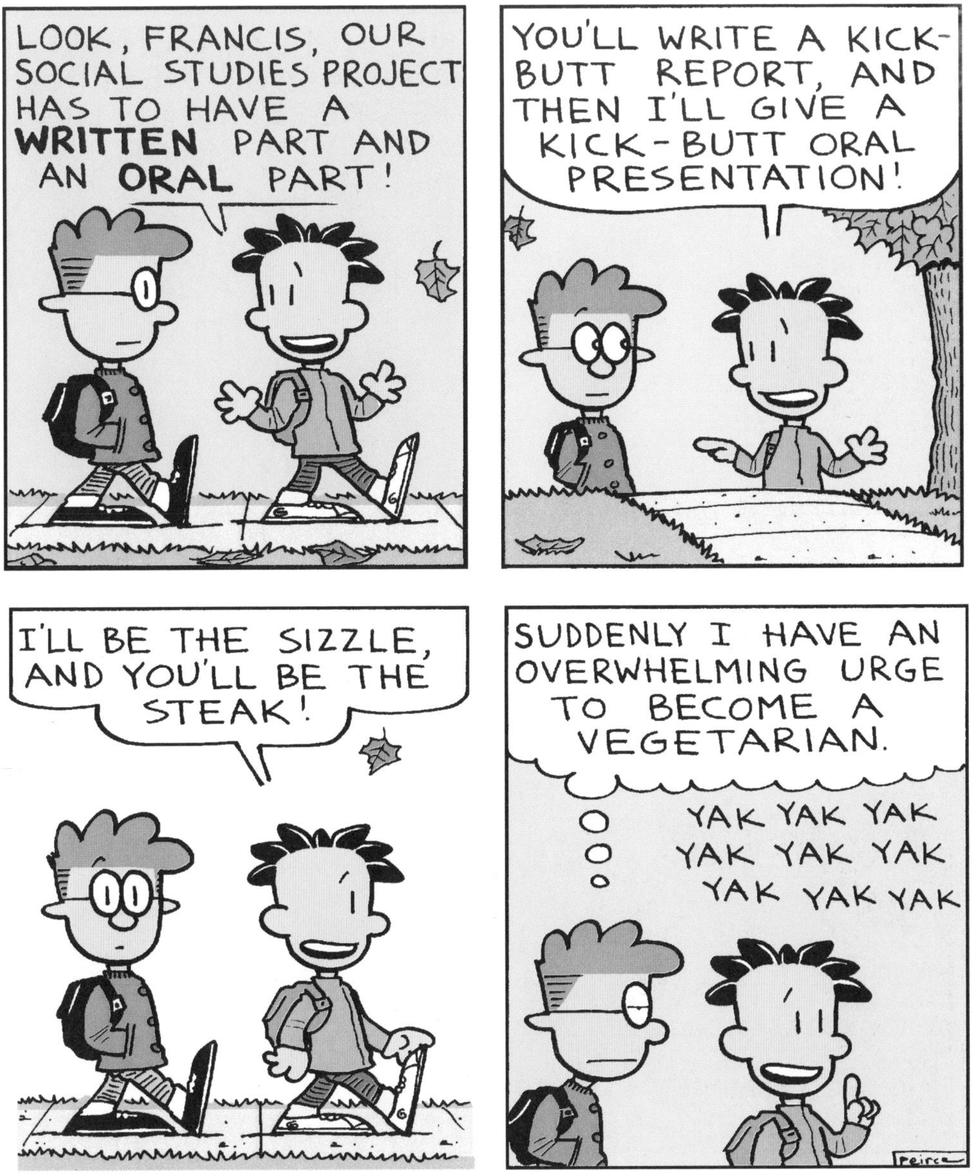
LOOK, FRANCIS, OUR SOCIAL STUDIES PROJECT HAS TO HAVE A **WRITTEN** PART AND AN **ORAL** PART!
YOU'LL WRITE A KICK-BUTT REPORT, AND THEN I'LL GIVE A KICK-BUTT ORAL PRESENTATION!
I'LL BE THE SIZZLE, AND YOU'LL BE THE STEAK!
SUDDENLY I HAVE AN OVERWHELMING URGE TO BECOME A VEGETARIAN.
YAK YAK YAK YAK YAK YAK YAK YAK YAK
peirce

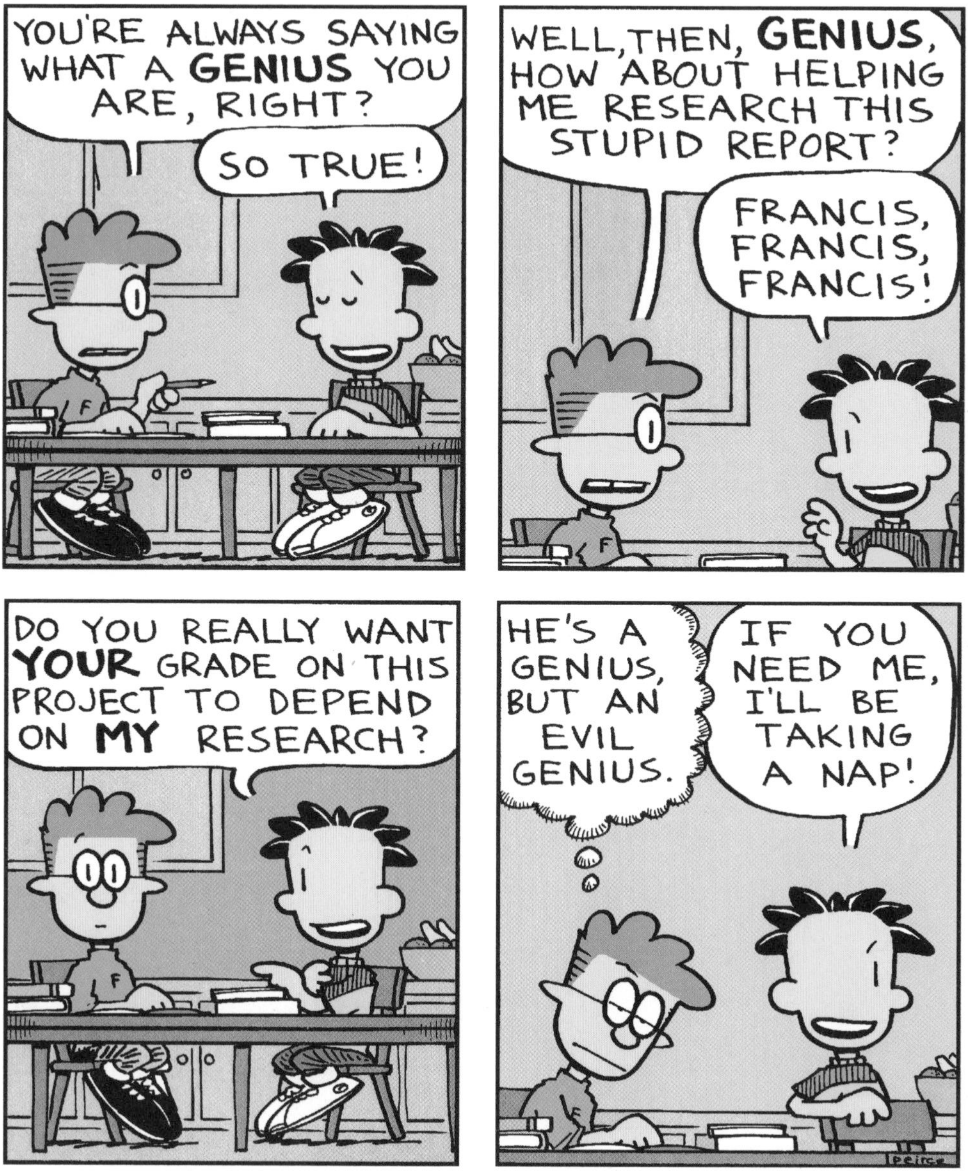
YOU'RE ALWAYS SAYING WHAT A **GENIUS** YOU ARE, RIGHT?
SO TRUE!
WELL, THEN, **GENIUS**, HOW ABOUT HELPING ME RESEARCH THIS STUPID REPORT?
FRANCIS, FRANCIS, FRANCIS!
DO YOU REALLY WANT **YOUR** GRADE ON THIS PROJECT TO DEPEND ON **MY** RESEARCH?
HE'S A GENIUS, BUT AN EVIL GENIUS.
IF YOU NEED ME, I'LL BE TAKING A NAP!
Lpeirce

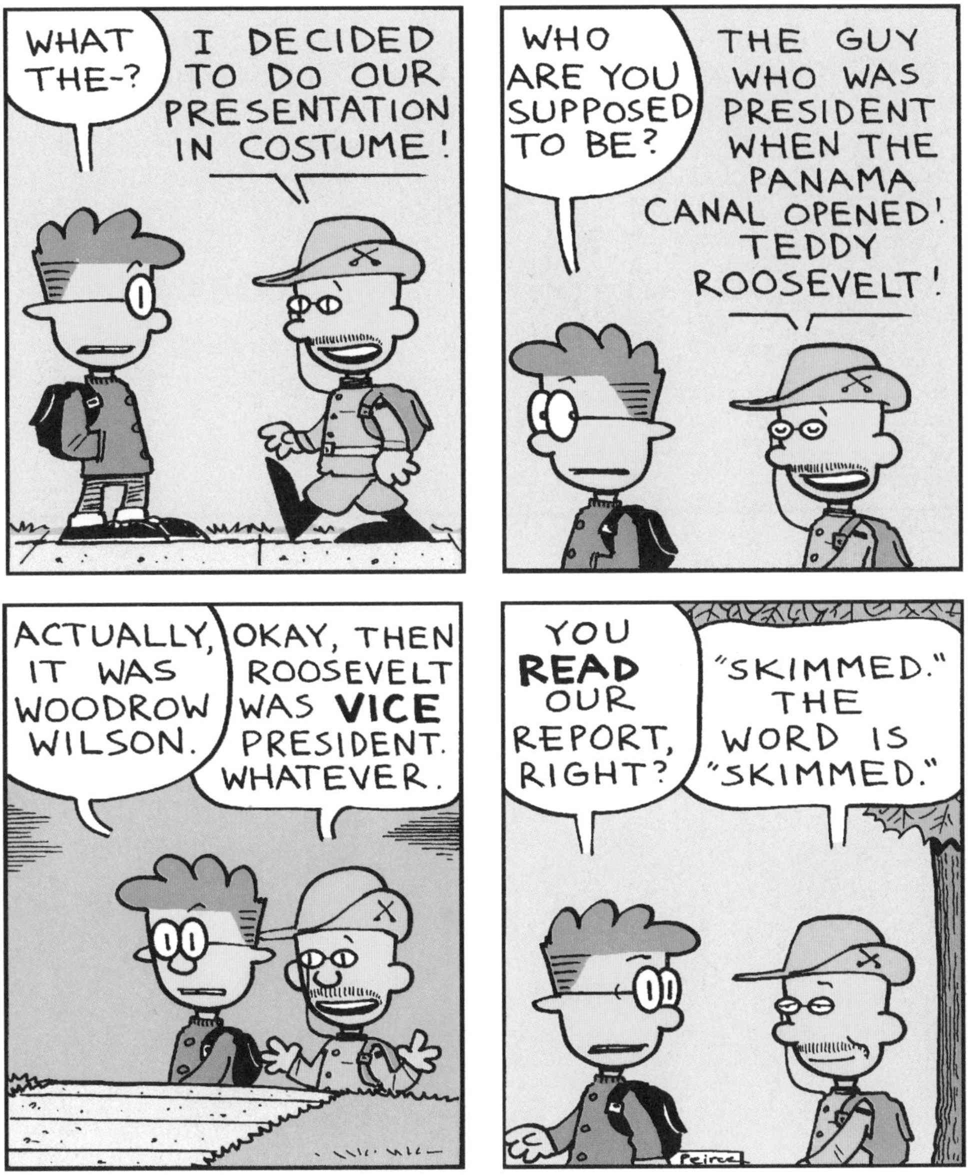
WHAT THE-?
I DECIDED TO DO OUR PRESENTATION IN COSTUME!
WHO ARE YOU SUPPOSED TO BE?
THE GUY WHO WAS PRESIDENT WHEN THE PANAMA CANAL OPENED! TEDDY ROOSEVELT!
ACTUALLY, IT WAS WOODROW WILSON.
OKAY, THEN ROOSEVELT WAS **VICE** PRESIDENT. WHATEVER.
YOU **READ** OUR REPORT, RIGHT?
"SKIMMED." THE WORD IS "SKIMMED."
Peirce

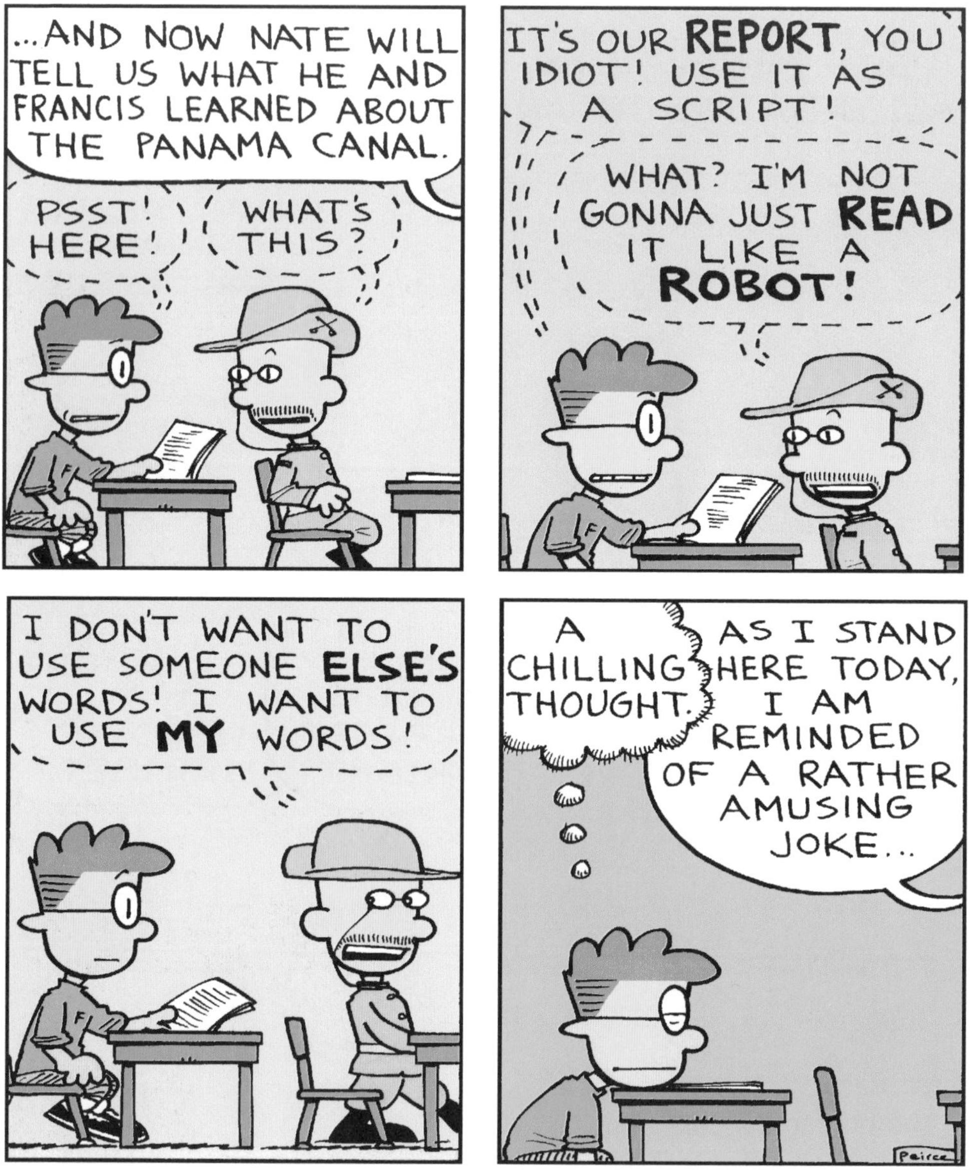
...AND NOW NATE WILL TELL US WHAT HE AND FRANCIS LEARNED ABOUT THE PANAMA CANAL.
PSST! HERE!
WHAT'S THIS?
IT'S OUR REPORT, YOU IDIOT! USE IT AS A SCRIPT!
WHAT? I'M NOT GONNA JUST READ IT LIKE A ROBOT!
I DON'T WANT TO USE SOMEONE ELSE'S WORDS! I WANT TO USE MY WORDS!
A CHILLING THOUGHT.
AS I STAND HERE TODAY, I AM REMINDED OF A RATHER AMUSING JOKE...
Peirce

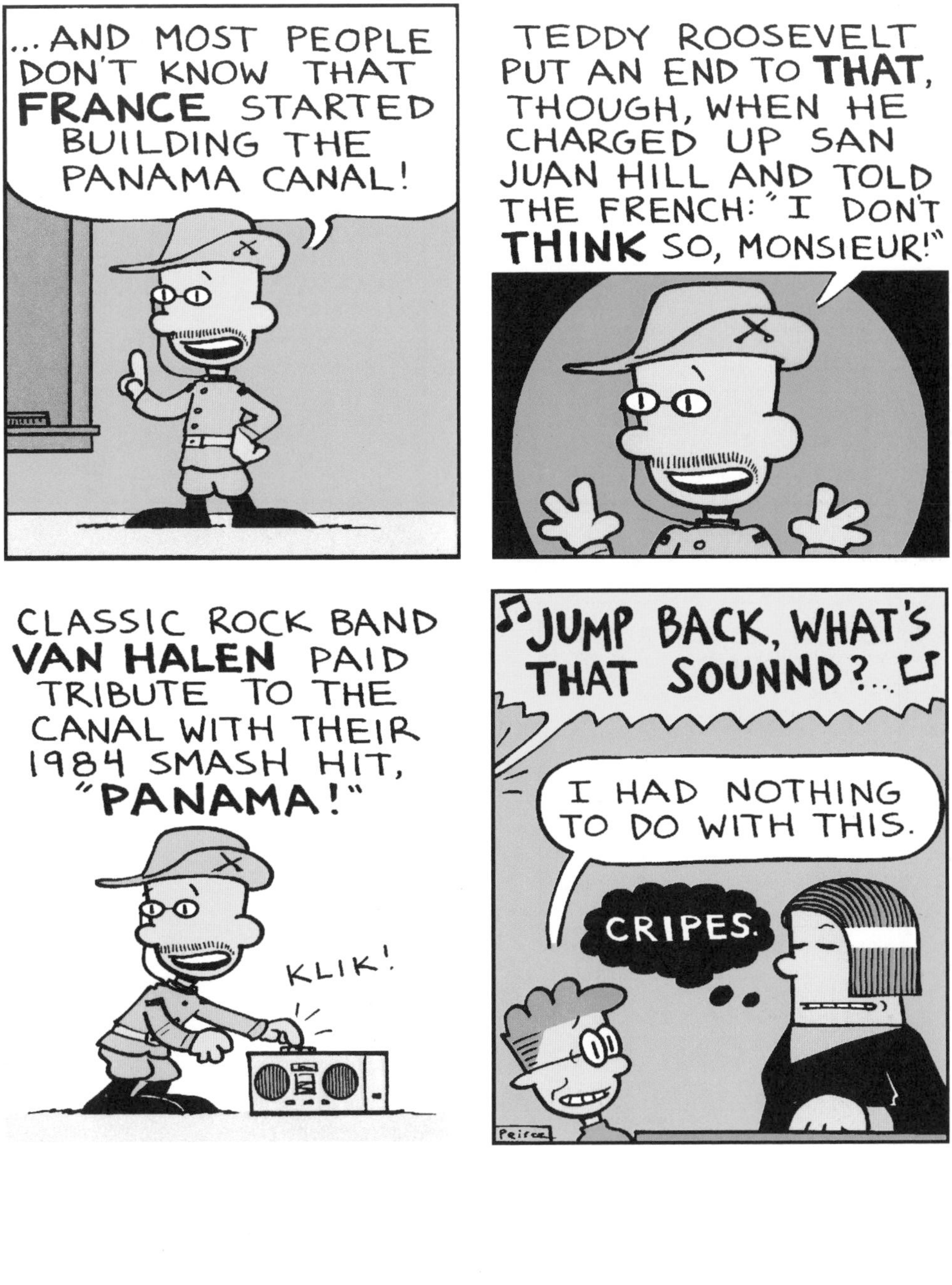
...AND MOST PEOPLE DON'T KNOW THAT **FRANCE** STARTED BUILDING THE PANAMA CANAL!
TEDDY ROOSEVELT PUT AN END TO **THAT**, THOUGH, WHEN HE CHARGED UP SAN JUAN HILL AND TOLD THE FRENCH: "I DON'T **THINK** SO, MONSIEUR!"
CLASSIC ROCK BAND **VAN HALEN** PAID TRIBUTE TO THE CANAL WITH THEIR 1984 SMASH HIT, "**PANAMA!**"
KLIK!
♪ JUMP BACK, WHAT'S THAT SOUNND?... ♫
I HAD NOTHING TO DO WITH THIS.
CRIPES.
Peirce

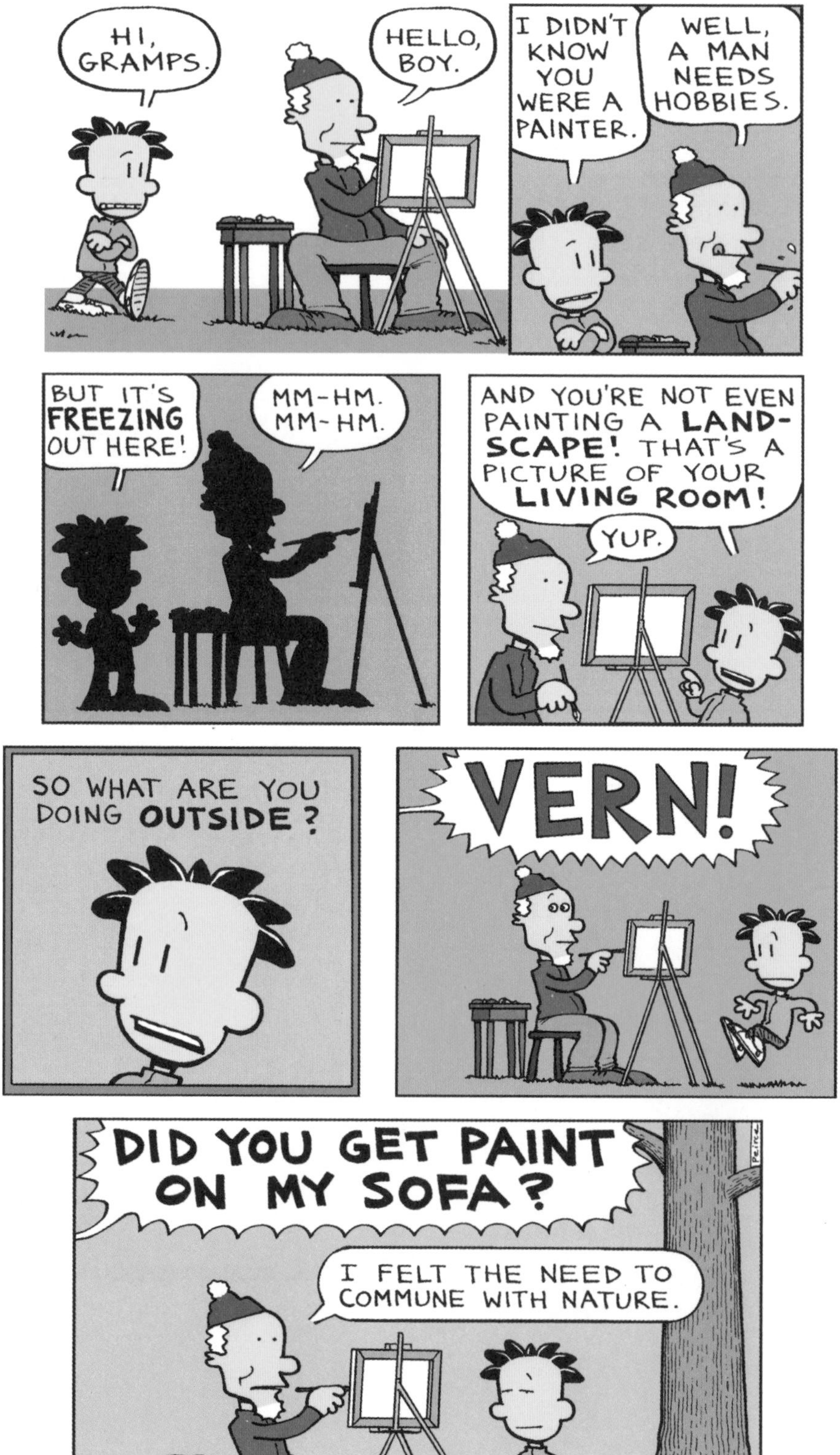
HI, GRAMPS.
HELLO, BOY.
I DIDN'T KNOW YOU WERE A PAINTER.
WELL, A MAN NEEDS HOBBIES.
BUT IT'S FREEZING OUT HERE!
MM-HM. MM-HM.
AND YOU'RE NOT EVEN PAINTING A LANDSCAPE! THAT'S A PICTURE OF YOUR LIVING ROOM!
YUP.
SO WHAT ARE YOU DOING OUTSIDE?
VERN!
DID YOU GET PAINT ON MY SOFA?
I FELT THE NEED TO COMMUNE WITH NATURE.
Peirce

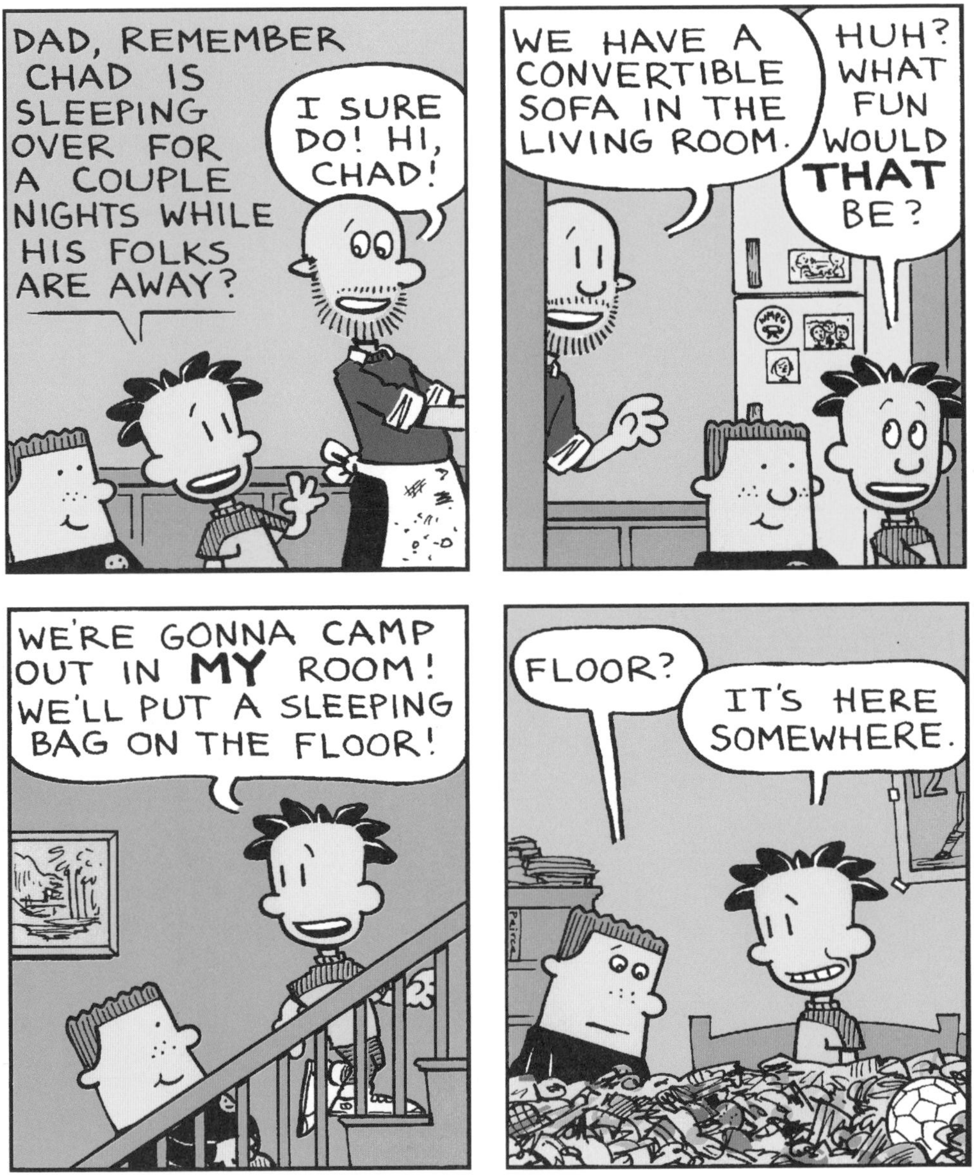
DAD, REMEMBER CHAD IS SLEEPING OVER FOR A COUPLE NIGHTS WHILE HIS FOLKS ARE AWAY?
I SURE DO! HI, CHAD!
WE HAVE A CONVERTIBLE SOFA IN THE LIVING ROOM.
HUH? WHAT FUN WOULD THAT BE?
WE'RE GONNA CAMP OUT IN MY ROOM! WE'LL PUT A SLEEPING BAG ON THE FLOOR!
FLOOR?
IT'S HERE SOMEWHERE.

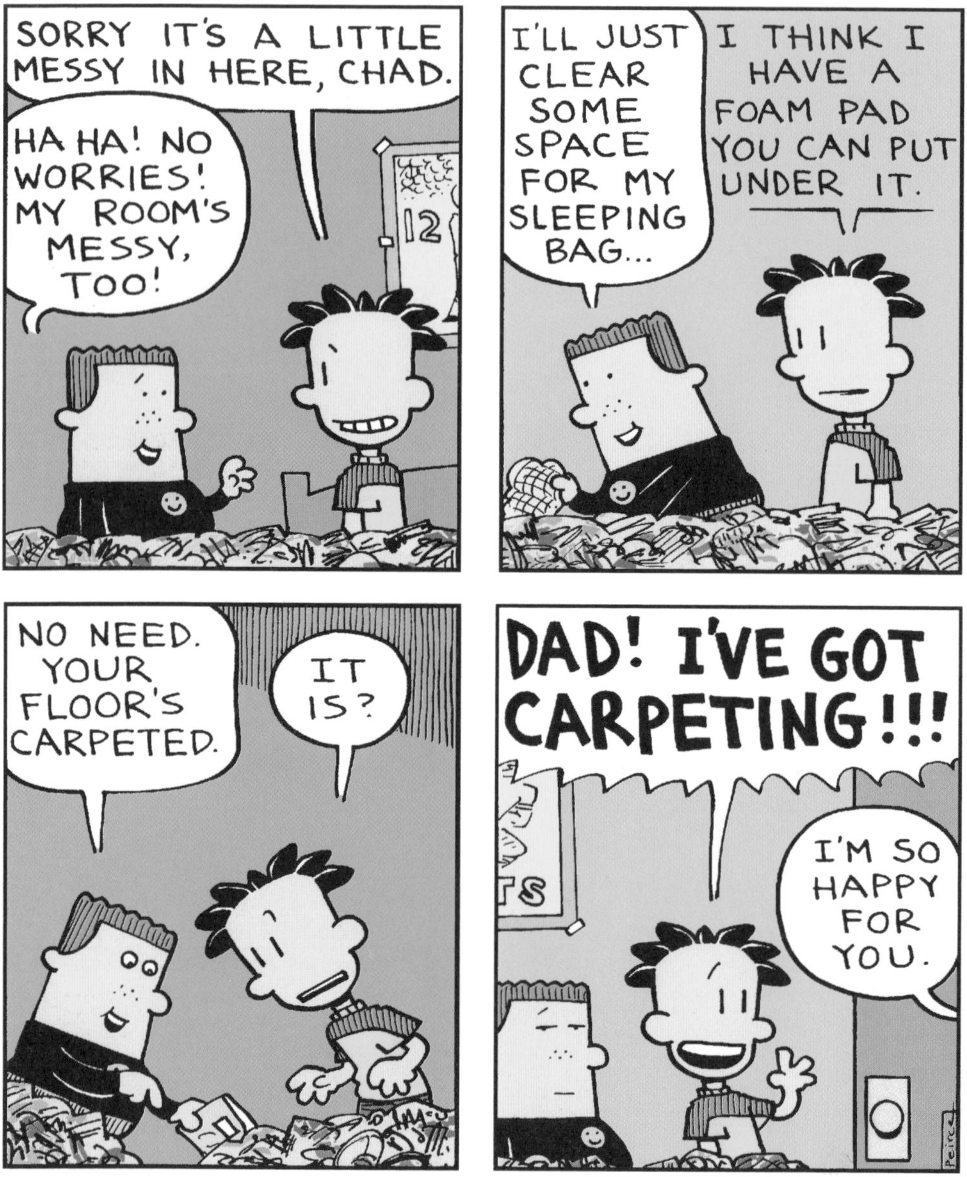
SORRY IT'S A LITTLE MESSY IN HERE, CHAD.
HA HA! NO WORRIES! MY ROOM'S MESSY, TOO!
12
I'LL JUST CLEAR SOME SPACE FOR MY SLEEPING BAG...
I THINK I HAVE A FOAM PAD YOU CAN PUT UNDER IT.
NO NEED. YOUR FLOOR'S CARPETED.
IT IS?
DAD! I'VE GOT CARPETING!!!
I'M SO HAPPY FOR YOU.
Peirce

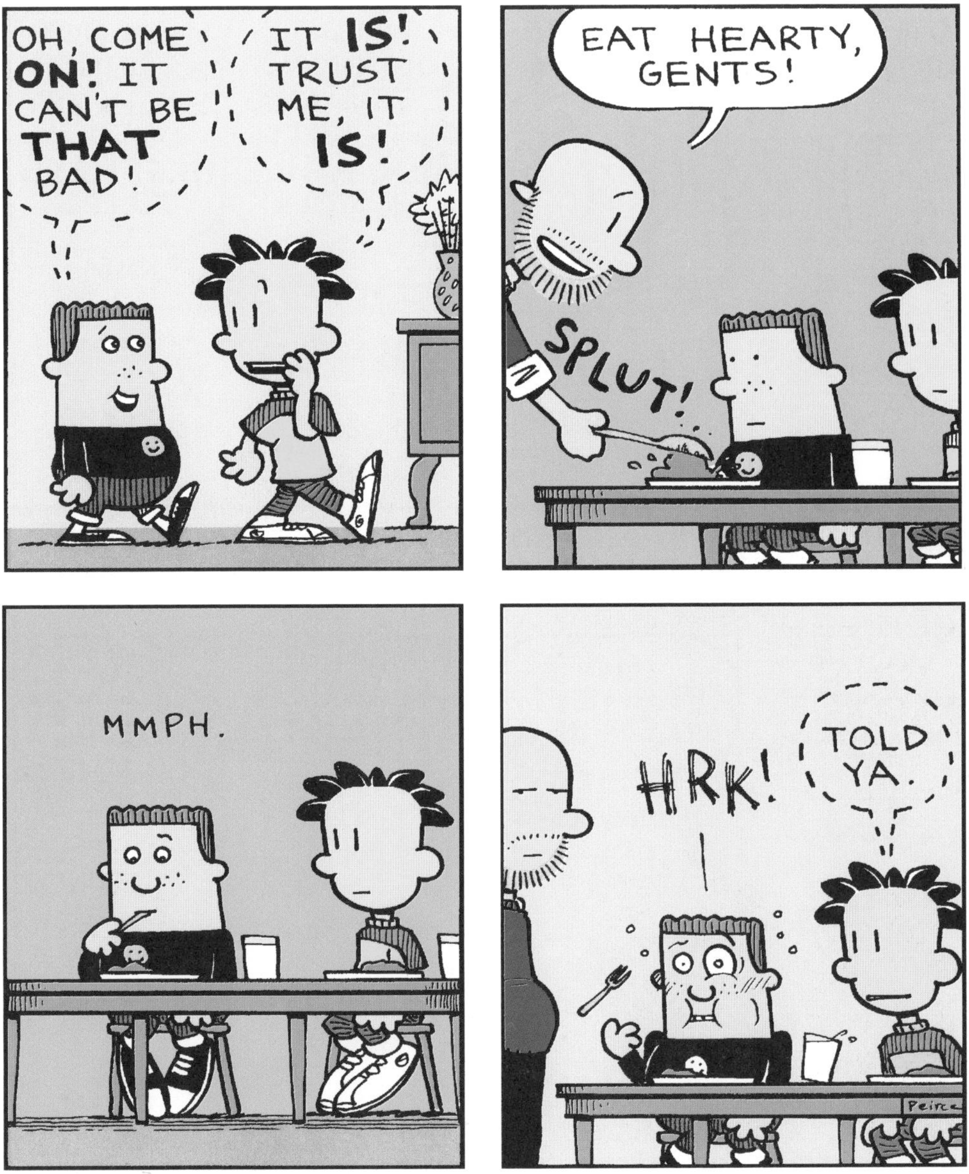
OH, COME ON! IT CAN'T BE THAT BAD!
IT IS! TRUST ME, IT IS!
EAT HEARTY, GENTS!
SPLUT!
MMPH.
HRK!
TOLD YA.

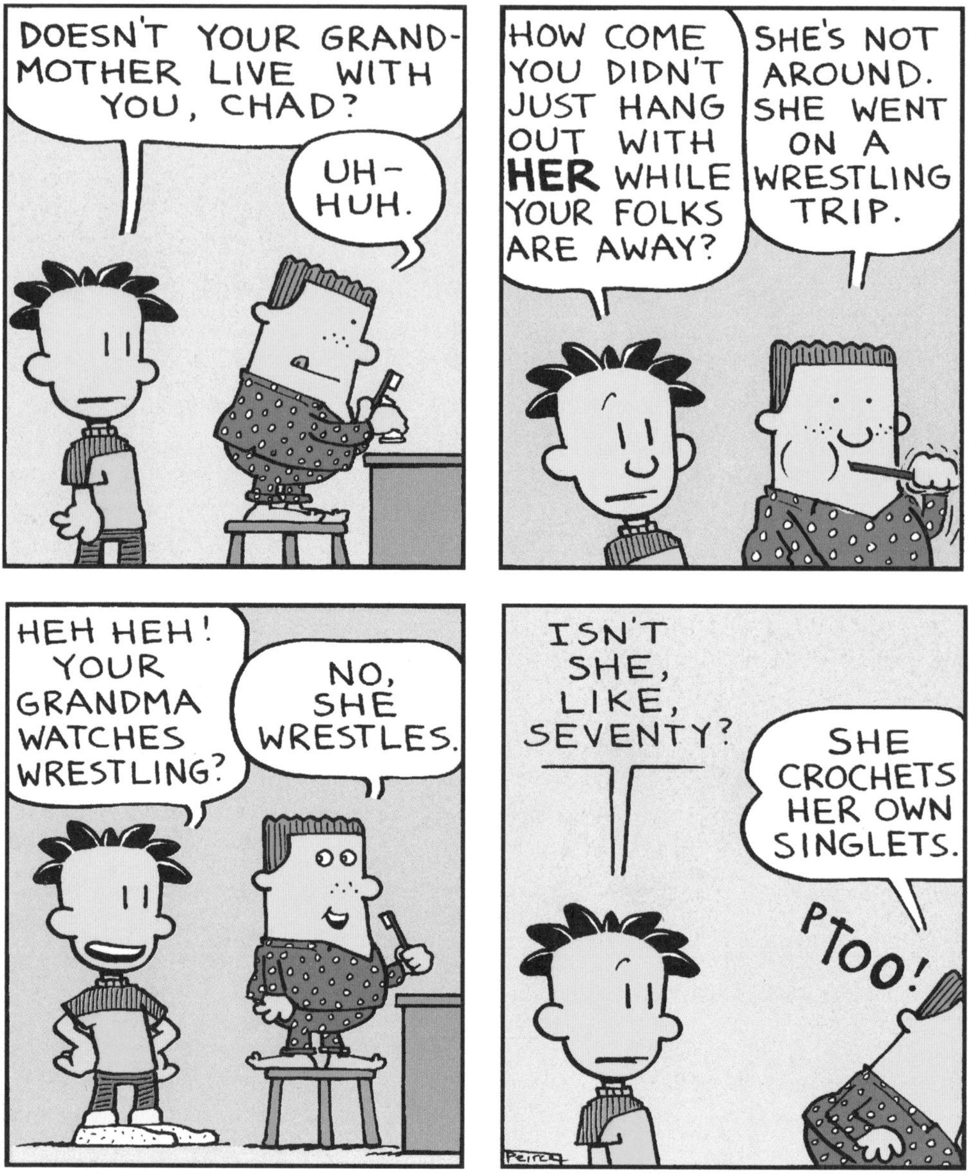
DOESN'T YOUR GRANDMOTHER LIVE WITH YOU, CHAD?
UH-HUH.
HOW COME YOU DIDN'T JUST HANG OUT WITH **HER** WHILE YOUR FOLKS ARE AWAY?
SHE'S NOT AROUND. SHE WENT ON A WRESTLING TRIP.
HEH HEH! YOUR GRANDMA WATCHES WRESTLING?
NO, SHE WRESTLES.
ISN'T SHE, LIKE, SEVENTY?
SHE CROCHETS HER OWN SINGLETS.
PTOO!
PEIRCE

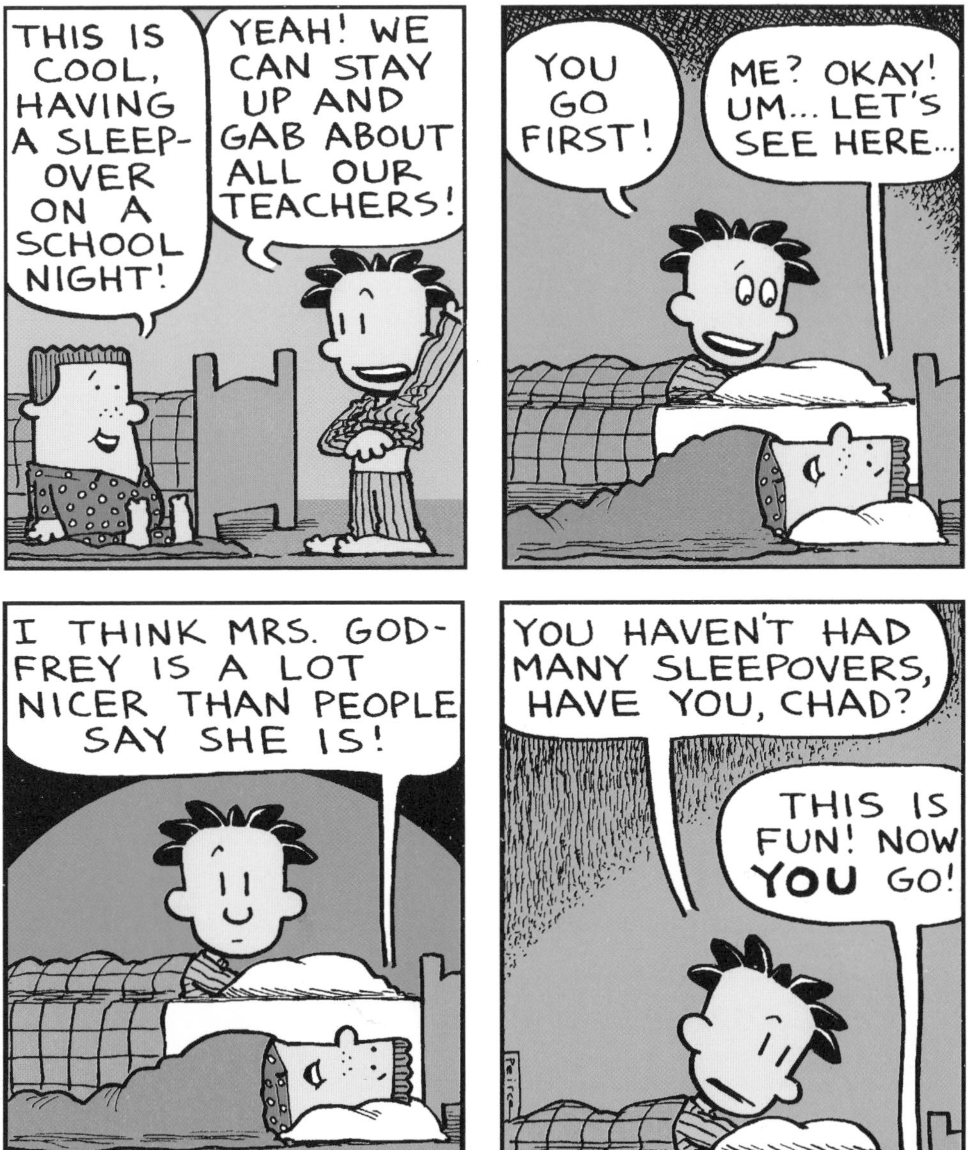
THIS IS COOL, HAVING A SLEEP-OVER ON A SCHOOL NIGHT!
YEAH! WE CAN STAY UP AND GAB ABOUT ALL OUR TEACHERS!
YOU GO FIRST!
ME? OKAY! UM... LET'S SEE HERE...
I THINK MRS. GOD-FREY IS A LOT NICER THAN PEOPLE SAY SHE IS!
YOU HAVEN'T HAD MANY SLEEPOVERS, HAVE YOU, CHAD?
THIS IS FUN! NOW **YOU** GO!
Peirce

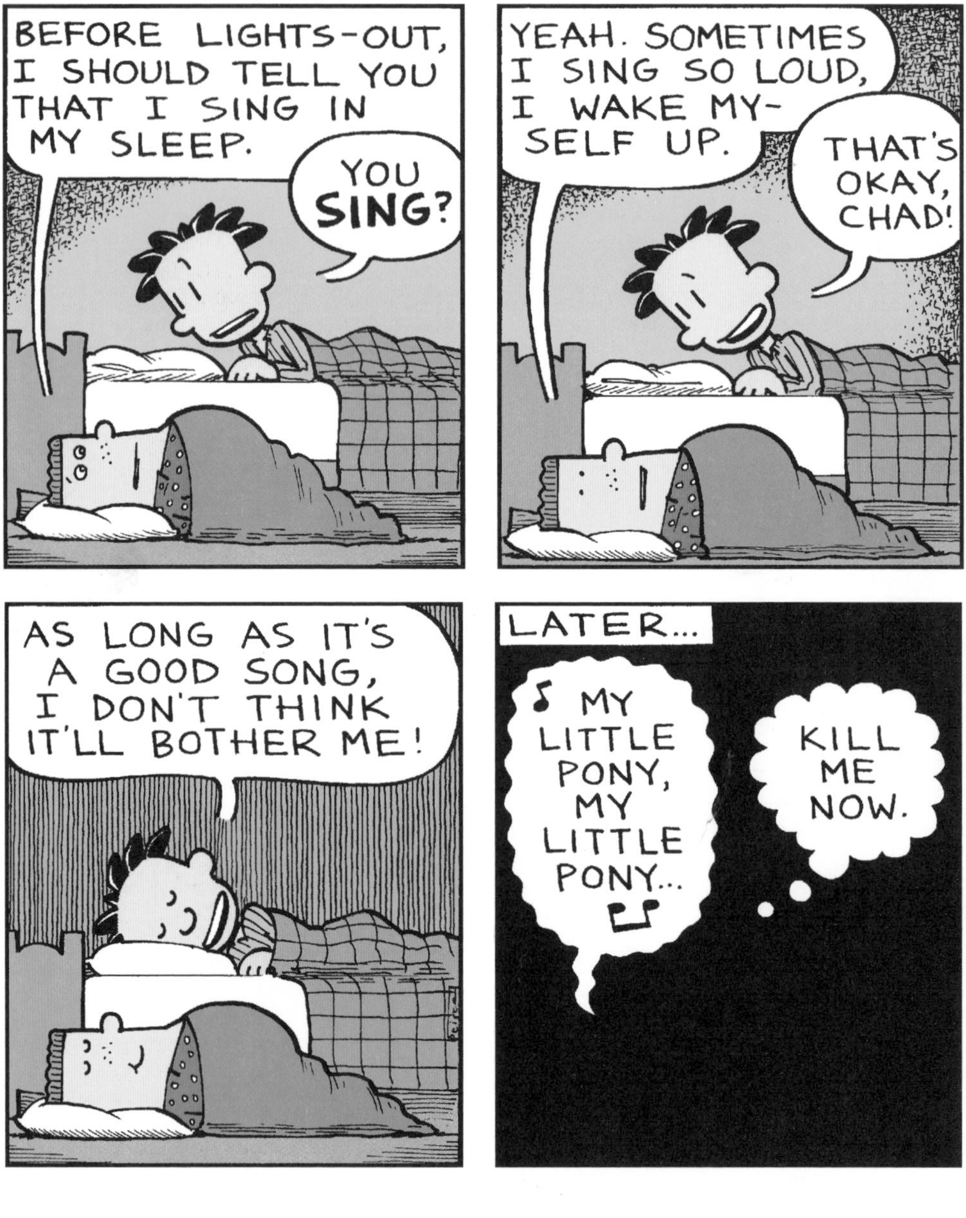
BEFORE LIGHTS-OUT, I SHOULD TELL YOU THAT I SING IN MY SLEEP.
YOU SING?
YEAH. SOMETIMES I SING SO LOUD, I WAKE MY-SELF UP.
THAT'S OKAY, CHAD!
AS LONG AS IT'S A GOOD SONG, I DON'T THINK IT'LL BOTHER ME!
LATER...
MY LITTLE PONY, MY LITTLE PONY...
KILL ME NOW.

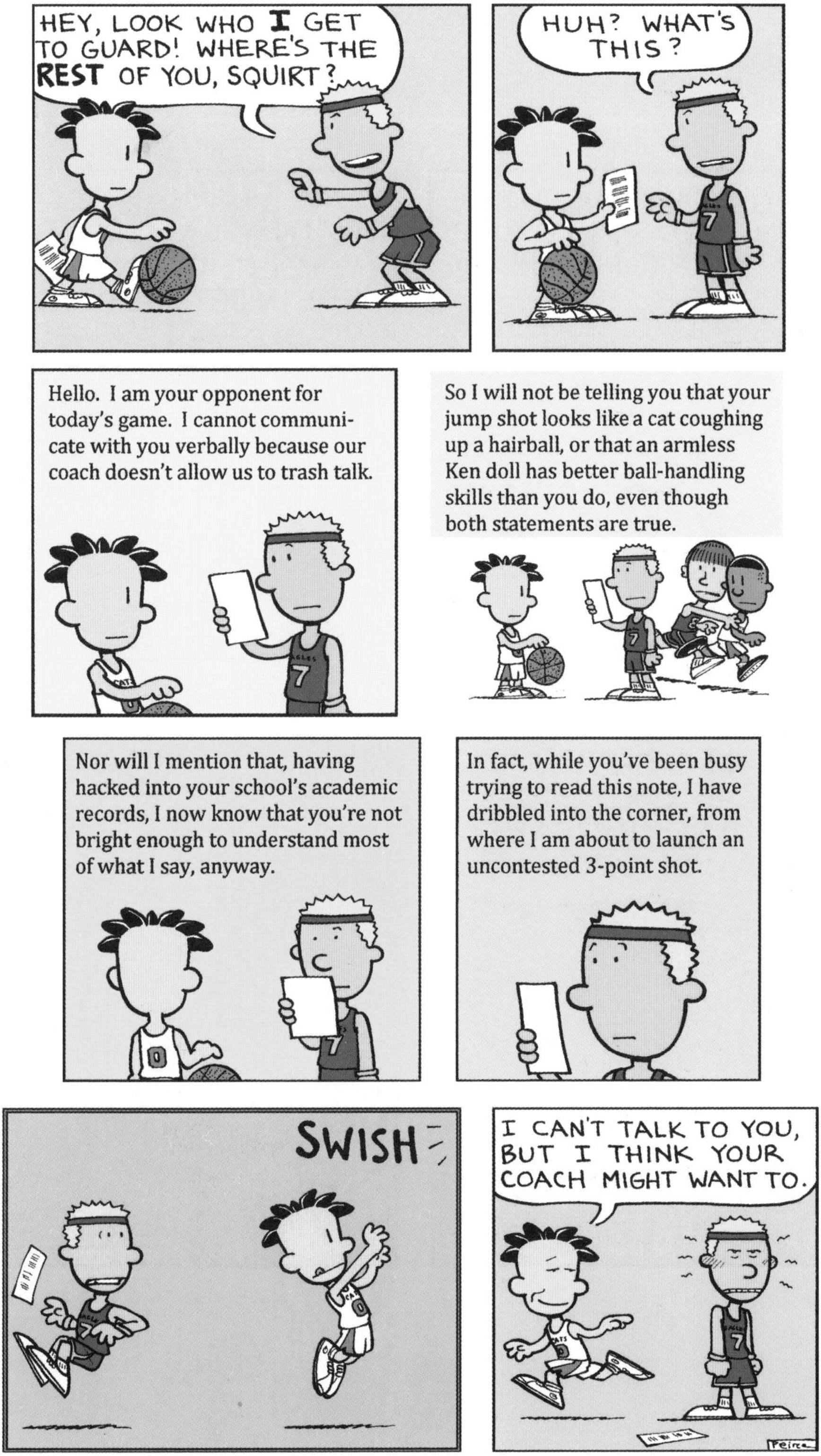
HEY, LOOK WHO I GET TO GUARD! WHERE'S THE REST OF YOU, SQUIRT?
HUH? WHAT'S THIS?
Hello. I am your opponent for today's game. I cannot communicate with you verbally because our coach doesn't allow us to trash talk.
So I will not be telling you that your jump shot looks like a cat coughing up a hairball, or that an armless Ken doll has better ball-handling skills than you do, even though both statements are true.
Nor will I mention that, having hacked into your school's academic records, I now know that you're not bright enough to understand most of what I say, anyway.
In fact, while you've been busy trying to read this note, I have dribbled into the corner, from where I am about to launch an uncontested 3-point shot.
SWISH
I CAN'T TALK TO YOU, BUT I THINK YOUR COACH MIGHT WANT TO.

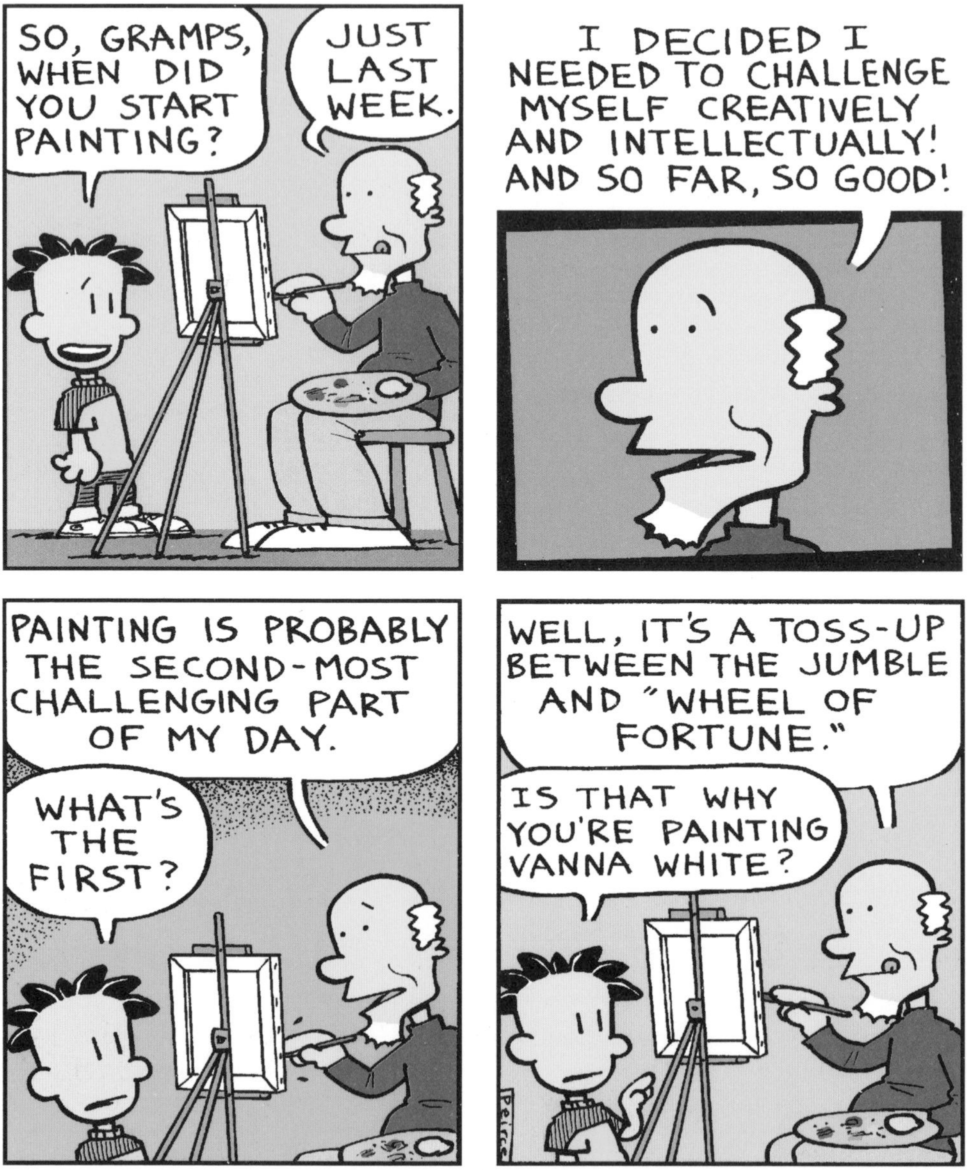
SO, GRAMPS, WHEN DID YOU START PAINTING?
JUST LAST WEEK.
I DECIDED I NEEDED TO CHALLENGE MYSELF CREATIVELY AND INTELLECTUALLY! AND SO FAR, SO GOOD!
PAINTING IS PROBABLY THE SECOND-MOST CHALLENGING PART OF MY DAY.
WHAT'S THE FIRST?
WELL, IT'S A TOSS-UP BETWEEN THE JUMBLE AND "WHEEL OF FORTUNE."
IS THAT WHY YOU'RE PAINTING VANNA WHITE?
Peirce

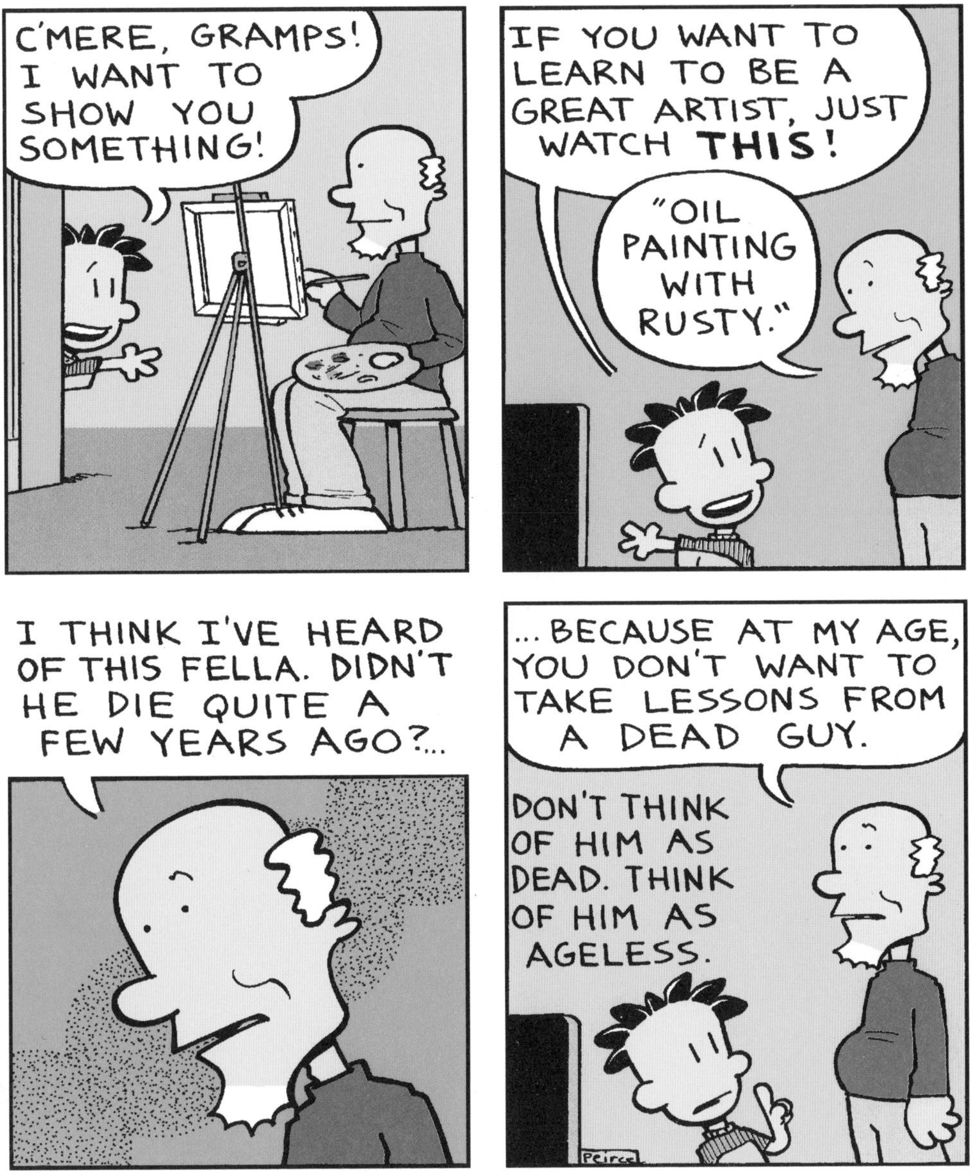
C'MERE, GRAMPS! I WANT TO SHOW YOU SOMETHING!
IF YOU WANT TO LEARN TO BE A GREAT ARTIST, JUST WATCH THIS!
"OIL PAINTING WITH RUSTY."
I THINK I'VE HEARD OF THIS FELLA. DIDN'T HE DIE QUITE A FEW YEARS AGO?...
...BECAUSE AT MY AGE, YOU DON'T WANT TO TAKE LESSONS FROM A DEAD GUY.
DON'T THINK OF HIM AS DEAD. THINK OF HIM AS AGELESS.
PEIRCE

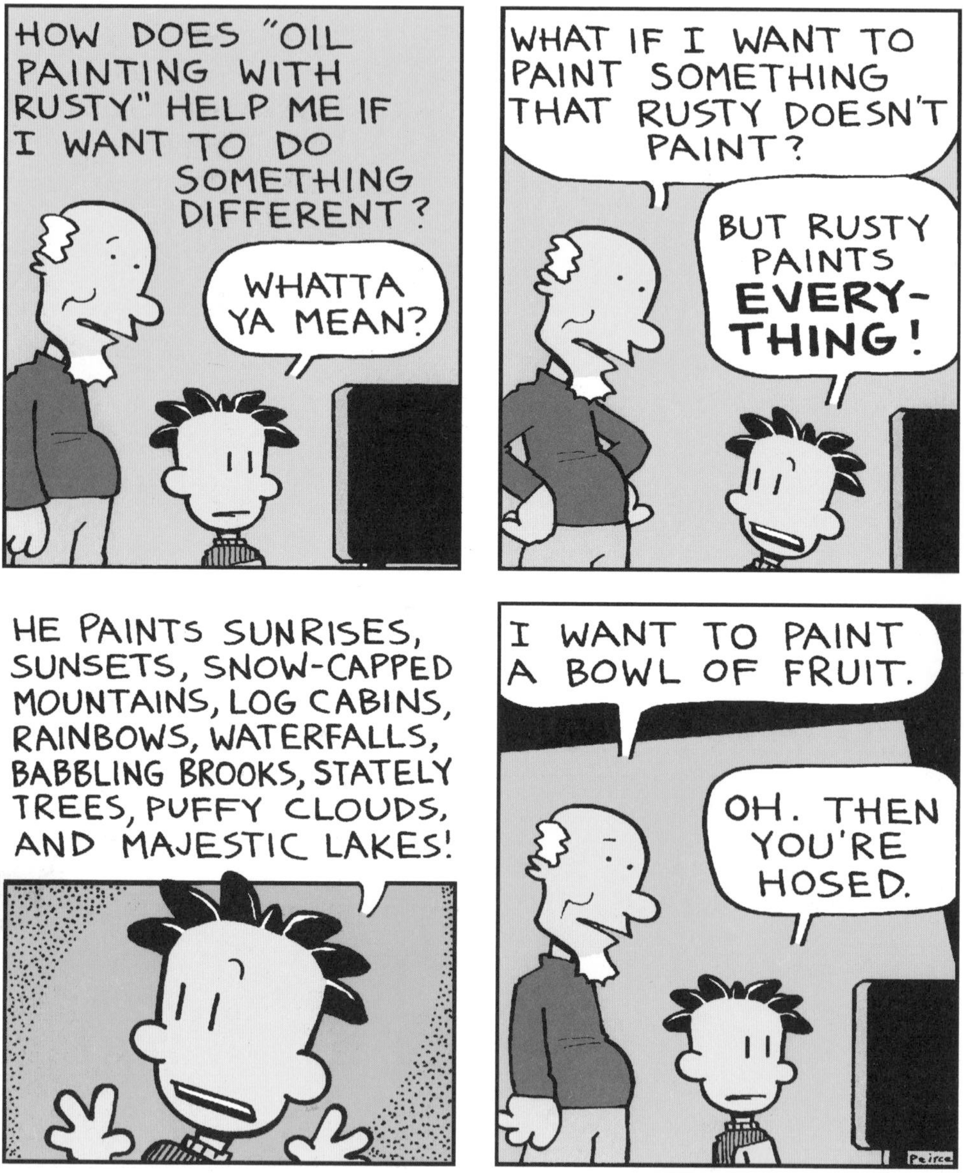
HOW DOES "OIL PAINTING WITH RUSTY" HELP ME IF I WANT TO DO SOMETHING DIFFERENT?
WHATTA YA MEAN?
WHAT IF I WANT TO PAINT SOMETHING THAT RUSTY DOESN'T PAINT?
BUT RUSTY PAINTS **EVERY-THING!**
HE PAINTS SUNRISES, SUNSETS, SNOW-CAPPED MOUNTAINS, LOG CABINS, RAINBOWS, WATERFALLS, BABBLING BROOKS, STATELY TREES, PUFFY CLOUDS, AND MAJESTIC LAKES!
I WANT TO PAINT A BOWL OF FRUIT.
OH. THEN YOU'RE HOSED.
Peirce

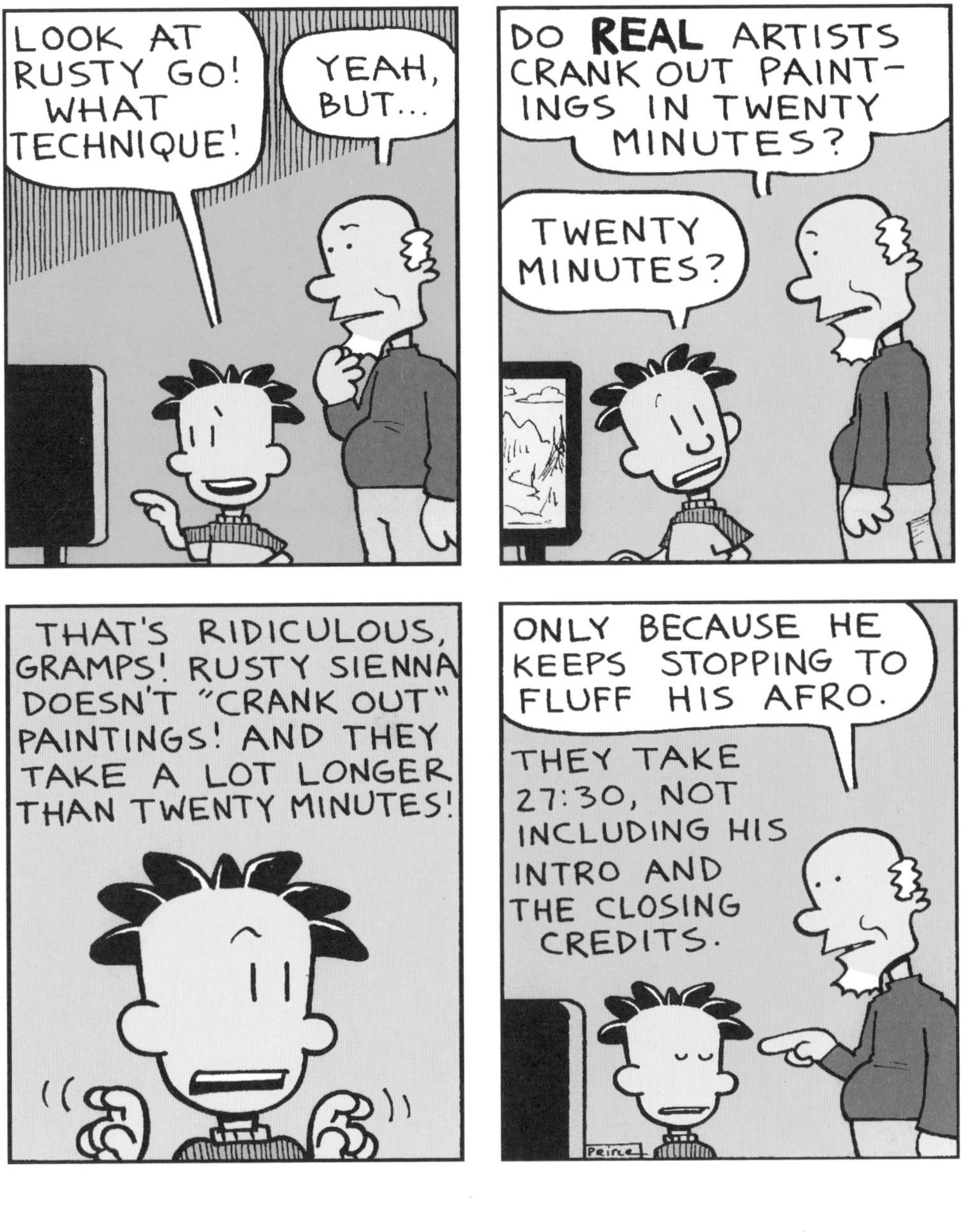
LOOK AT RUSTY GO! WHAT TECHNIQUE!
YEAH, BUT...
DO **REAL** ARTISTS CRANK OUT PAINTINGS IN TWENTY MINUTES?
TWENTY MINUTES?
THAT'S RIDICULOUS, GRAMPS! RUSTY SIENNA DOESN'T "CRANK OUT" PAINTINGS! AND THEY TAKE A LOT LONGER THAN TWENTY MINUTES!
ONLY BECAUSE HE KEEPS STOPPING TO FLUFF HIS AFRO.
THEY TAKE 27:30, NOT INCLUDING HIS INTRO AND THE CLOSING CREDITS.
PEIRCE

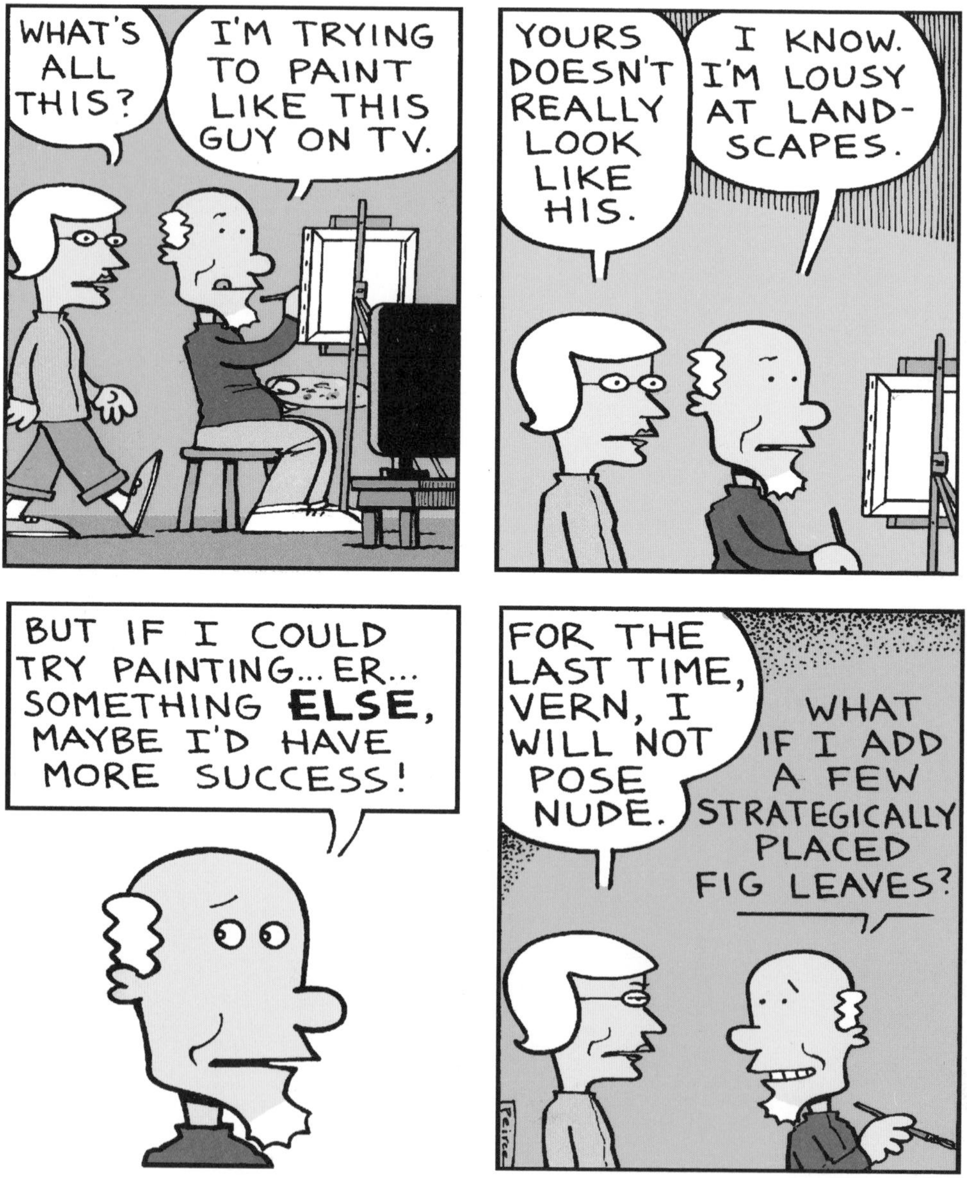
WHAT'S ALL THIS?
I'M TRYING TO PAINT LIKE THIS GUY ON TV.
YOURS DOESN'T REALLY LOOK LIKE HIS.
I KNOW. I'M LOUSY AT LAND-SCAPES.
BUT IF I COULD TRY PAINTING... ER... SOMETHING ELSE, MAYBE I'D HAVE MORE SUCCESS!
FOR THE LAST TIME, VERN, I WILL NOT POSE NUDE.
WHAT IF I ADD A FEW STRATEGICALLY PLACED FIG LEAVES?
Peirce

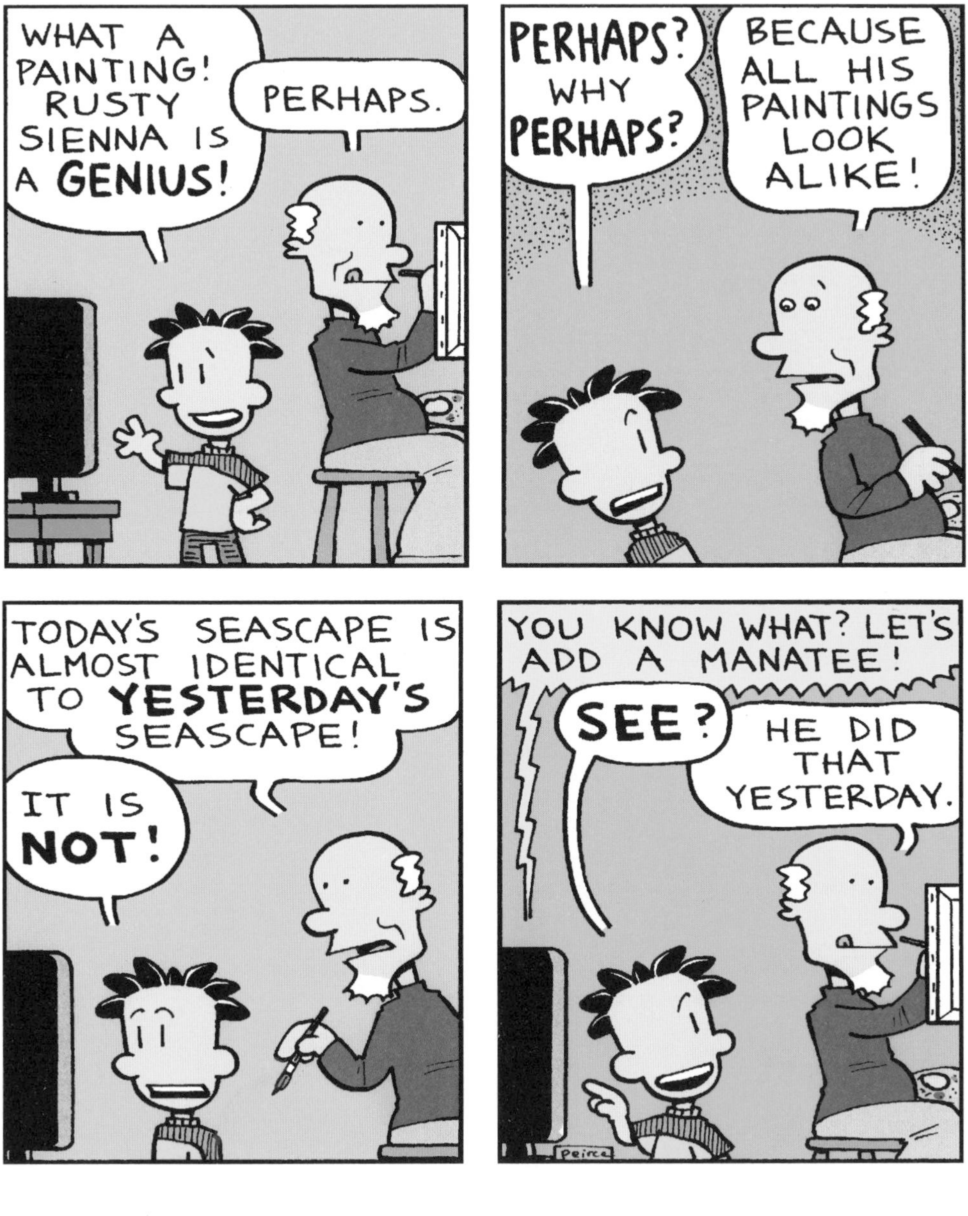
WHAT A PAINTING! RUSTY SIENNA IS A **GENIUS**!
PERHAPS.
PERHAPS? WHY **PERHAPS?**
BECAUSE ALL HIS PAINTINGS LOOK ALIKE!
TODAY'S SEASCAPE IS ALMOST IDENTICAL TO **YESTERDAY'S** SEASCAPE!
IT IS **NOT**!
YOU KNOW WHAT? LET'S ADD A MANATEE!
SEE?
HE DID THAT YESTERDAY.
Peirce

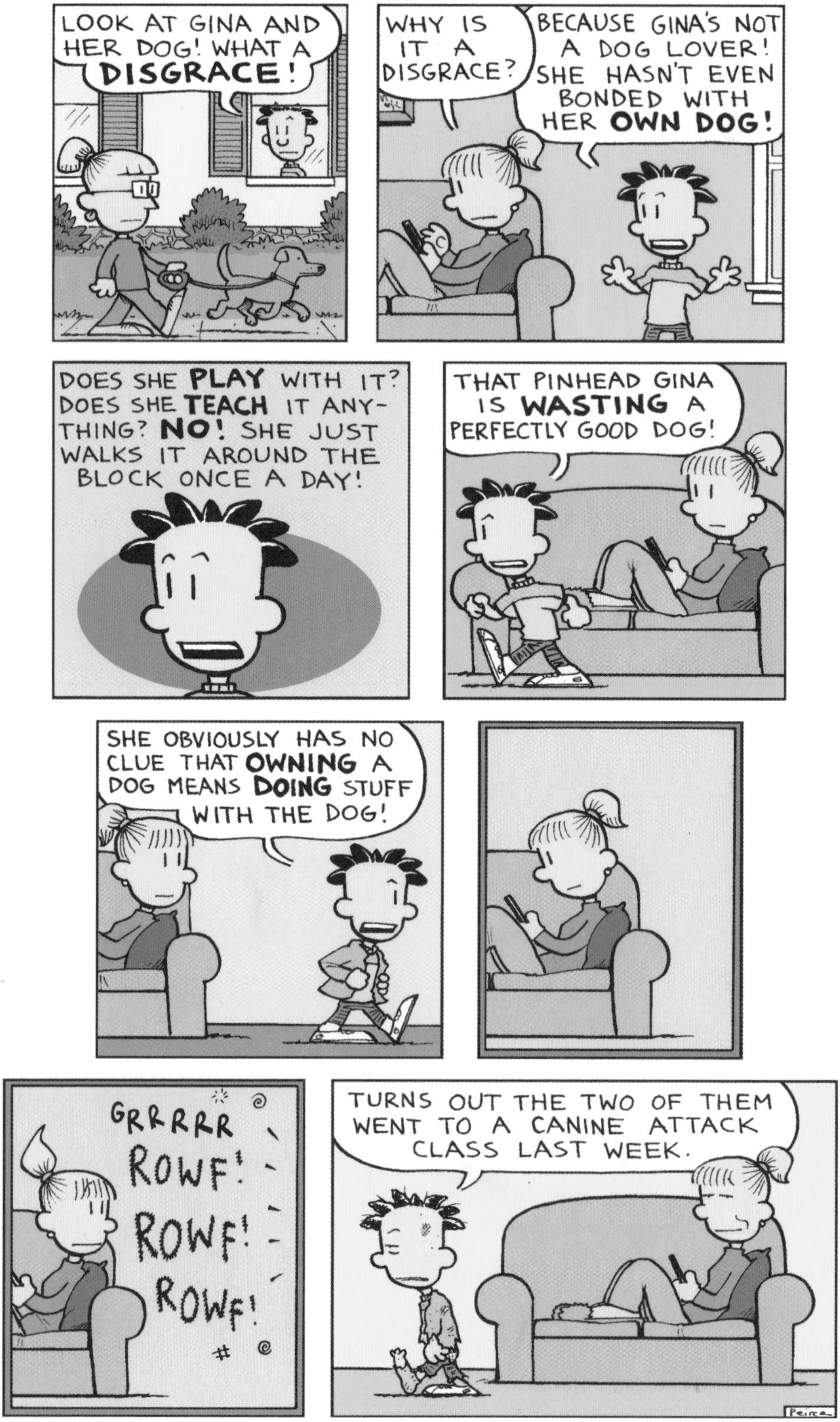
LOOK AT GINA AND HER DOG! WHAT A DISGRACE!
WHY IS IT A DISGRACE?
BECAUSE GINA'S NOT A DOG LOVER! SHE HASN'T EVEN BONDED WITH HER OWN DOG!
DOES SHE PLAY WITH IT? DOES SHE TEACH IT ANY-THING? NO! SHE JUST WALKS IT AROUND THE BLOCK ONCE A DAY!
THAT PINHEAD GINA IS WASTING A PERFECTLY GOOD DOG!
SHE OBVIOUSLY HAS NO CLUE THAT OWNING A DOG MEANS DOING STUFF WITH THE DOG!
GRRRRR
ROWF!
ROWF!
ROWF!
TURNS OUT THE TWO OF THEM WENT TO A CANINE ATTACK CLASS LAST WEEK.
Peirce

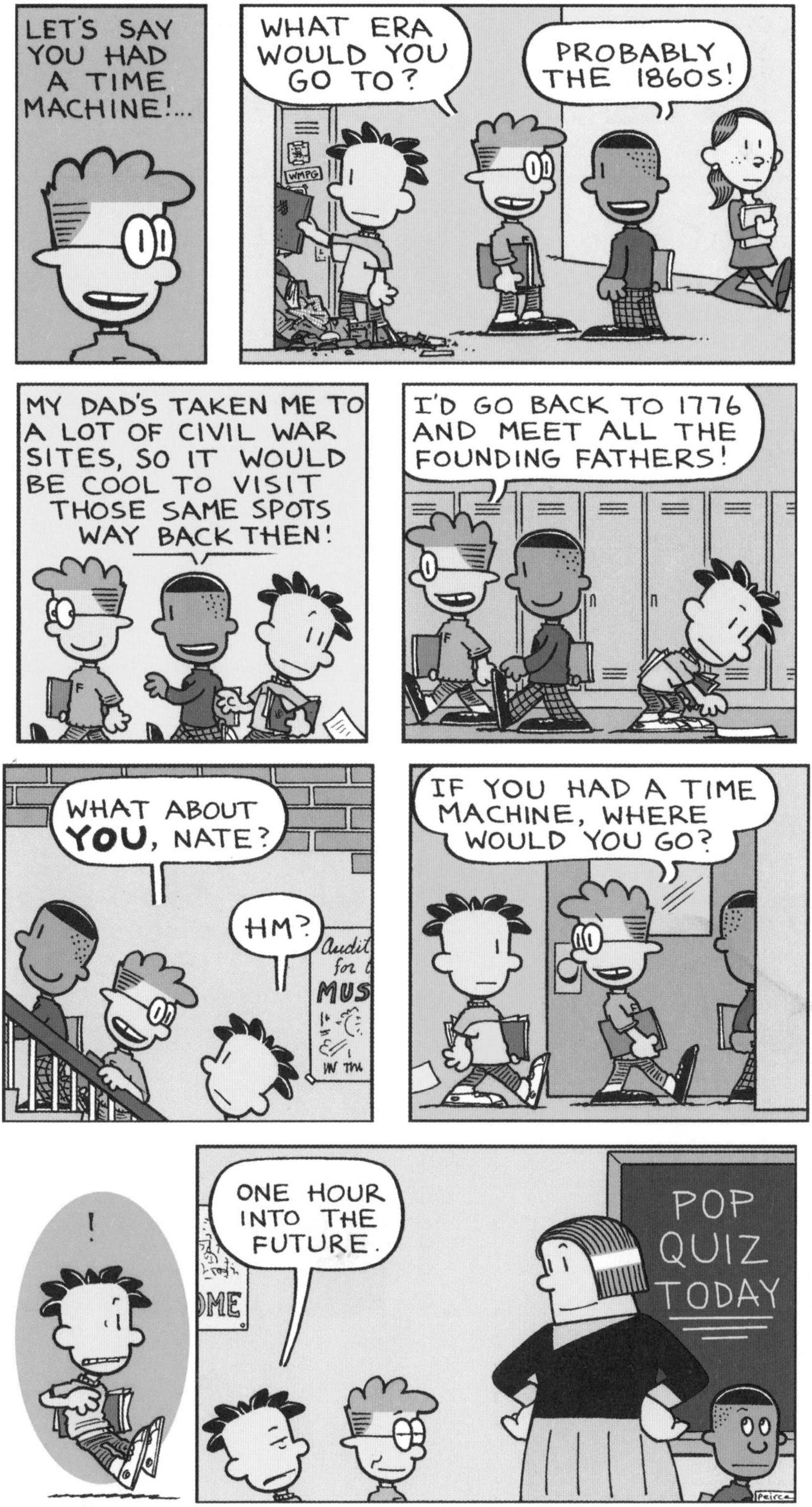
LET'S SAY YOU HAD A TIME MACHINE!...
WHAT ERA WOULD YOU GO TO?
PROBABLY THE 1860S!
WMPG
MY DAD'S TAKEN ME TO A LOT OF CIVIL WAR SITES, SO IT WOULD BE COOL TO VISIT THOSE SAME SPOTS WAY BACK THEN!
I'D GO BACK TO 1776 AND MEET ALL THE FOUNDING FATHERS!
WHAT ABOUT **YOU**, NATE?
HM?
MUS
IF YOU HAD A TIME MACHINE, WHERE WOULD YOU GO?
!
ONE HOUR INTO THE FUTURE.
POP QUIZ TODAY
Peirce

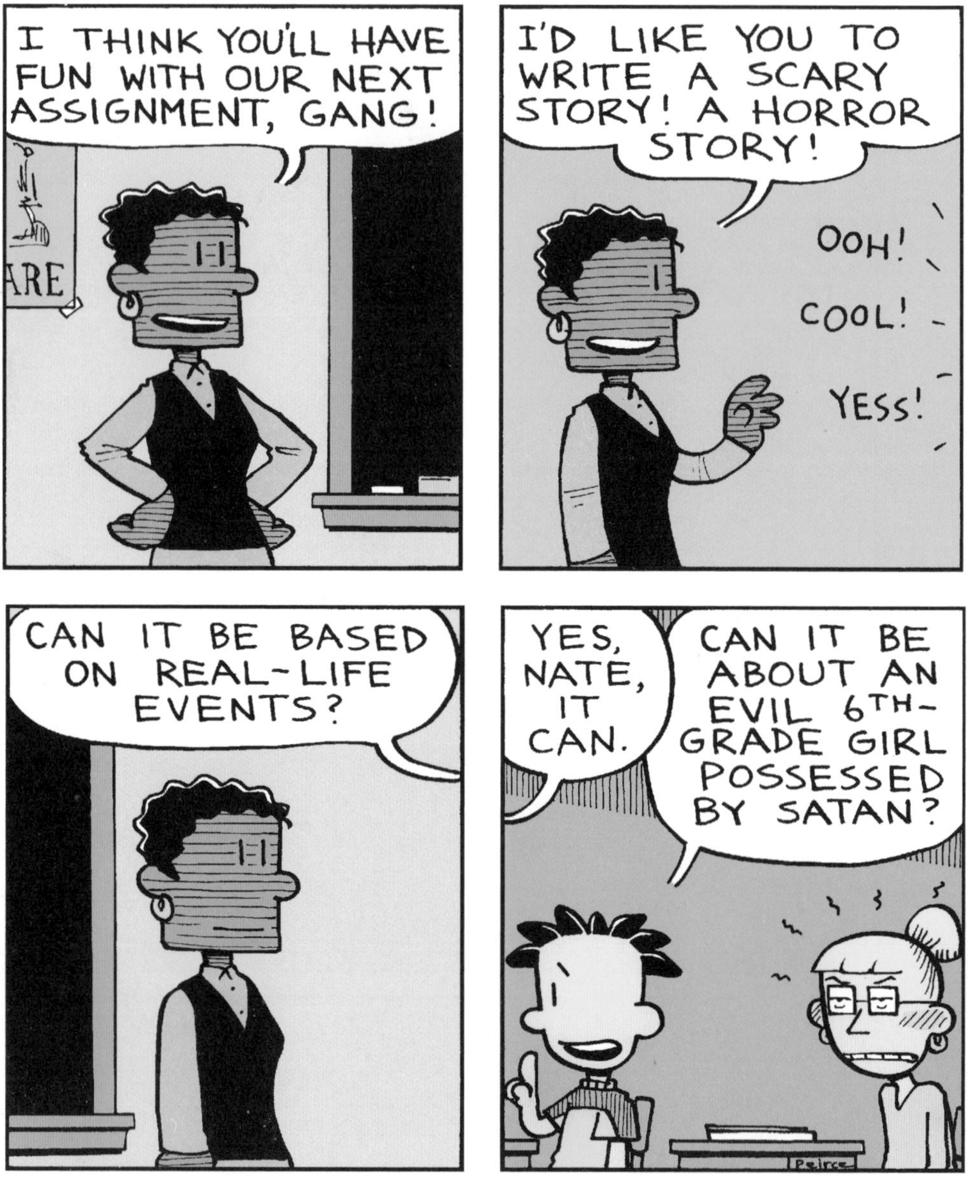
I THINK YOU'LL HAVE FUN WITH OUR NEXT ASSIGNMENT, GANG!
ARE
I'D LIKE YOU TO WRITE A SCARY STORY! A HORROR STORY!
OOH!
COOL!
YESS!
CAN IT BE BASED ON REAL-LIFE EVENTS?
YES, NATE, IT CAN.
CAN IT BE ABOUT AN EVIL 6TH-GRADE GIRL POSSESSED BY SATAN?
Peirce

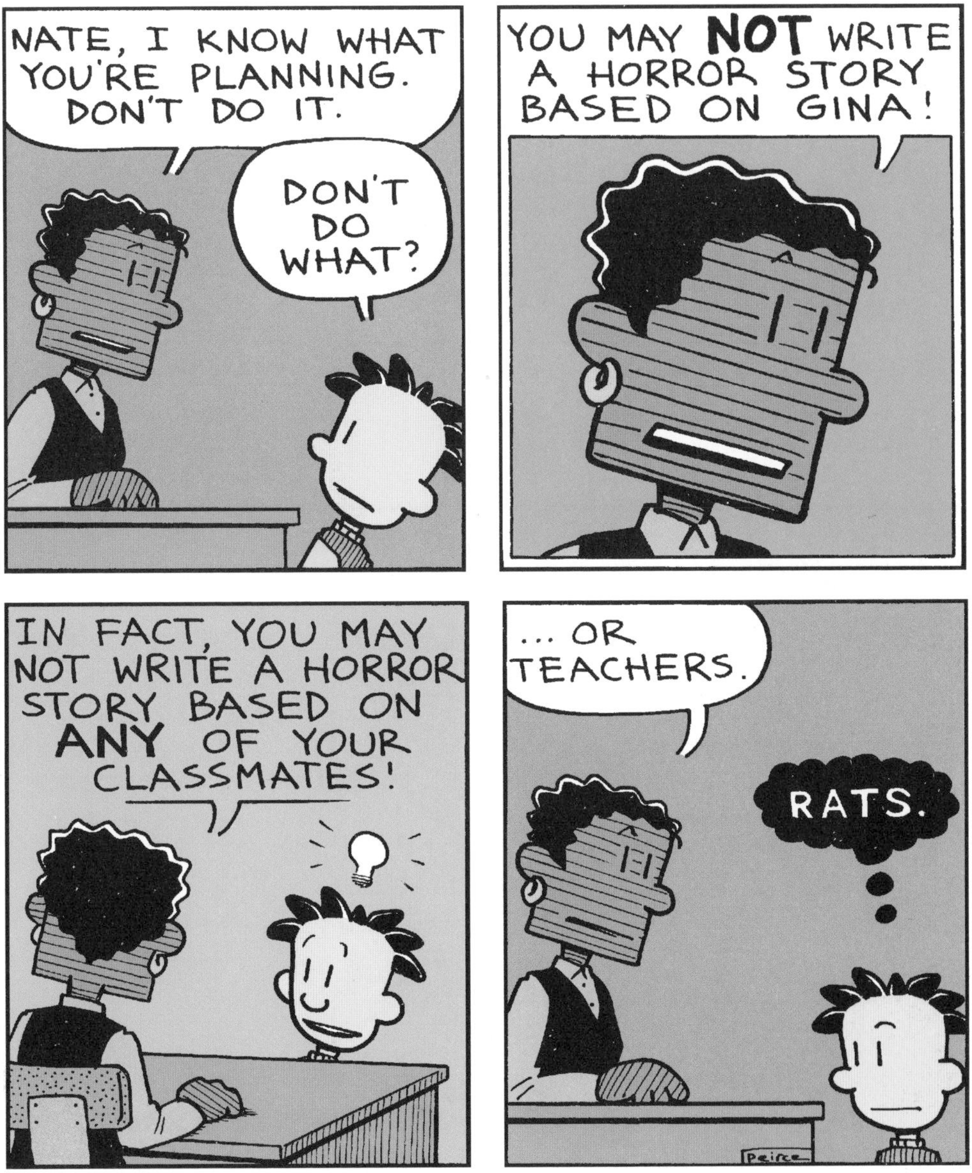
NATE, I KNOW WHAT YOU'RE PLANNING. DON'T DO IT.
DON'T DO WHAT?
YOU MAY **NOT** WRITE A HORROR STORY BASED ON GINA!
IN FACT, YOU MAY NOT WRITE A HORROR STORY BASED ON **ANY** OF YOUR CLASSMATES!
... OR TEACHERS.
RATS.
Peirce

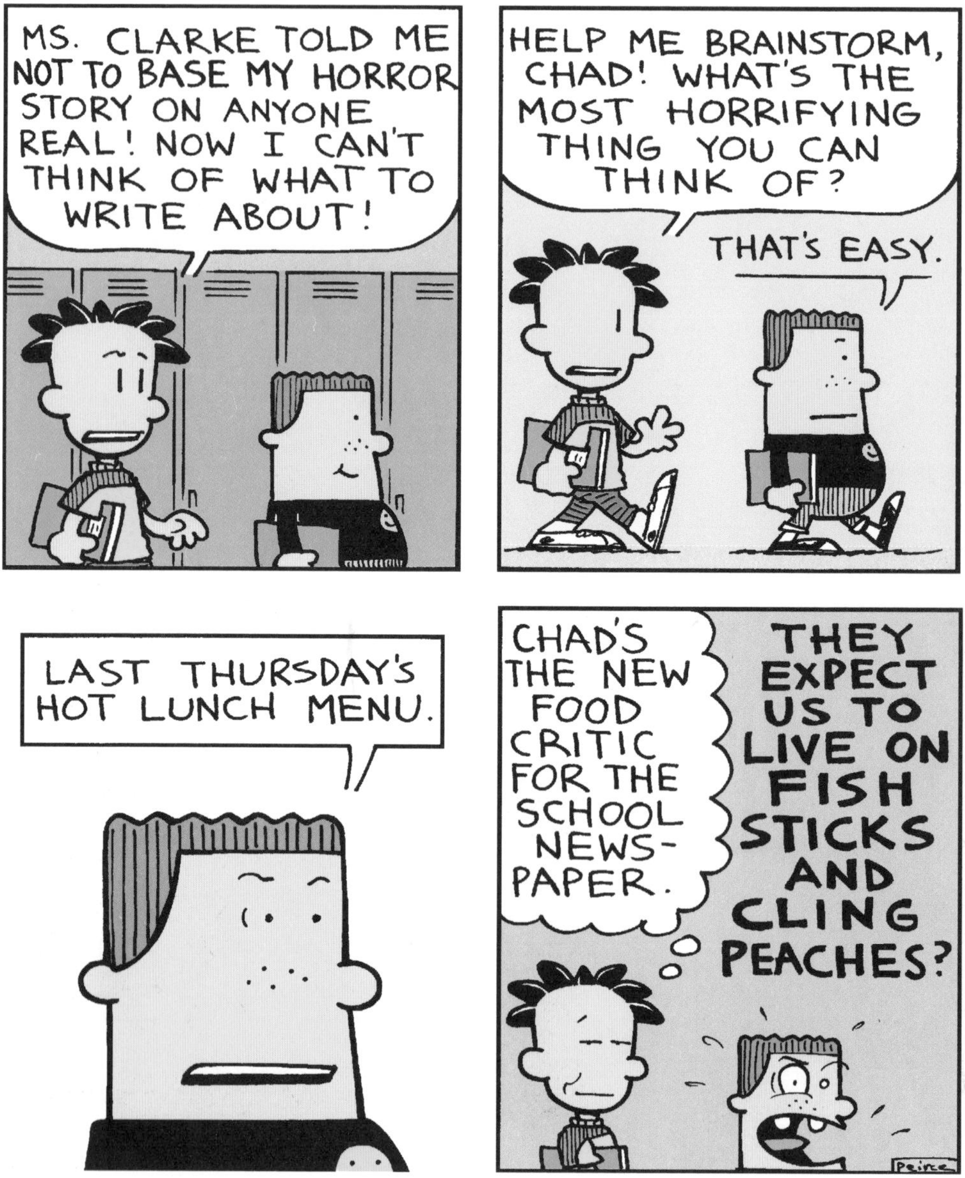
MS. CLARKE TOLD ME NOT TO BASE MY HORROR STORY ON ANYONE REAL! NOW I CAN'T THINK OF WHAT TO WRITE ABOUT!
HELP ME BRAINSTORM, CHAD! WHAT'S THE MOST HORRIFYING THING YOU CAN THINK OF?
THAT'S EASY.
LAST THURSDAY'S HOT LUNCH MENU.
CHAD'S THE NEW FOOD CRITIC FOR THE SCHOOL NEWS-PAPER.
THEY EXPECT US TO LIVE ON FISH STICKS AND CLING PEACHES?
Peirce

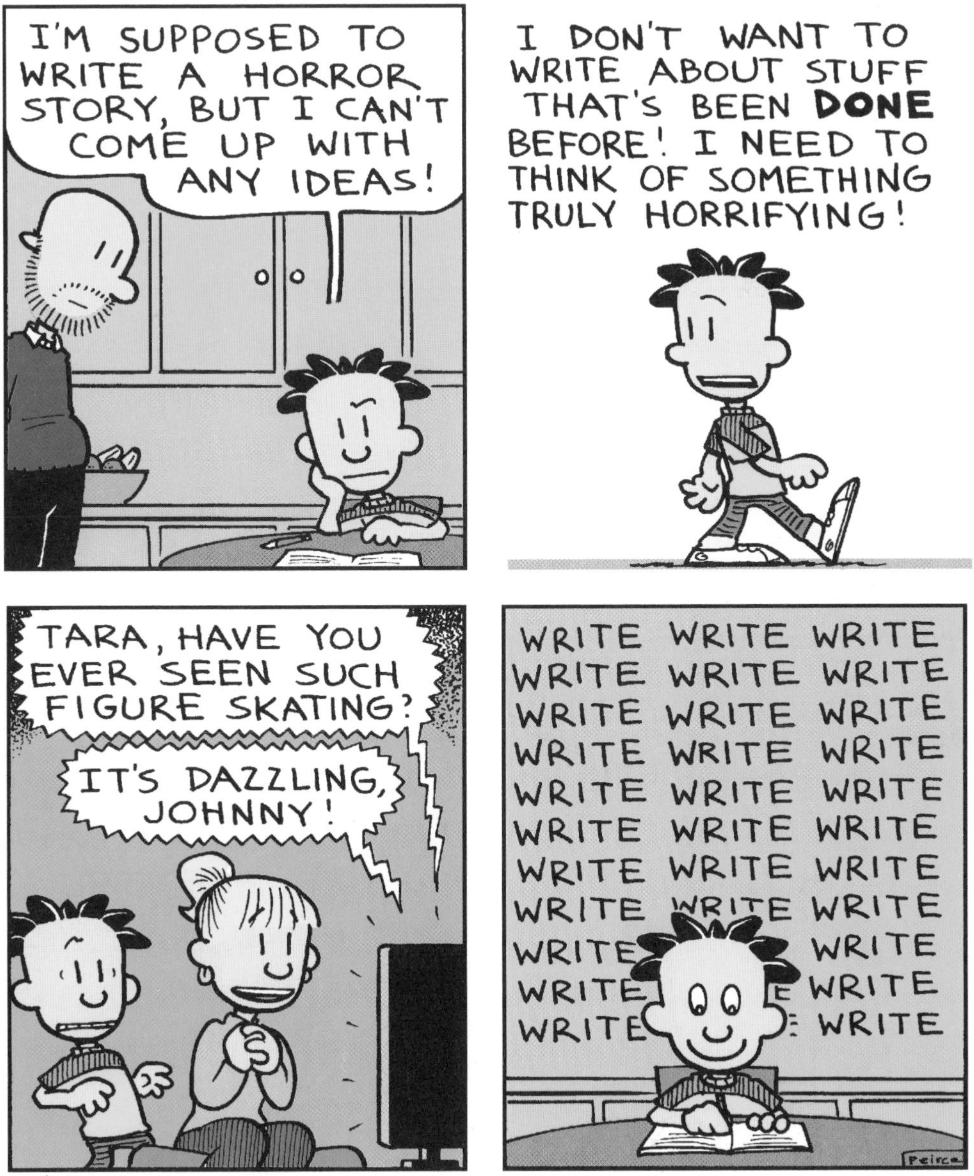
I'M SUPPOSED TO WRITE A HORROR STORY, BUT I CAN'T COME UP WITH ANY IDEAS!
I DON'T WANT TO WRITE ABOUT STUFF THAT'S BEEN **DONE** BEFORE! I NEED TO THINK OF SOMETHING TRULY HORRIFYING!
TARA, HAVE YOU EVER SEEN SUCH FIGURE SKATING?
IT'S DAZZLING, JOHNNY!
WRITE WRITE WRITE
WRITE WRITE WRITE
WRITE WRITE WRITE
WRITE WRITE WRITE
WRITE WRITE WRITE
WRITE WRITE WRITE
WRITE WRITE WRITE
WRITE WRITE WRITE
WRITE WRITE
WRITE WRITE
WRITE WRITE
Peirce

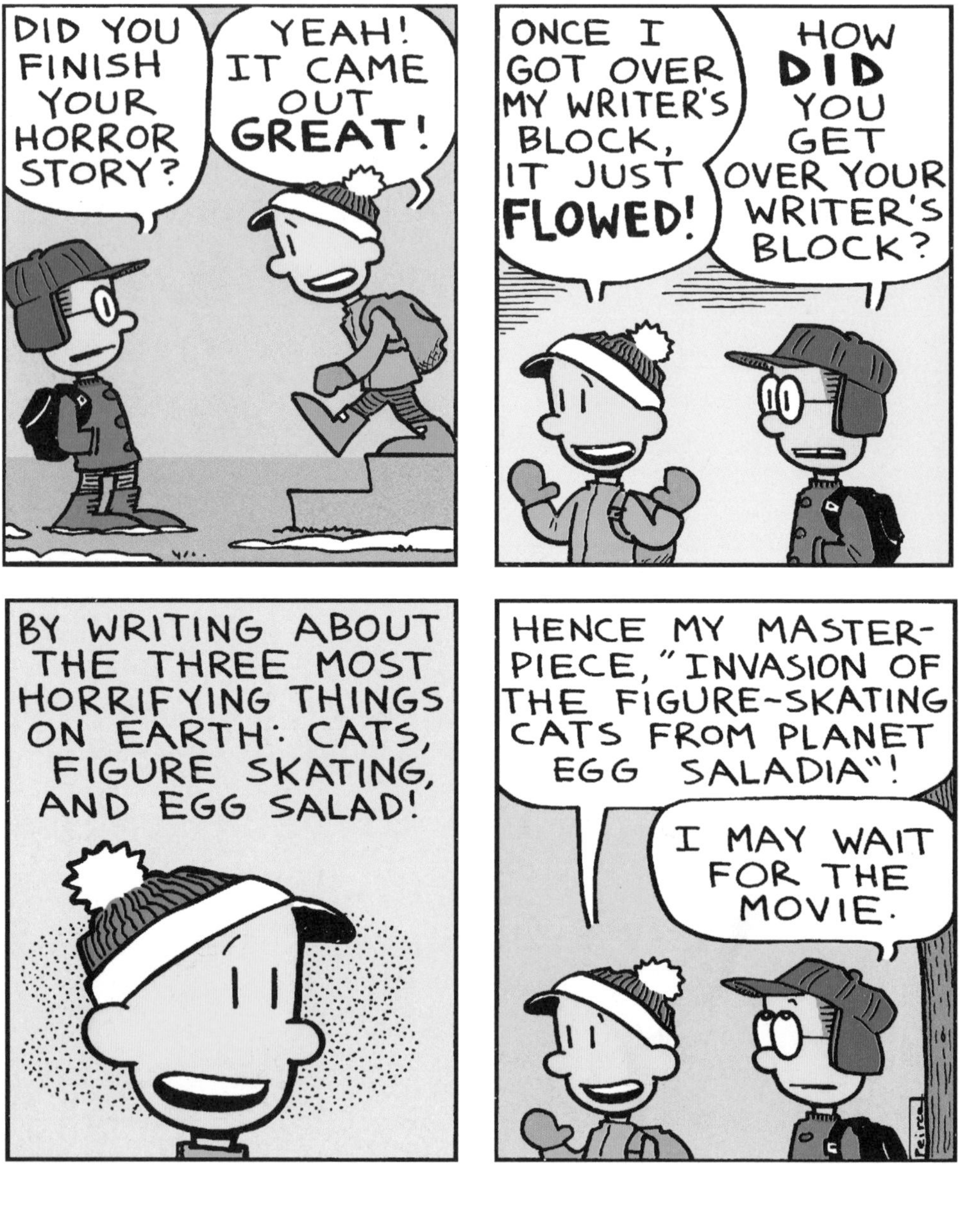
DID YOU FINISH YOUR HORROR STORY?
YEAH! IT CAME OUT GREAT!
ONCE I GOT OVER MY WRITER'S BLOCK, IT JUST FLOWED!
HOW DID YOU GET OVER YOUR WRITER'S BLOCK?
BY WRITING ABOUT THE THREE MOST HORRIFYING THINGS ON EARTH: CATS, FIGURE SKATING, AND EGG SALAD!
HENCE MY MASTER-PIECE, "INVASION OF THE FIGURE-SKATING CATS FROM PLANET EGG SALADIA"!
I MAY WAIT FOR THE MOVIE.
Peirce

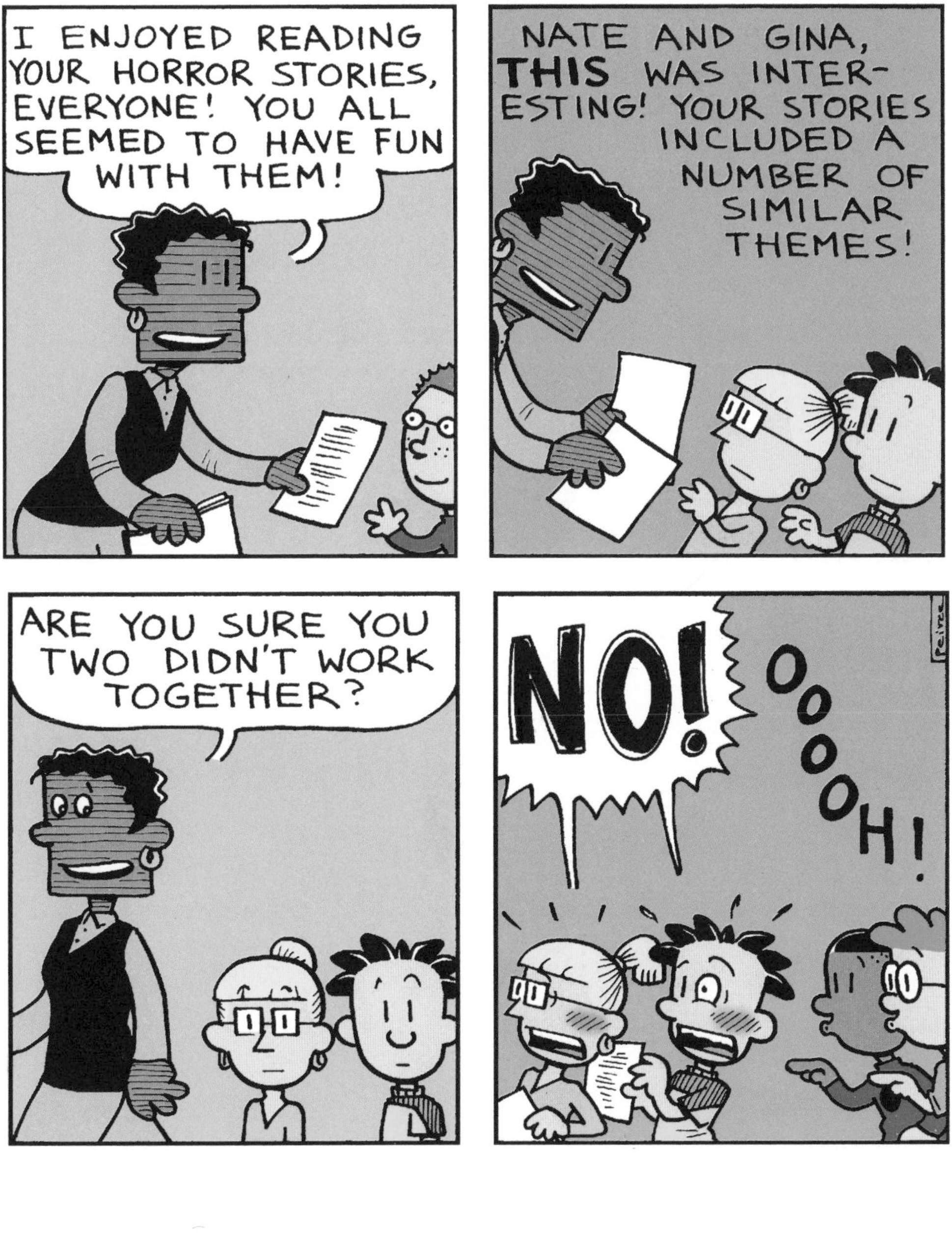
I ENJOYED READING YOUR HORROR STORIES, EVERYONE! YOU ALL SEEMED TO HAVE FUN WITH THEM!
NATE AND GINA, THIS WAS INTERESTING! YOUR STORIES INCLUDED A NUMBER OF SIMILAR THEMES!
ARE YOU SURE YOU TWO DIDN'T WORK TOGETHER?
NO!
OOOOOH!
Peirce

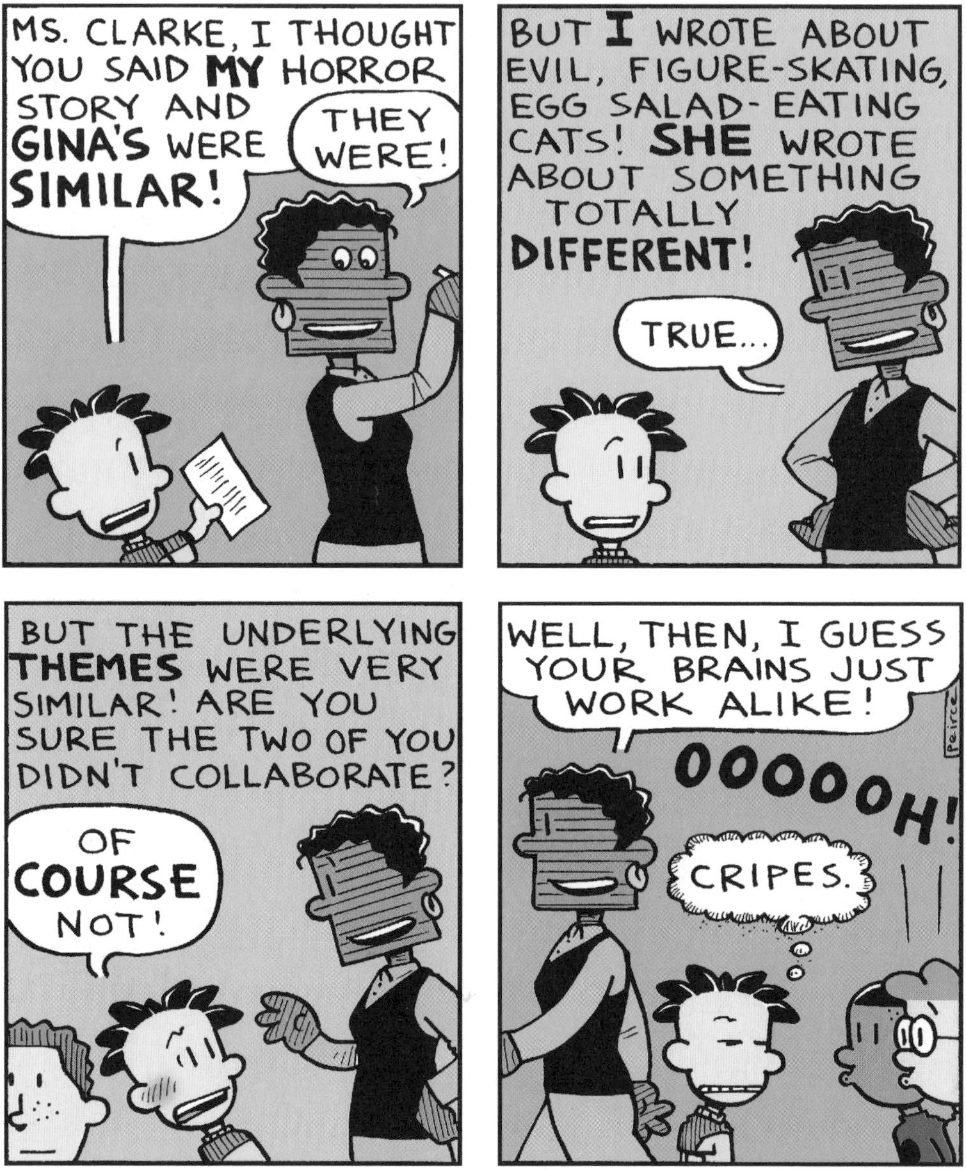
MS. CLARKE, I THOUGHT YOU SAID MY HORROR STORY AND GINA'S WERE SIMILAR!
THEY WERE!
BUT I WROTE ABOUT EVIL, FIGURE-SKATING, EGG SALAD-EATING CATS! SHE WROTE ABOUT SOMETHING TOTALLY DIFFERENT!
TRUE...
BUT THE UNDERLYING THEMES WERE VERY SIMILAR! ARE YOU SURE THE TWO OF YOU DIDN'T COLLABORATE?
OF COURSE NOT!
WELL, THEN, I GUESS YOUR BRAINS JUST WORK ALIKE!
OOOOOOH!
CRIPES.
Peirce

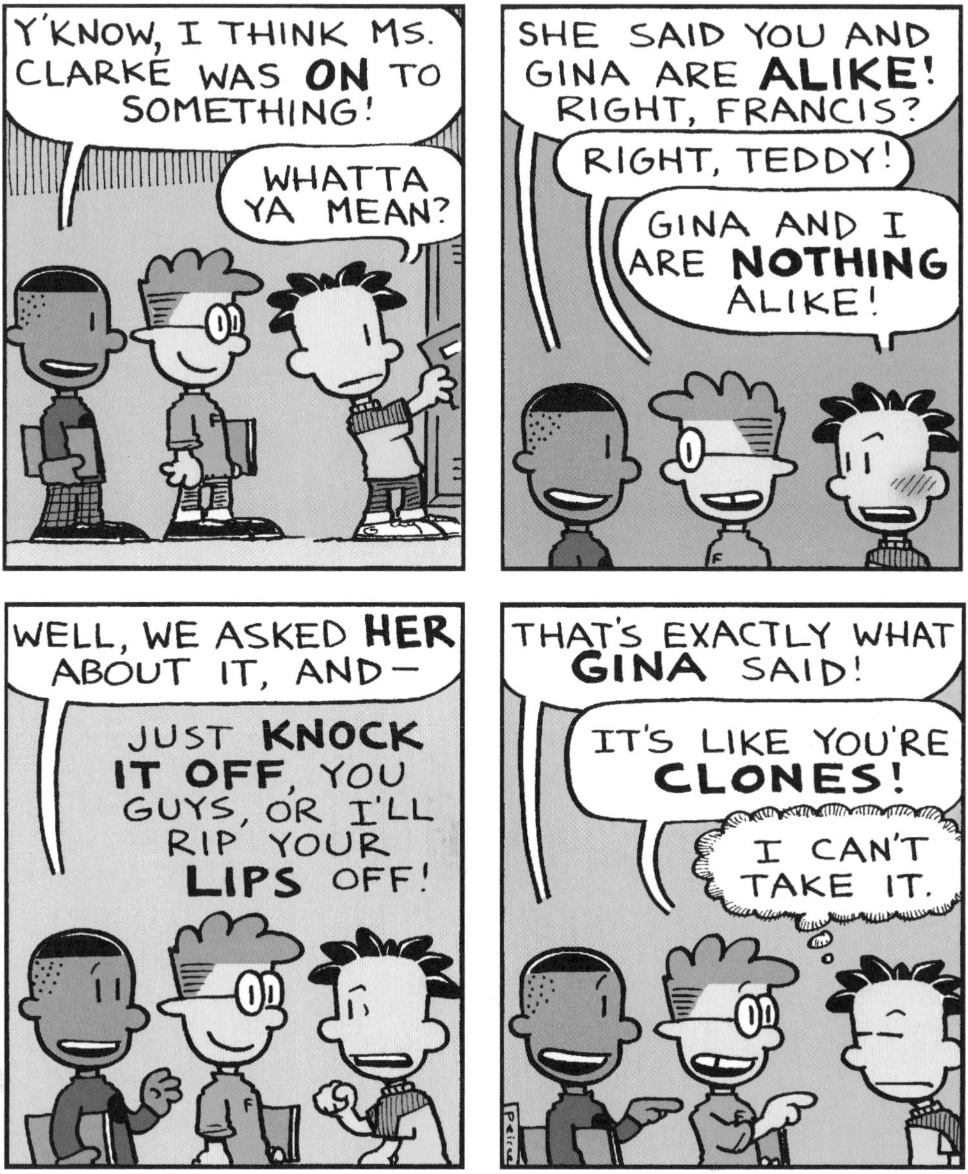
Y'KNOW, I THINK MS. CLARKE WAS **ON** TO SOMETHING!
WHATTA YA MEAN?
SHE SAID YOU AND GINA ARE **ALIKE**! RIGHT, FRANCIS?
RIGHT, TEDDY!
GINA AND I ARE **NOTHING** ALIKE!
WELL, WE ASKED **HER** ABOUT IT, AND—
JUST **KNOCK IT OFF**, YOU GUYS, OR I'LL RIP YOUR **LIPS** OFF!
THAT'S EXACTLY WHAT **GINA** SAID!
IT'S LIKE YOU'RE **CLONES**!
I CAN'T TAKE IT.
Peirce

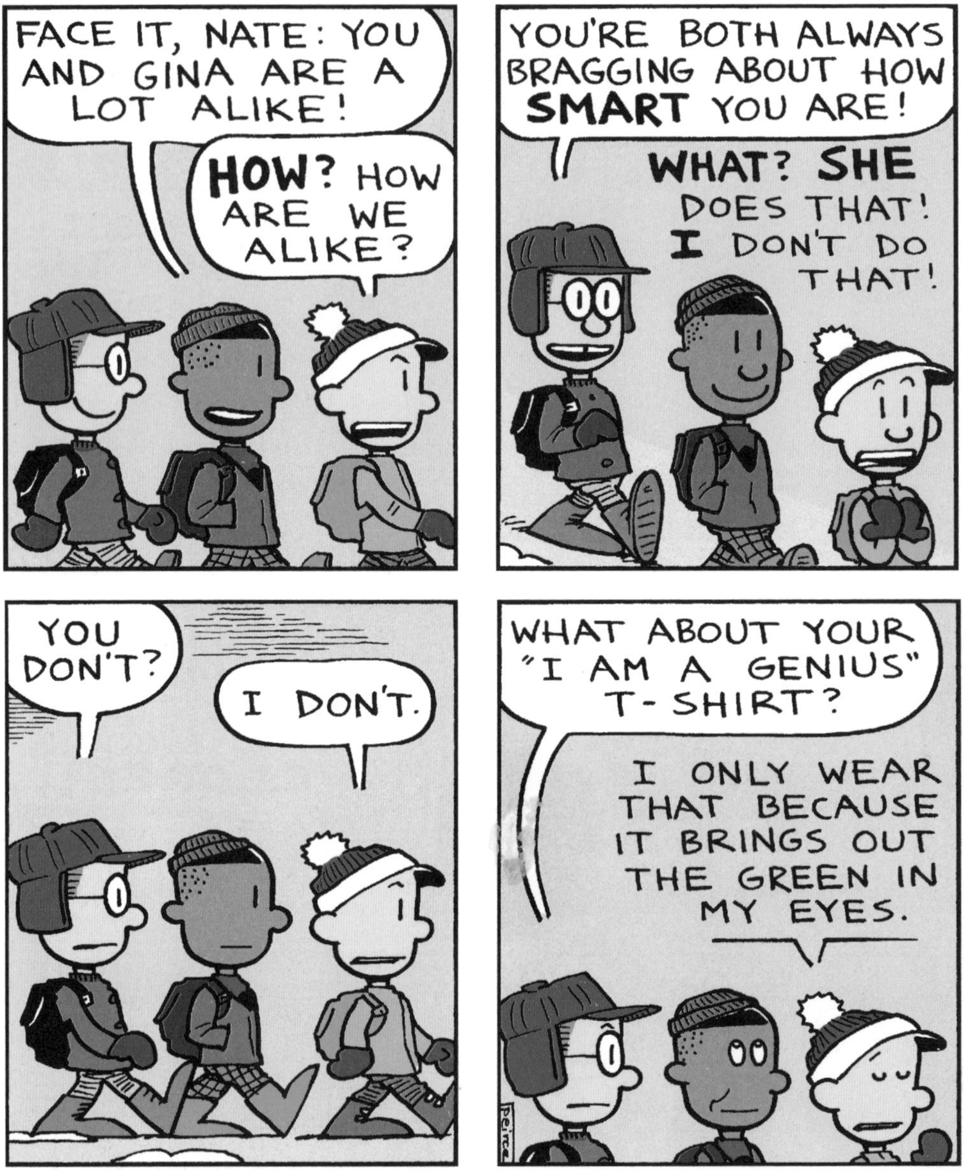
FACE IT, NATE: YOU AND GINA ARE A LOT ALIKE!
HOW? HOW ARE WE ALIKE?
YOU'RE BOTH ALWAYS BRAGGING ABOUT HOW SMART YOU ARE!
WHAT? SHE DOES THAT! I DON'T DO THAT!
YOU DON'T?
I DON'T.
WHAT ABOUT YOUR "I AM A GENIUS" T-SHIRT?
I ONLY WEAR THAT BECAUSE IT BRINGS OUT THE GREEN IN MY EYES.
peirce

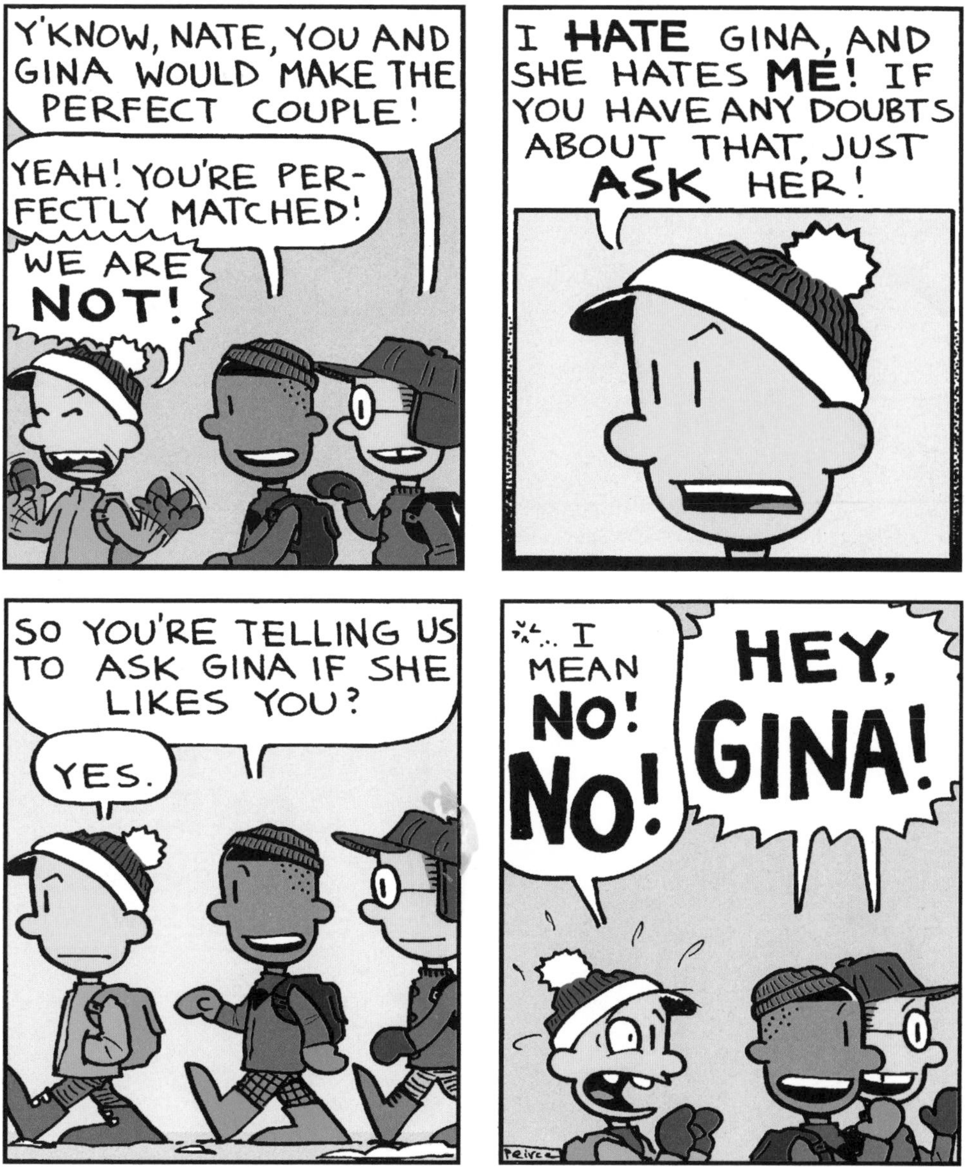
Y'KNOW, NATE, YOU AND GINA WOULD MAKE THE PERFECT COUPLE!
YEAH! YOU'RE PERFECTLY MATCHED!
WE ARE NOT!
I HATE GINA, AND SHE HATES ME! IF YOU HAVE ANY DOUBTS ABOUT THAT, JUST ASK HER!
SO YOU'RE TELLING US TO ASK GINA IF SHE LIKES YOU?
YES.
I MEAN NO! NO!
HEY, GINA!
PEIRCE

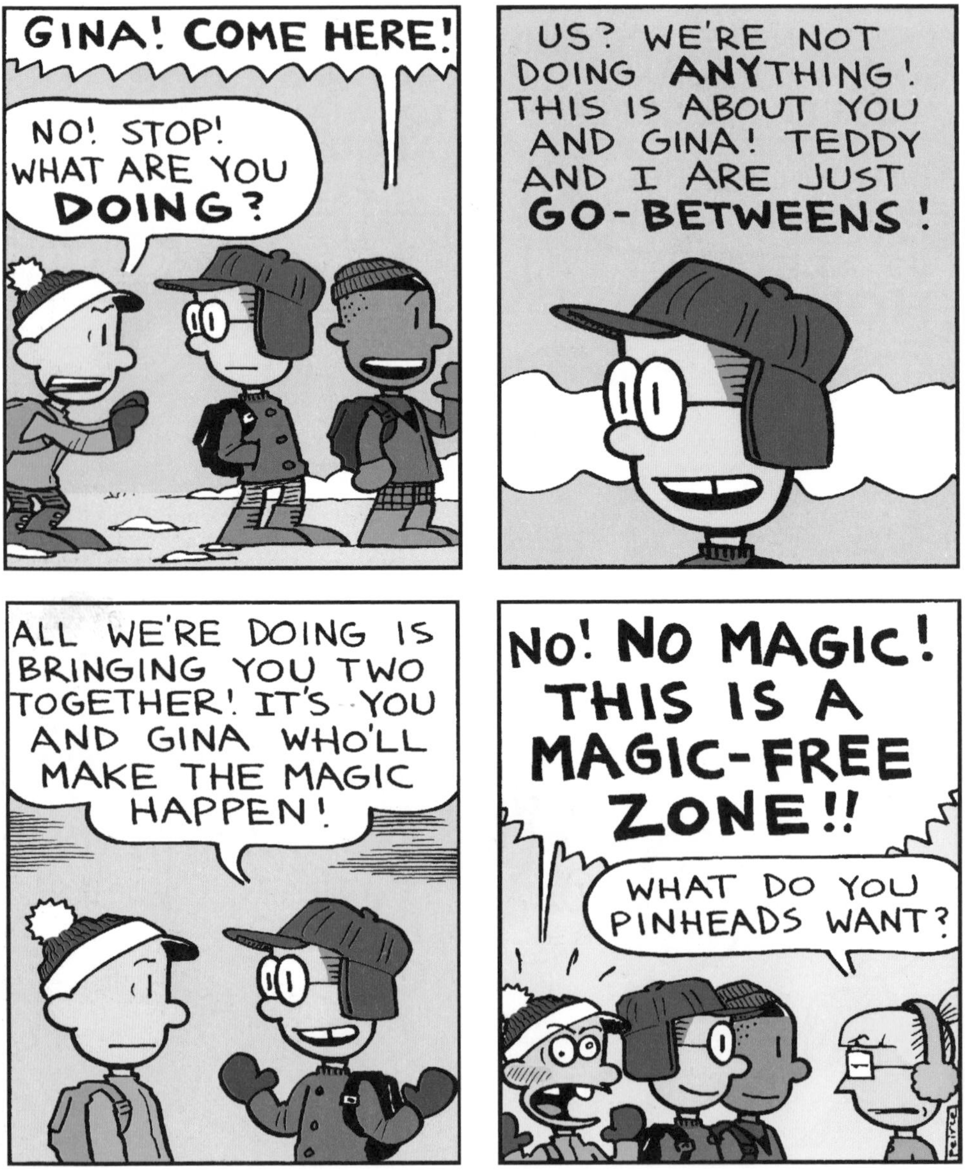
GINA! COME HERE!
NO! STOP! WHAT ARE YOU DOING?
US? WE'RE NOT DOING ANYTHING! THIS IS ABOUT YOU AND GINA! TEDDY AND I ARE JUST GO-BETWEENS!
ALL WE'RE DOING IS BRINGING YOU TWO TOGETHER! IT'S YOU AND GINA WHO'LL MAKE THE MAGIC HAPPEN!
NO! NO MAGIC! THIS IS A MAGIC-FREE ZONE!!
WHAT DO YOU PINHEADS WANT?
PEIRCE

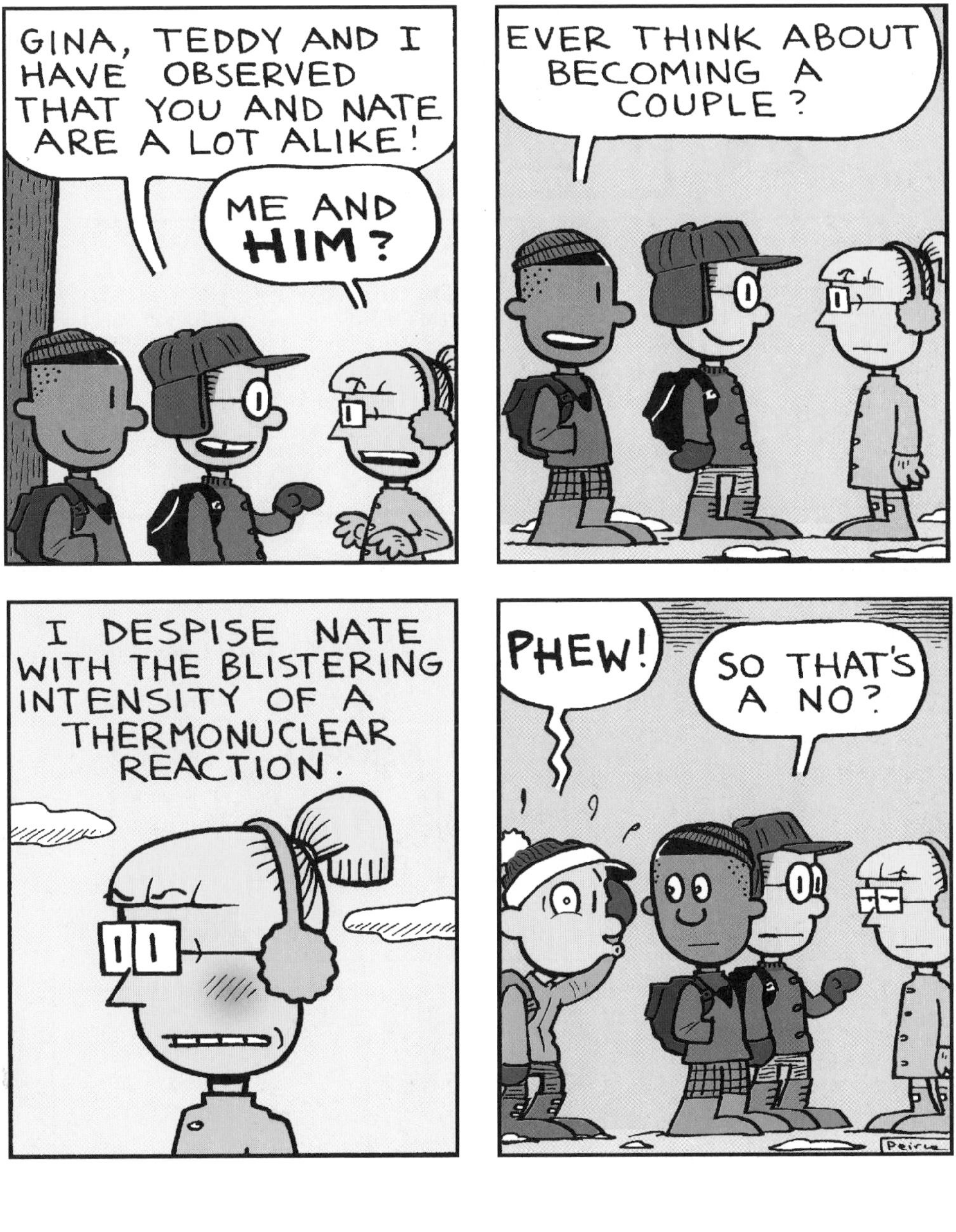
GINA, TEDDY AND I HAVE OBSERVED THAT YOU AND NATE ARE A LOT ALIKE!
ME AND HIM?
EVER THINK ABOUT BECOMING A COUPLE?
I DESPISE NATE WITH THE BLISTERING INTENSITY OF A THERMONUCLEAR REACTION.
PHEW!
SO THAT'S A NO?
Peirce

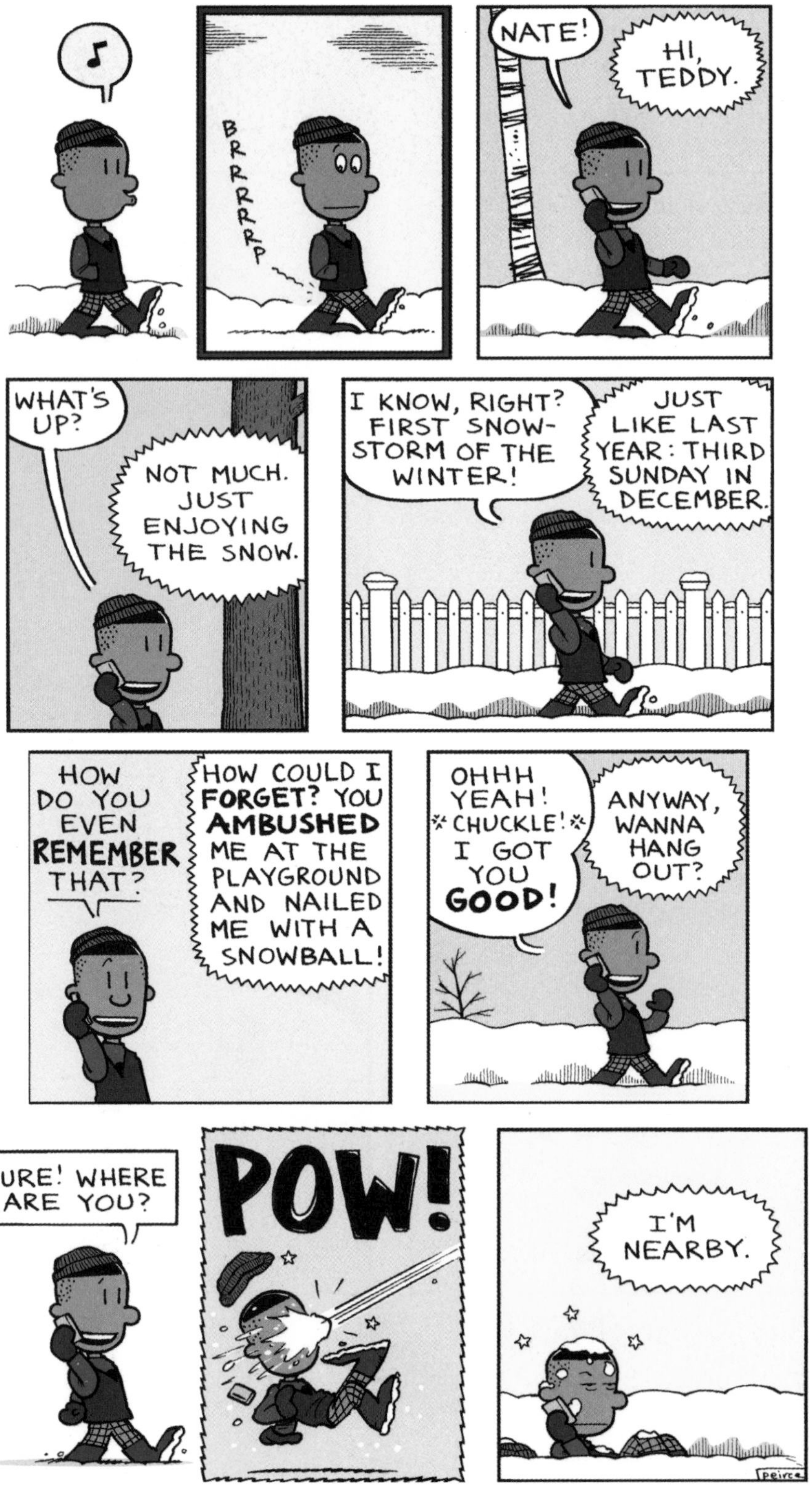
♪
BRRRRRRP
NATE!
HI, TEDDY.
WHAT'S UP?
NOT MUCH. JUST ENJOYING THE SNOW.
I KNOW, RIGHT? FIRST SNOW-STORM OF THE WINTER!
JUST LIKE LAST YEAR: THIRD SUNDAY IN DECEMBER.
HOW DO YOU EVEN **REMEMBER** THAT?
HOW COULD I **FORGET**? YOU **AMBUSHED** ME AT THE PLAYGROUND AND NAILED ME WITH A SNOWBALL!
OHHH YEAH! *CHUCKLE!* I GOT YOU **GOOD**!
ANYWAY, WANNA HANG OUT?
SURE! WHERE ARE YOU?
POW!
I'M NEARBY.
peirce

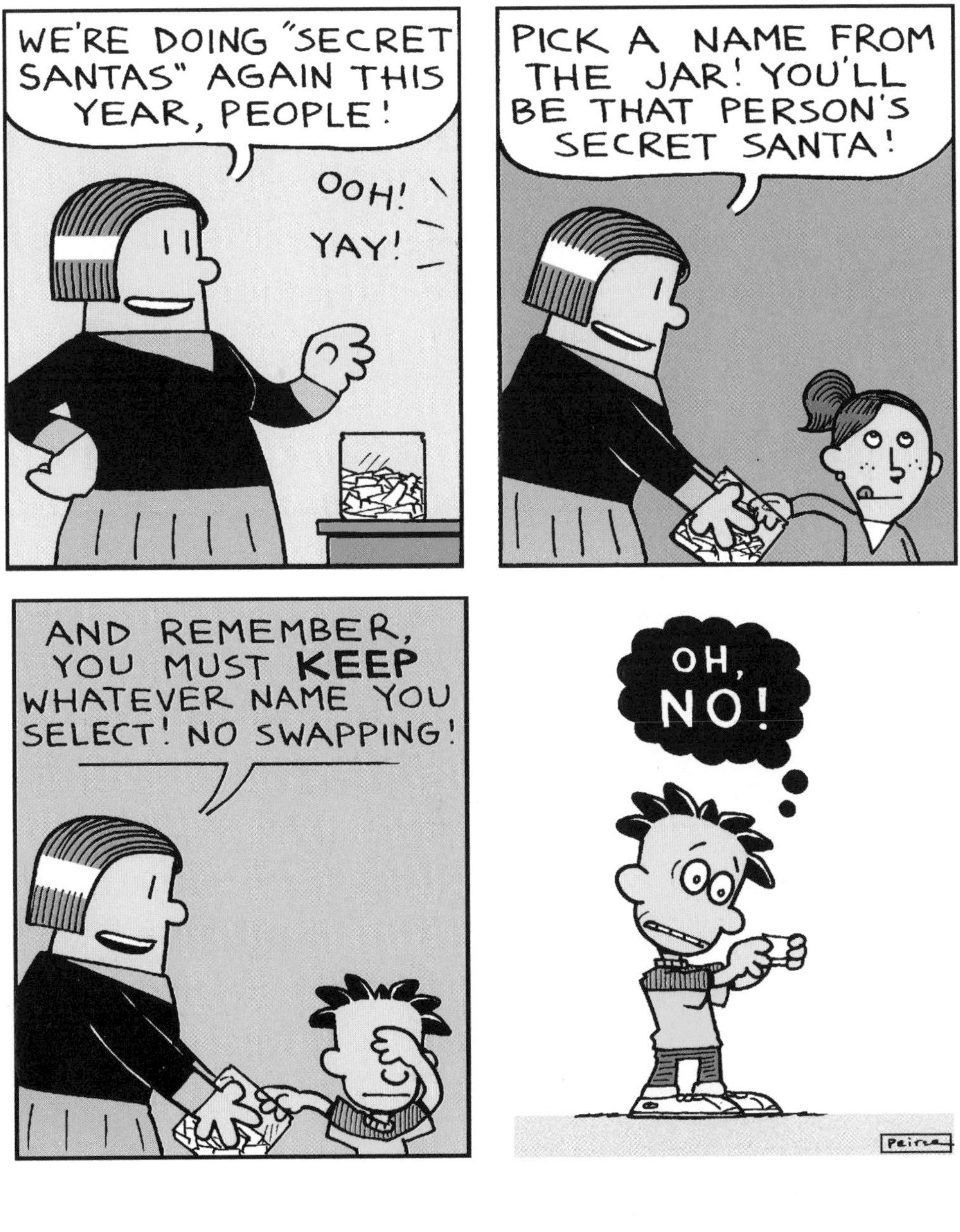
WE'RE DOING "SECRET SANTAS" AGAIN THIS YEAR, PEOPLE!
OOH!
YAY!
PICK A NAME FROM THE JAR! YOU'LL BE THAT PERSON'S SECRET SANTA!
AND REMEMBER, YOU MUST **KEEP** WHATEVER NAME YOU SELECT! NO SWAPPING!
OH, NO!
Peirce

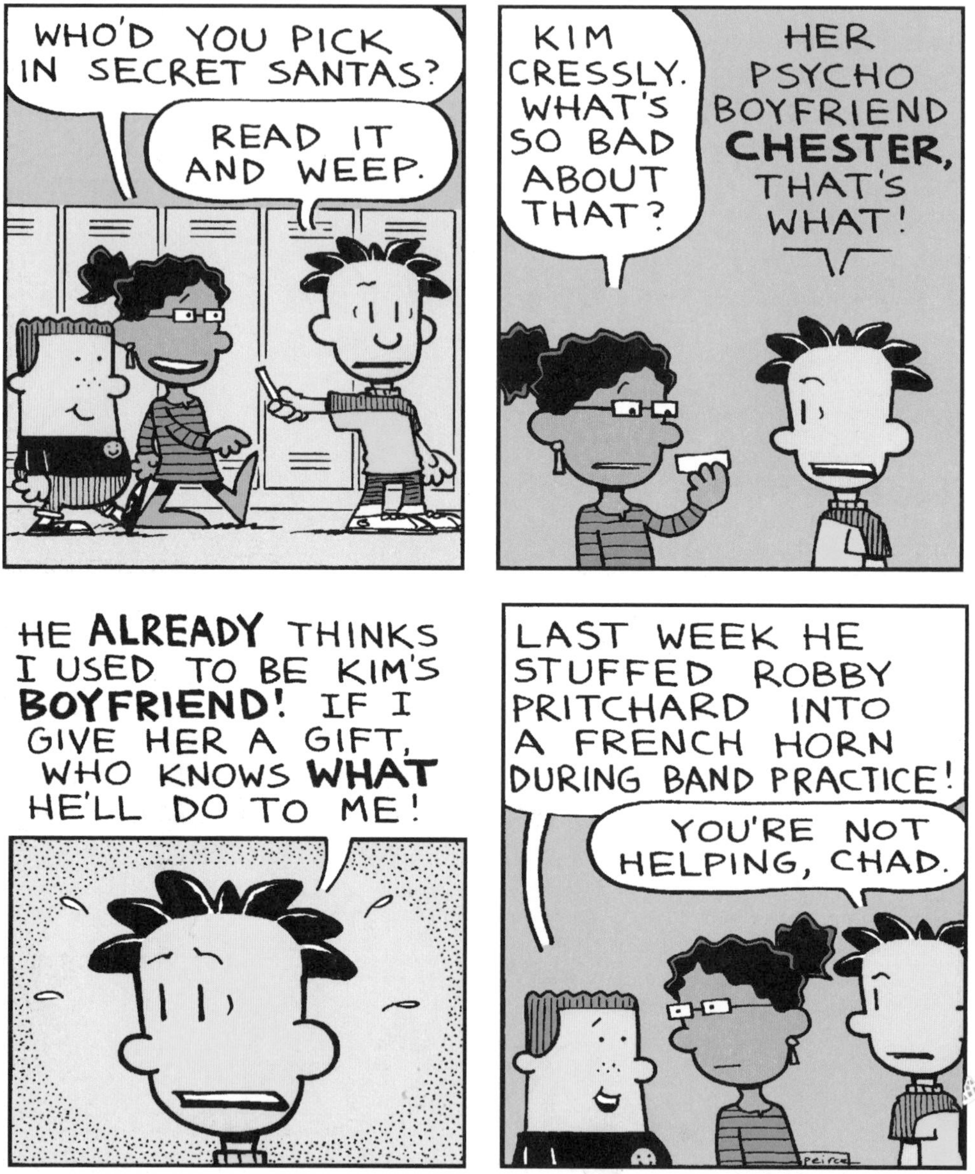
WHO'D YOU PICK IN SECRET SANTAS?
READ IT AND WEEP.
KIM CRESSLY. WHAT'S SO BAD ABOUT THAT?
HER PSYCHO BOYFRIEND CHESTER, THAT'S WHAT!
HE ALREADY THINKS I USED TO BE KIM'S BOYFRIEND! IF I GIVE HER A GIFT, WHO KNOWS WHAT HE'LL DO TO ME!
LAST WEEK HE STUFFED ROBBY PRITCHARD INTO A FRENCH HORN DURING BAND PRACTICE!
YOU'RE NOT HELPING, CHAD.
peirce

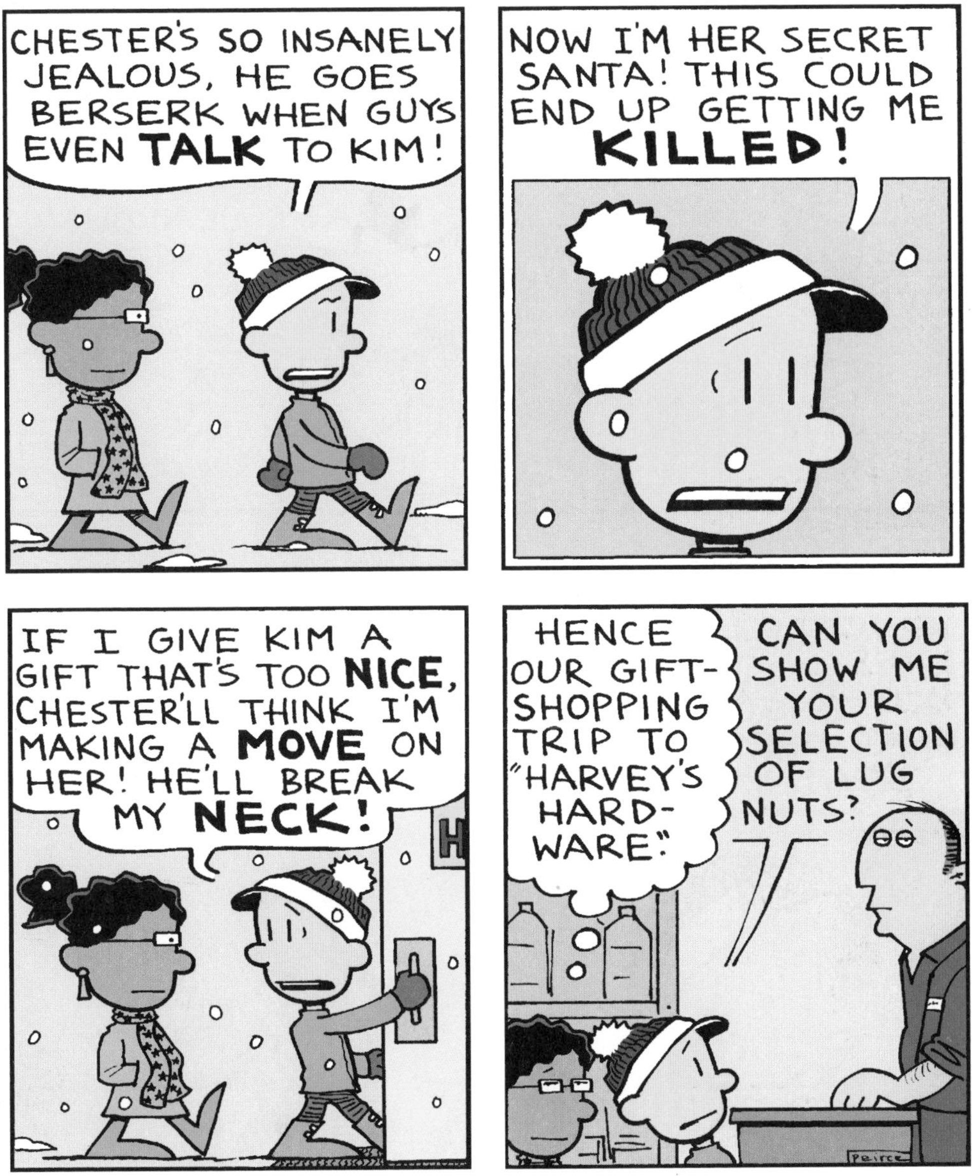
CHESTER'S SO INSANELY JEALOUS, HE GOES BERSERK WHEN GUYS EVEN **TALK** TO KIM!
NOW I'M HER SECRET SANTA! THIS COULD END UP GETTING ME **KILLED**!
IF I GIVE KIM A GIFT THAT'S TOO **NICE**, CHESTER'LL THINK I'M MAKING A **MOVE** ON HER! HE'LL BREAK MY **NECK**!
HENCE OUR GIFT-SHOPPING TRIP TO "HARVEY'S HARD-WARE."
CAN YOU SHOW ME YOUR SELECTION OF LUG NUTS?
PEIRCE

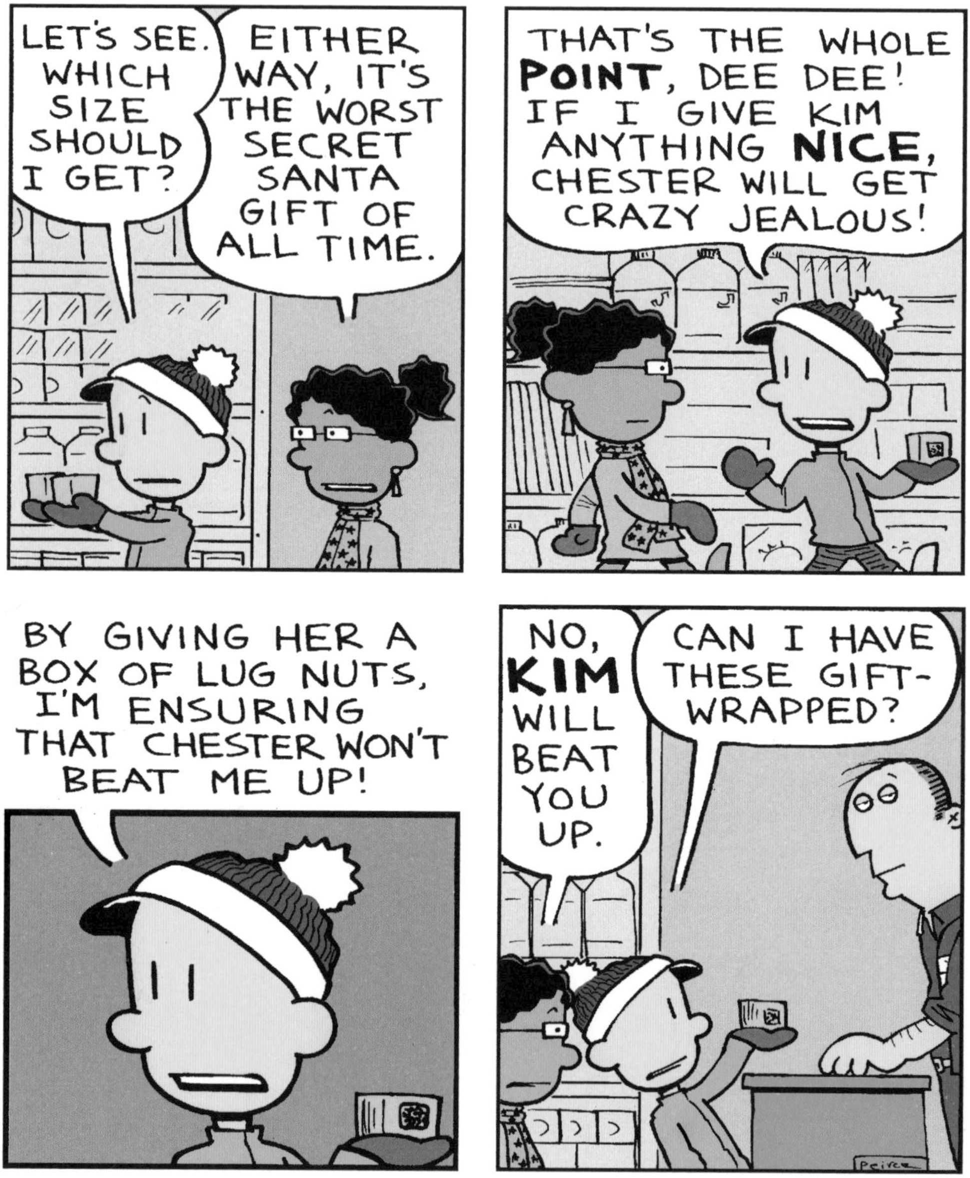

LET'S SEE. WHICH SIZE SHOULD I GET?
EITHER WAY, IT'S THE WORST SECRET SANTA GIFT OF ALL TIME.
THAT'S THE WHOLE **POINT**, DEE DEE! IF I GIVE KIM ANYTHING **NICE**, CHESTER WILL GET CRAZY JEALOUS!
BY GIVING HER A BOX OF LUG NUTS, I'M ENSURING THAT CHESTER WON'T BEAT ME UP!
NO, **KIM** WILL BEAT YOU UP.
CAN I HAVE THESE GIFT-WRAPPED?
Peirce

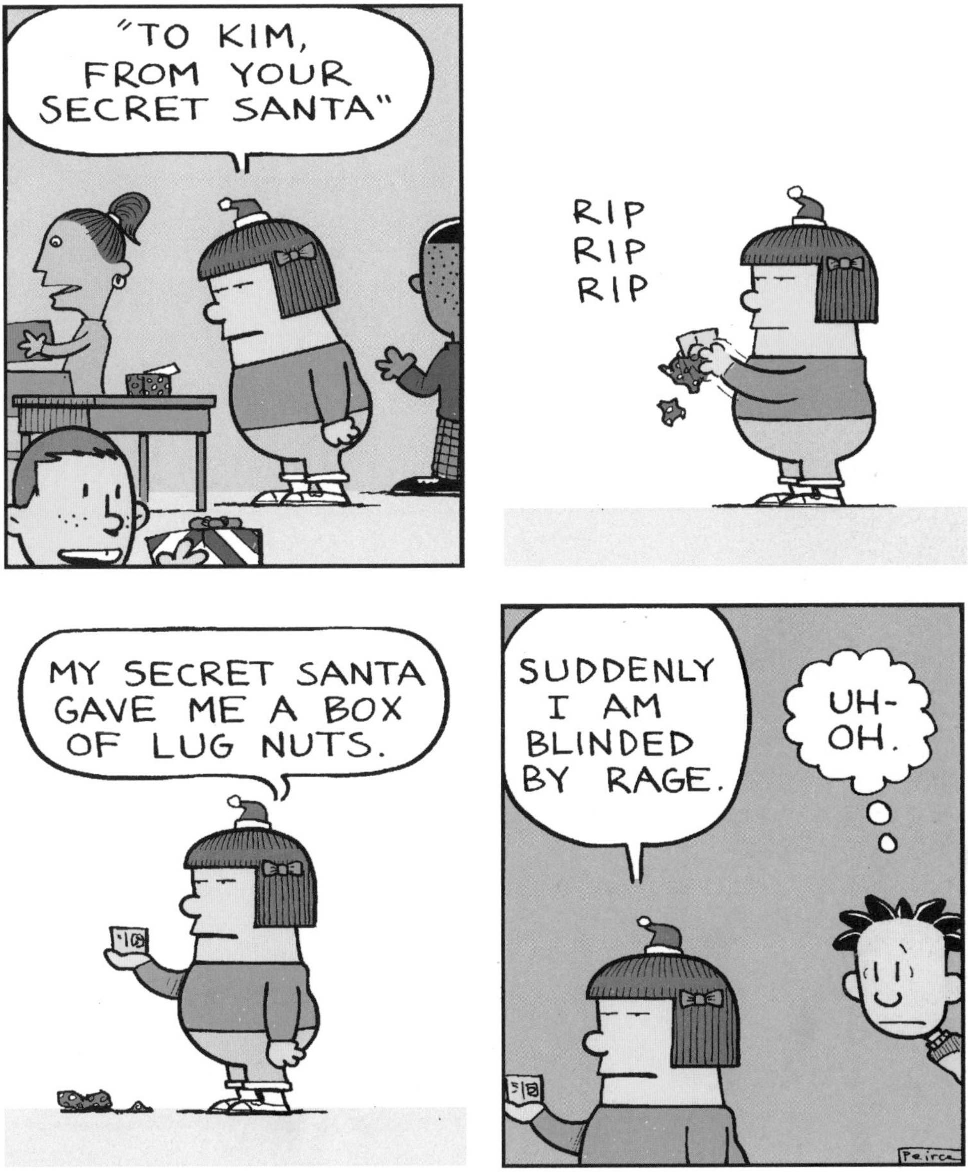
"TO KIM, FROM YOUR SECRET SANTA"
RIP RIP RIP
MY SECRET SANTA GAVE ME A BOX OF LUG NUTS.
SUDDENLY I AM BLINDED BY RAGE.
UH-OH.
Peirce

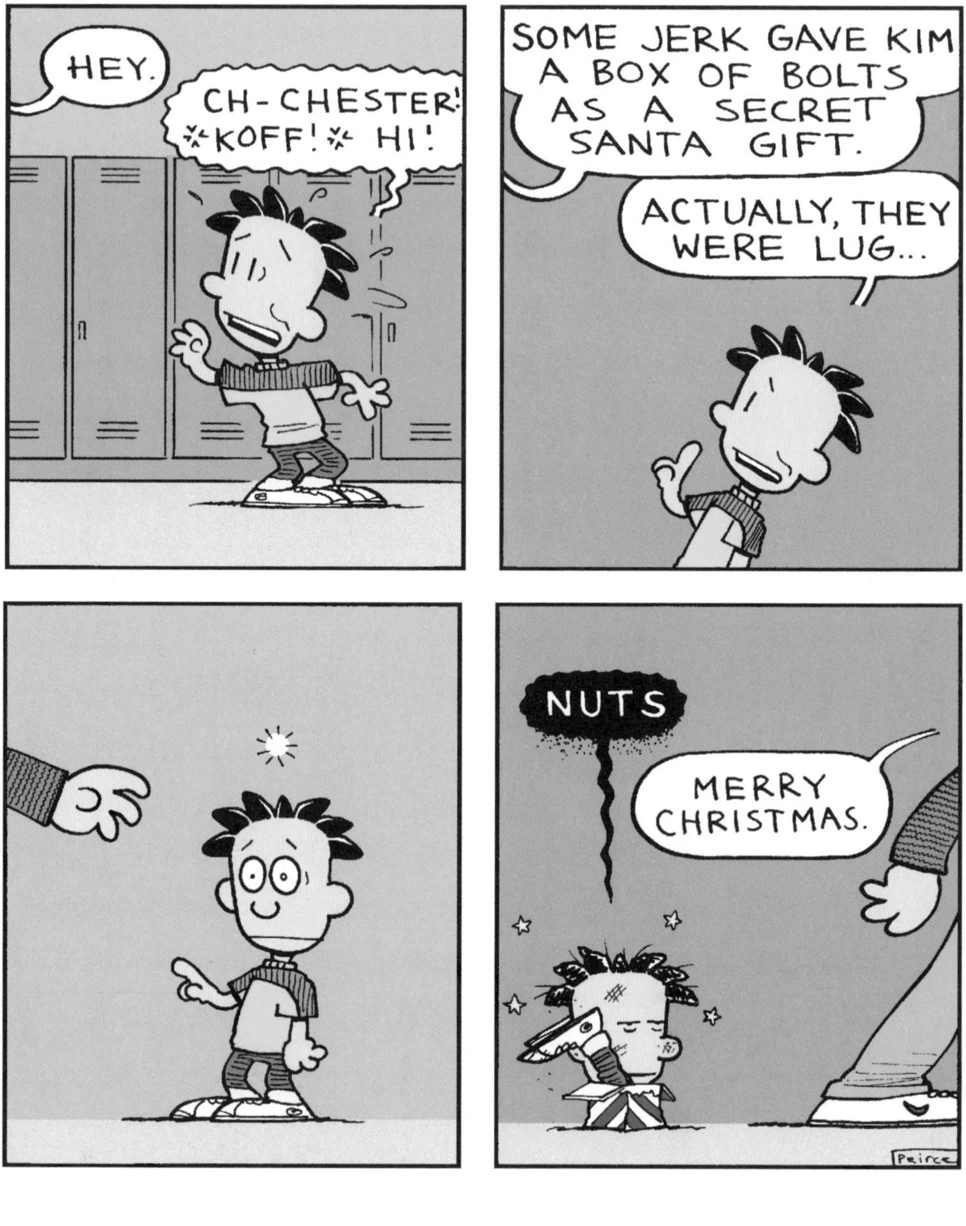
HEY.
CH-CHESTER! *KOFF!* HI!
SOME JERK GAVE KIM A BOX OF BOLTS AS A SECRET SANTA GIFT.
ACTUALLY, THEY WERE LUG...
NUTS
MERRY CHRISTMAS.
Peirce

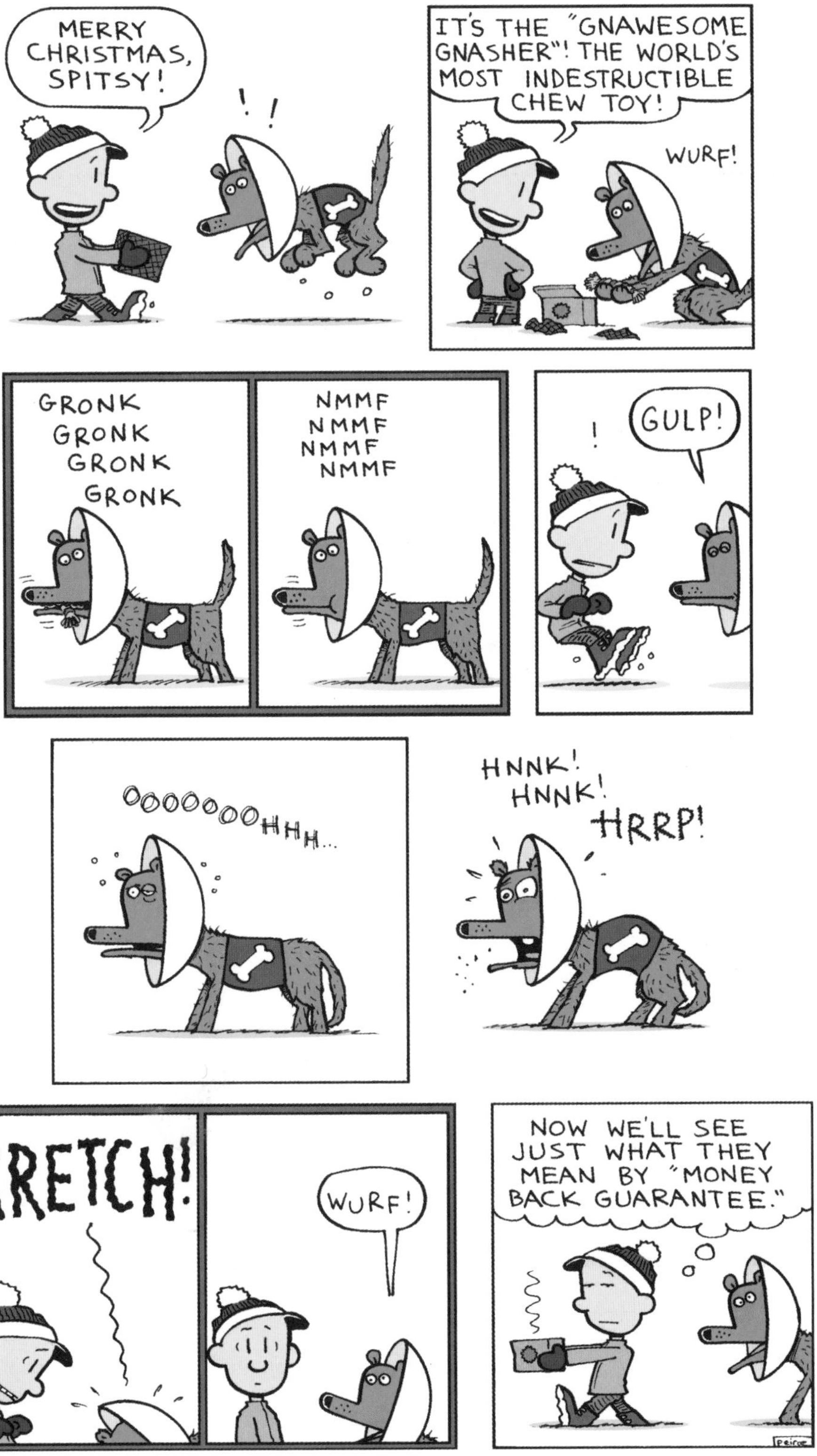
MERRY CHRISTMAS, SPITSY!
! !
IT'S THE "GNAWESOME GNASHER"! THE WORLD'S MOST INDESTRUCTIBLE CHEW TOY!
WURF!
GRONK GRONK GRONK GRONK
NMMF NMMF NMMF NMMF
!
GULP!
OOOOOOOOHHH...
HNNK! HNNK! HRRP!
RRETCH!
WURF!
NOW WE'LL SEE JUST WHAT THEY MEAN BY "MONEY BACK GUARANTEE."
peirce

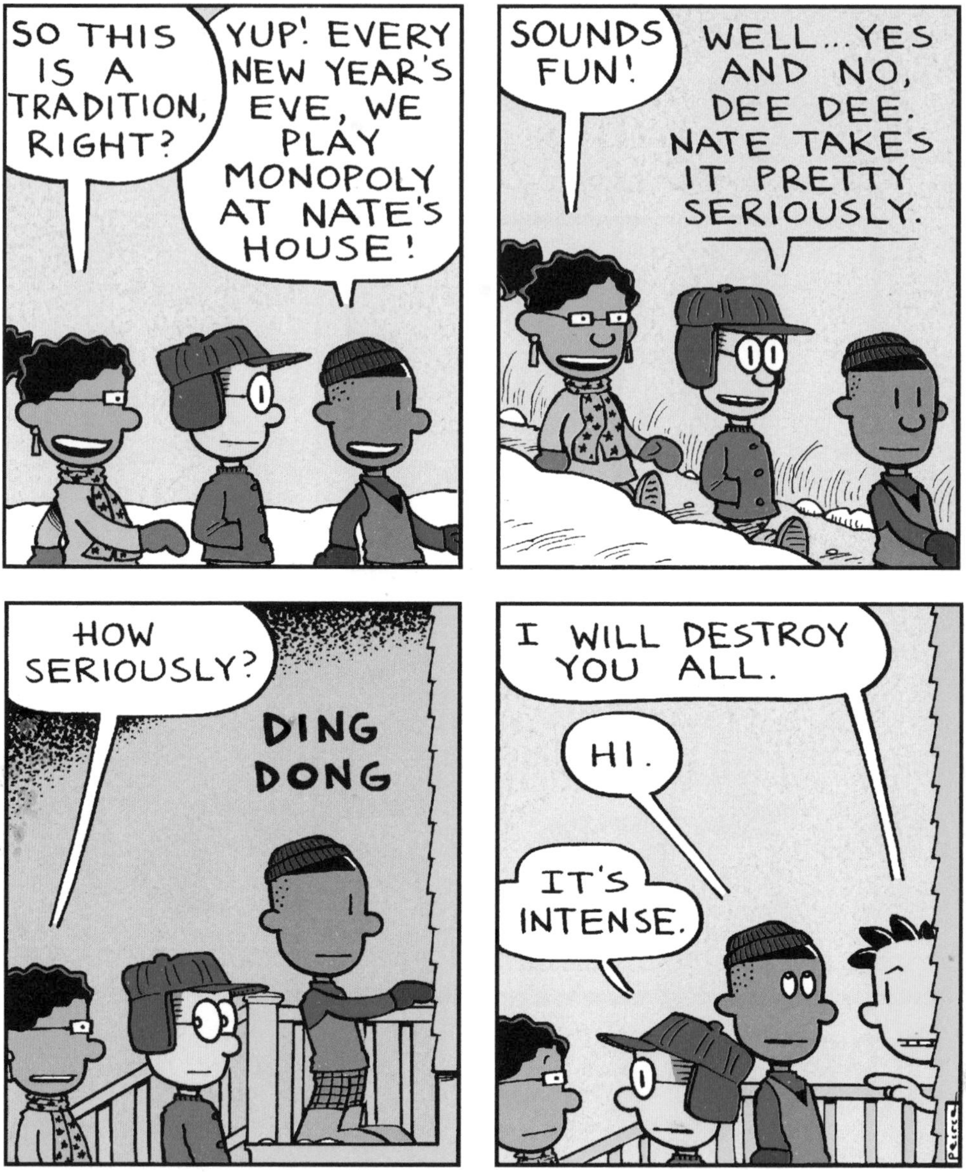
SO THIS IS A TRADITION, RIGHT?
YUP! EVERY NEW YEAR'S EVE, WE PLAY MONOPOLY AT NATE'S HOUSE!
SOUNDS FUN!
WELL... YES AND NO, DEE DEE. NATE TAKES IT PRETTY SERIOUSLY.
HOW SERIOUSLY?
DING DONG
I WILL DESTROY YOU ALL.
HI.
IT'S INTENSE.

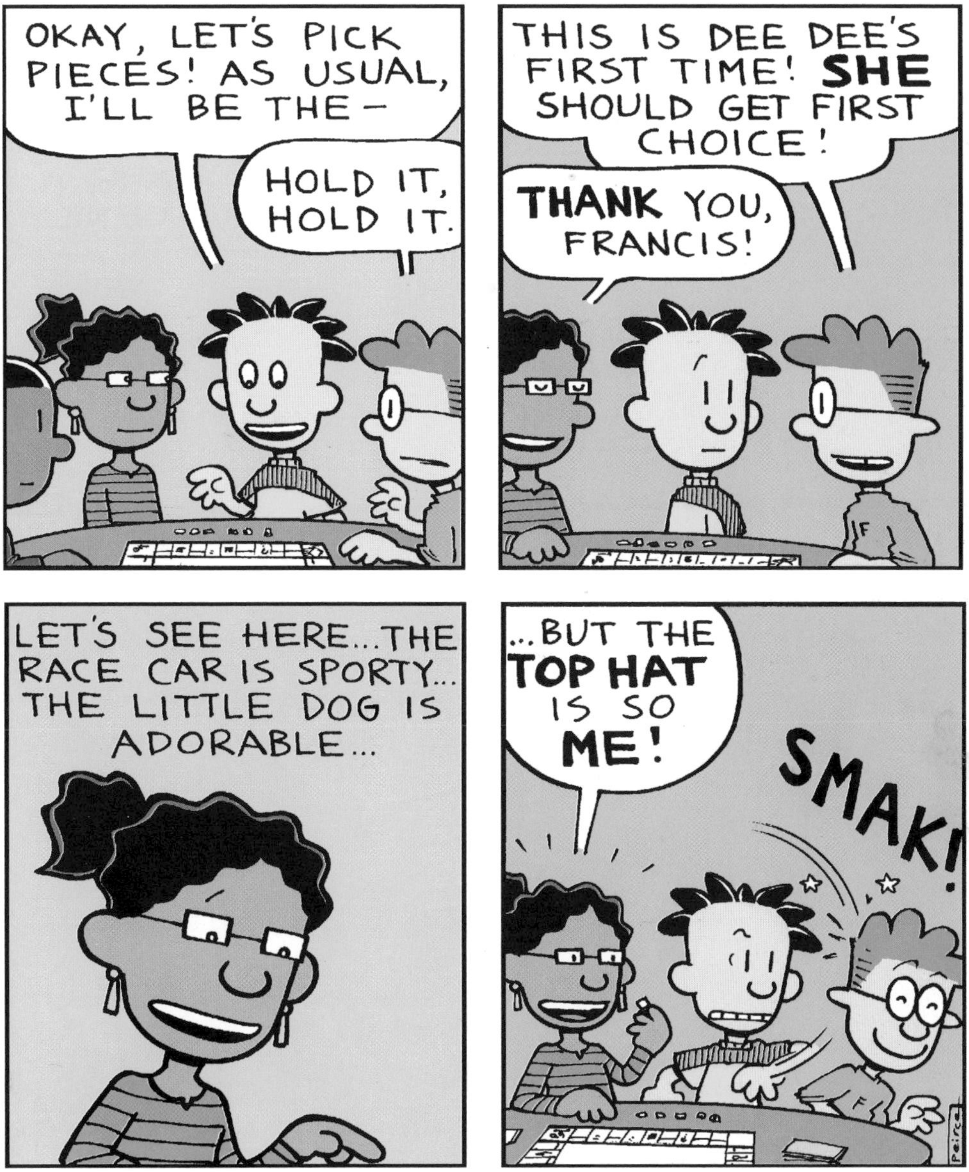
OKAY, LET'S PICK PIECES! AS USUAL, I'LL BE THE-
HOLD IT, HOLD IT.
THIS IS DEE DEE'S FIRST TIME! SHE SHOULD GET FIRST CHOICE!
THANK YOU, FRANCIS!
LET'S SEE HERE... THE RACE CAR IS SPORTY... THE LITTLE DOG IS ADORABLE...
...BUT THE TOP HAT IS SO ME!
SMAK!
Peirce

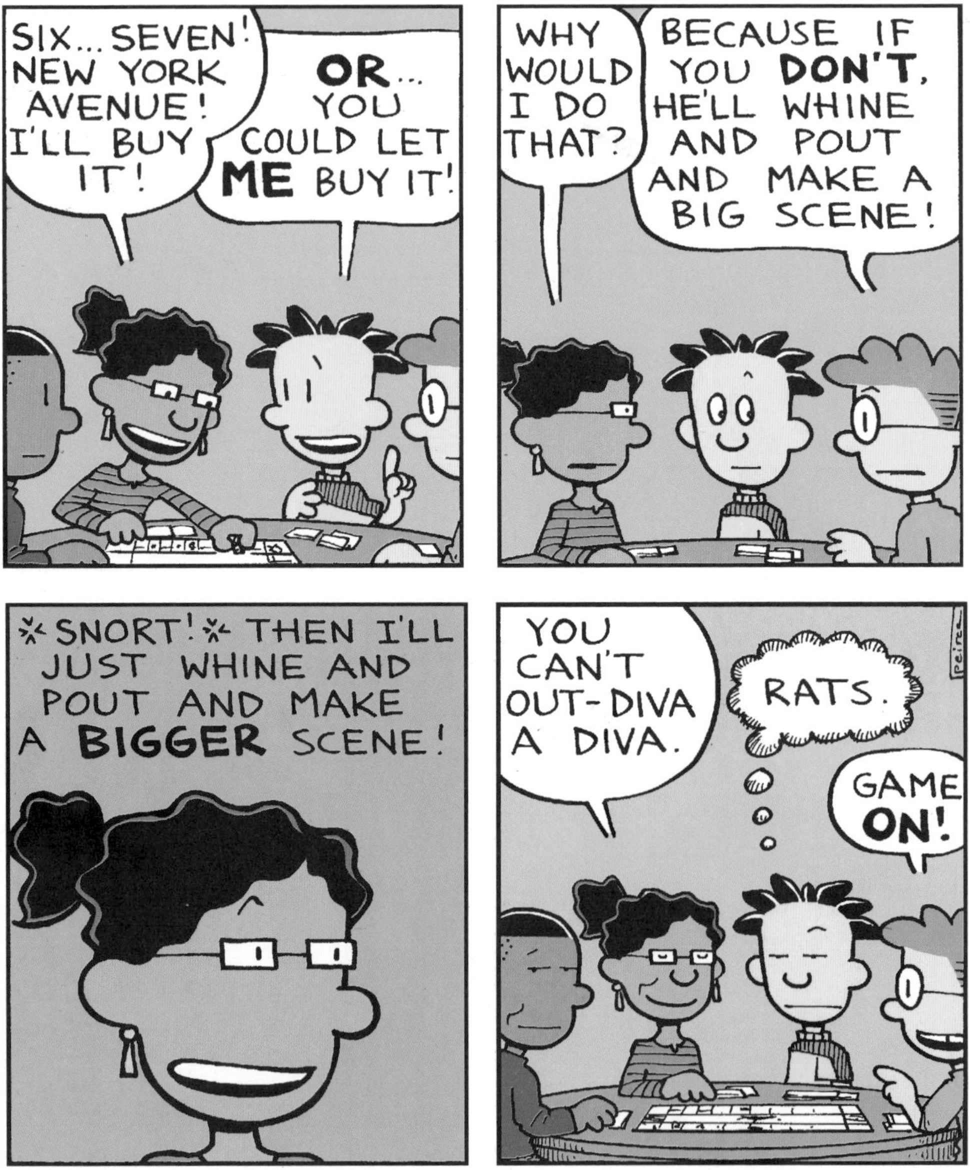
SIX... SEVEN! NEW YORK AVENUE! I'LL BUY IT!
OR... YOU COULD LET **ME** BUY IT!
WHY WOULD I DO THAT?
BECAUSE IF YOU **DON'T**, HE'LL WHINE AND POUT AND MAKE A BIG SCENE!
SNORT! THEN I'LL JUST WHINE AND POUT AND MAKE A **BIGGER** SCENE!
YOU CAN'T OUT-DIVA A DIVA.
RATS.
GAME **ON**!
peirce

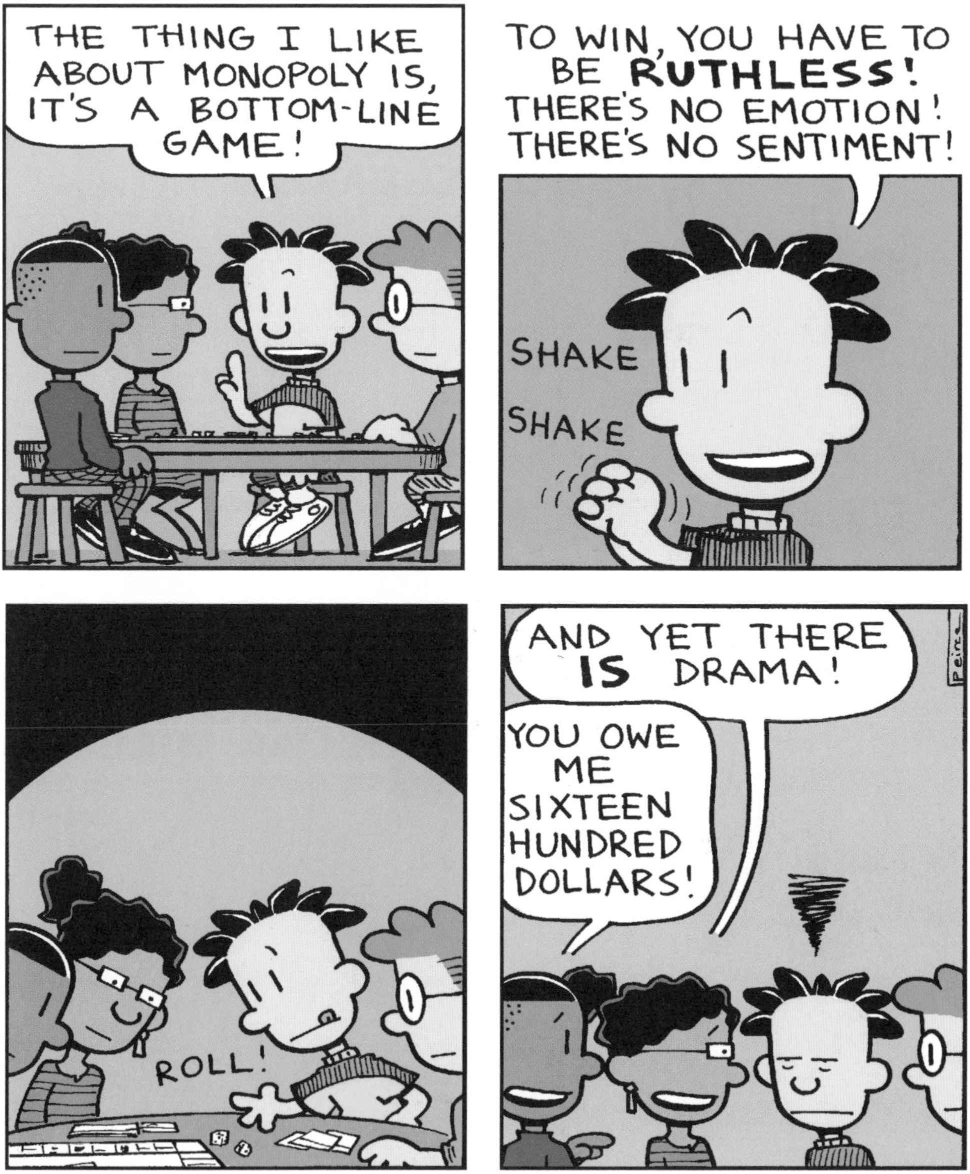
THE THING I LIKE ABOUT MONOPOLY IS, IT'S A BOTTOM-LINE GAME!
TO WIN, YOU HAVE TO BE **RUTHLESS!** THERE'S NO EMOTION! THERE'S NO SENTIMENT!
SHAKE
SHAKE
ROLL!
AND YET THERE **IS** DRAMA!
YOU OWE ME SIXTEEN HUNDRED DOLLARS!
Peirce

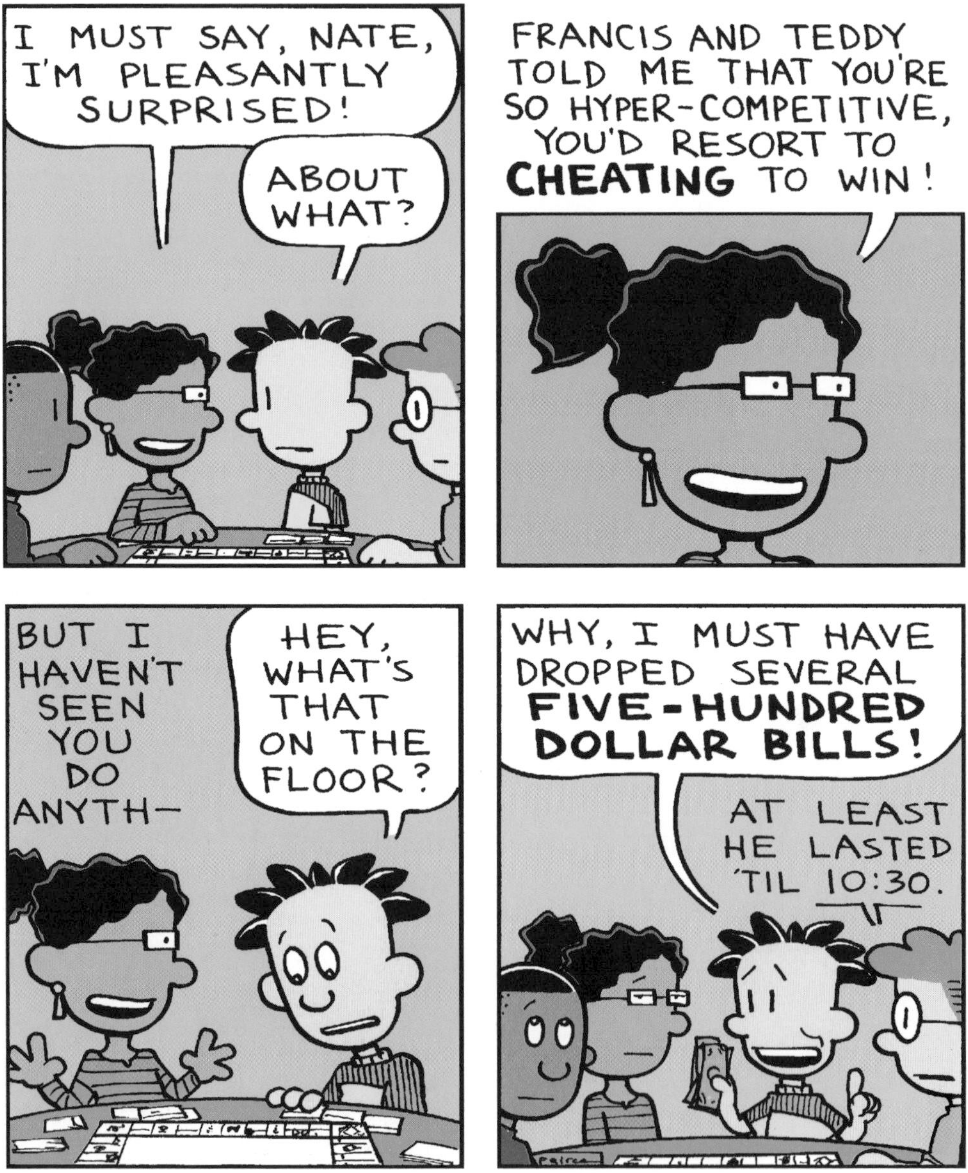
I MUST SAY, NATE, I'M PLEASANTLY SURPRISED!
ABOUT WHAT?
FRANCIS AND TEDDY TOLD ME THAT YOU'RE SO HYPER-COMPETITIVE, YOU'D RESORT TO **CHEATING** TO WIN!
BUT I HAVEN'T SEEN YOU DO ANYTH—
HEY, WHAT'S THAT ON THE FLOOR?
WHY, I MUST HAVE DROPPED SEVERAL **FIVE-HUNDRED DOLLAR BILLS!**
AT LEAST HE LASTED 'TIL 10:30.

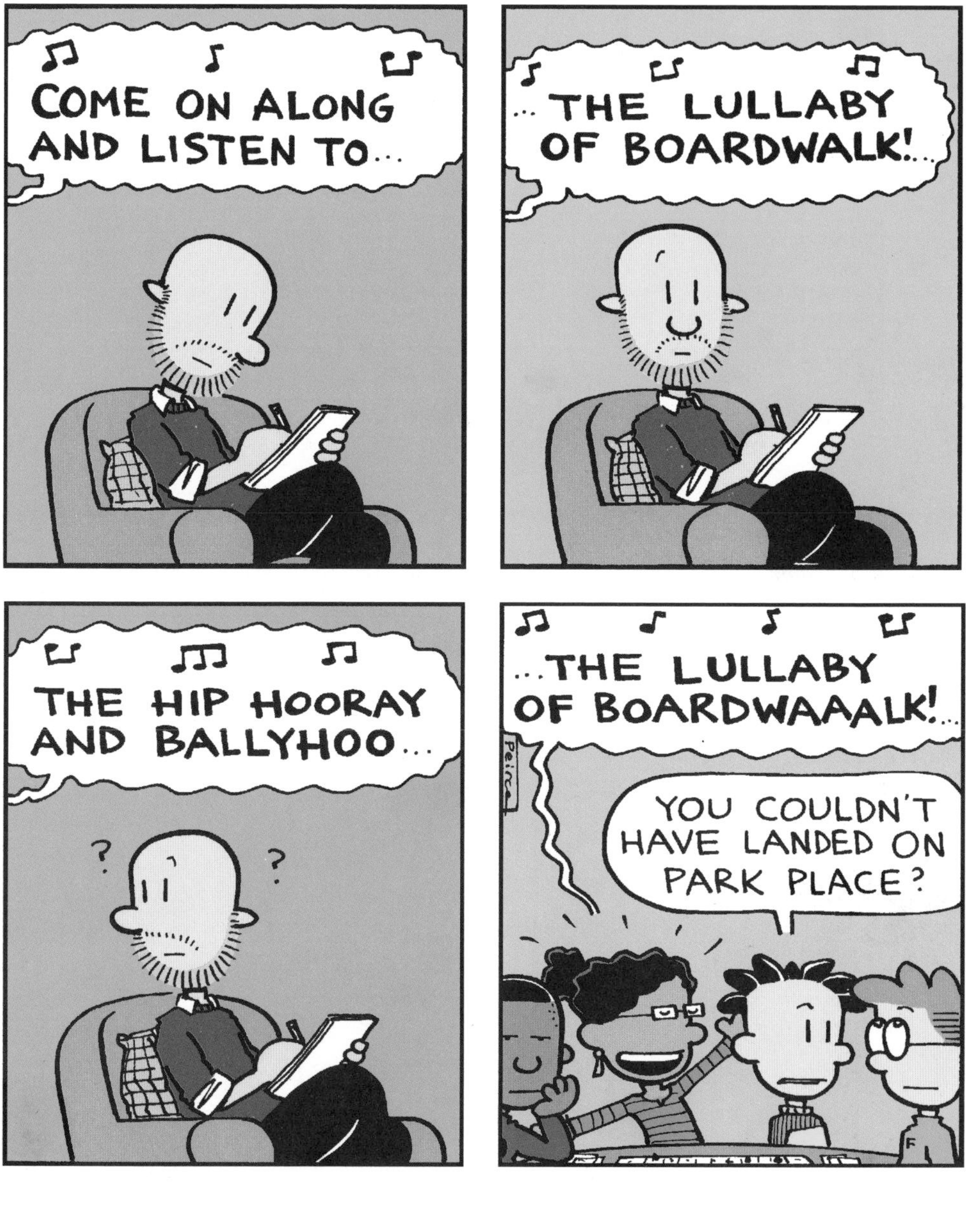
COME ON ALONG AND LISTEN TO...
...THE LULLABY OF BOARDWALK!...
THE HIP HOORAY AND BALLYHOO...
...THE LULLABY OF BOARDWAAALK!...
Peirce
YOU COULDN'T HAVE LANDED ON PARK PLACE?

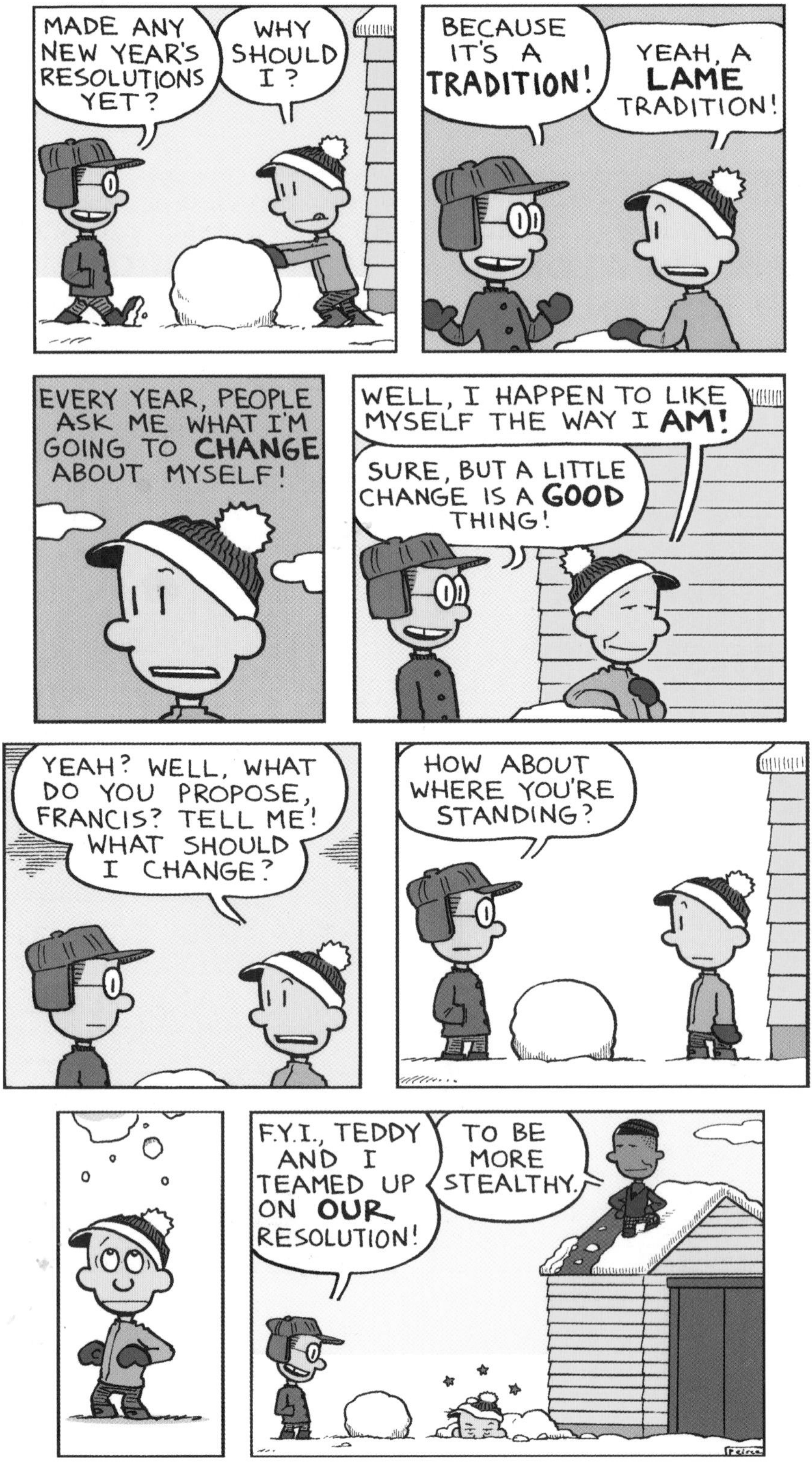
MADE ANY NEW YEAR'S RESOLUTIONS YET?
WHY SHOULD I?
BECAUSE IT'S A TRADITION!
YEAH, A LAME TRADITION!
EVERY YEAR, PEOPLE ASK ME WHAT I'M GOING TO CHANGE ABOUT MYSELF!
WELL, I HAPPEN TO LIKE MYSELF THE WAY I AM!
SURE, BUT A LITTLE CHANGE IS A GOOD THING!
YEAH? WELL, WHAT DO YOU PROPOSE, FRANCIS? TELL ME! WHAT SHOULD I CHANGE?
HOW ABOUT WHERE YOU'RE STANDING?
F.Y.I., TEDDY AND I TEAMED UP ON OUR RESOLUTION!
TO BE MORE STEALTHY.

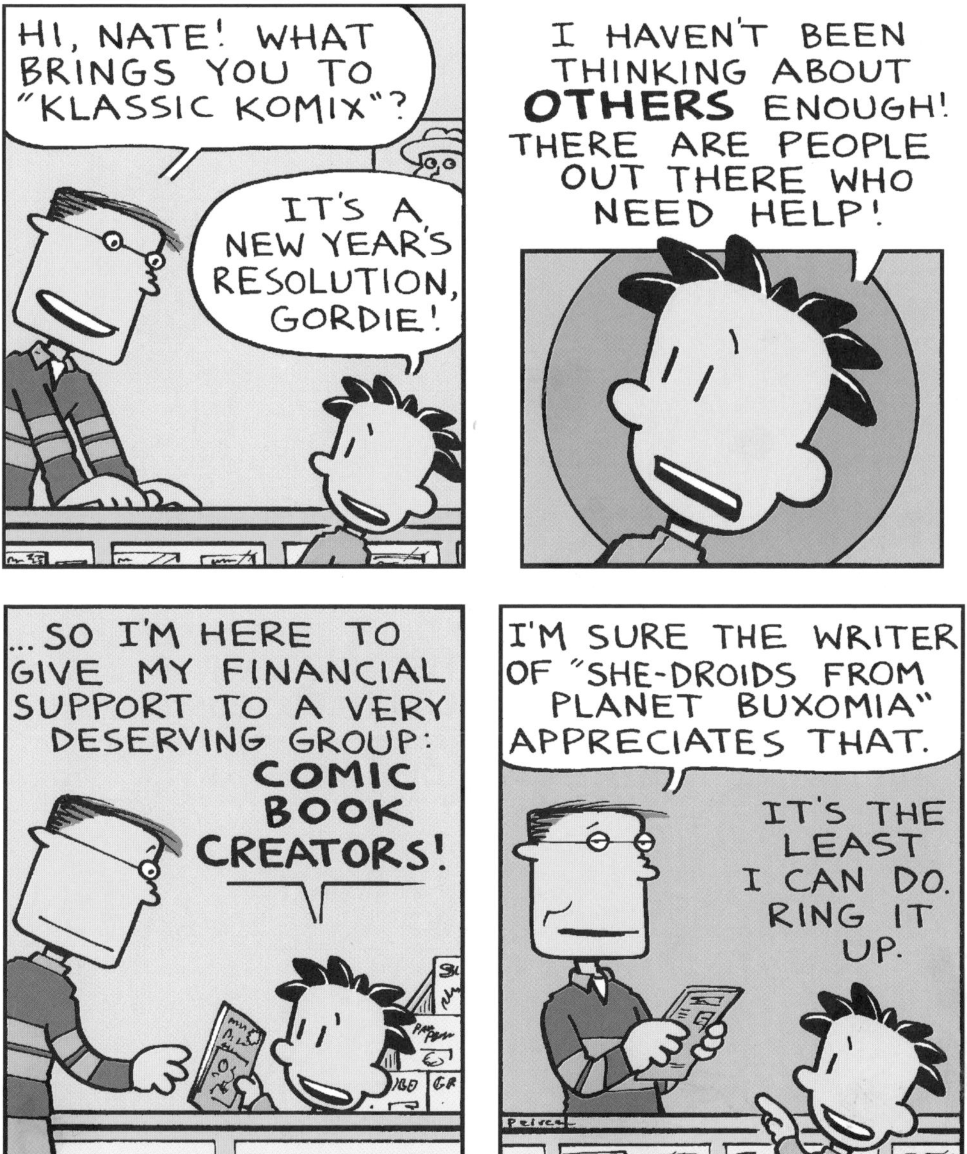
HI, NATE! WHAT BRINGS YOU TO "KLASSIC KOMIX"?
IT'S A NEW YEAR'S RESOLUTION, GORDIE!
I HAVEN'T BEEN THINKING ABOUT **OTHERS** ENOUGH! THERE ARE PEOPLE OUT THERE WHO NEED HELP!
...SO I'M HERE TO GIVE MY FINANCIAL SUPPORT TO A VERY DESERVING GROUP: **COMIC BOOK CREATORS!**
I'M SURE THE WRITER OF "SHE-DROIDS FROM PLANET BUXOMIA" APPRECIATES THAT.
IT'S THE LEAST I CAN DO. RING IT UP.

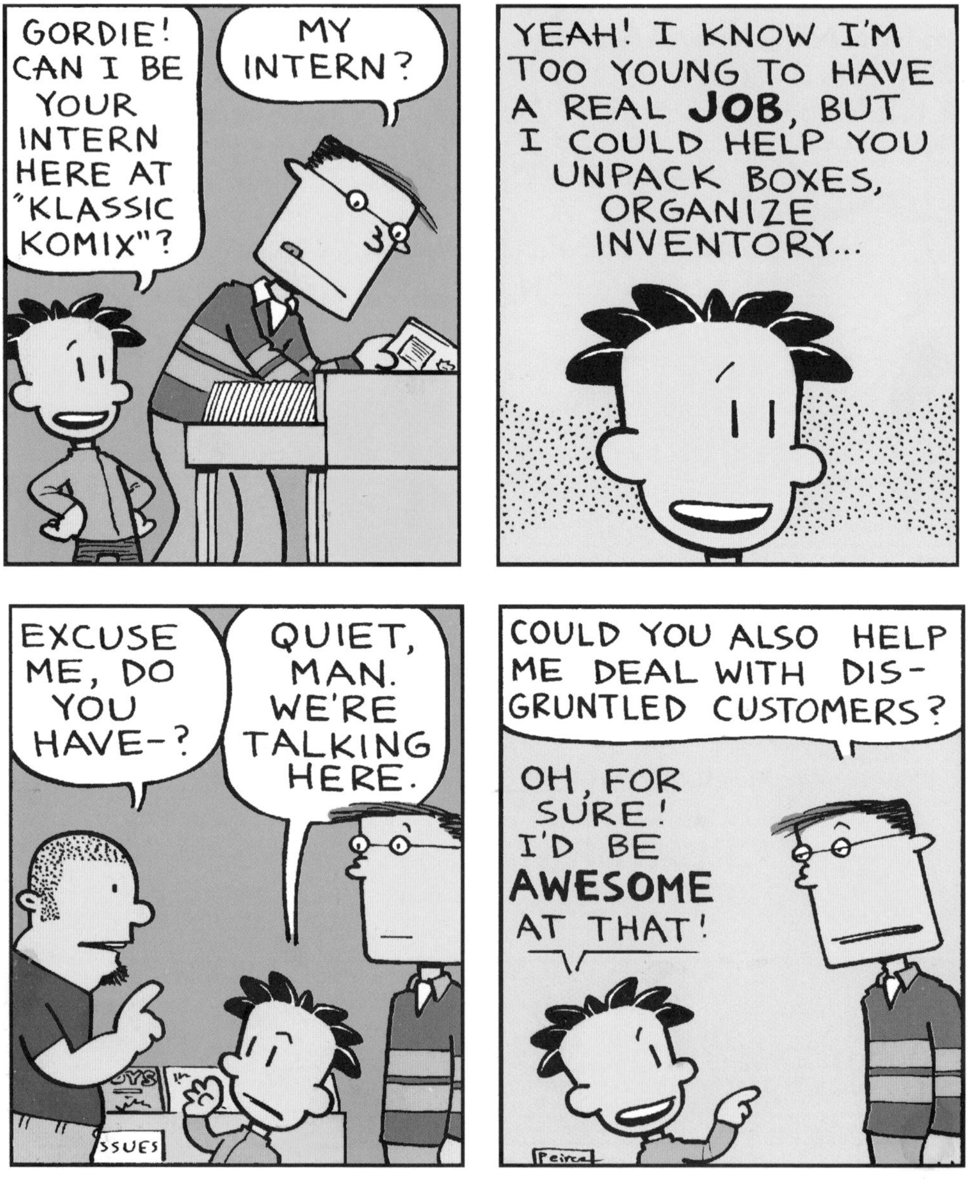
GORDIE! CAN I BE YOUR INTERN HERE AT "KLASSIC KOMIX"?
MY INTERN?
YEAH! I KNOW I'M TOO YOUNG TO HAVE A REAL **JOB**, BUT I COULD HELP YOU UNPACK BOXES, ORGANIZE INVENTORY...
EXCUSE ME, DO YOU HAVE-?
QUIET, MAN. WE'RE TALKING HERE.
COULD YOU ALSO HELP ME DEAL WITH DIS-GRUNTLED CUSTOMERS?
OH, FOR SURE! I'D BE **AWESOME** AT THAT!

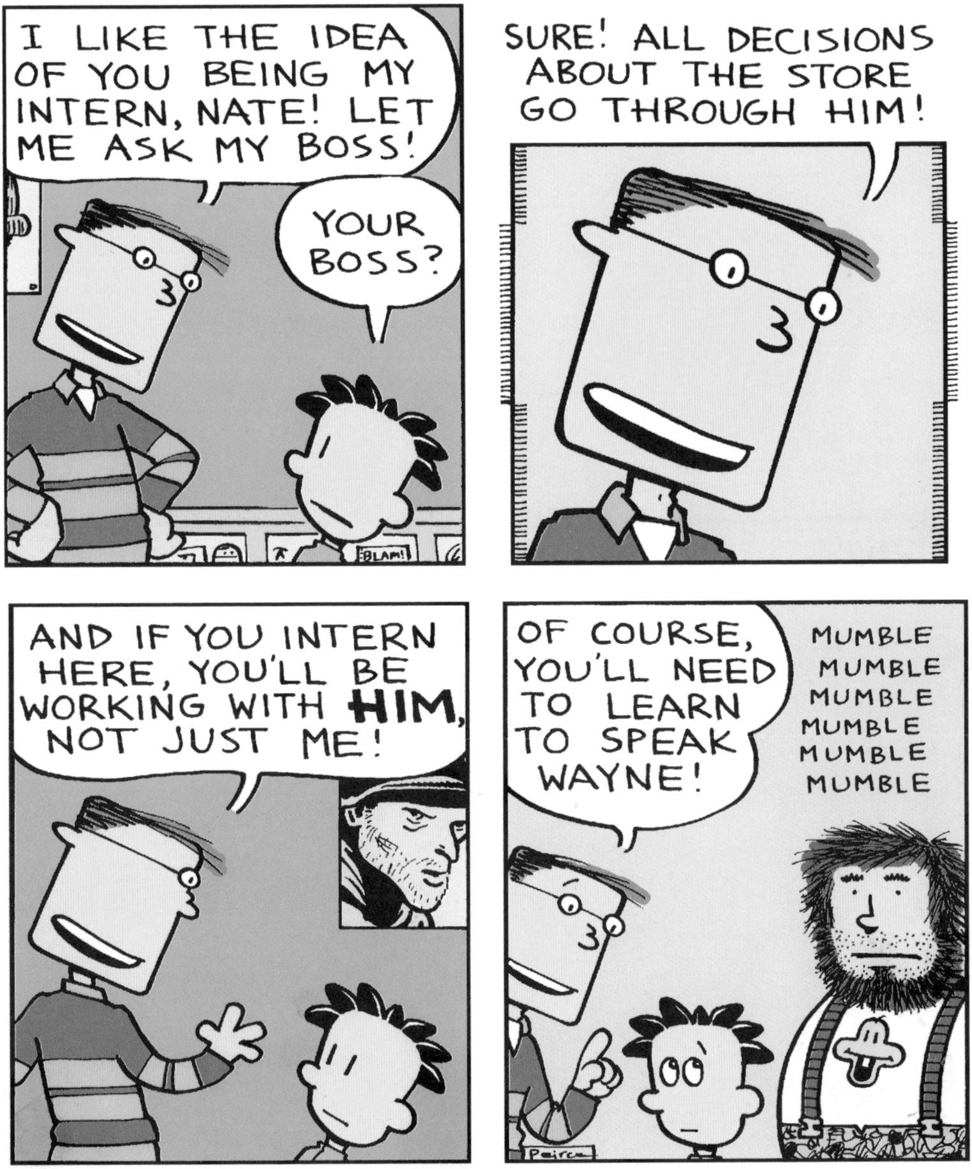
I LIKE THE IDEA OF YOU BEING MY INTERN, NATE! LET ME ASK MY BOSS!
YOUR BOSS?
BLAM!
SURE! ALL DECISIONS ABOUT THE STORE GO THROUGH HIM!
AND IF YOU INTERN HERE, YOU'LL BE WORKING WITH HIM, NOT JUST ME!
OF COURSE, YOU'LL NEED TO LEARN TO SPEAK WAYNE!
MUMBLE MUMBLE MUMBLE MUMBLE MUMBLE MUMBLE
Peirce

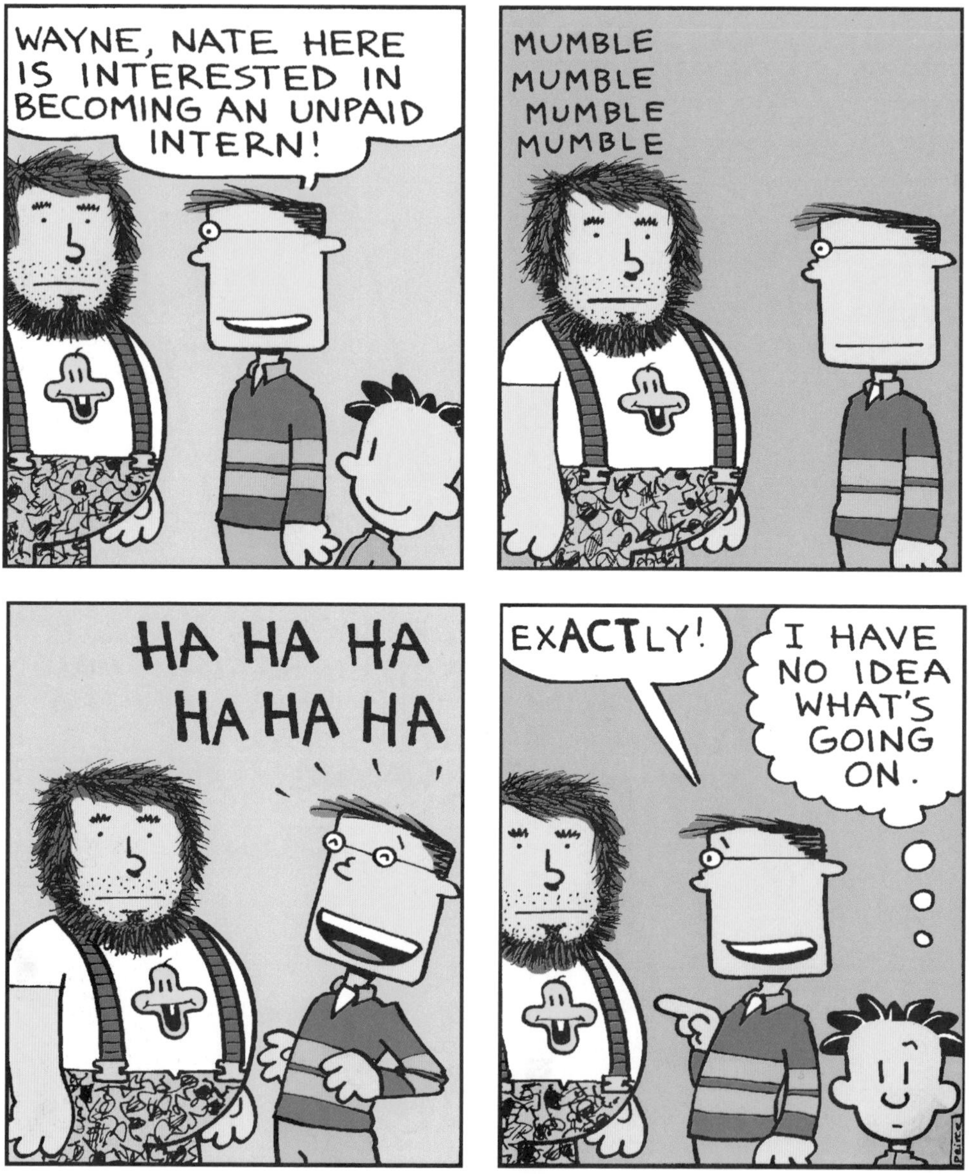
WAYNE, NATE HERE IS INTERESTED IN BECOMING AN UNPAID INTERN!
MUMBLE MUMBLE MUMBLE MUMBLE
HA HA HA HA HA HA
EXACTLY!
I HAVE NO IDEA WHAT'S GOING ON.

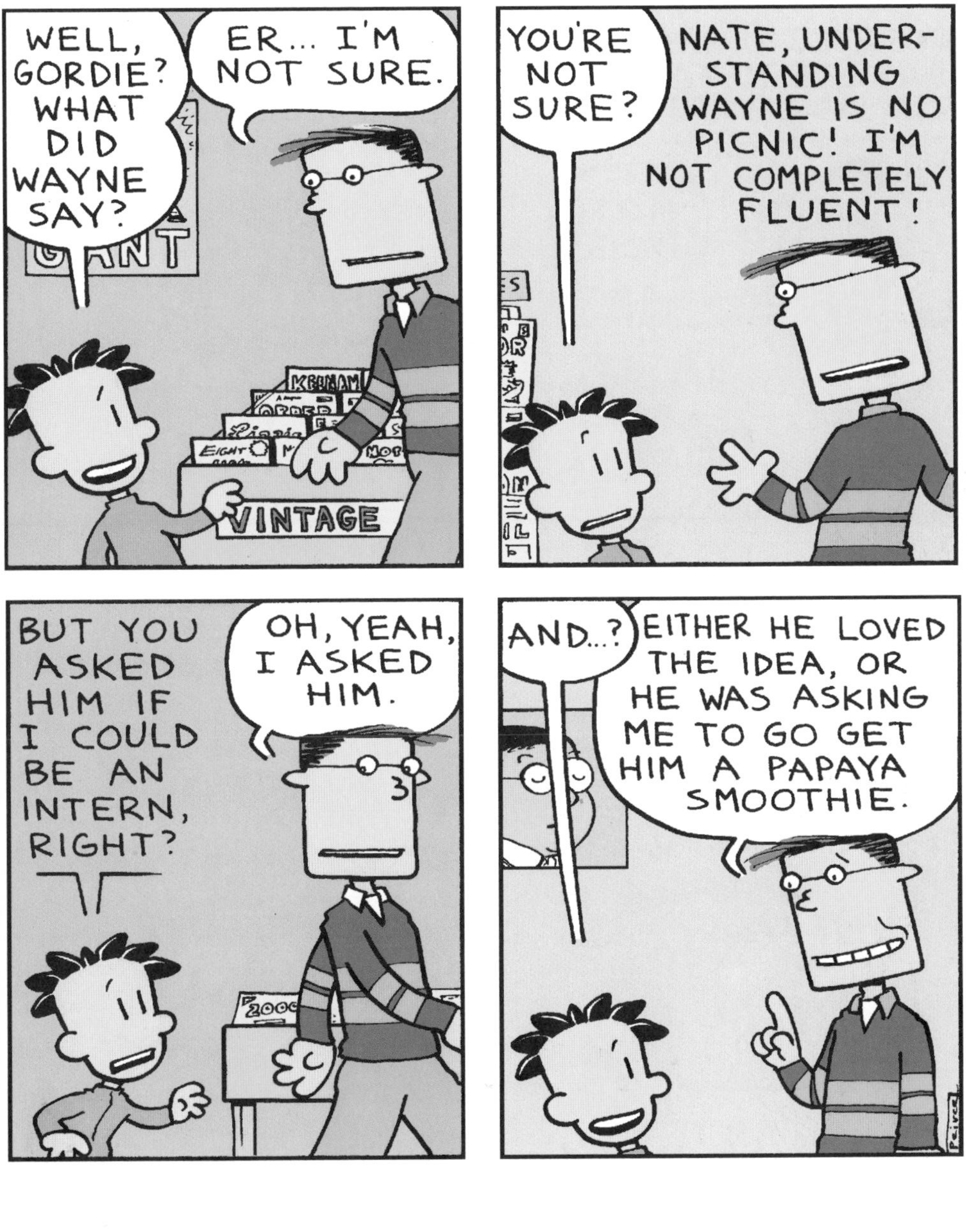
WELL, GORDIE? WHAT DID WAYNE SAY?
ER... I'M NOT SURE.
VINTAGE
YOU'RE NOT SURE?
NATE, UNDER-STANDING WAYNE IS NO PICNIC! I'M NOT COMPLETELY FLUENT!
BUT YOU ASKED HIM IF I COULD BE AN INTERN, RIGHT?
OH, YEAH, I ASKED HIM.
AND...?
EITHER HE LOVED THE IDEA, OR HE WAS ASKING ME TO GO GET HIM A PAPAYA SMOOTHIE.

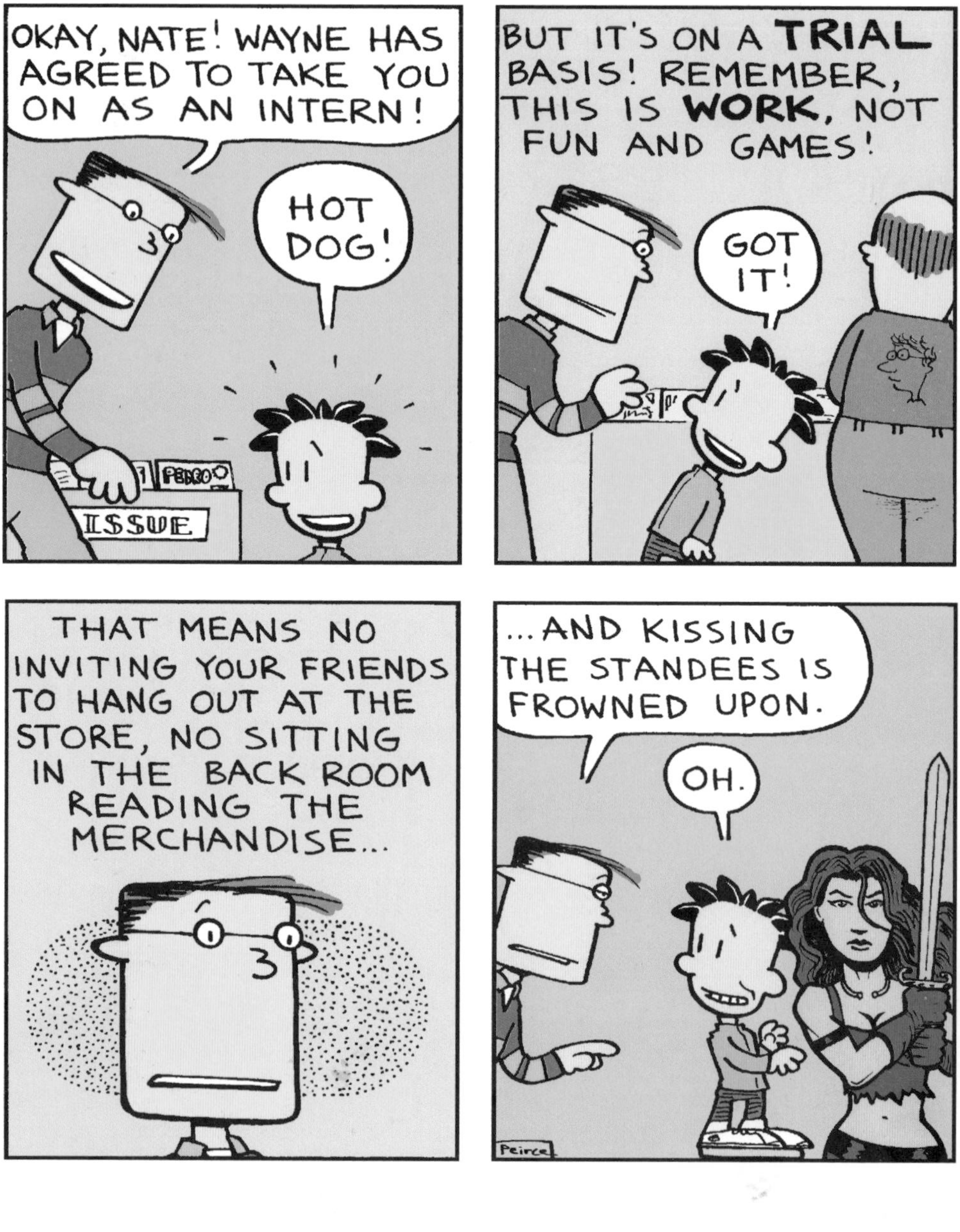
OKAY, NATE! WAYNE HAS AGREED TO TAKE YOU ON AS AN INTERN!
HOT DOG!
ISSUE
BUT IT'S ON A TRIAL BASIS! REMEMBER, THIS IS WORK, NOT FUN AND GAMES!
GOT IT!
THAT MEANS NO INVITING YOUR FRIENDS TO HANG OUT AT THE STORE, NO SITTING IN THE BACK ROOM READING THE MERCHANDISE...
...AND KISSING THE STANDEES IS FROWNED UPON.
OH.
Peirce

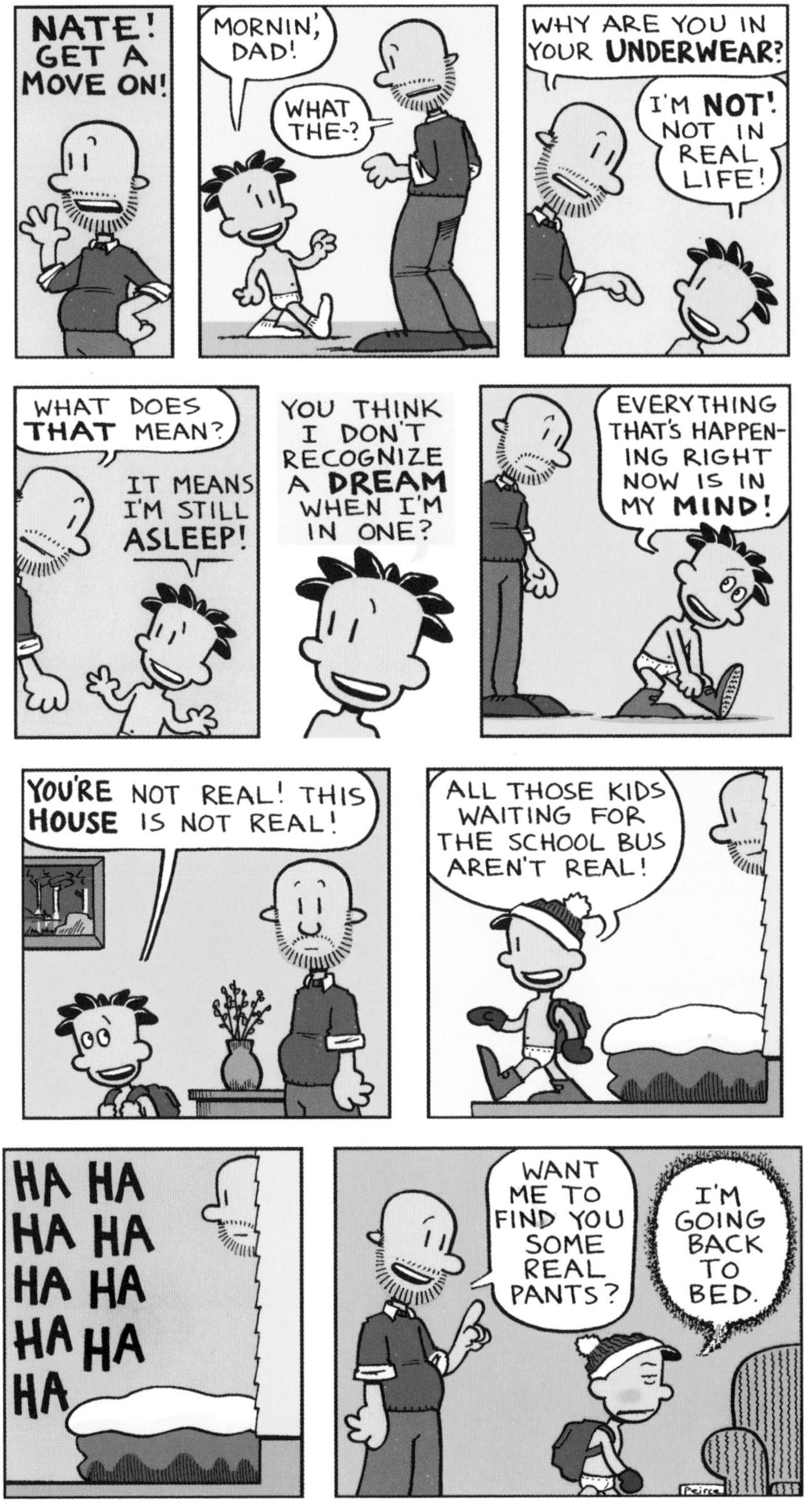
NATE! GET A MOVE ON!
MORNIN', DAD!
WHAT THE-?
WHY ARE YOU IN YOUR UNDERWEAR?
I'M NOT! NOT IN REAL LIFE!
WHAT DOES THAT MEAN?
IT MEANS I'M STILL ASLEEP!
YOU THINK I DON'T RECOGNIZE A DREAM WHEN I'M IN ONE?
EVERYTHING THAT'S HAPPENING RIGHT NOW IS IN MY MIND!
YOU'RE NOT REAL! THIS HOUSE IS NOT REAL!
ALL THOSE KIDS WAITING FOR THE SCHOOL BUS AREN'T REAL!
HA HA HA HA HA HA HA HA HA
WANT ME TO FIND YOU SOME REAL PANTS?
I'M GOING BACK TO BED.
Peirce

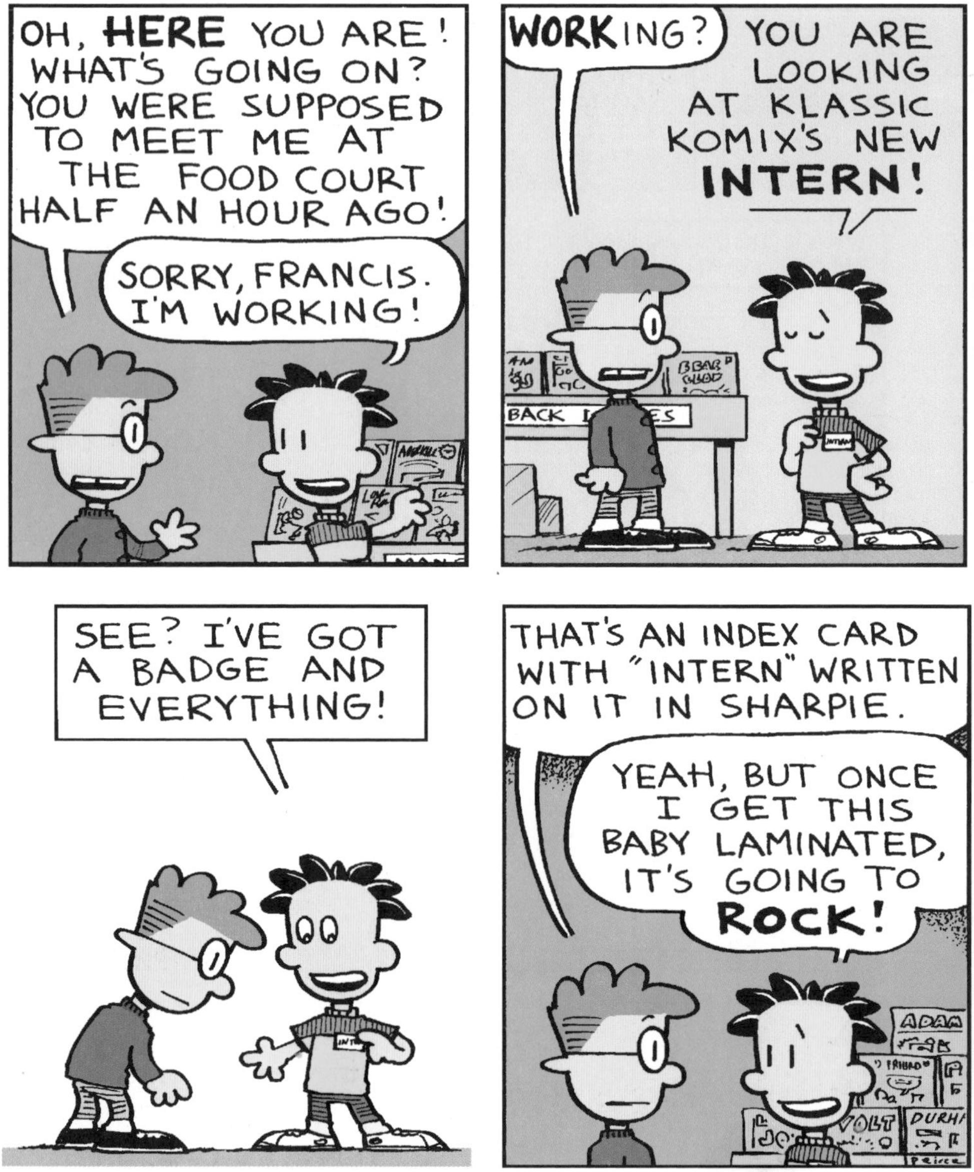

OH, HERE YOU ARE! WHAT'S GOING ON? YOU WERE SUPPOSED TO MEET ME AT THE FOOD COURT HALF AN HOUR AGO!
SORRY, FRANCIS. I'M WORKING!
WORKING?
YOU ARE LOOKING AT KLASSIC KOMIX'S NEW INTERN!
SEE? I'VE GOT A BADGE AND EVERYTHING!
THAT'S AN INDEX CARD WITH "INTERN" WRITTEN ON IT IN SHARPIE.
YEAH, BUT ONCE I GET THIS BABY LAMINATED, IT'S GOING TO ROCK!

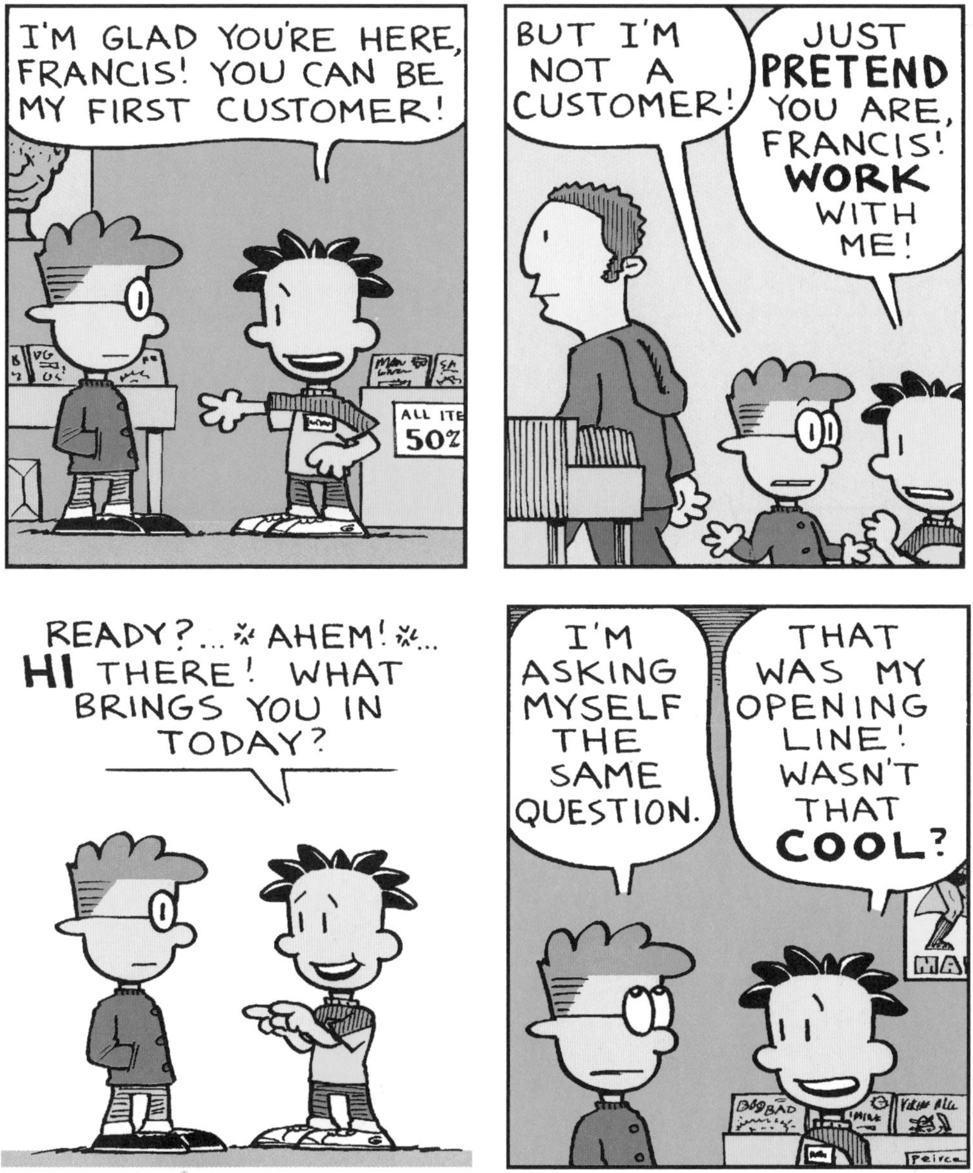

I'M GLAD YOU'RE HERE, FRANCIS! YOU CAN BE MY FIRST CUSTOMER!
ALL ITE
50%
BUT I'M NOT A CUSTOMER!
JUST **PRETEND** YOU ARE, FRANCIS! **WORK** WITH ME!
READY?... *AHEM!*... **HI** THERE! WHAT BRINGS YOU IN TODAY?
I'M ASKING MYSELF THE SAME QUESTION.
THAT WAS MY OPENING LINE! WASN'T THAT **COOL**?
Peirce

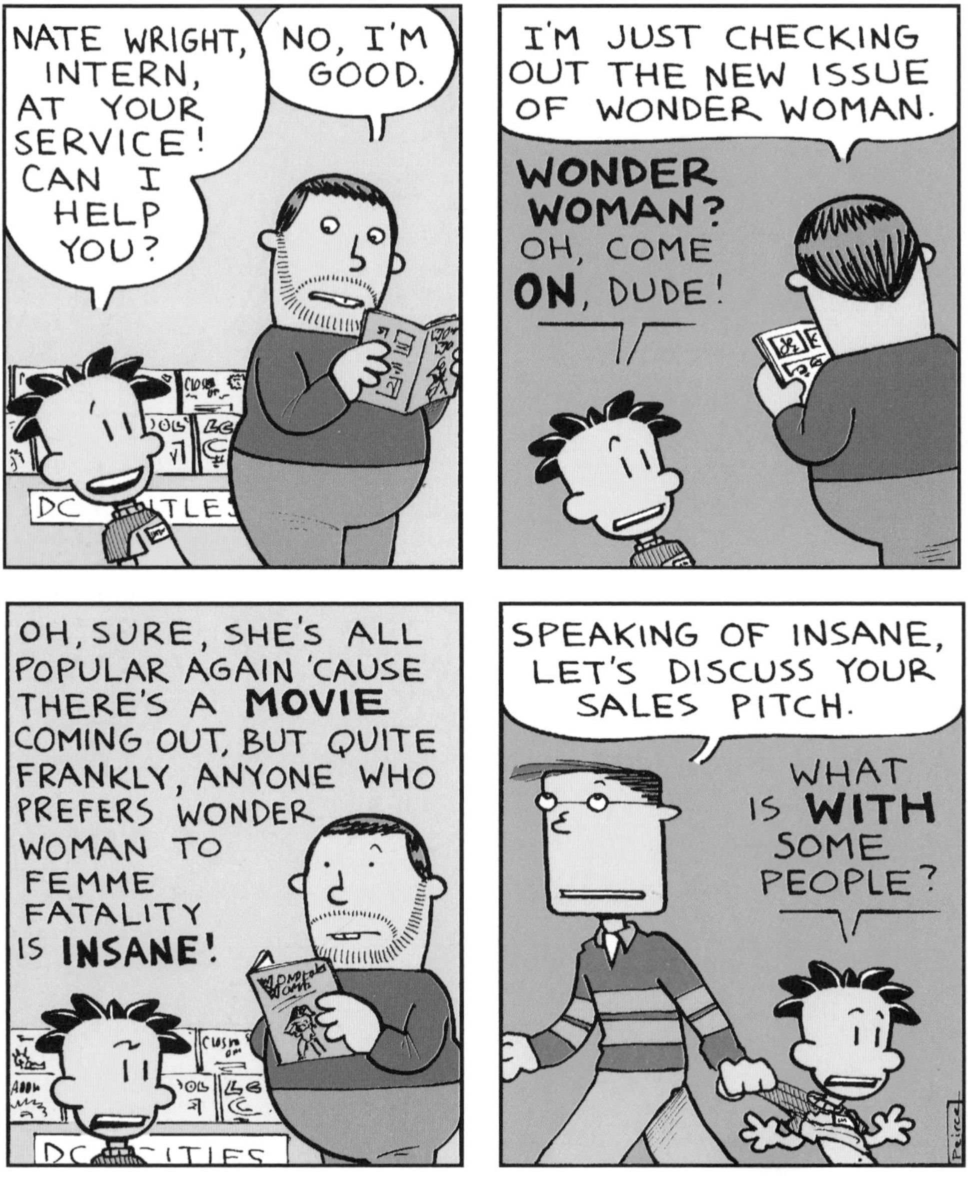
NATE WRIGHT, INTERN, AT YOUR SERVICE! CAN I HELP YOU?
NO, I'M GOOD.
DC TITLES
I'M JUST CHECKING OUT THE NEW ISSUE OF WONDER WOMAN.
WONDER WOMAN? OH, COME ON, DUDE!
OH, SURE, SHE'S ALL POPULAR AGAIN 'CAUSE THERE'S A MOVIE COMING OUT, BUT QUITE FRANKLY, ANYONE WHO PREFERS WONDER WOMAN TO FEMME FATALITY IS INSANE!
DC TITLES
SPEAKING OF INSANE, LET'S DISCUSS YOUR SALES PITCH.
WHAT IS WITH SOME PEOPLE?
Peirce

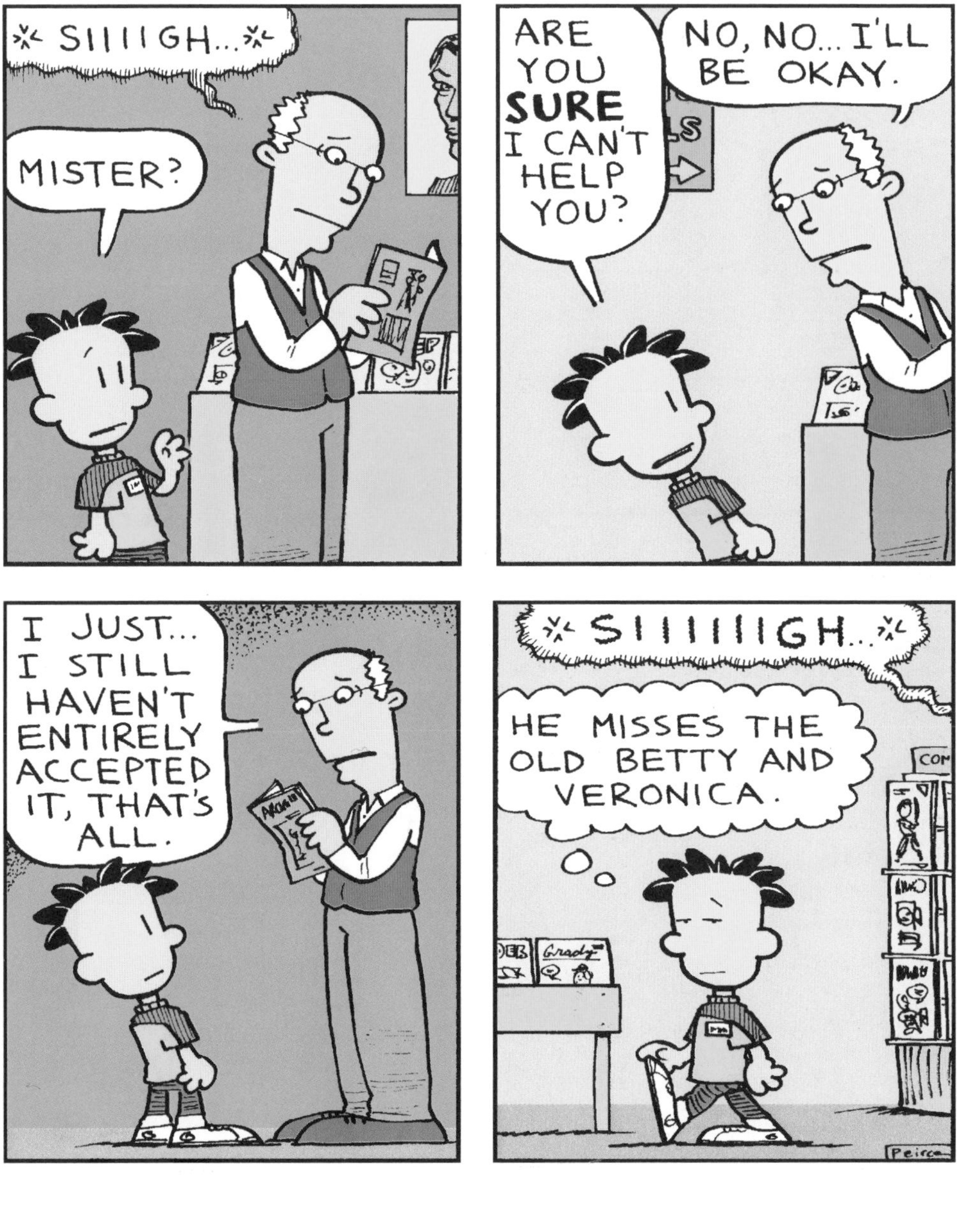
SIIIIGH...
MISTER?
ARE YOU SURE I CAN'T HELP YOU?
NO, NO... I'LL BE OKAY.
I JUST... I STILL HAVEN'T ENTIRELY ACCEPTED IT, THAT'S ALL.
SIIIIIIGH...
HE MISSES THE OLD BETTY AND VERONICA.
Peirce

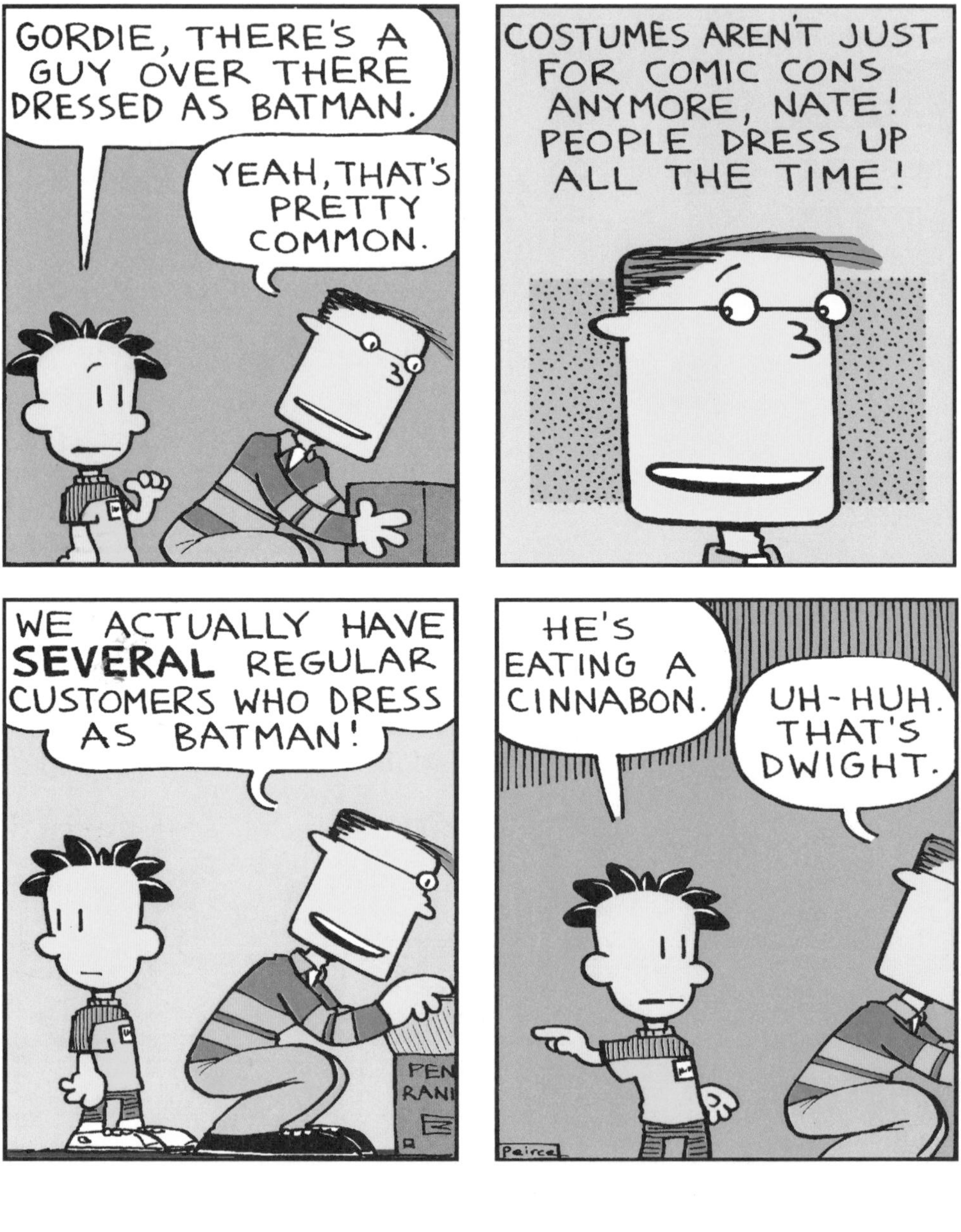

GORDIE, THERE'S A GUY OVER THERE DRESSED AS BATMAN.
YEAH, THAT'S PRETTY COMMON.
COSTUMES AREN'T JUST FOR COMIC CONS ANYMORE, NATE! PEOPLE DRESS UP ALL THE TIME!
WE ACTUALLY HAVE **SEVERAL** REGULAR CUSTOMERS WHO DRESS AS BATMAN!
HE'S EATING A CINNABON.
UH-HUH. THAT'S DWIGHT.
Peirce

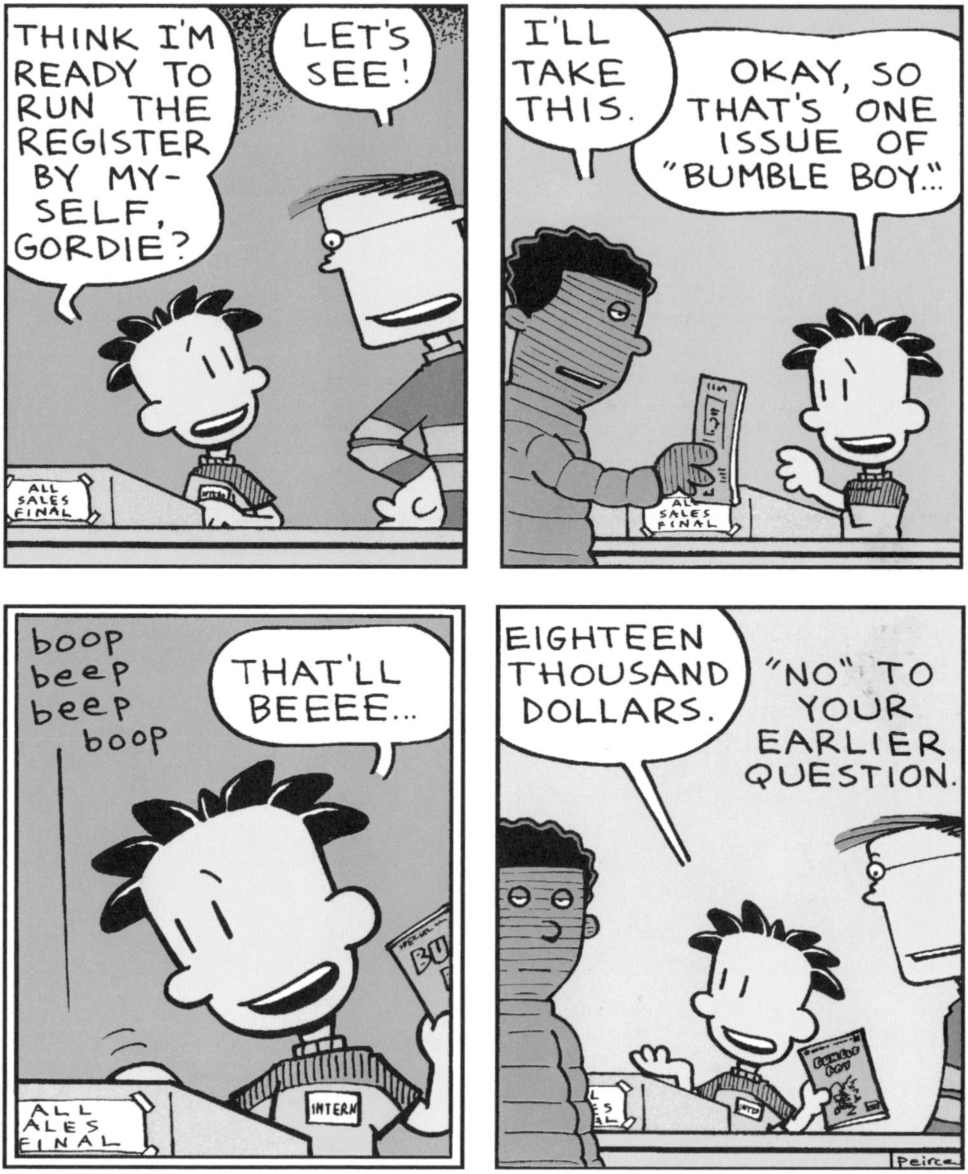

THINK I'M READY TO RUN THE REGISTER BY MY-SELF, GORDIE?
LET'S SEE!
ALL SALES FINAL
I'LL TAKE THIS.
OKAY, SO THAT'S ONE ISSUE OF "BUMBLE BOY."
boop beep beep boop
THAT'LL BEEEE...
INTERN
EIGHTEEN THOUSAND DOLLARS.
"NO" TO YOUR EARLIER QUESTION.
Peirce

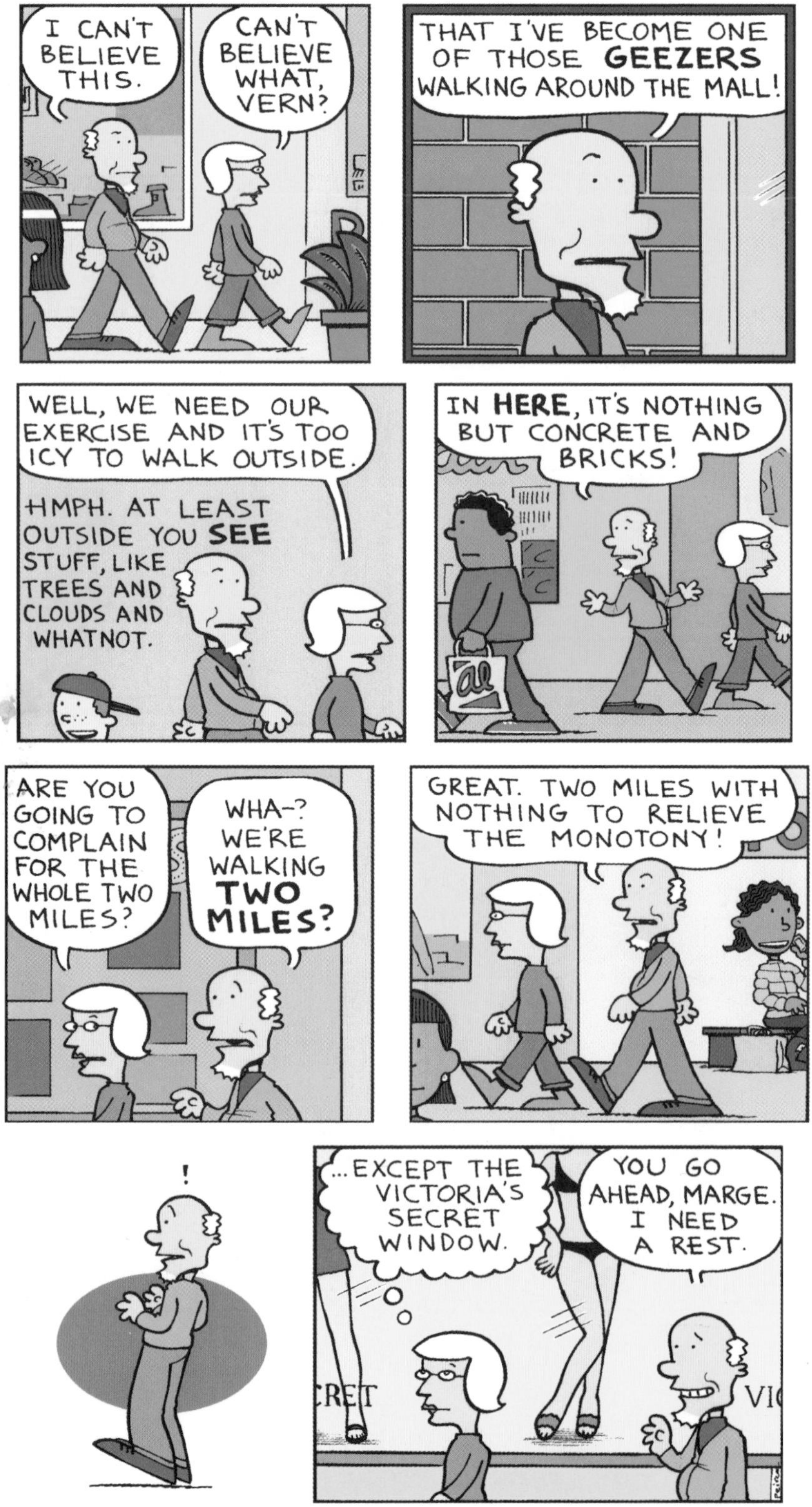
I CAN'T BELIEVE THIS.
CAN'T BELIEVE WHAT, VERN?
THAT I'VE BECOME ONE OF THOSE **GEEZERS** WALKING AROUND THE MALL!
WELL, WE NEED OUR EXERCISE AND IT'S TOO ICY TO WALK OUTSIDE.
HMPH. AT LEAST OUTSIDE YOU **SEE** STUFF, LIKE TREES AND CLOUDS AND WHATNOT.
IN **HERE**, IT'S NOTHING BUT CONCRETE AND BRICKS!
ARE YOU GOING TO COMPLAIN FOR THE WHOLE TWO MILES?
WHA-? WE'RE WALKING **TWO MILES?**
GREAT. TWO MILES WITH NOTHING TO RELIEVE THE MONOTONY!
!
...EXCEPT THE VICTORIA'S SECRET WINDOW.
YOU GO AHEAD, MARGE. I NEED A REST.
CRET
VI

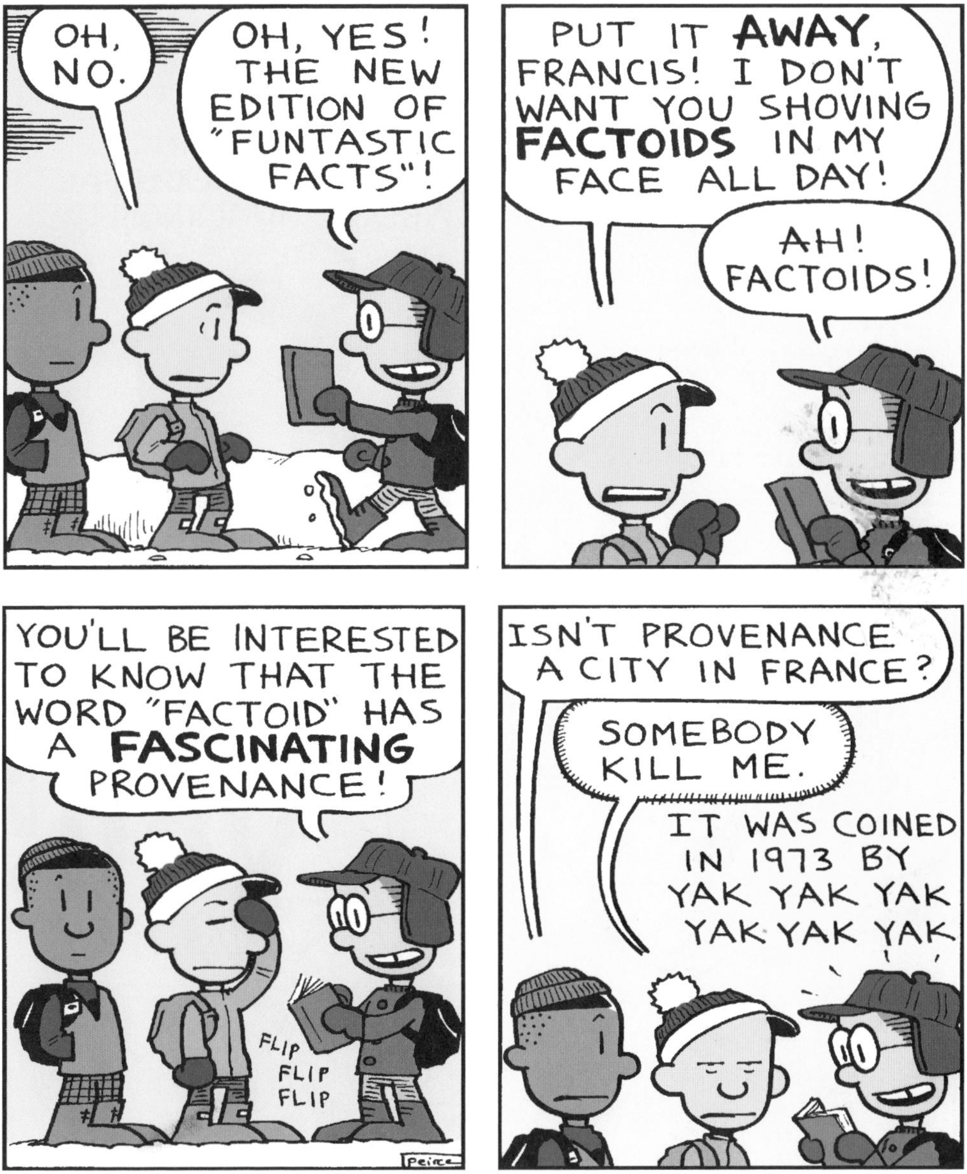
OH, NO.
OH, YES! THE NEW EDITION OF "FUNTASTIC FACTS"!
PUT IT **AWAY**, FRANCIS! I DON'T WANT YOU SHOVING **FACTOIDS** IN MY FACE ALL DAY!
AH! FACTOIDS!
YOU'LL BE INTERESTED TO KNOW THAT THE WORD "FACTOID" HAS A **FASCINATING** PROVENANCE!
FLIP FLIP FLIP
Peirce
ISN'T PROVENANCE A CITY IN FRANCE?
SOMEBODY KILL ME.
IT WAS COINED IN 1973 BY YAK YAK YAK YAK YAK YAK

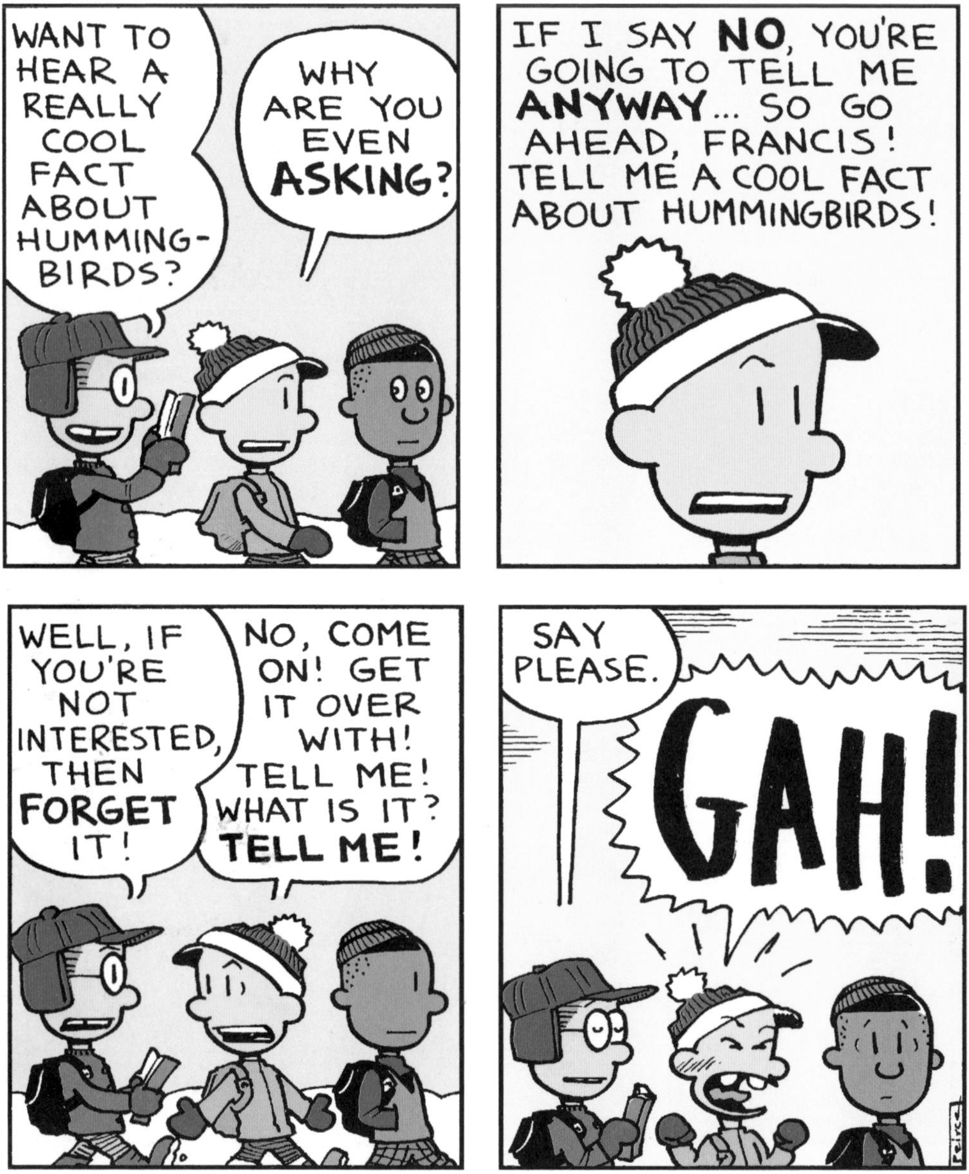
WANT TO HEAR A REALLY COOL FACT ABOUT HUMMING-BIRDS?
WHY ARE YOU EVEN ASKING?
IF I SAY NO, YOU'RE GOING TO TELL ME ANYWAY... SO GO AHEAD, FRANCIS! TELL ME A COOL FACT ABOUT HUMMINGBIRDS!
WELL, IF YOU'RE NOT INTERESTED, THEN FORGET IT!
NO, COME ON! GET IT OVER WITH! TELL ME! WHAT IS IT? TELL ME!
SAY PLEASE.
GAH!
Peirce

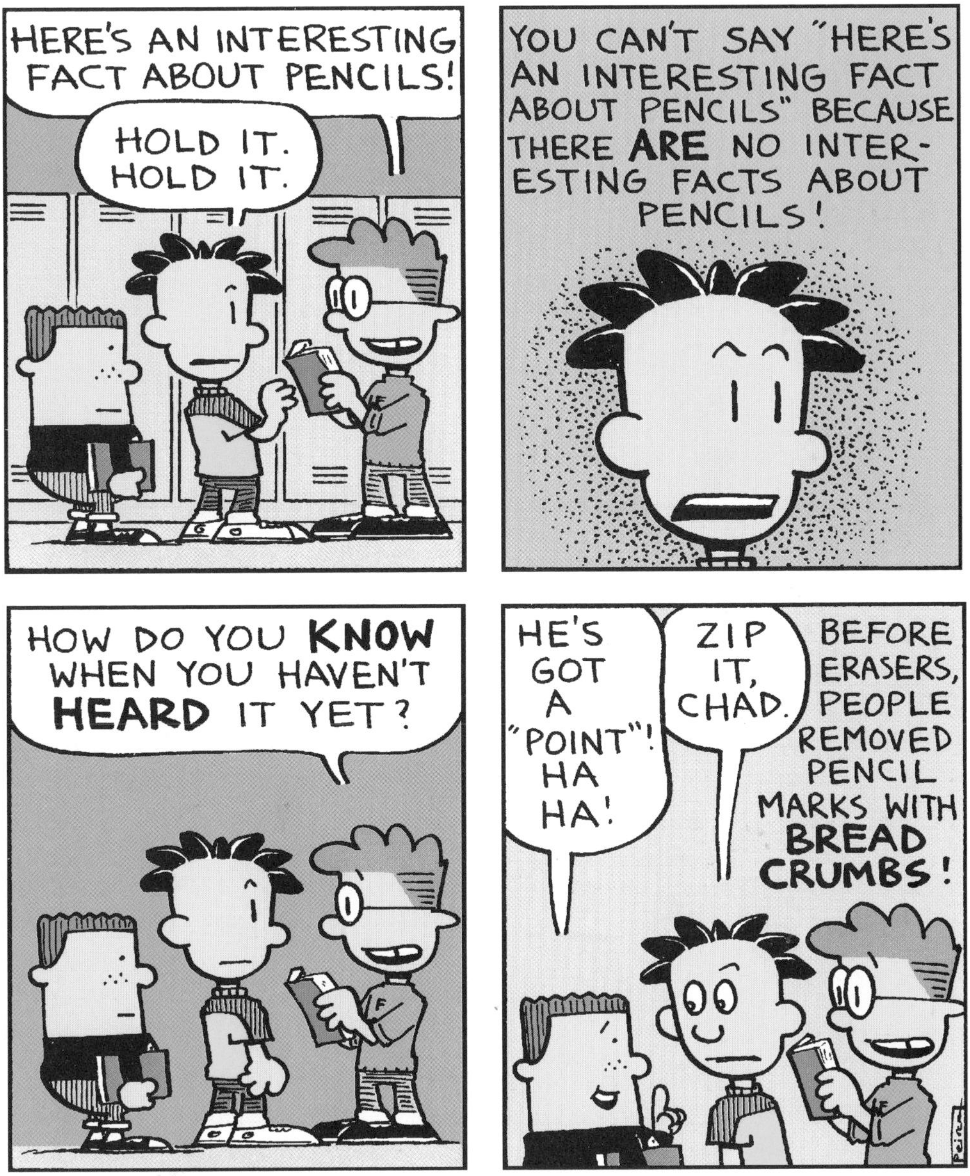
HERE'S AN INTERESTING FACT ABOUT PENCILS!
HOLD IT. HOLD IT.
YOU CAN'T SAY "HERE'S AN INTERESTING FACT ABOUT PENCILS" BECAUSE THERE **ARE** NO INTERESTING FACTS ABOUT PENCILS!
HOW DO YOU **KNOW** WHEN YOU HAVEN'T **HEARD** IT YET?
HE'S GOT A "POINT"! HA HA!
ZIP IT, CHAD.
BEFORE ERASERS, PEOPLE REMOVED PENCIL MARKS WITH **BREAD CRUMBS**!

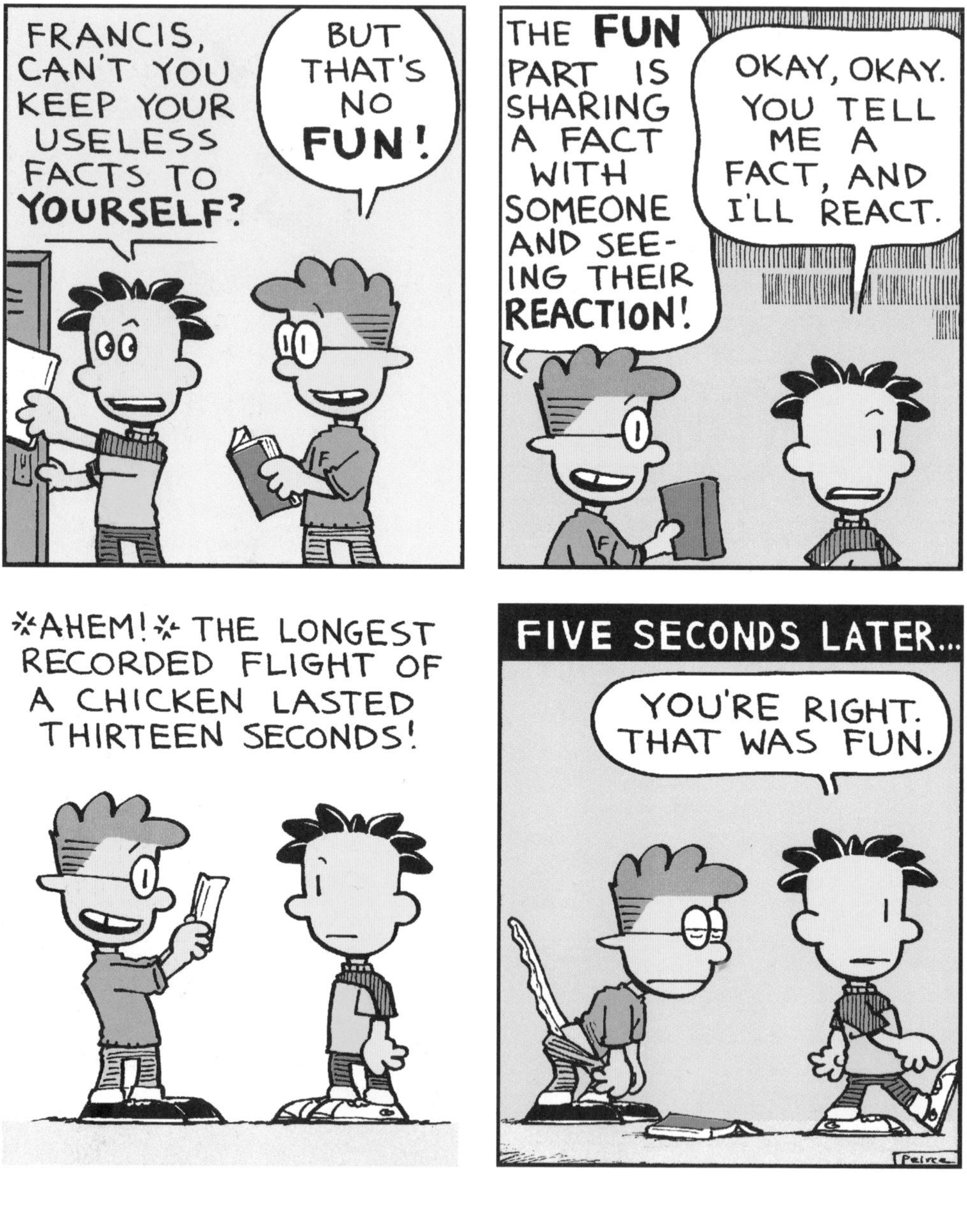
FRANCIS, CAN'T YOU KEEP YOUR USELESS FACTS TO **YOURSELF**?
BUT THAT'S NO **FUN**!
THE **FUN** PART IS SHARING A FACT WITH SOMEONE AND SEE-ING THEIR **REACTION**!
OKAY, OKAY. YOU TELL ME A FACT, AND I'LL REACT.
AHEM! THE LONGEST RECORDED FLIGHT OF A CHICKEN LASTED THIRTEEN SECONDS!
FIVE SECONDS LATER...
YOU'RE RIGHT. THAT WAS FUN.
Peirce

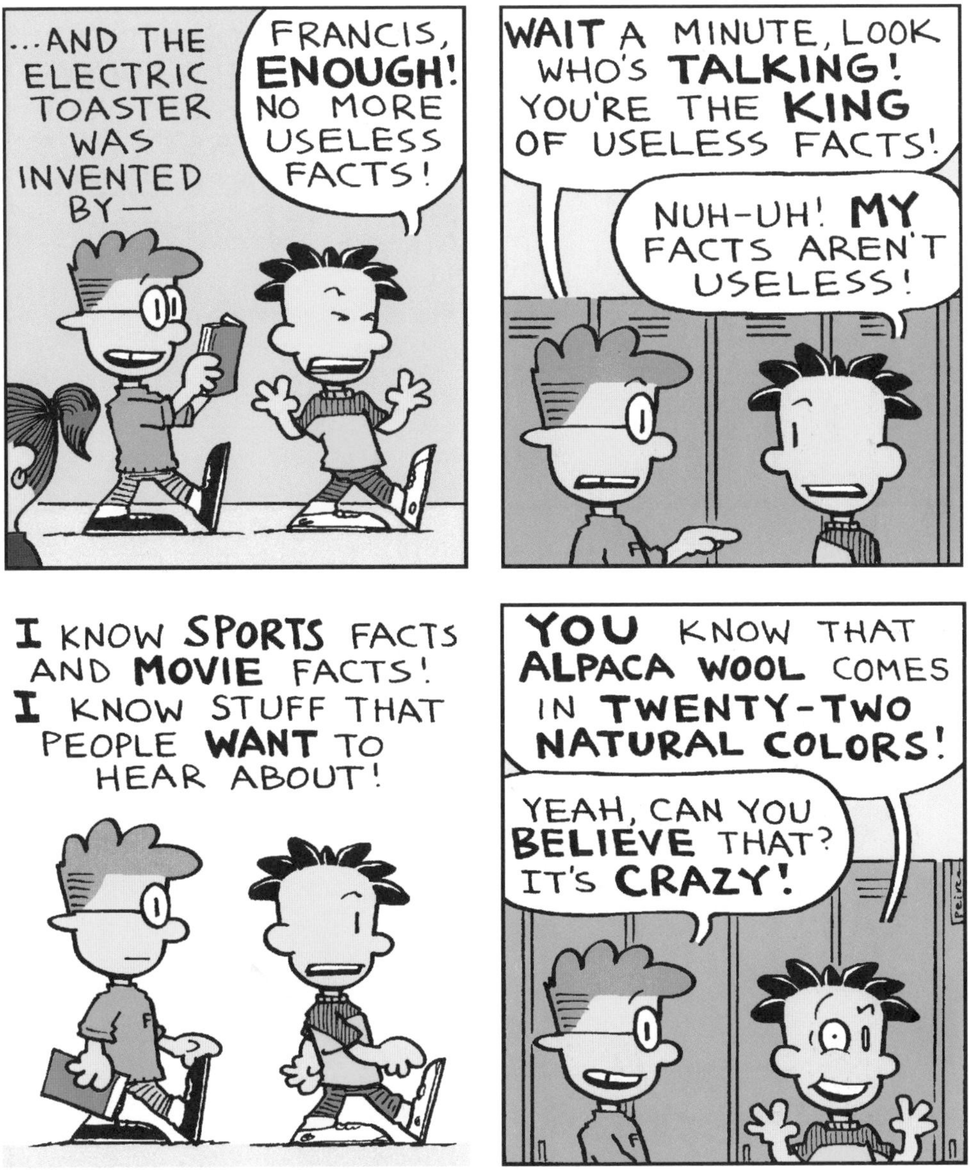

...AND THE ELECTRIC TOASTER WAS INVENTED BY—
FRANCIS, ENOUGH! NO MORE USELESS FACTS!
WAIT A MINUTE, LOOK WHO'S TALKING! YOU'RE THE KING OF USELESS FACTS!
NUH-UH! MY FACTS AREN'T USELESS!
I KNOW SPORTS FACTS AND MOVIE FACTS! I KNOW STUFF THAT PEOPLE WANT TO HEAR ABOUT!
YOU KNOW THAT ALPACA WOOL COMES IN TWENTY-TWO NATURAL COLORS!
YEAH, CAN YOU BELIEVE THAT? IT'S CRAZY!

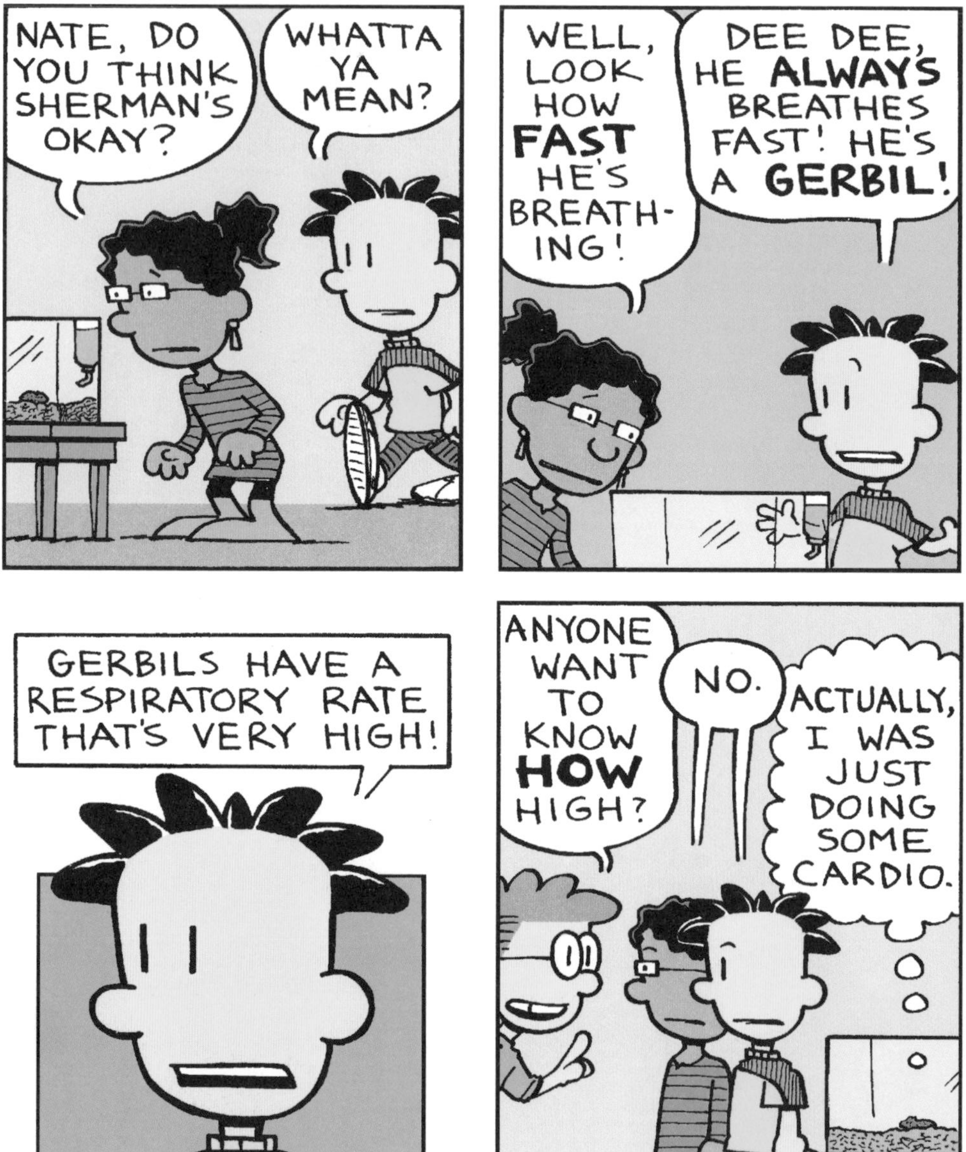
NATE, DO YOU THINK SHERMAN'S OKAY?
WHATTA YA MEAN?
WELL, LOOK HOW **FAST** HE'S BREATH-ING!
DEE DEE, HE **ALWAYS** BREATHES FAST! HE'S A **GERBIL**!
GERBILS HAVE A RESPIRATORY RATE THAT'S VERY HIGH!
ANYONE WANT TO KNOW **HOW** HIGH?
NO.
ACTUALLY, I WAS JUST DOING SOME CARDIO.

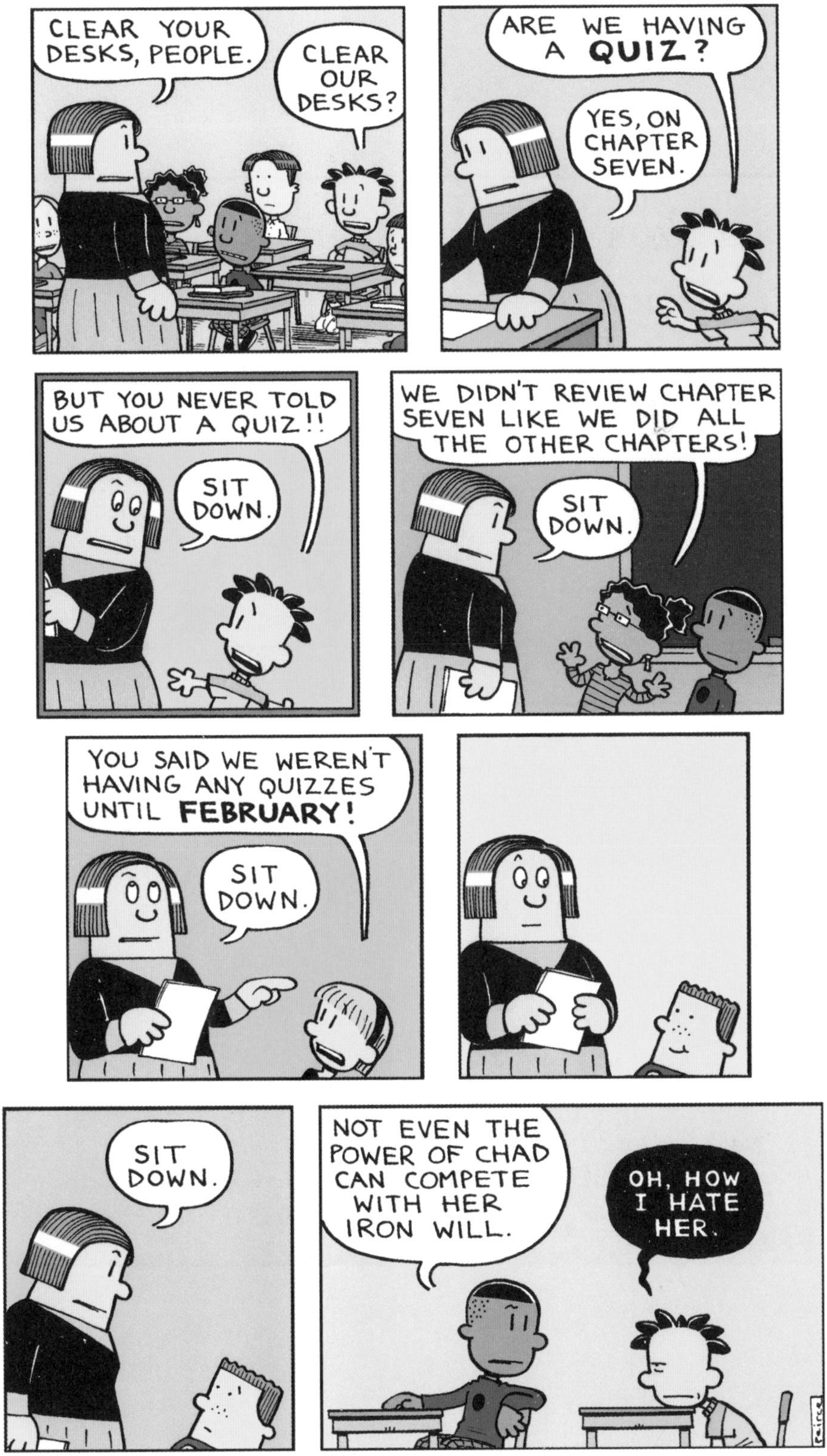
CLEAR YOUR DESKS, PEOPLE.
CLEAR OUR DESKS?
ARE WE HAVING A **QUIZ**?
YES, ON CHAPTER SEVEN.
BUT YOU NEVER TOLD US ABOUT A QUIZ!!
SIT DOWN.
WE DIDN'T REVIEW CHAPTER SEVEN LIKE WE DID ALL THE OTHER CHAPTERS!
SIT DOWN.
YOU SAID WE WEREN'T HAVING ANY QUIZZES UNTIL **FEBRUARY**!
SIT DOWN.
SIT DOWN.
NOT EVEN THE POWER OF CHAD CAN COMPETE WITH HER IRON WILL.
OH, HOW I HATE HER.
peirce

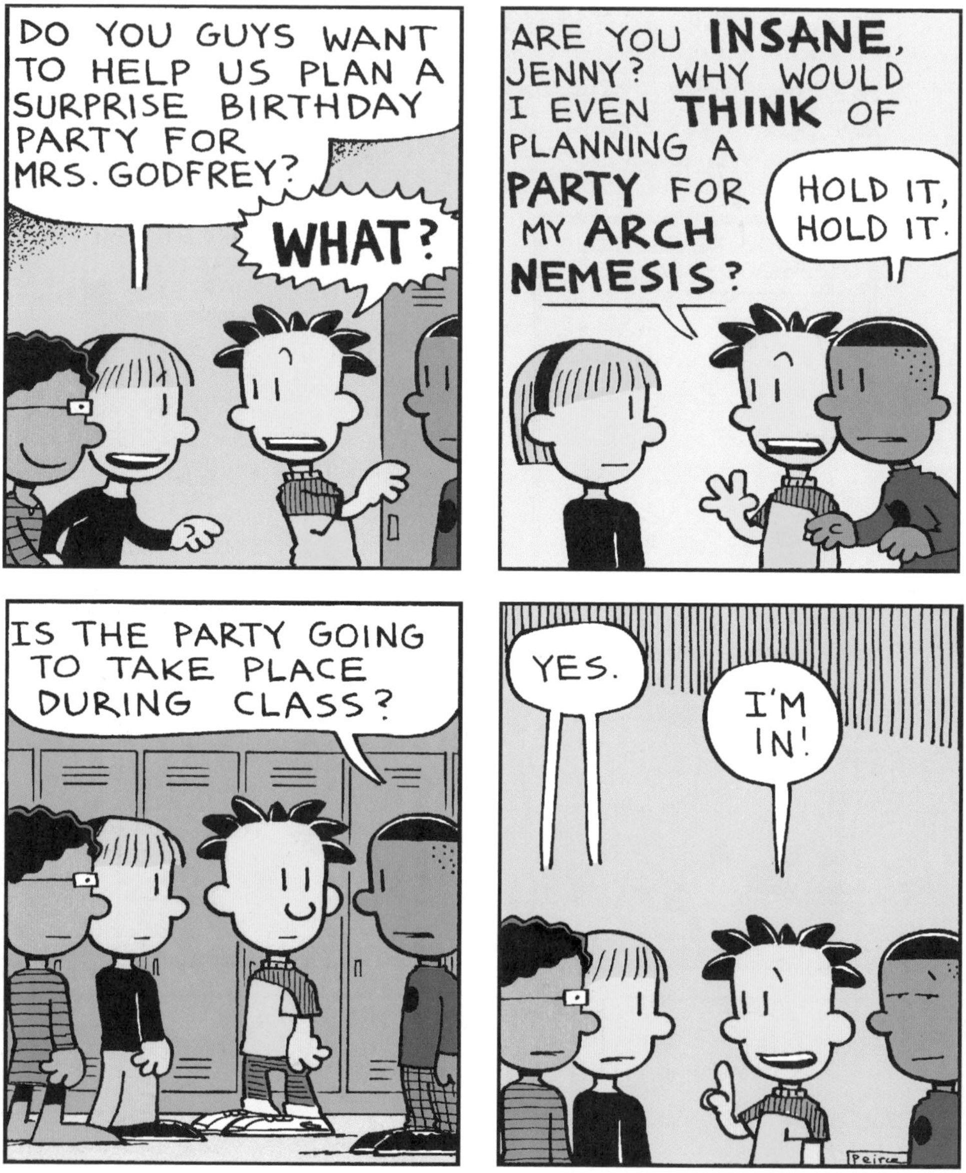
DO YOU GUYS WANT TO HELP US PLAN A SURPRISE BIRTHDAY PARTY FOR MRS. GODFREY?
WHAT?
ARE YOU INSANE, JENNY? WHY WOULD I EVEN THINK OF PLANNING A PARTY FOR MY ARCH NEMESIS?
HOLD IT, HOLD IT.
IS THE PARTY GOING TO TAKE PLACE DURING CLASS?
YES.
I'M IN!
Peirce

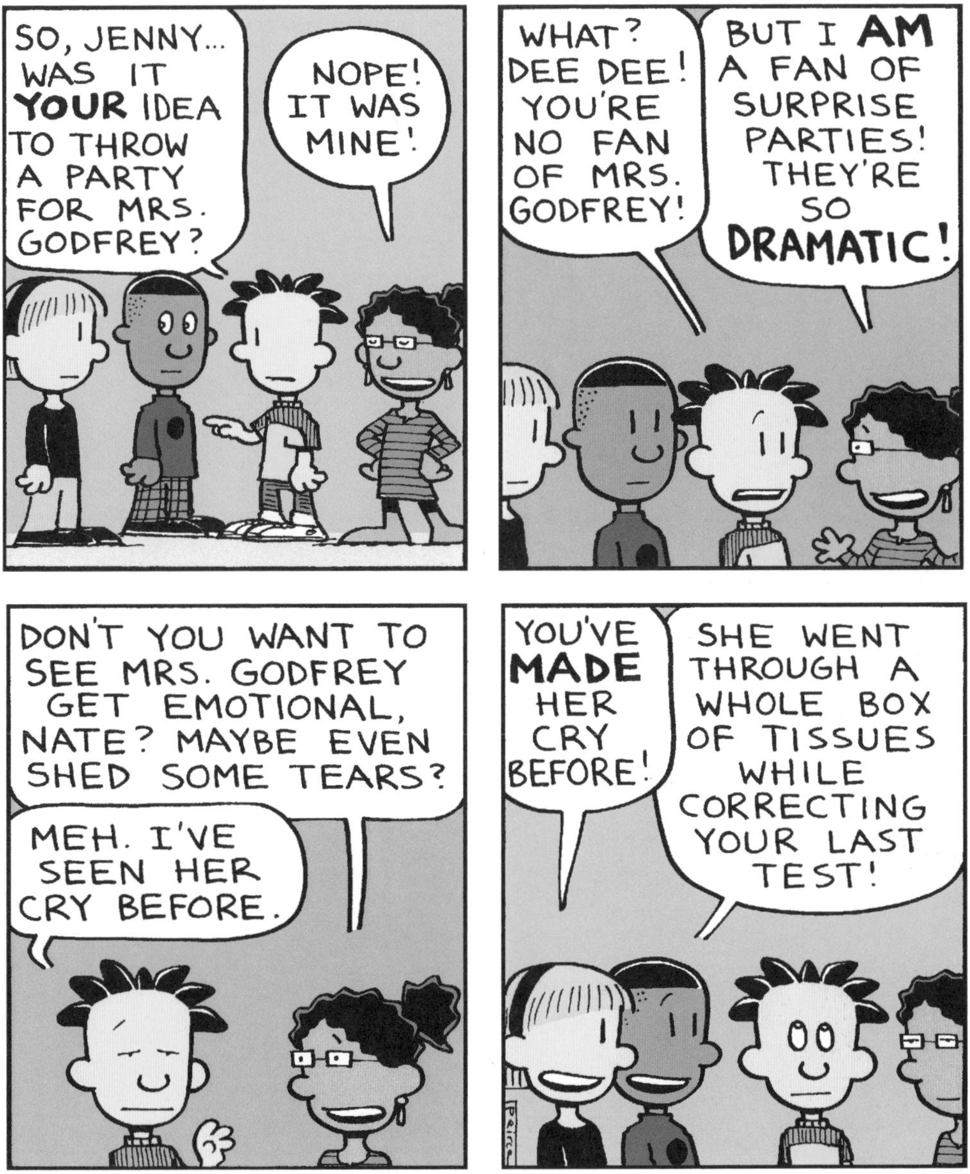
SO, JENNY... WAS IT YOUR IDEA TO THROW A PARTY FOR MRS. GODFREY?
NOPE! IT WAS MINE!
WHAT? DEE DEE! YOU'RE NO FAN OF MRS. GODFREY!
BUT I AM A FAN OF SURPRISE PARTIES! THEY'RE SO DRAMATIC!
DON'T YOU WANT TO SEE MRS. GODFREY GET EMOTIONAL, NATE? MAYBE EVEN SHED SOME TEARS?
MEH. I'VE SEEN HER CRY BEFORE.
YOU'VE MADE HER CRY BEFORE!
SHE WENT THROUGH A WHOLE BOX OF TISSUES WHILE CORRECTING YOUR LAST TEST!
PEIRCE

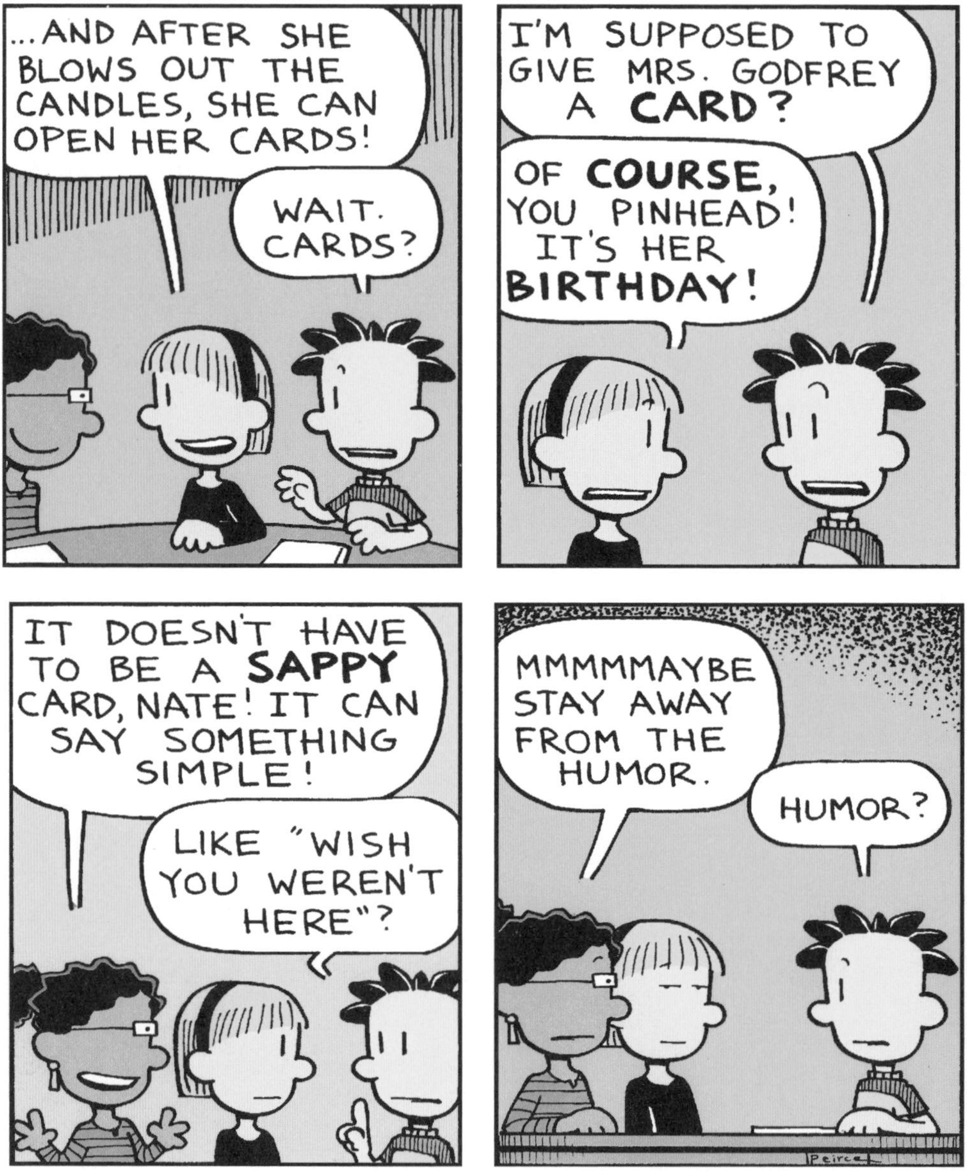
...AND AFTER SHE BLOWS OUT THE CANDLES, SHE CAN OPEN HER CARDS!
WAIT. CARDS?
I'M SUPPOSED TO GIVE MRS. GODFREY A **CARD**?
OF **COURSE**, YOU PINHEAD! IT'S HER **BIRTHDAY**!
IT DOESN'T HAVE TO BE A **SAPPY** CARD, NATE! IT CAN SAY SOMETHING SIMPLE!
LIKE "WISH YOU WEREN'T HERE"?
MMMMMAYBE STAY AWAY FROM THE HUMOR.
HUMOR?
Peirce

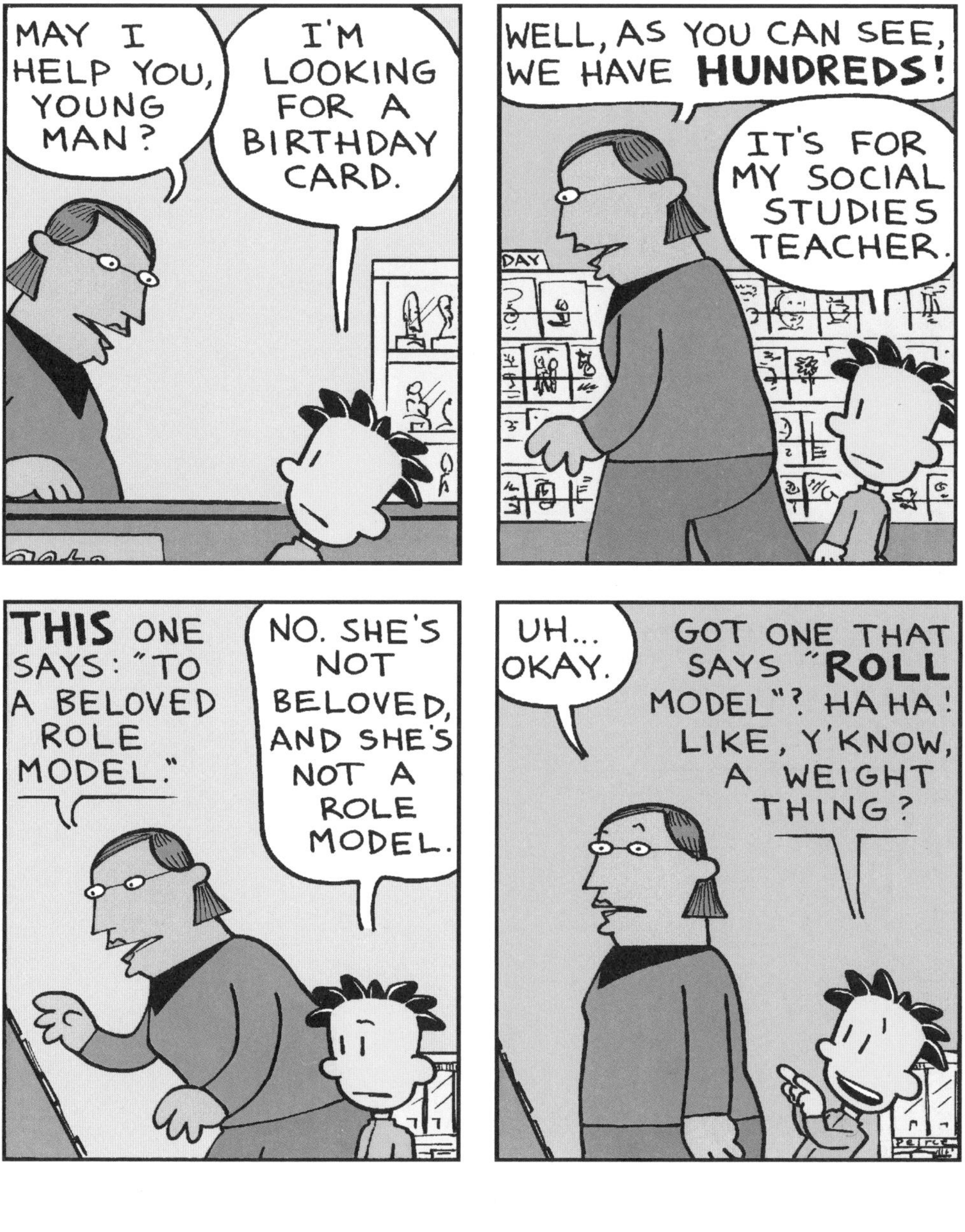
MAY I HELP YOU, YOUNG MAN?
I'M LOOKING FOR A BIRTHDAY CARD.
WELL, AS YOU CAN SEE, WE HAVE **HUNDREDS**!
IT'S FOR MY SOCIAL STUDIES TEACHER.
THIS ONE SAYS: "TO A BELOVED ROLE MODEL."
NO. SHE'S NOT BELOVED, AND SHE'S NOT A ROLE MODEL.
UH... OKAY.
GOT ONE THAT SAYS "**ROLL** MODEL"? HA HA! LIKE, Y'KNOW, A WEIGHT THING?

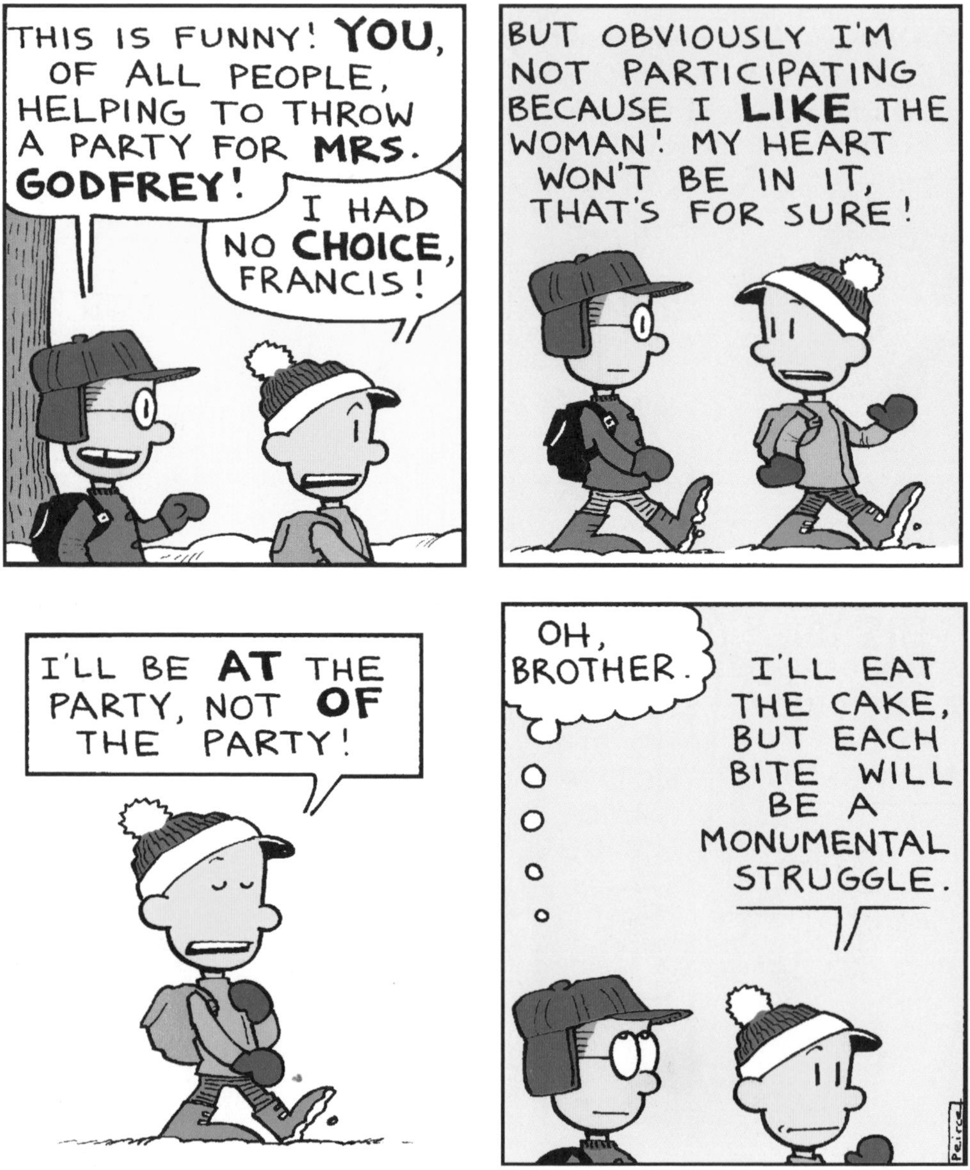
THIS IS FUNNY! YOU, OF ALL PEOPLE, HELPING TO THROW A PARTY FOR MRS. GODFREY!
I HAD NO CHOICE, FRANCIS!
BUT OBVIOUSLY I'M NOT PARTICIPATING BECAUSE I LIKE THE WOMAN! MY HEART WON'T BE IN IT, THAT'S FOR SURE!
I'LL BE AT THE PARTY, NOT OF THE PARTY!
I'LL EAT THE CAKE, BUT EACH BITE WILL BE A MONUMENTAL STRUGGLE.
OH, BROTHER.
Peirce

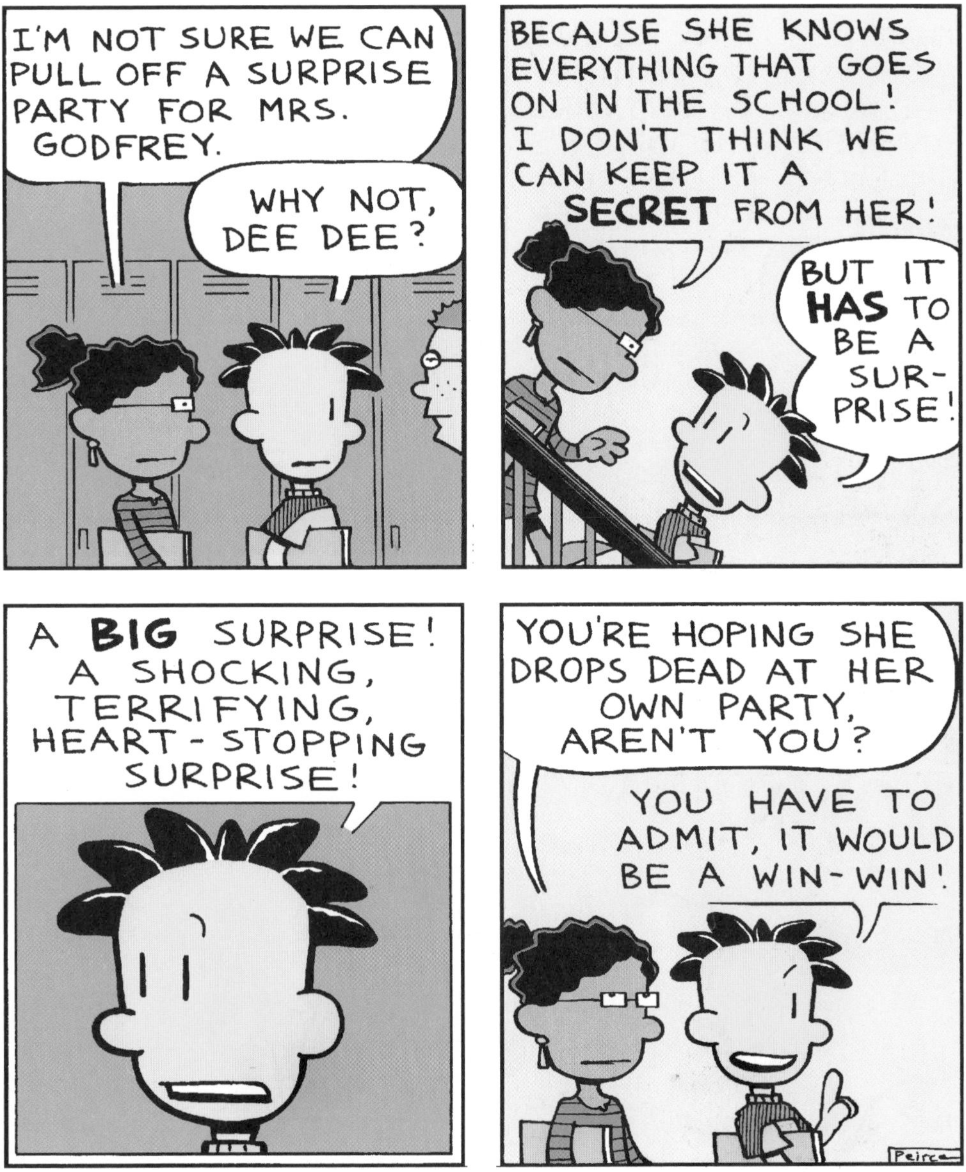
I'M NOT SURE WE CAN PULL OFF A SURPRISE PARTY FOR MRS. GODFREY.
WHY NOT, DEE DEE?
BECAUSE SHE KNOWS EVERYTHING THAT GOES ON IN THE SCHOOL! I DON'T THINK WE CAN KEEP IT A **SECRET** FROM HER!
BUT IT **HAS** TO BE A SURPRISE!
A **BIG** SURPRISE! A SHOCKING, TERRIFYING, HEART-STOPPING SURPRISE!
YOU'RE HOPING SHE DROPS DEAD AT HER OWN PARTY, AREN'T YOU?
YOU HAVE TO ADMIT, IT WOULD BE A WIN-WIN!
Peirce

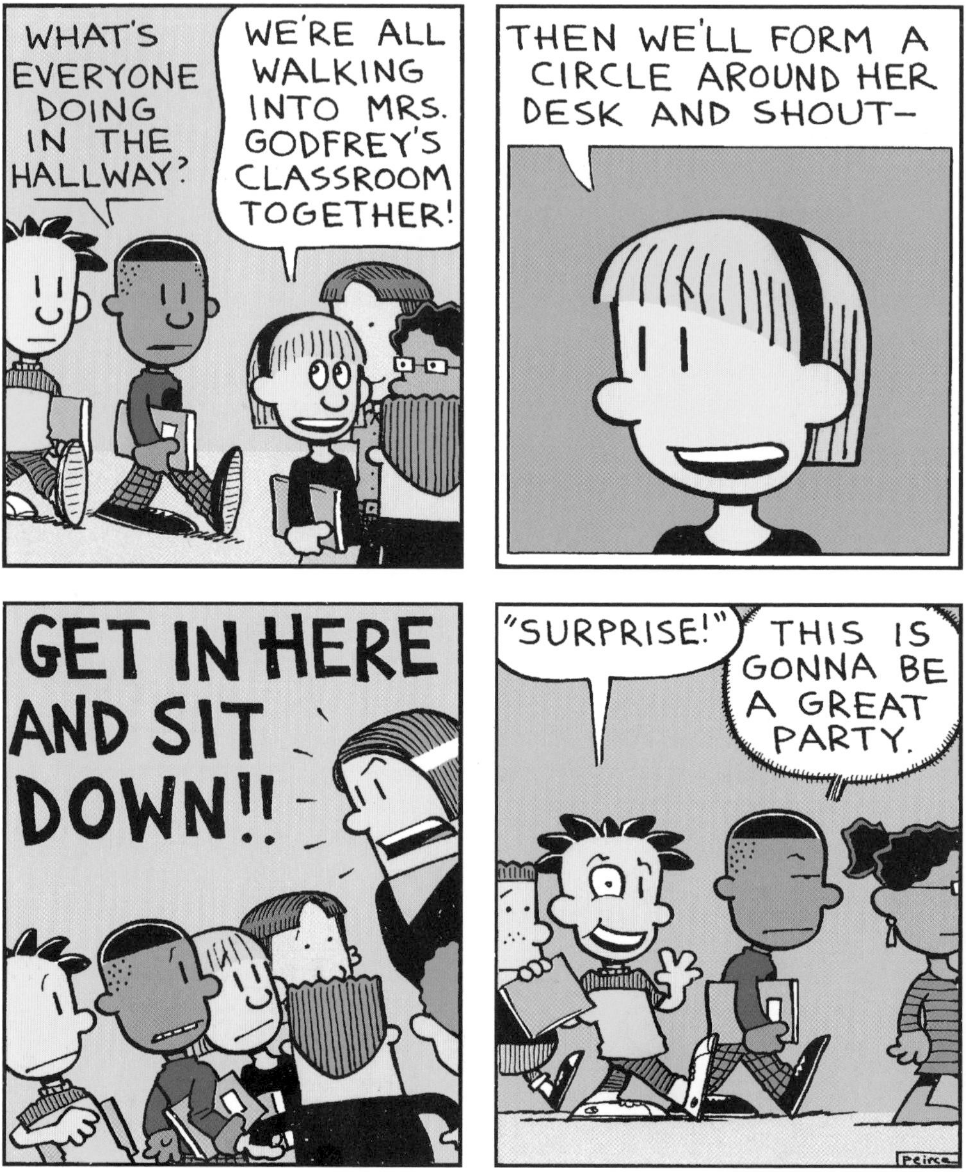
WHAT'S EVERYONE DOING IN THE HALLWAY?
WE'RE ALL WALKING INTO MRS. GODFREY'S CLASSROOM TOGETHER!
THEN WE'LL FORM A CIRCLE AROUND HER DESK AND SHOUT–
GET IN HERE AND SIT DOWN!!
"SURPRISE!"
THIS IS GONNA BE A GREAT PARTY.
Peirce

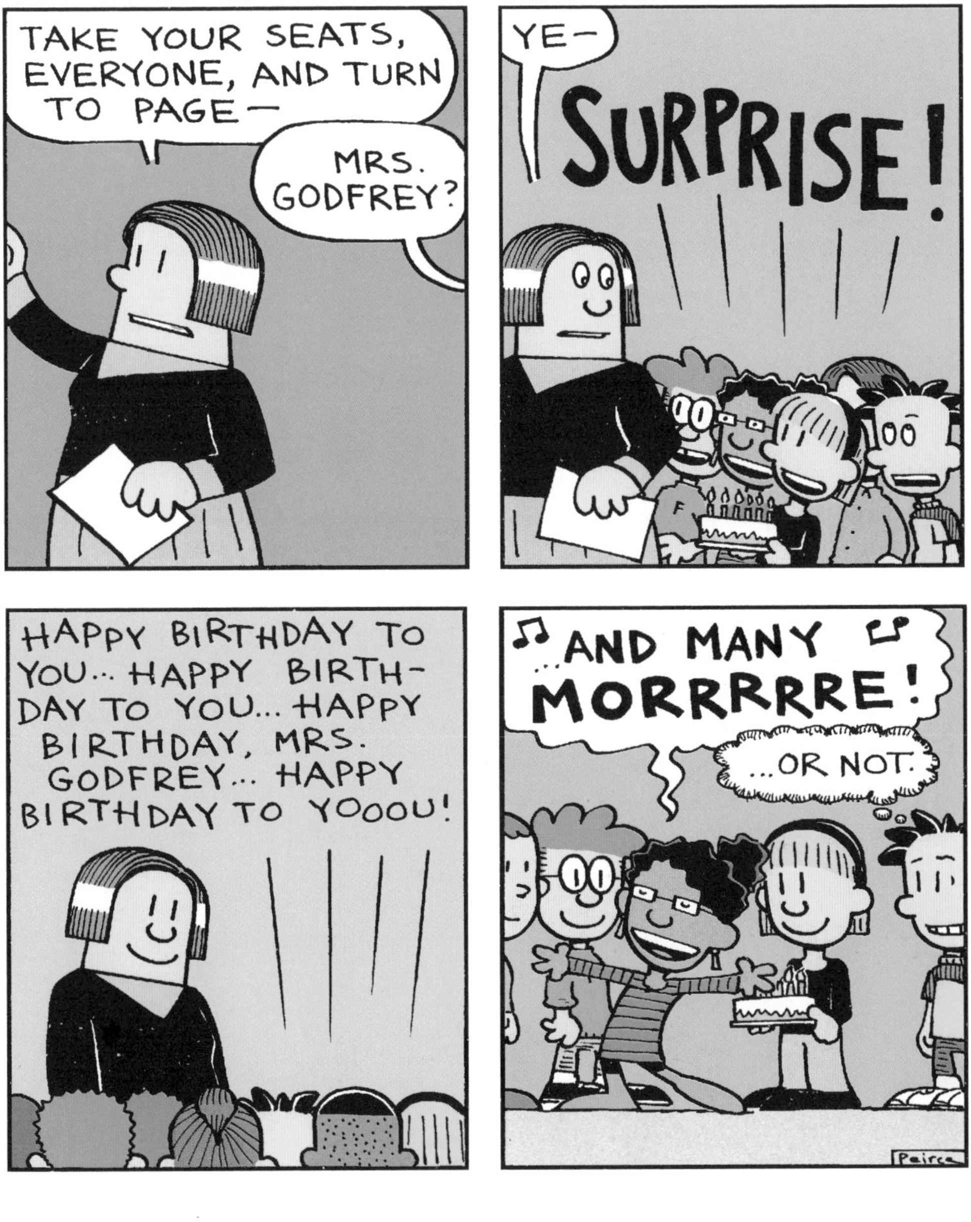
TAKE YOUR SEATS, EVERYONE, AND TURN TO PAGE—
MRS. GODFREY?
YE—
SURPRISE!
HAPPY BIRTHDAY TO YOU... HAPPY BIRTHDAY TO YOU... HAPPY BIRTHDAY, MRS. GODFREY... HAPPY BIRTHDAY TO YOOOU!
...AND MANY MORRRRRE!
...OR NOT.
Peirce

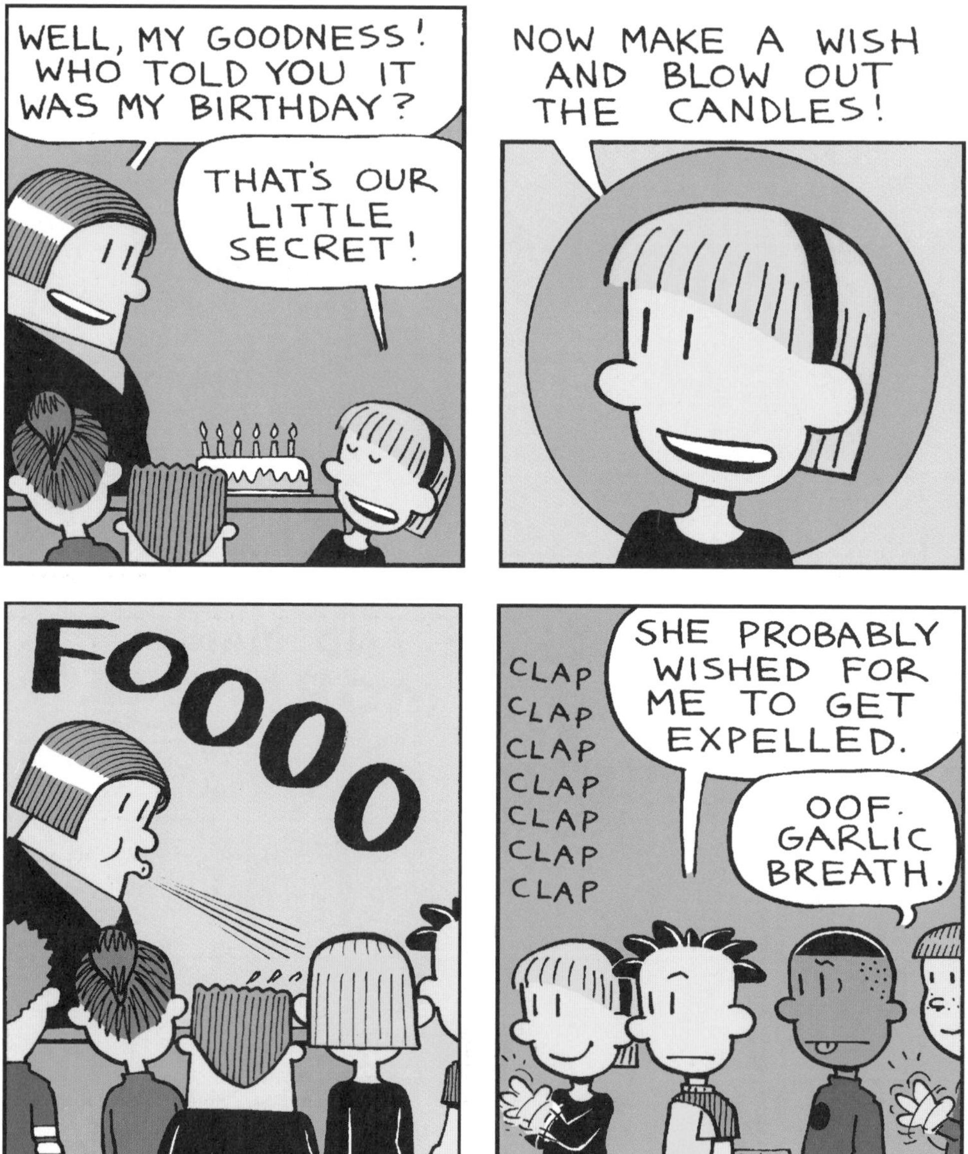

WELL, MY GOODNESS! WHO TOLD YOU IT WAS MY BIRTHDAY?
THAT'S OUR LITTLE SECRET!
NOW MAKE A WISH AND BLOW OUT THE CANDLES!
FOOOO
CLAP CLAP CLAP CLAP CLAP CLAP CLAP
SHE PROBABLY WISHED FOR ME TO GET EXPELLED.
OOF. GARLIC BREATH.
Peirce

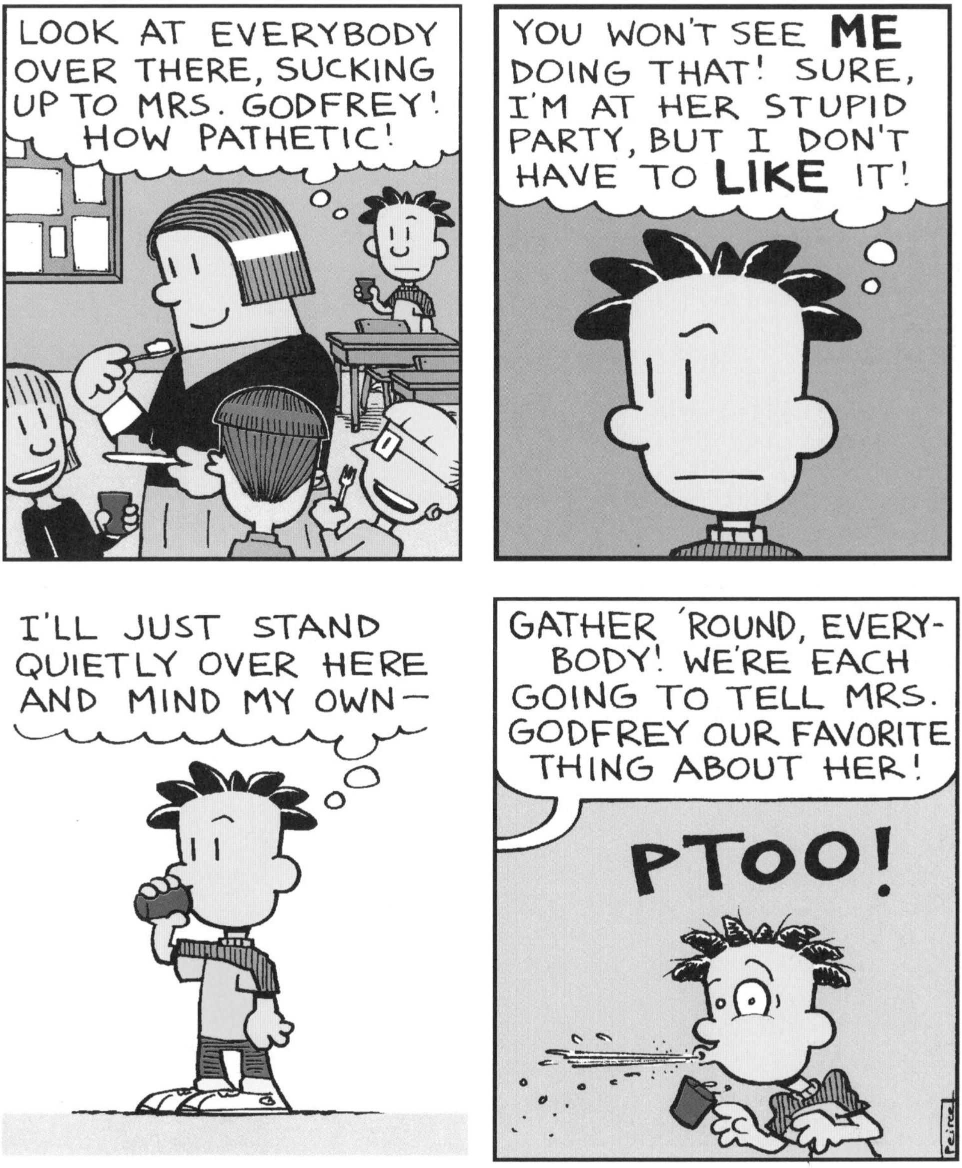
LOOK AT EVERYBODY OVER THERE, SUCKING UP TO MRS. GODFREY! HOW PATHETIC!
YOU WON'T SEE **ME** DOING THAT! SURE, I'M AT HER STUPID PARTY, BUT I DON'T HAVE TO **LIKE** IT!
I'LL JUST STAND QUIETLY OVER HERE AND MIND MY OWN—
GATHER 'ROUND, EVERYBODY! WE'RE EACH GOING TO TELL MRS. GODFREY OUR FAVORITE THING ABOUT HER!
PTOO!
Peirce

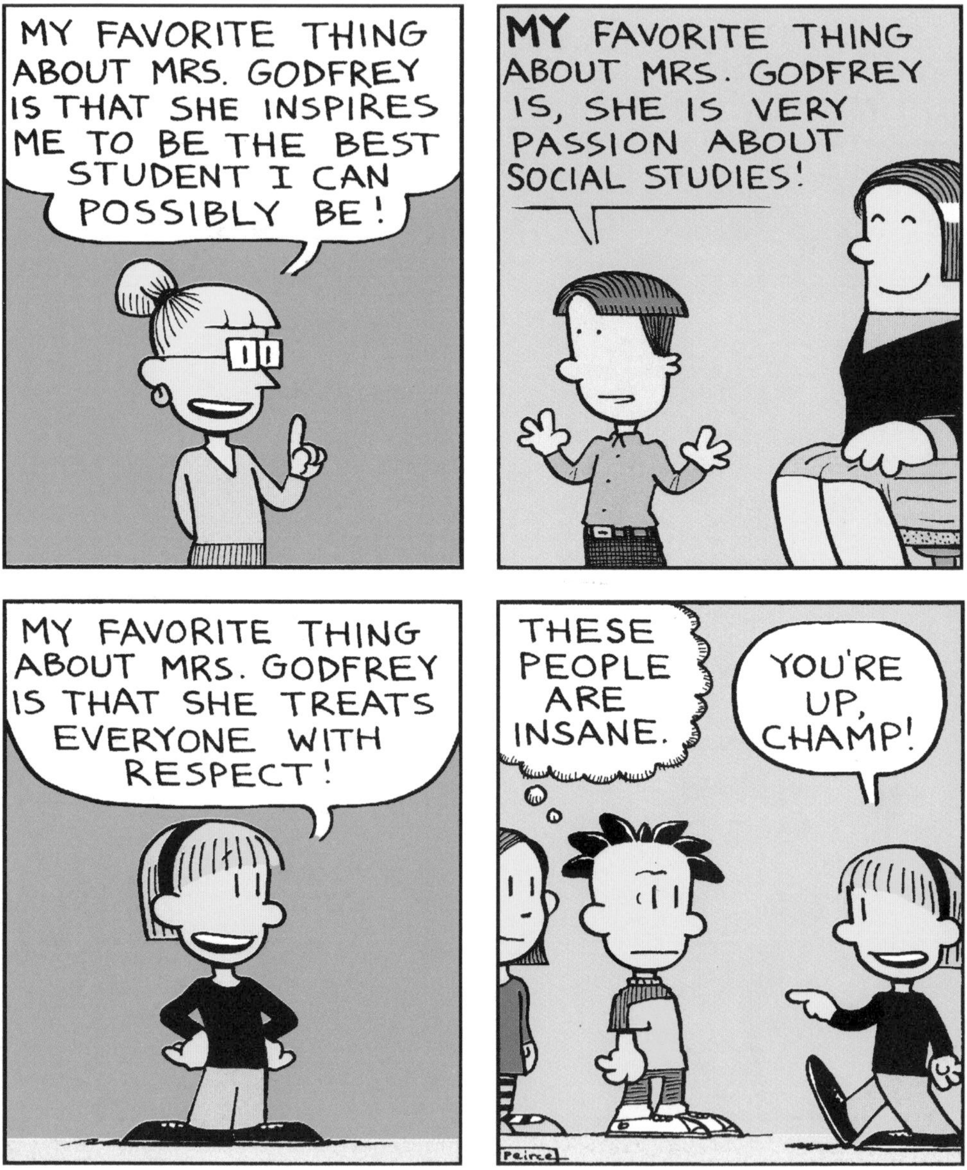
MY FAVORITE THING ABOUT MRS. GODFREY IS THAT SHE INSPIRES ME TO BE THE BEST STUDENT I CAN POSSIBLY BE!
MY FAVORITE THING ABOUT MRS. GODFREY IS, SHE IS VERY PASSION ABOUT SOCIAL STUDIES!
MY FAVORITE THING ABOUT MRS. GODFREY IS THAT SHE TREATS EVERYONE WITH RESPECT!
THESE PEOPLE ARE INSANE.
YOU'RE UP, CHAMP!
Peirce

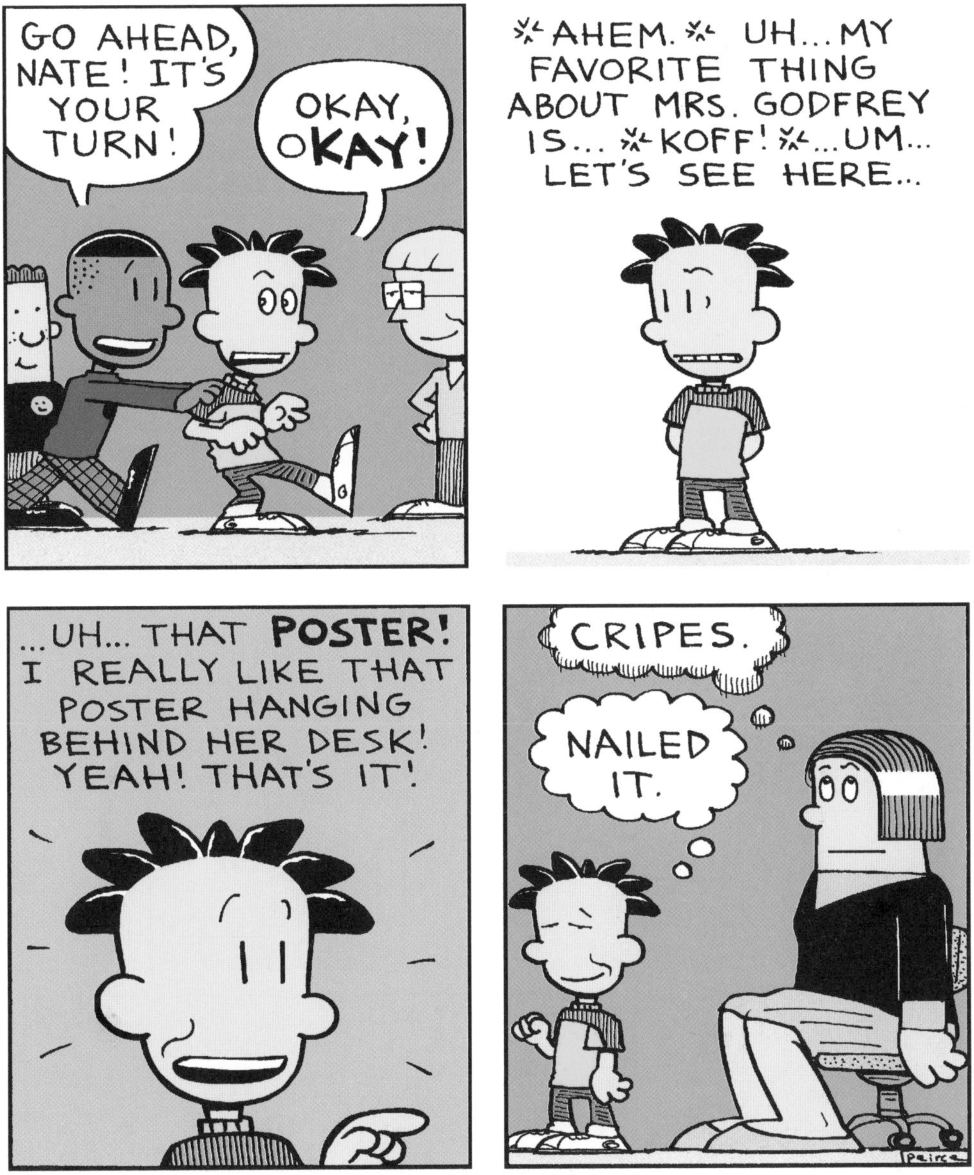
GO AHEAD, NATE! IT'S YOUR TURN!
OKAY, OKAY!
AHEM. UH... MY FAVORITE THING ABOUT MRS. GODFREY IS... KOFF! ...UM... LET'S SEE HERE...
...UH... THAT POSTER! I REALLY LIKE THAT POSTER HANGING BEHIND HER DESK! YEAH! THAT'S IT!
CRIPES.
NAILED IT.
Peirce

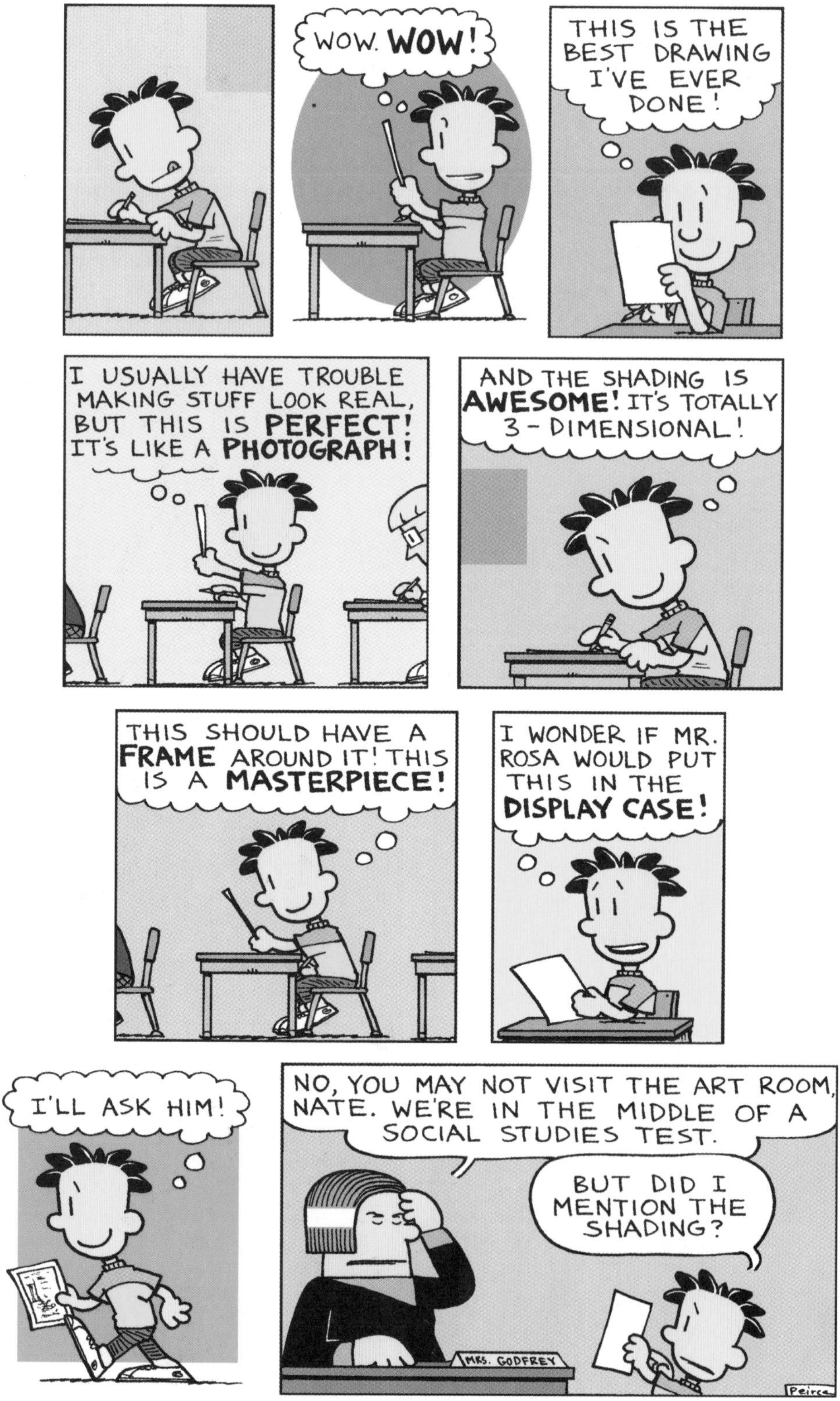
WOW. WOW!
THIS IS THE BEST DRAWING I'VE EVER DONE!
I USUALLY HAVE TROUBLE MAKING STUFF LOOK REAL, BUT THIS IS PERFECT! IT'S LIKE A PHOTOGRAPH!
AND THE SHADING IS AWESOME! IT'S TOTALLY 3-DIMENSIONAL!
THIS SHOULD HAVE A FRAME AROUND IT! THIS IS A MASTERPIECE!
I WONDER IF MR. ROSA WOULD PUT THIS IN THE DISPLAY CASE!
I'LL ASK HIM!
NO, YOU MAY NOT VISIT THE ART ROOM, NATE. WE'RE IN THE MIDDLE OF A SOCIAL STUDIES TEST.
BUT DID I MENTION THE SHADING?
MRS. GODFREY
Peirce

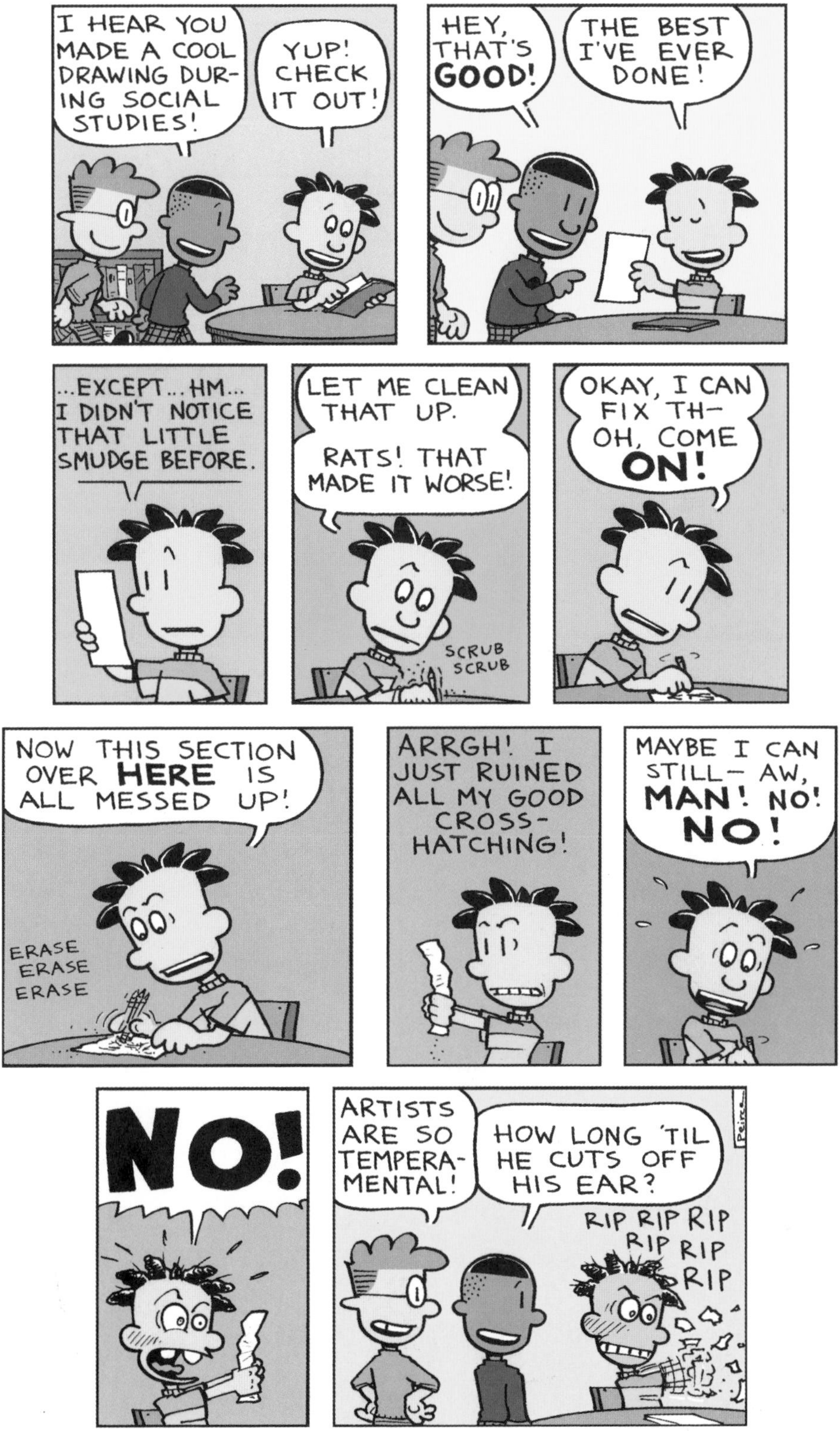
I HEAR YOU MADE A COOL DRAWING DURING SOCIAL STUDIES!
YUP! CHECK IT OUT!
HEY, THAT'S **GOOD**!
THE BEST I'VE EVER DONE!
...EXCEPT...HM... I DIDN'T NOTICE THAT LITTLE SMUDGE BEFORE.
LET ME CLEAN THAT UP.
RATS! THAT MADE IT WORSE!
SCRUB SCRUB
OKAY, I CAN FIX TH– OH, COME **ON**!
NOW THIS SECTION OVER **HERE** IS ALL MESSED UP!
ERASE ERASE ERASE
ARRGH! I JUST RUINED ALL MY GOOD CROSS-HATCHING!
MAYBE I CAN STILL– AW, **MAN**! NO! **NO**!
NO!
ARTISTS ARE SO TEMPERAMENTAL!
HOW LONG 'TIL HE CUTS OFF HIS EAR?
RIP RIP RIP RIP RIP RIP
Peirce

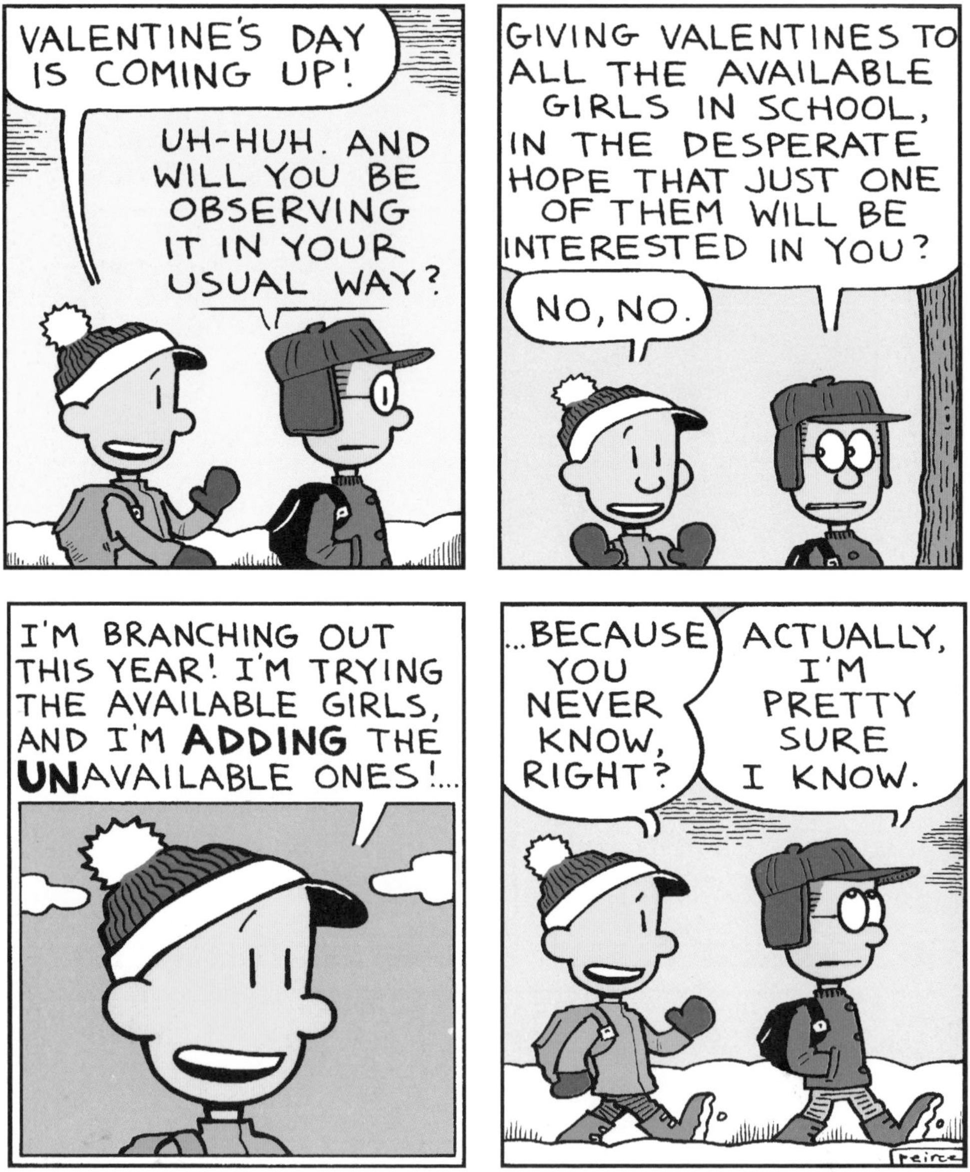
VALENTINE'S DAY IS COMING UP!
UH-HUH. AND WILL YOU BE OBSERVING IT IN YOUR USUAL WAY?
GIVING VALENTINES TO ALL THE AVAILABLE GIRLS IN SCHOOL, IN THE DESPERATE HOPE THAT JUST ONE OF THEM WILL BE INTERESTED IN YOU?
NO, NO.
I'M BRANCHING OUT THIS YEAR! I'M TRYING THE AVAILABLE GIRLS, AND I'M ADDING THE UNAVAILABLE ONES!...
...BECAUSE YOU NEVER KNOW, RIGHT?
ACTUALLY, I'M PRETTY SURE I KNOW.
peirce

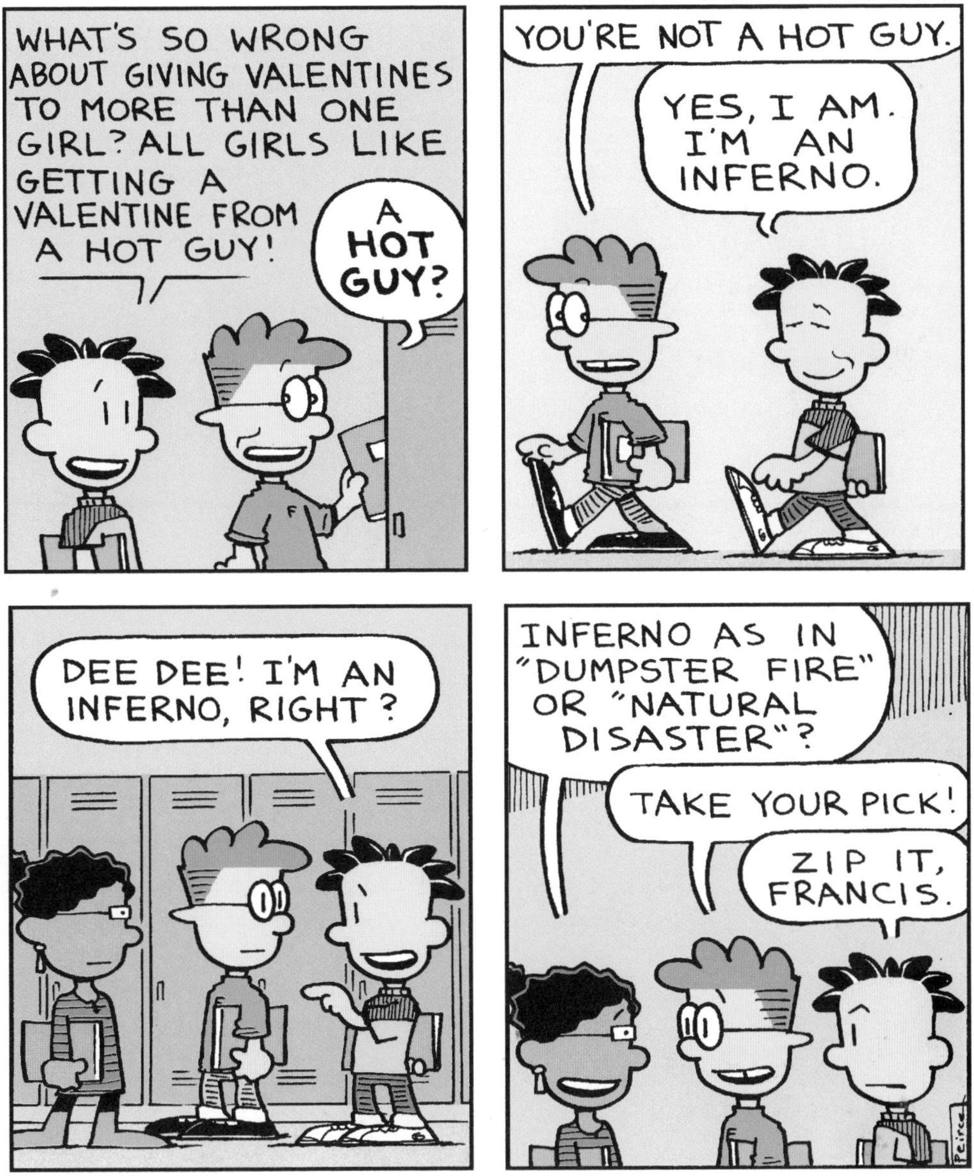
WHAT'S SO WRONG ABOUT GIVING VALENTINES TO MORE THAN ONE GIRL? ALL GIRLS LIKE GETTING A VALENTINE FROM A HOT GUY!
A HOT GUY?
YOU'RE NOT A HOT GUY.
YES, I AM. I'M AN INFERNO.
DEE DEE! I'M AN INFERNO, RIGHT?
INFERNO AS IN "DUMPSTER FIRE" OR "NATURAL DISASTER"?
TAKE YOUR PICK!
ZIP IT, FRANCIS.
Peirce

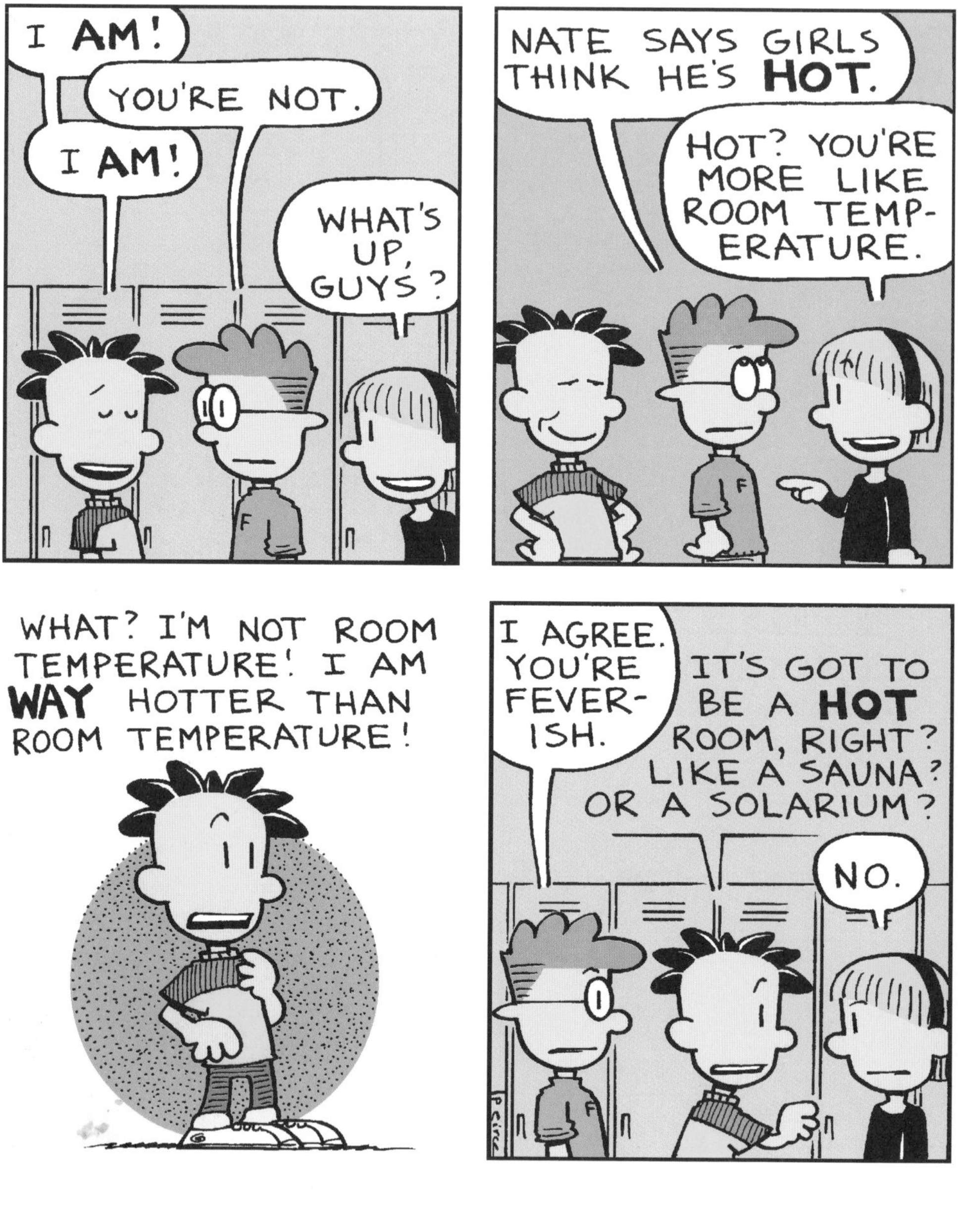
I AM!
YOU'RE NOT.
I AM!
WHAT'S UP, GUYS?
NATE SAYS GIRLS THINK HE'S **HOT**.
HOT? YOU'RE MORE LIKE ROOM TEMP-ERATURE.
WHAT? I'M NOT ROOM TEMPERATURE! I AM **WAY** HOTTER THAN ROOM TEMPERATURE!
I AGREE. YOU'RE FEVER-ISH.
IT'S GOT TO BE A **HOT** ROOM, RIGHT? LIKE A SAUNA? OR A SOLARIUM?
NO.

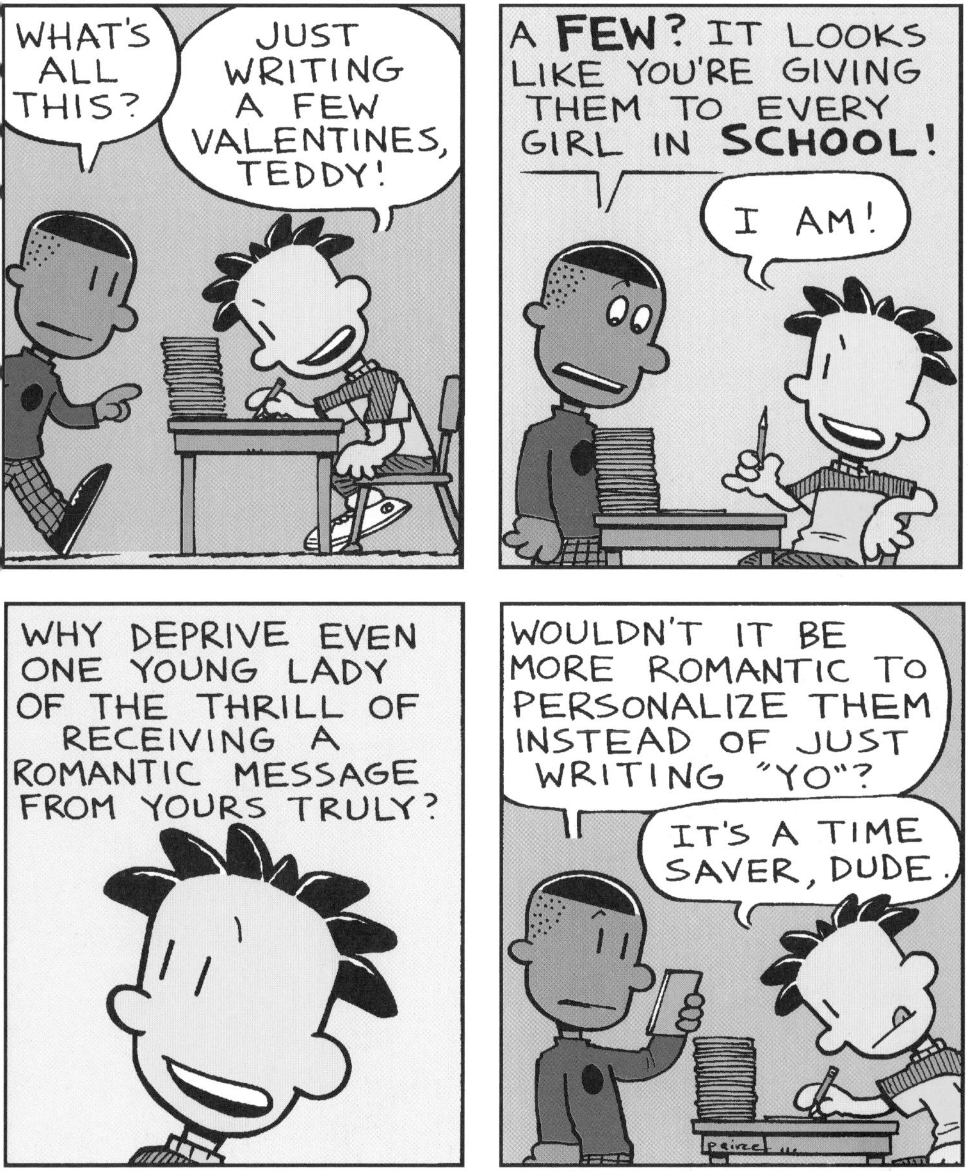

WHAT'S ALL THIS?
JUST WRITING A FEW VALENTINES, TEDDY!
A FEW? IT LOOKS LIKE YOU'RE GIVING THEM TO EVERY GIRL IN SCHOOL!
I AM!
WHY DEPRIVE EVEN ONE YOUNG LADY OF THE THRILL OF RECEIVING A ROMANTIC MESSAGE FROM YOURS TRULY?
WOULDN'T IT BE MORE ROMANTIC TO PERSONALIZE THEM INSTEAD OF JUST WRITING "YO"?
IT'S A TIME SAVER, DUDE.

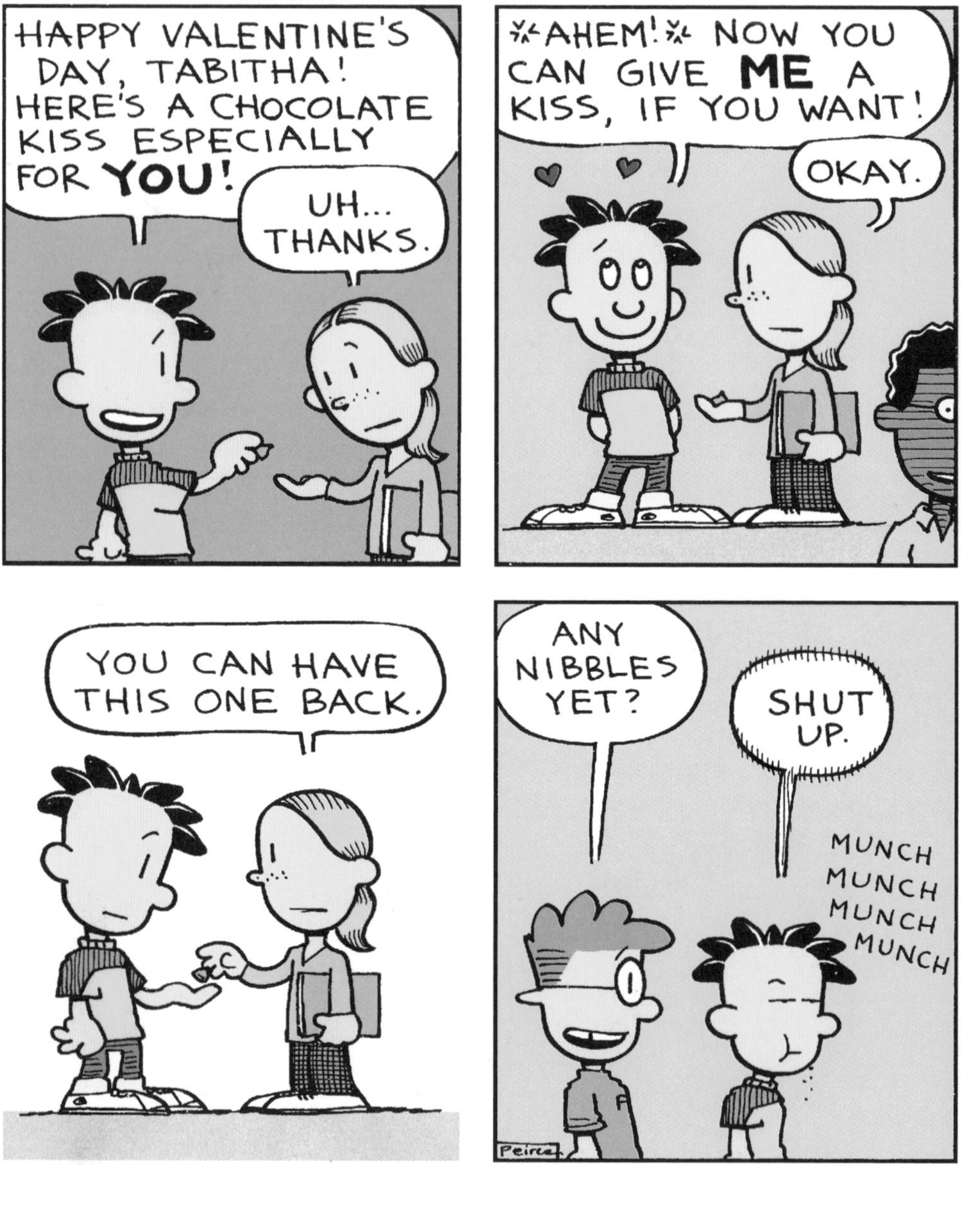
HAPPY VALENTINE'S DAY, TABITHA! HERE'S A CHOCOLATE KISS ESPECIALLY FOR **YOU**!
UH... THANKS.
AHEM! NOW YOU CAN GIVE **ME** A KISS, IF YOU WANT!
OKAY.
YOU CAN HAVE THIS ONE BACK.
ANY NIBBLES YET?
SHUT UP.
MUNCH MUNCH MUNCH MUNCH
Peirce

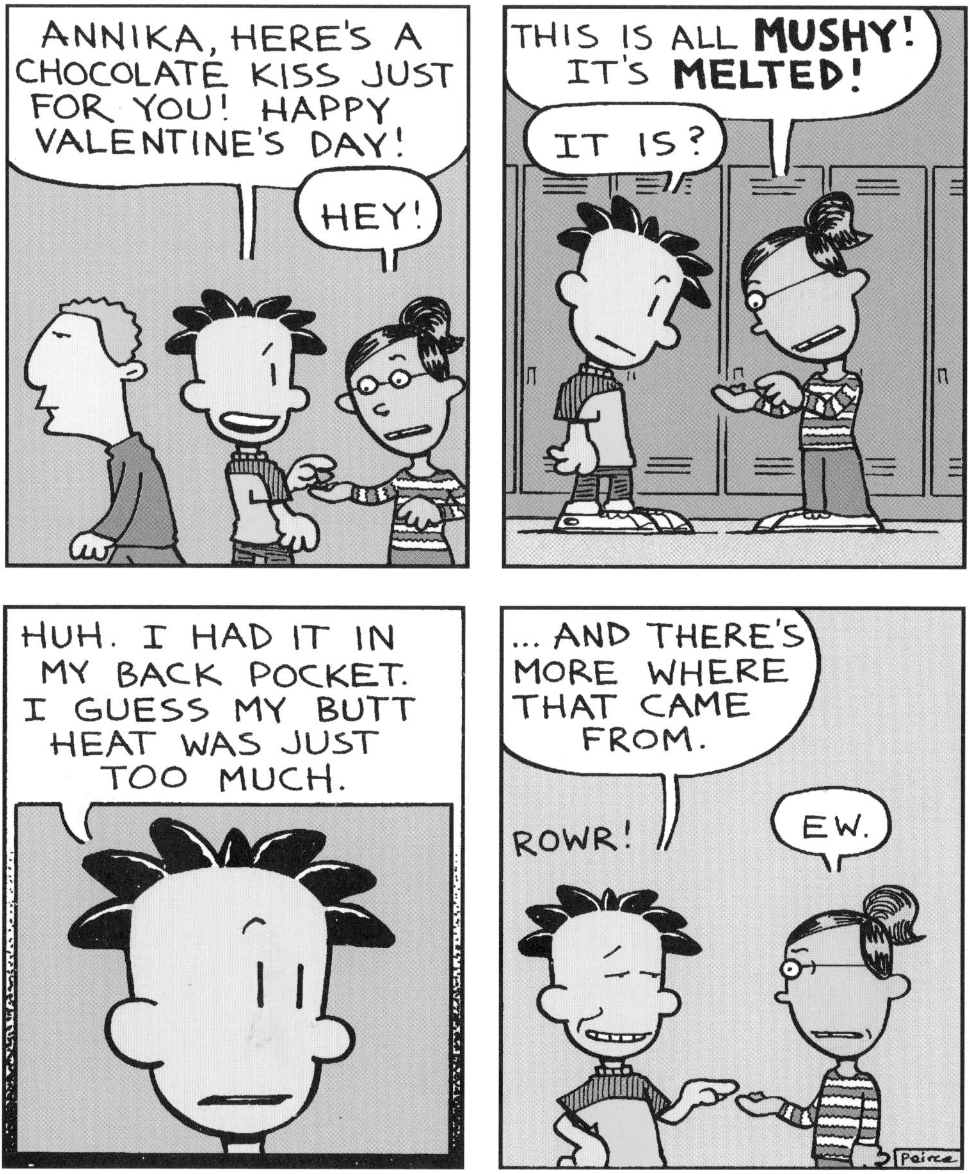
ANNIKA, HERE'S A CHOCOLATE KISS JUST FOR YOU! HAPPY VALENTINE'S DAY!
HEY!
THIS IS ALL **MUSHY!** IT'S **MELTED!**
IT IS?
HUH. I HAD IT IN MY BACK POCKET. I GUESS MY BUTT HEAT WAS JUST TOO MUCH.
... AND THERE'S MORE WHERE THAT CAME FROM.
ROWR!
EW.
Peirce

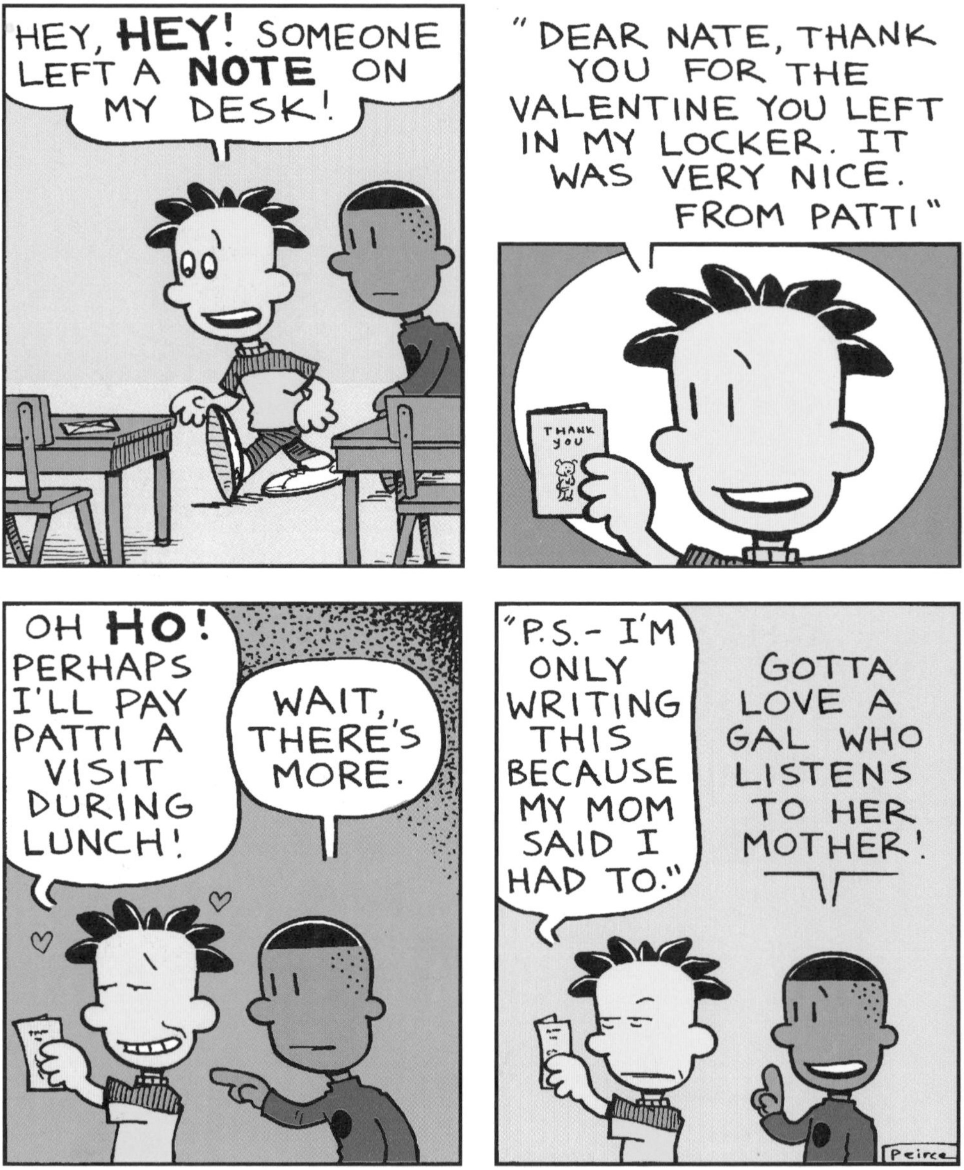
HEY, **HEY**! SOMEONE LEFT A **NOTE** ON MY DESK!
"DEAR NATE, THANK YOU FOR THE VALENTINE YOU LEFT IN MY LOCKER. IT WAS VERY NICE. FROM PATTI"
THANK YOU
OH **HO**! PERHAPS I'LL PAY PATTI A VISIT DURING LUNCH!
WAIT, THERE'S MORE.
"P.S. - I'M ONLY WRITING THIS BECAUSE MY MOM SAID I HAD TO."
GOTTA LOVE A GAL WHO LISTENS TO HER MOTHER!
Peirce

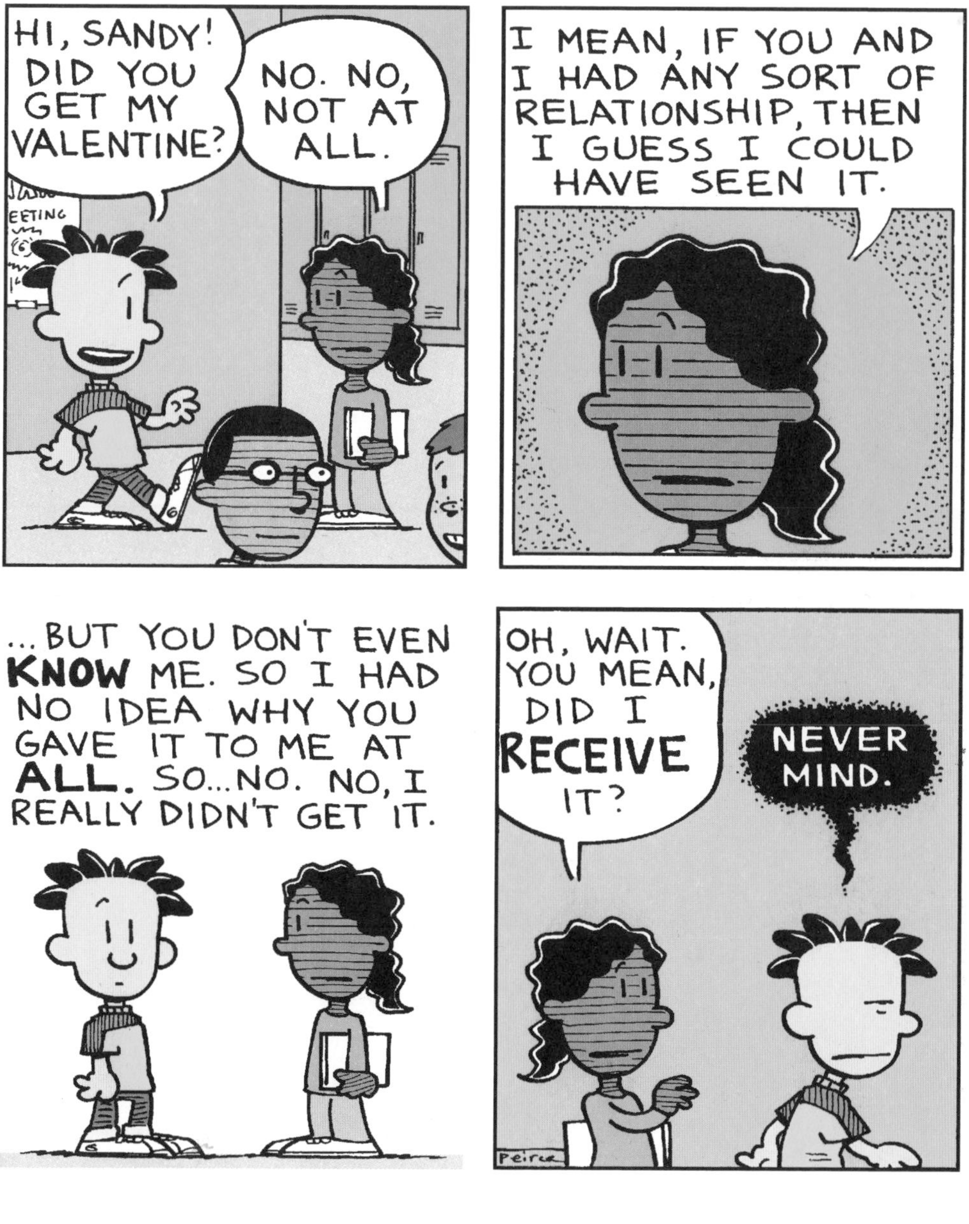
HI, SANDY! DID YOU GET MY VALENTINE?
NO. NO, NOT AT ALL.
I MEAN, IF YOU AND I HAD ANY SORT OF RELATIONSHIP, THEN I GUESS I COULD HAVE SEEN IT.
...BUT YOU DON'T EVEN **KNOW** ME. SO I HAD NO IDEA WHY YOU GAVE IT TO ME AT **ALL**. SO...NO. NO, I REALLY DIDN'T GET IT.
OH, WAIT. YOU MEAN, DID I **RECEIVE** IT?
NEVER MIND.
Peirce

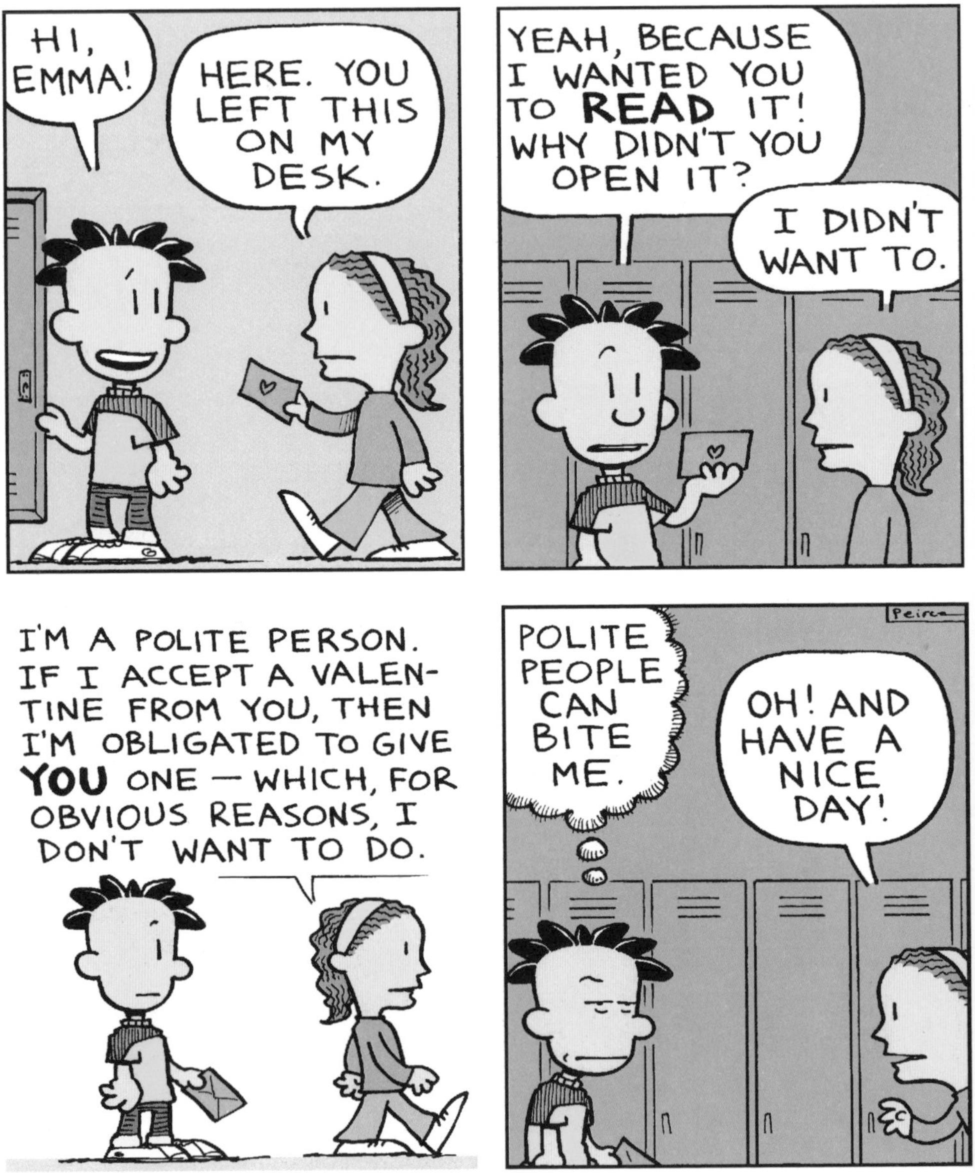
HI, EMMA!
HERE. YOU LEFT THIS ON MY DESK.
YEAH, BECAUSE I WANTED YOU TO **READ** IT! WHY DIDN'T YOU OPEN IT?
I DIDN'T WANT TO.
I'M A POLITE PERSON. IF I ACCEPT A VALEN-TINE FROM YOU, THEN I'M OBLIGATED TO GIVE **YOU** ONE — WHICH, FOR OBVIOUS REASONS, I DON'T WANT TO DO.
POLITE PEOPLE CAN BITE ME.
OH! AND HAVE A NICE DAY!
Peirce

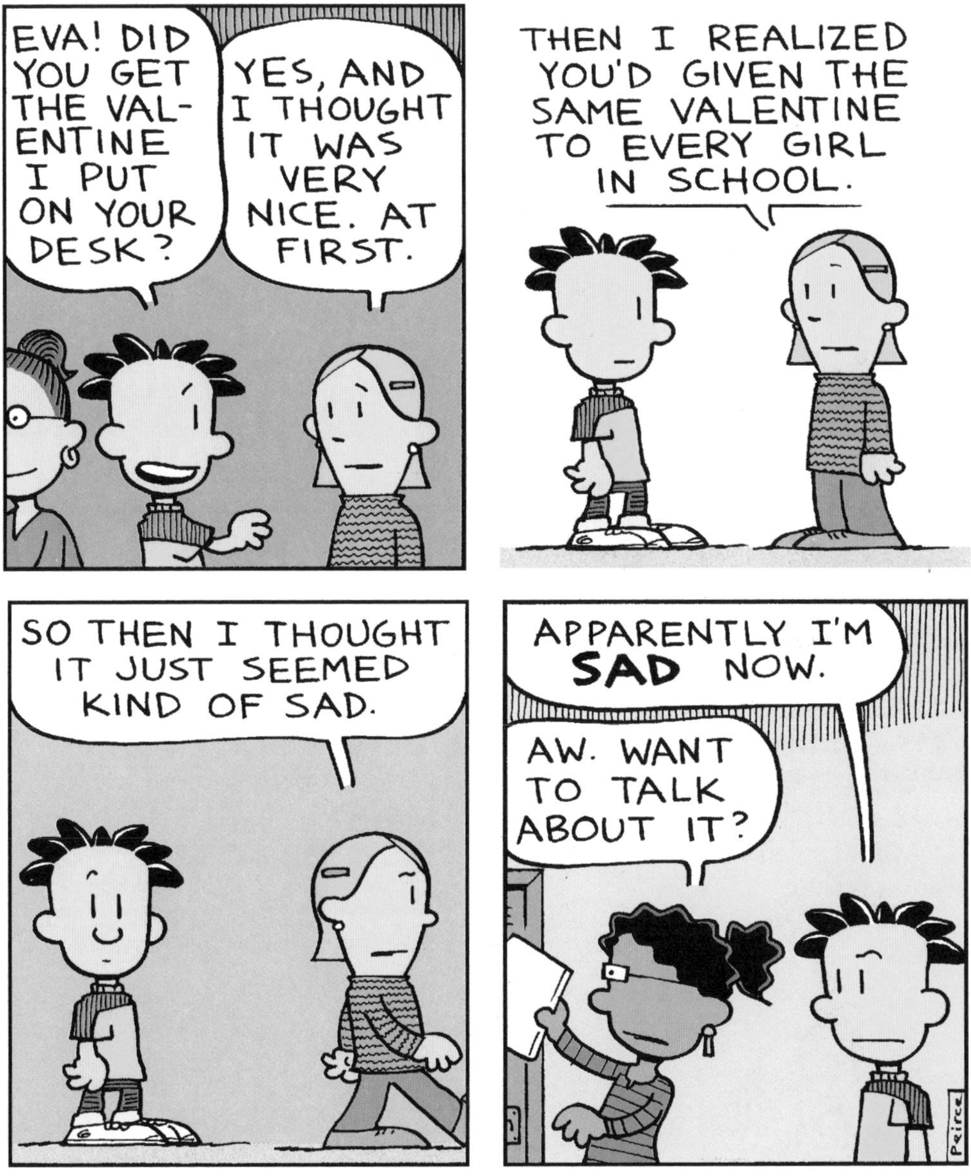
EVA! DID YOU GET THE VAL- ENTINE I PUT ON YOUR DESK?
YES, AND I THOUGHT IT WAS VERY NICE. AT FIRST.
THEN I REALIZED YOU'D GIVEN THE SAME VALENTINE TO EVERY GIRL IN SCHOOL.
SO THEN I THOUGHT IT JUST SEEMED KIND OF SAD.
APPARENTLY I'M **SAD** NOW.
AW. WANT TO TALK ABOUT IT?
Peirce

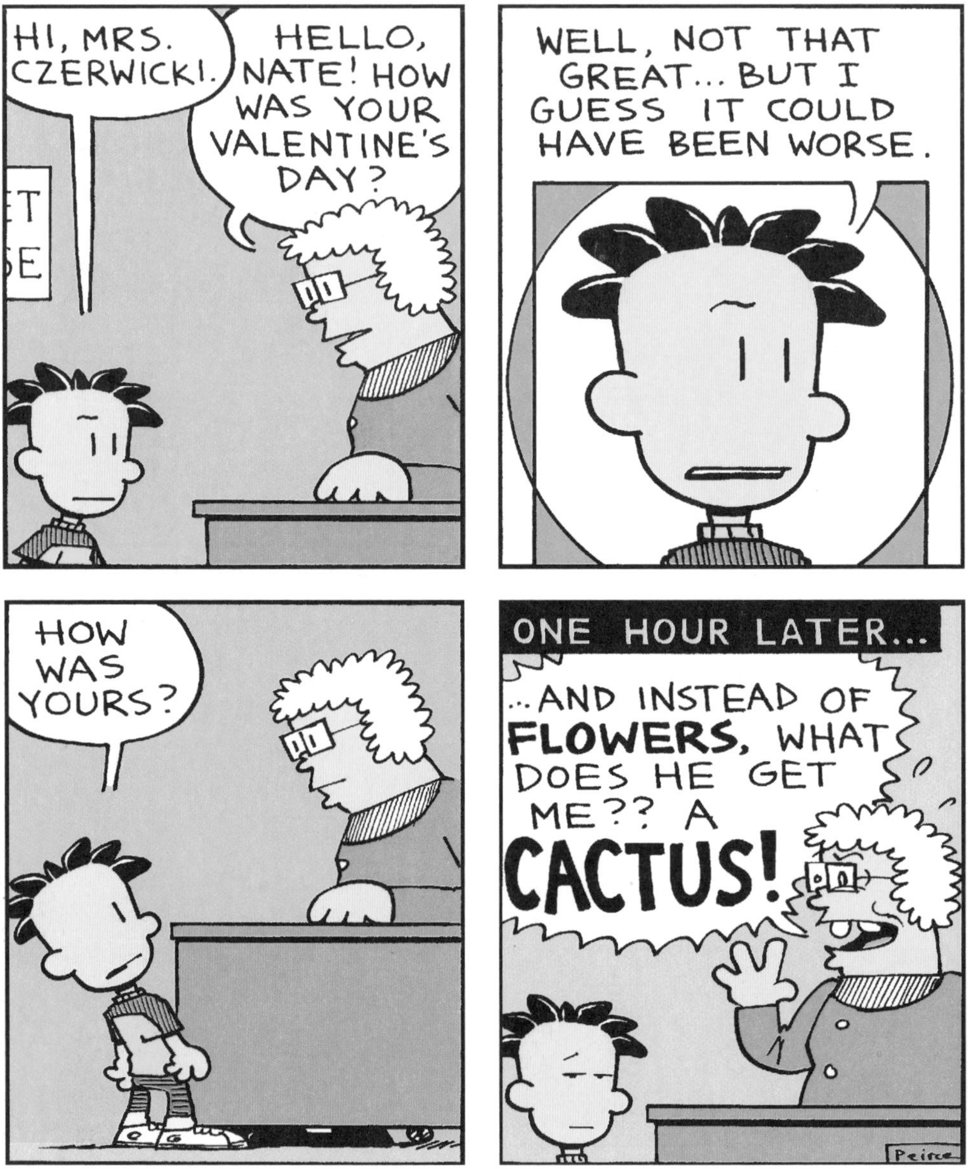
HI, MRS. CZERWICKI.
HELLO, NATE! HOW WAS YOUR VALENTINE'S DAY?
WELL, NOT THAT GREAT... BUT I GUESS IT COULD HAVE BEEN WORSE.
HOW WAS YOURS?
ONE HOUR LATER...
...AND INSTEAD OF FLOWERS, WHAT DOES HE GET ME?? A CACTUS!
Peirce

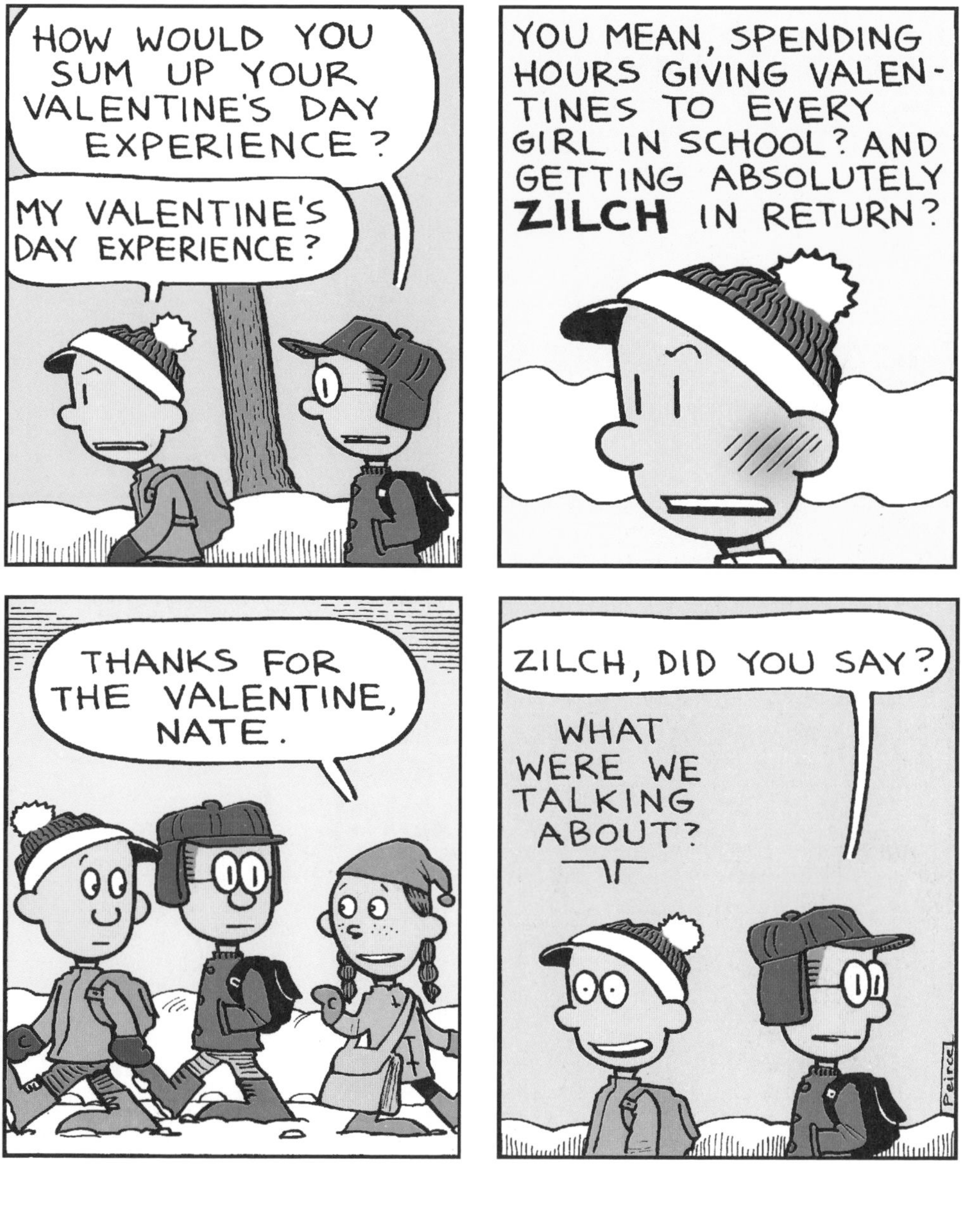
HOW WOULD YOU SUM UP YOUR VALENTINE'S DAY EXPERIENCE?
MY VALENTINE'S DAY EXPERIENCE?
YOU MEAN, SPENDING HOURS GIVING VALEN-TINES TO EVERY GIRL IN SCHOOL? AND GETTING ABSOLUTELY **ZILCH** IN RETURN?
THANKS FOR THE VALENTINE, NATE.
ZILCH, DID YOU SAY?
WHAT WERE WE TALKING ABOUT?
Peirce

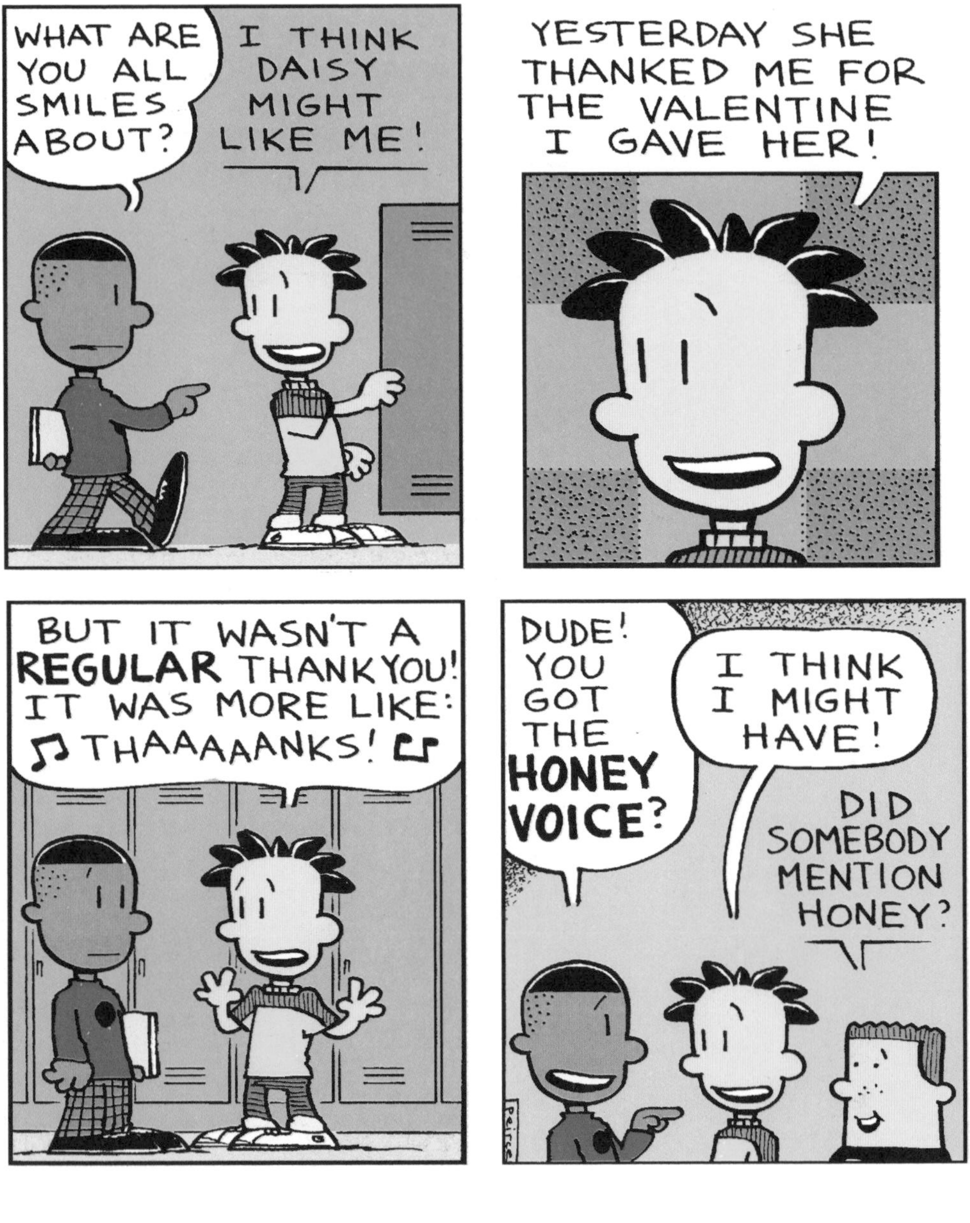
WHAT ARE YOU ALL SMILES ABOUT?
I THINK DAISY MIGHT LIKE ME!
YESTERDAY SHE THANKED ME FOR THE VALENTINE I GAVE HER!
BUT IT WASN'T A **REGULAR** THANK YOU! IT WAS MORE LIKE: ♫ THAAAAANKS! ♫
DUDE! YOU GOT THE **HONEY VOICE**?
I THINK I MIGHT HAVE!
DID SOMEBODY MENTION HONEY?
Peirce

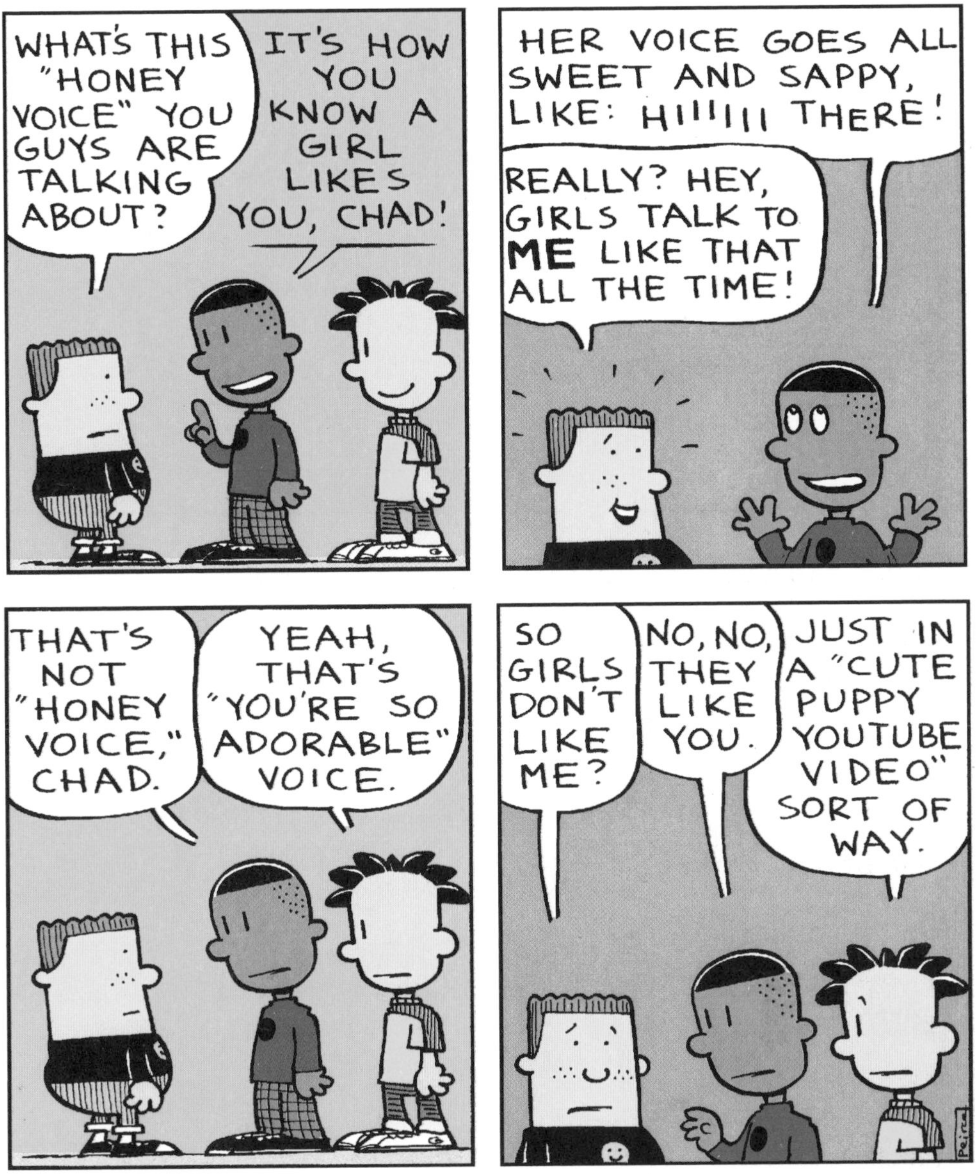
WHAT'S THIS "HONEY VOICE" YOU GUYS ARE TALKING ABOUT?
IT'S HOW YOU KNOW A GIRL LIKES YOU, CHAD!
HER VOICE GOES ALL SWEET AND SAPPY, LIKE: HIIIIII THERE!
REALLY? HEY, GIRLS TALK TO ME LIKE THAT ALL THE TIME!
THAT'S NOT "HONEY VOICE," CHAD.
YEAH, THAT'S "YOU'RE SO ADORABLE" VOICE.
SO GIRLS DON'T LIKE ME?
NO, NO, THEY LIKE YOU.
JUST IN A "CUTE PUPPY YOUTUBE VIDEO" SORT OF WAY.
Peirce

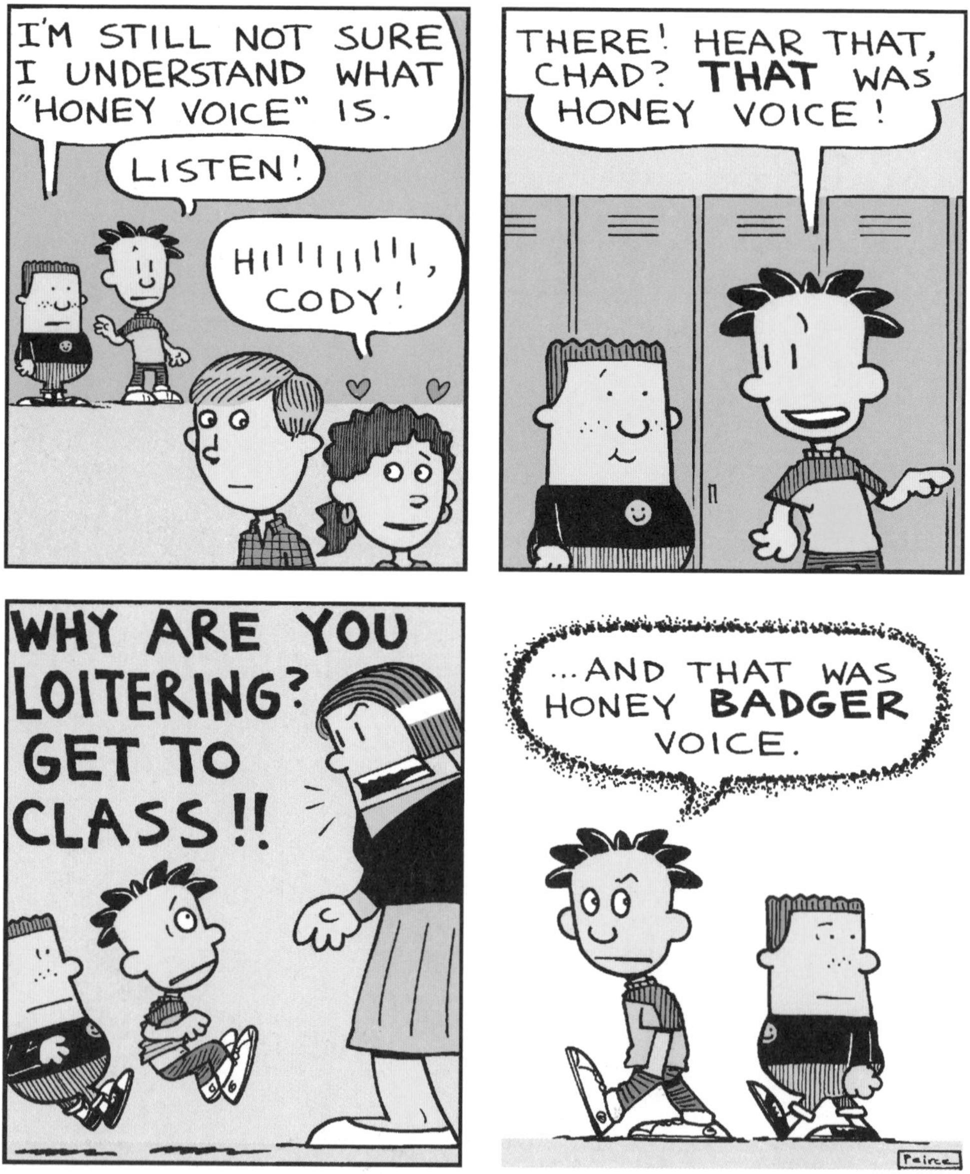

I'M STILL NOT SURE I UNDERSTAND WHAT "HONEY VOICE" IS.
LISTEN!
HIIIIIIIII, CODY!
THERE! HEAR THAT, CHAD? THAT WAS HONEY VOICE!
WHY ARE YOU LOITERING? GET TO CLASS!!
...AND THAT WAS HONEY BADGER VOICE.
Peirce

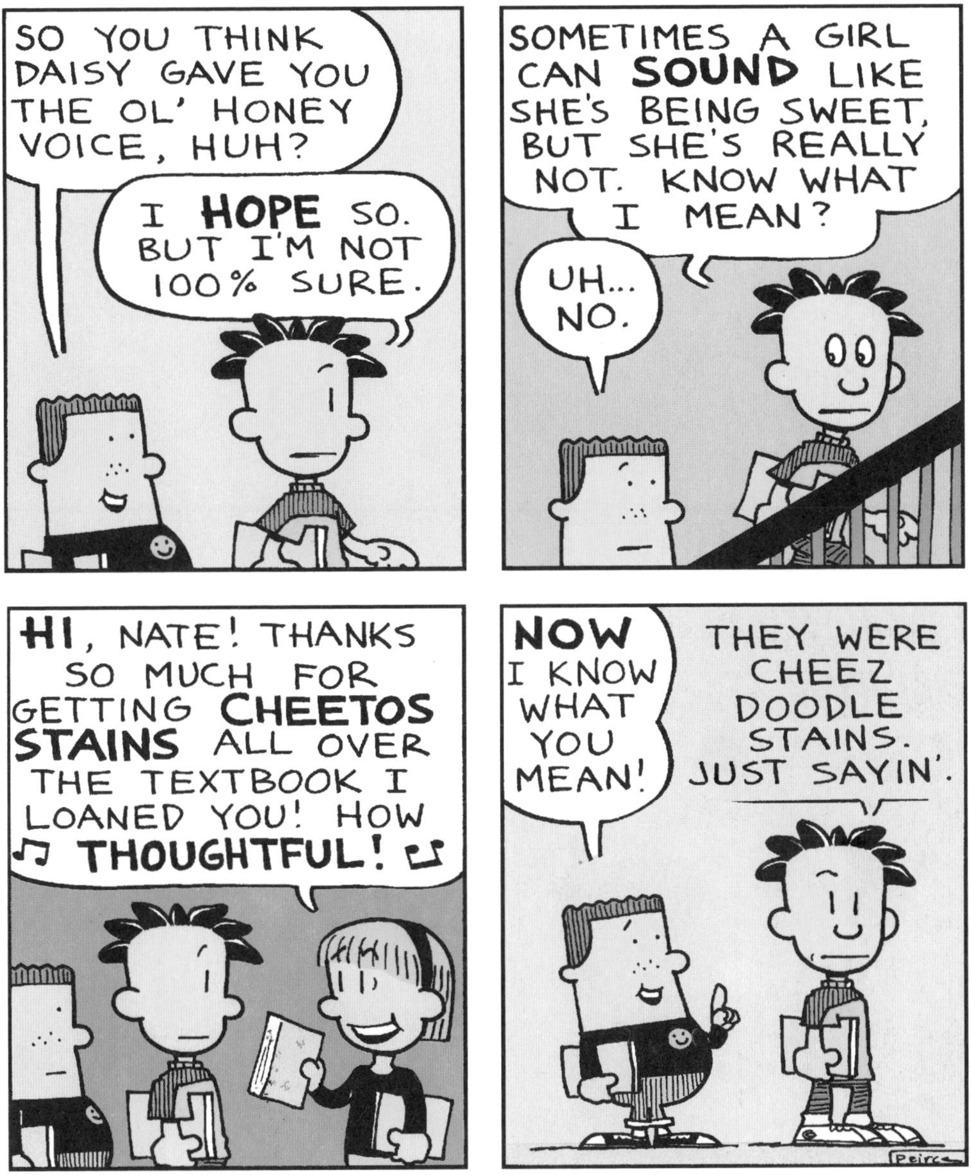
SO YOU THINK DAISY GAVE YOU THE OL' HONEY VOICE, HUH?
I **HOPE** SO. BUT I'M NOT 100% SURE.
SOMETIMES A GIRL CAN **SOUND** LIKE SHE'S BEING SWEET, BUT SHE'S REALLY NOT. KNOW WHAT I MEAN?
UH... NO.
HI, NATE! THANKS SO MUCH FOR GETTING **CHEETOS STAINS** ALL OVER THE TEXTBOOK I LOANED YOU! HOW ♫ **THOUGHTFUL!** ♫
NOW I KNOW WHAT YOU MEAN!
THEY WERE CHEEZ DOODLE STAINS. JUST SAYIN'.
Peirce

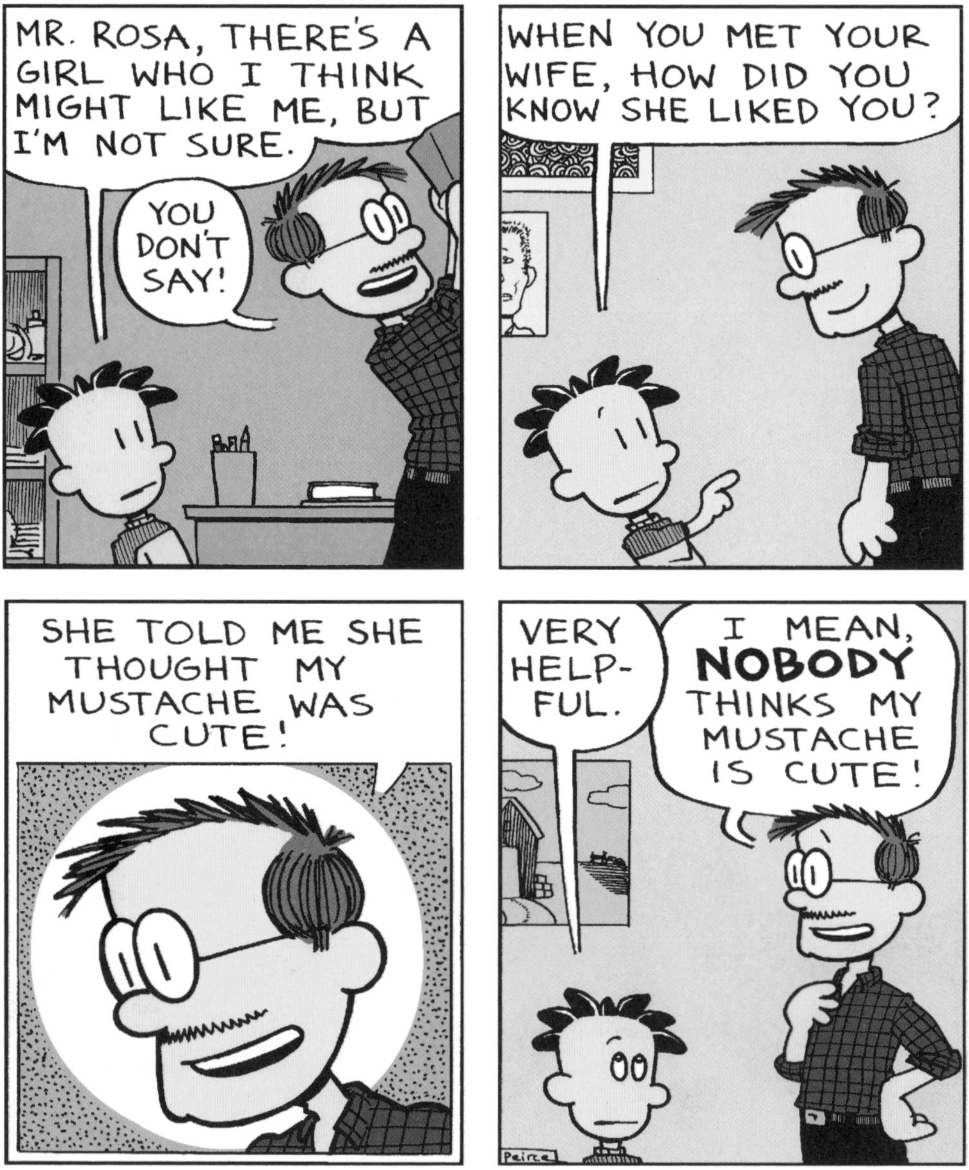
MR. ROSA, THERE'S A GIRL WHO I THINK MIGHT LIKE ME, BUT I'M NOT SURE.
YOU DON'T SAY!
WHEN YOU MET YOUR WIFE, HOW DID YOU KNOW SHE LIKED YOU?
SHE TOLD ME SHE THOUGHT MY MUSTACHE WAS CUTE!
VERY HELP-FUL.
I MEAN, **NOBODY** THINKS MY MUSTACHE IS CUTE!
Peirce

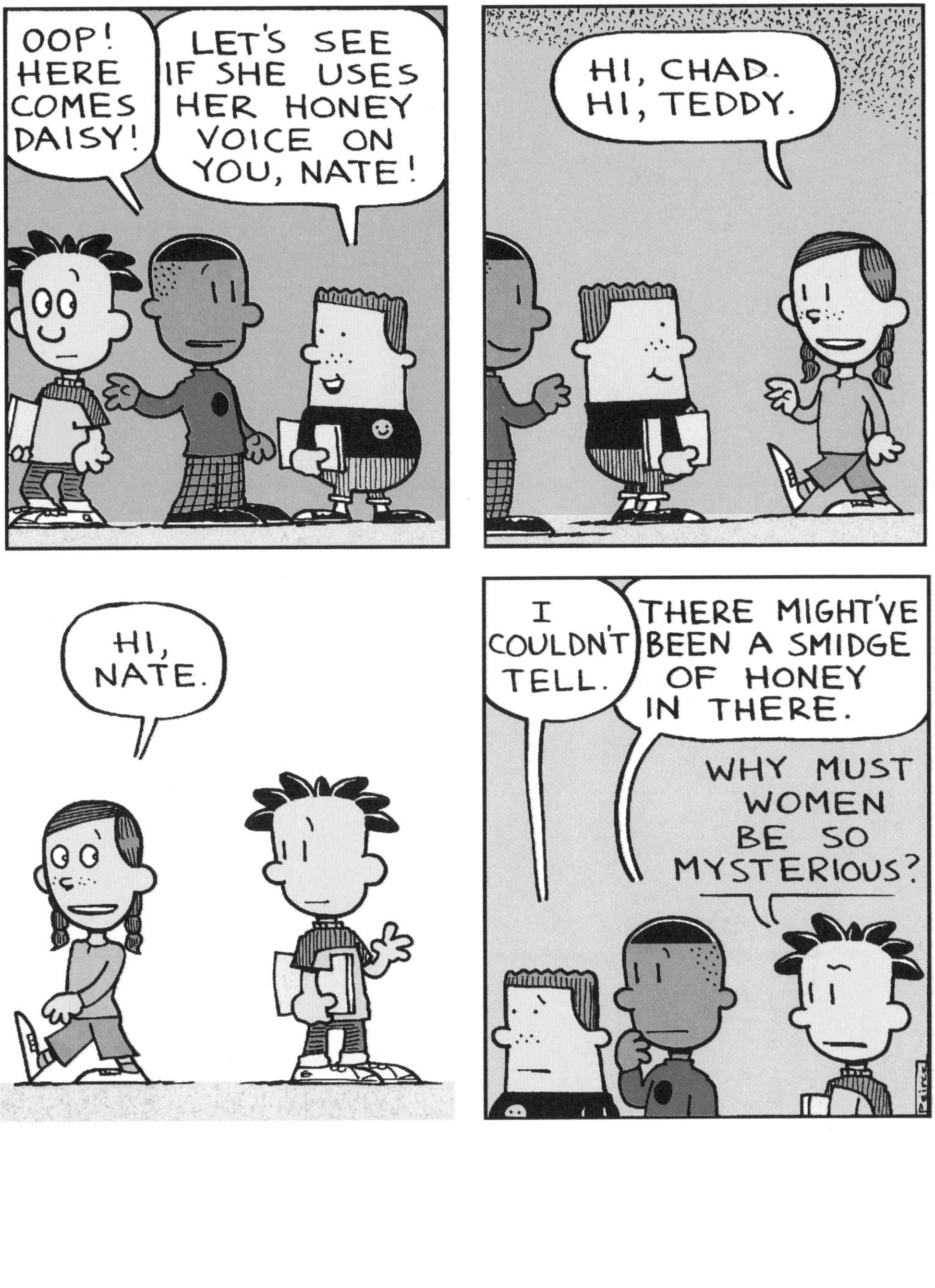
OOP! HERE COMES DAISY!
LET'S SEE IF SHE USES HER HONEY VOICE ON YOU, NATE!
HI, CHAD. HI, TEDDY.
HI, NATE.
I COULDN'T TELL.
THERE MIGHT'VE BEEN A SMIDGE OF HONEY IN THERE.
WHY MUST WOMEN BE SO MYSTERIOUS?
Peirce

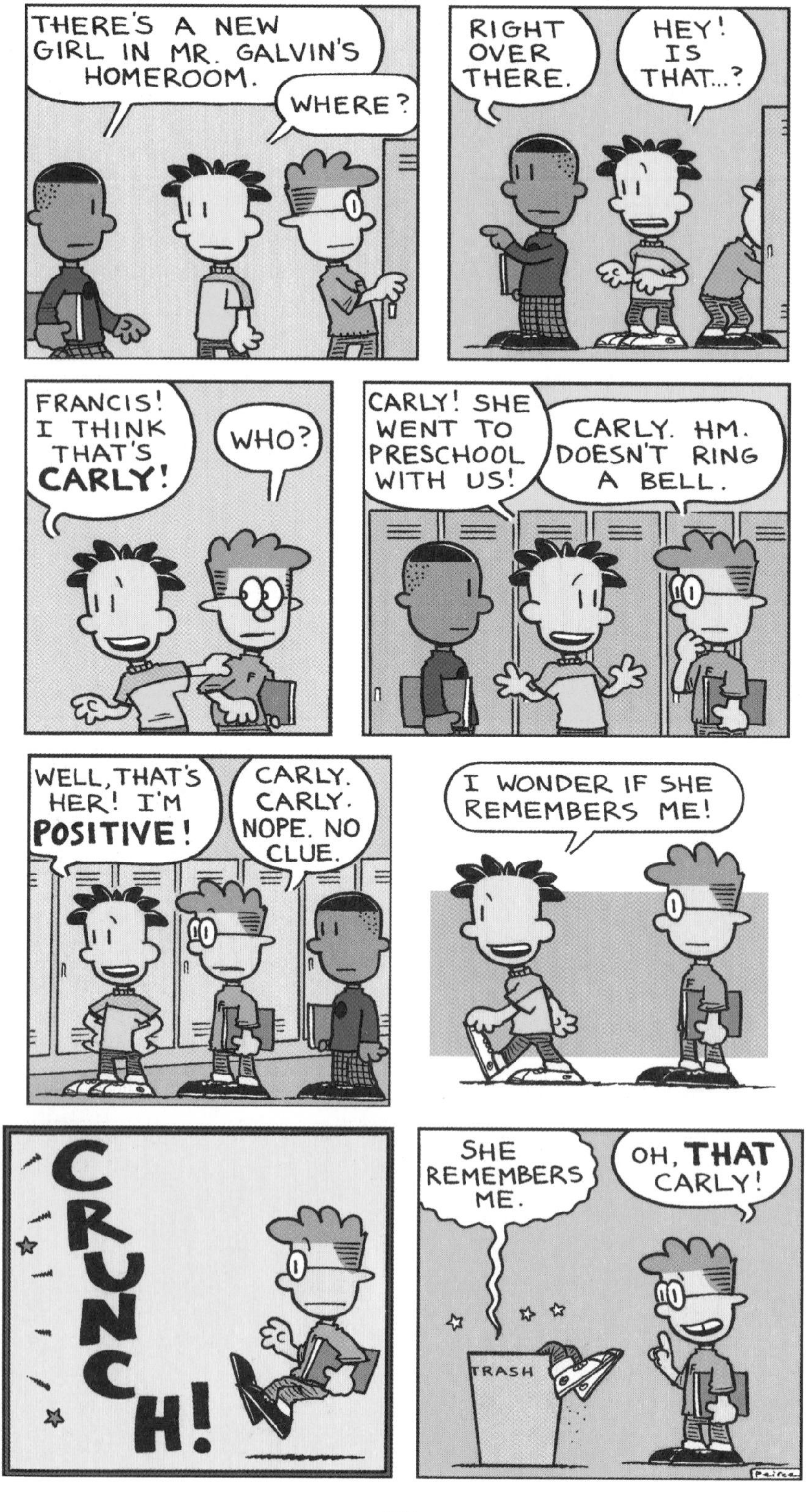
THERE'S A NEW GIRL IN MR. GALVIN'S HOMEROOM.
WHERE?
RIGHT OVER THERE.
HEY! IS THAT...?
FRANCIS! I THINK THAT'S CARLY!
WHO?
CARLY! SHE WENT TO PRESCHOOL WITH US!
CARLY. HM. DOESN'T RING A BELL.
WELL, THAT'S HER! I'M POSITIVE!
CARLY. CARLY. NOPE. NO CLUE.
I WONDER IF SHE REMEMBERS ME!
CRUNCH!
SHE REMEMBERS ME.
OH, THAT CARLY!
TRASH
Peirce

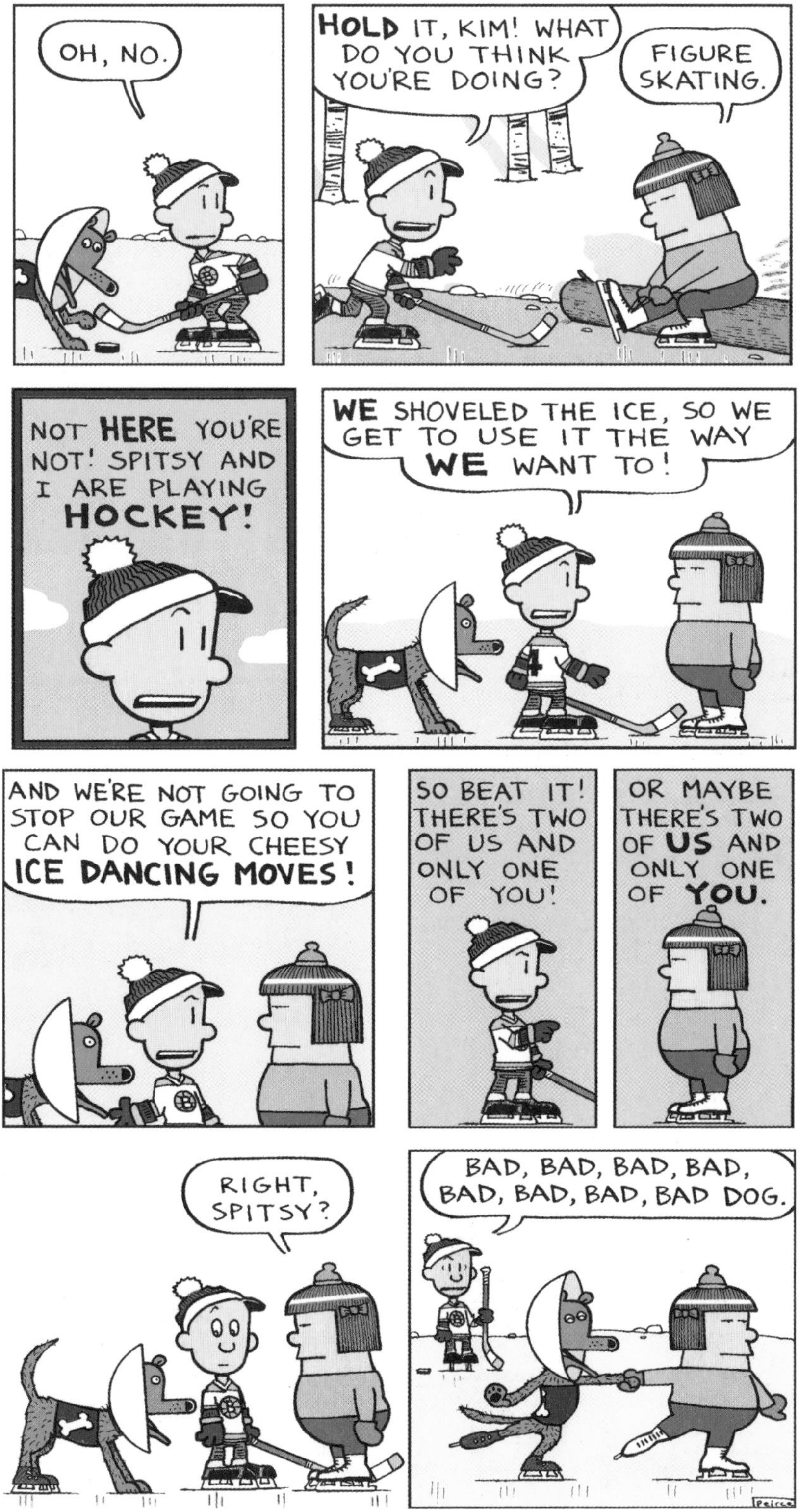

OH, NO.
HOLD IT, KIM! WHAT DO YOU THINK YOU'RE DOING?
FIGURE SKATING.
NOT HERE YOU'RE NOT! SPITSY AND I ARE PLAYING HOCKEY!
WE SHOVELED THE ICE, SO WE GET TO USE IT THE WAY WE WANT TO!
AND WE'RE NOT GOING TO STOP OUR GAME SO YOU CAN DO YOUR CHEESY ICE DANCING MOVES!
SO BEAT IT! THERE'S TWO OF US AND ONLY ONE OF YOU!
OR MAYBE THERE'S TWO OF US AND ONLY ONE OF YOU.
RIGHT, SPITSY?
BAD, BAD, BAD, BAD, BAD, BAD, BAD, BAD DOG.
Peirce

Look for these books!

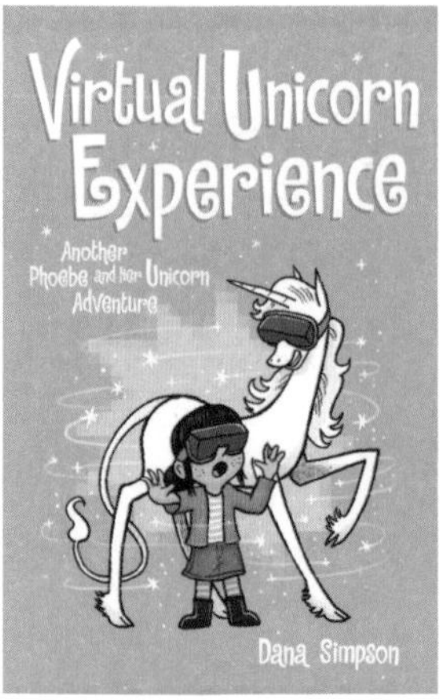
Virtual Unicorn Experience
Another Phoebe and her Unicorn Adventure
Dana Simpson

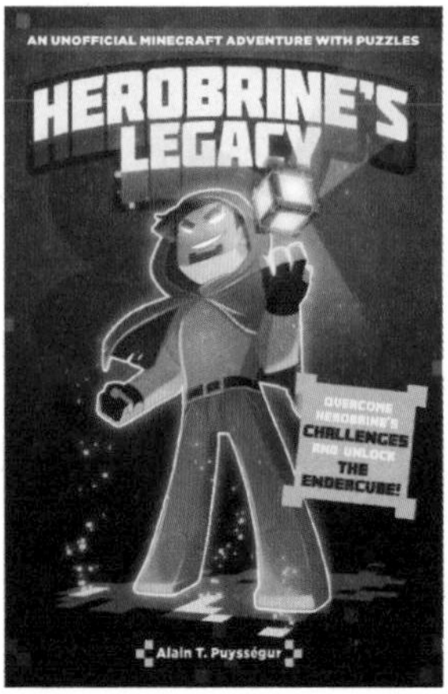
AN UNOFFICIAL MINECRAFT ADVENTURE WITH PUZZLES
HEROBRINE'S LEGACY
OVERCOME HEROBRINE'S CHALLENGES AND UNLOCK THE ENDERCUBE!
Alain T. Puysségur

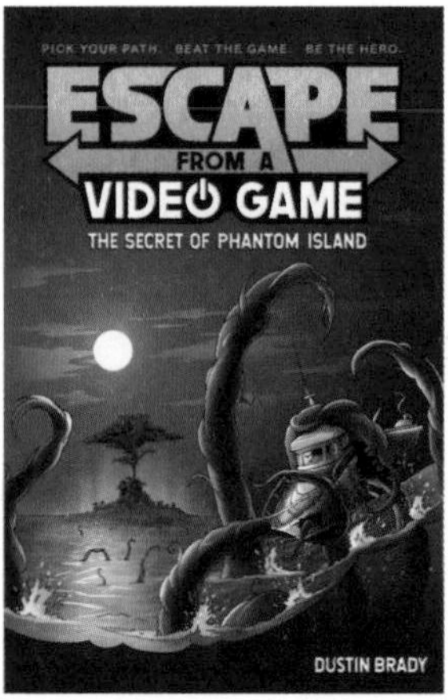
PICK YOUR PATH. BEAT THE GAME. BE THE HERO.
ESCAPE FROM A VIDEO GAME
THE SECRET OF PHANTOM ISLAND
DUSTIN BRADY

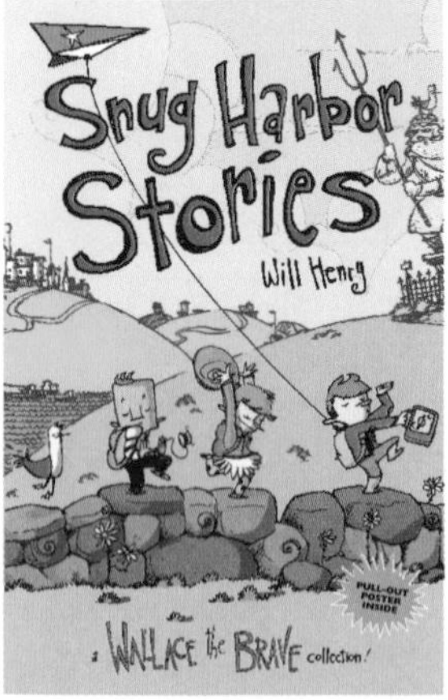
Snug Harbor Stories
Will Henry
PULL-OUT POSTER INSIDE
a WALLACE the BRAVE collection!

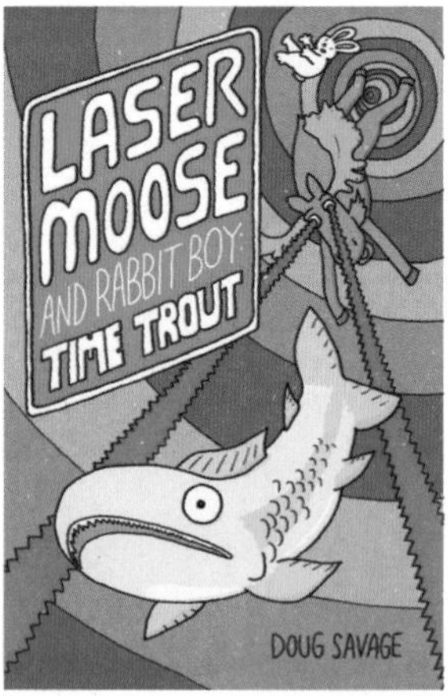
LASER MOOSE AND RABBIT BOY: TIME TROUT
DOUG SAVAGE

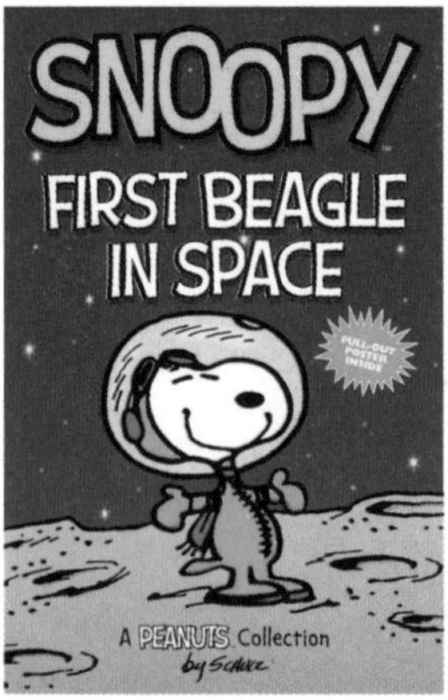
SNOOPY
FIRST BEAGLE IN SPACE
PULL-OUT POSTER INSIDE
A PEANUTS Collection
by Schulz

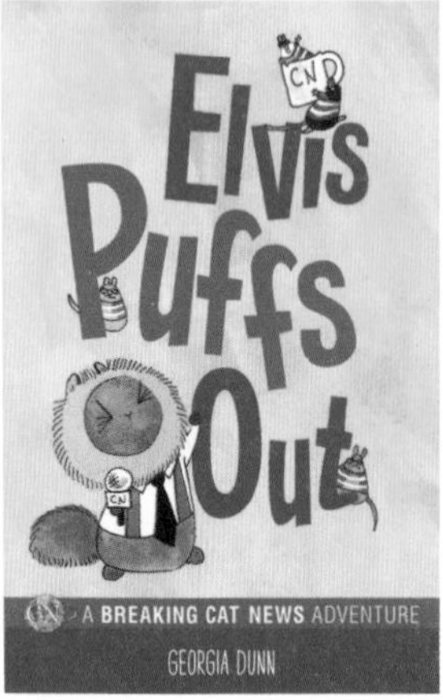
Elvis Puffs Out
A BREAKING CAT NEWS ADVENTURE
GEORGIA DUNN

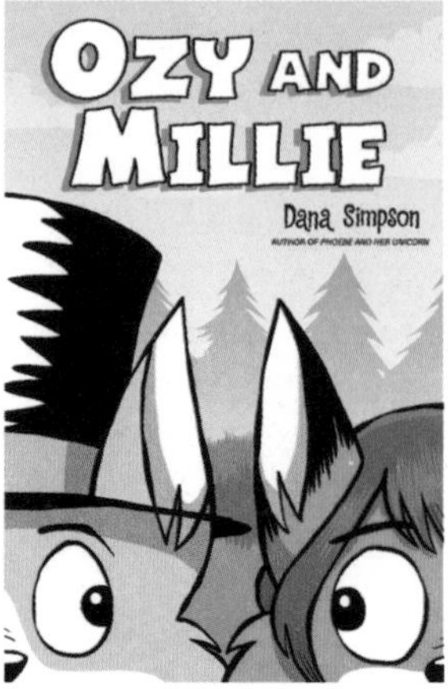
OZY AND MILLIE
Dana Simpson

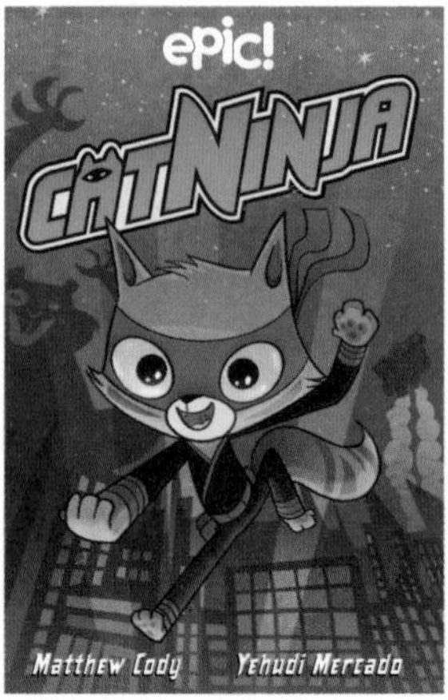
epic!
CATNINJA
Matthew Cody
Yehudi Mercado

Big Nate is distributed internationally by Andrews McMeel Syndication.

Andrews McMeel Publishing
a division of Andrews McMeel Universal
1130 Walnut Street, Kansas City, Missouri 64106

www.andrewsmcmeel.com

21 22 23 24 25 SDB 10 9 8 7 6 5 4 3 2 1

ISBN: 978-1-5248-6477-4

Library of Congress Control Number: 2020943994

Made by:
King Yip (Dongguan) Printing & Packaging Factory Ltd.
Address and location of manufacturer:
Daning Administrative District, Humen Town
Dongguan Guangdong, China 523930
1st Printing—11/23/20

These strips appeared in newspapers from
September 5, 2016, through February 25, 2017.

Big Nate can be viewed on the Internet at
www.gocomics.com/big_nate.